Shadows
of
Atonement

B. Edward Blackmon

DEDICATION

To Courtney,
My wife, my muse, and the love of my life.
Through every high and every low, you've
shaped the man I am today. Though our
journey hasn't been easy, it's been ours, and for
that, I'm grateful. This story, in its rawness and
pain, is as much about love as it is about loss.
Thank you for the memories we built, the
lessons I've learned, and for being the spark that
still burns within me.

Always.

To Clark,
My pride and my strength.
You are the reason I keep going, the light that
cuts through even the darkest moments. May
you always know your worth, and may you
never be afraid to chase your dreams. This story
is for you, too—because it's about survival,
resilience, and finding yourself even when the
world tries to tear you apart. Keep fighting, son.

You're more than enough.

Shadows of Atonement

Table Of Contents

ACKNOWLEDGMENTS

Writing this book has been an intense journey, and I owe so many people a debt of gratitude for their support and encouragement along the way. Your encouragement kept me going when the words were hard to find.

A special thank you to Elizabeth, whose input and perspective helped shape the emotional depth of this story. Your insight, even during the most difficult moments, was invaluable.

To Alex, my son, for your feedback and constant presence. You inspire me every day, and this book is as much yours as it is mine.

I also want to thank my former students for their thoughtful feedback and for taking the time to read early drafts. Your insights made all the difference and pushed me to improve with each revision.

To everyone who has been a part of this journey, whether through your direct feedback, late-night conversations, or simple words of encouragement—thank you. This book is a testament to the power of persistence, love, and finding light even in the darkest of stories.

B. Edward Blackmon

Shadows of Atonement

1 Prologue:

The end?

To those who might care enough to read this,

I've spent 44 years trying to be someone—someone who mattered, someone worth loving, someone who made a difference, and someone to make you proud. I've failed at literally every turn. Teaching was supposed to be my purpose, my way of giving back, but all I did was waste my time. I never reached them, never made the impact I dreamed of but that was my calling and I even failed at that. Maybe that's the real reason why you left me, why you found comfort in other men. We all make choices, but I don't blame her, though. How could she love a man who couldn't even love himself?

I tried to be a good man, to live by the values I thought were right. I never strayed, never let my eyes wander, even when the world around me offered temptations. Other women may have shown interest, but it never meant anything to

1

me—because I only ever had eyes for you. Every advance was met with silence or politely turned away, because in my heart, you were the only one. I never wanted anyone else, never needed anything more than what I thought we had. I thought that if I could just stay true, if I could be the man I promised to be, it would be enough. But I see now that I wasn't enough—not for you, not for our marriage, not even for myself.

To my love—Elizabeth, my one and only connection, my soulmate, my person—I want you to know that no matter what happened between us, you have always been the love of my life. From the moment I met you, I knew there was no one else for me. You walked into my life, and everything shifted; it was as if the world finally made sense. I couldn't imagine my life without you, and even now, I can't fathom what it would have been without you in it. Even in my darkest moments, when it felt like everything was falling apart, my love for you never wavered.

I know I wasn't enough. I know I failed you in so many ways, and I carry that weight with me every day. I wasn't the perfect husband, and I couldn't give you the happiness you deserve. But none of that ever changed how I felt about you. I loved you more than life itself—more than anything I've ever known. I hope one day, you'll find the happiness I couldn't give you, that you'll find the peace I always wished for you. I never gave up on you or on us, and I'll try again in the next life to fulfill the love I know we were meant to have.

But it's hard to express how much I fought for us, how much I believed in us, even after everything.

When I found out the truth—about you and Bishop, and the others from before—it broke me in ways I didn't know I could be broken. The betrayal felt like a burning knife being thrust continuously into my heart, and there were nights I would lie awake, out of my mind, wondering how we had ended up here. How the woman I loved, the one I had built my life around, could seek comfort in the arms of another. But even then, even when the truth came crashing down on me, I couldn't walk away.

I stayed right by your side when you were sick dying with Covid and soon after when everyone else gave up on you. I was the one, the only one who fought for you when no one else would. Do you remember when your own mother turned her back on you, when the doctors said there was no hope? I didn't listen to them. I fought with everyone—your mother, the doctors, the hospitals as I pushed and pleaded, refusing to let them keep you institutionalized in that Hell-like place that was making you worse. They said you were too far gone, but I knew better. I was the one who got you out, who won that battle for your freedom.

When you finally came home, when you pretended to reconcile with me, I thought maybe—just maybe—I'd brought you back for us. That somehow, I'd saved us. But you weren't really coming back to me, were you? You were just making sure you were still taken care of, using that fake reconciliation so you wouldn't have to face this life alone because I was helpful.

I still remember every single one of the ninety minutes that morning when you said we would try and that you were done with the divorce and Bishop. We made out and held each other's naked bodies and you apologized for it all, and I bought in. For thirty minutes out of four months I had a real sense of hope for our future together. Afterwards, you treated me like some friend or a girlfriend—someone to help you, but never close enough to truly love. You even told your family we were going to try again, but like always you never let anyone in on the truth.

And after everything I did, after getting you healthy enough to go back to work, to have your life back... you wouldn't even share your body heat with me when I needed it most. Do you remember that night in the freezing rain, when I was soaked through, shaking with cold, standing there with your dog while you looked at me through the window and turned away? You were inside, warm and safe, and I came in from out there, I was broken and freezing, needing just a little bit of comfort. But you wouldn't even give me that, not even to share your body heat lying beside me.

That was the moment I realized how far you'd gone, how little I really meant to you. I fought for you when no one else did, I gave everything I had, and you couldn't even offer me the most-minimal basic human connection when I was at my lowest. And still, I couldn't walk away. Even then, I stayed. Because despite it all, despite the betrayals and the lies, I loved you with every part of me and I still do.

Everyone told me to leave, to give up. They said I was a fool for staying, for trying to fix something that was shattered beyond repair. Even my own friends abandoned me, siding with you, believing your version of the story. I became the villain in everyone's eyes, the man who wasn't good enough, the man who failed his wife. No one wanted to hear my side, to understand that I was still fighting for us, that I believed in our love even when no one else did.

I stayed, Liz. I stayed when everyone said I shouldn't, when they told me I deserved better, that you weren't worth the fight anymore. But I knew you were, I always believed that. I knew that what we had wasn't something I could walk away from. I believed, in my heart, that we could find our way back to each other, that there was something left worth saving. I fought and found a way for us but you didn't want it. I was loving, dependable, helpful, and did everything for you but I wasn't exciting enough.

I forgave you. I forgave you for everything, because I couldn't bear the thought of losing you. I couldn't let go of the life we had built, of the memories we shared, of the dreams we once had together. I clung to the hope that we could rebuild, that somehow, through all the pain, we could find a way to heal.

And yet, it wasn't enough. No matter how hard I tried, no matter how much I loved you, I couldn't change the way things had fallen apart. I couldn't undo the damage, and I couldn't stop you from drifting further away. I watched as the distance between us grew, and I felt powerless to stop it. It tore me apart inside, but I stayed. When you were put into the psyche ward and everyone wanted to leave you there, I fought for you until I got you out. I stayed and fought because I loved you. Because I couldn't imagine a life without you in it, even if that meant enduring the hurt, the betrayal, and the constant reminders of what we had lost.

I know I wasn't perfect. I know I made mistakes, and I take responsibility for my part in what happened to us. I hope you know that I really tried to be a better provider for you and Alex. But I need you to understand that, through it all, my love for you never faltered. Not once. Even when you were with him, even when you left me standing in the wreckage of our marriage, I still loved you. I still wanted to fight for you and I did. I still wanted us, but a new version to be built on the ashes of what was with all of the new knowledge and understanding we had of each other.

You were my everything, Elizabeth. My one and only. And even though we didn't make it, even though we couldn't find our way back, I want you to know that I never gave up on you. I never stopped believing in the love we shared, the love I still carry with me. I hope that one day, you'll find the happiness I couldn't give you, but please know that my love for you was real. It was the truest thing I've ever known, and it always will be.

I never gave up on us, Elizabeth, and I never will. In this life or the next, I will love you forever.

Always.

————————————————————————————————————

To My son, Alexander, if you read this, know that I'm truly sorry. Sorry for not being the father, the man, and the role model you deserved. Sorry for the disappointment I know I've been to you. I have seen the way you look at me when you don't think I am looking—pity mixed with disgust—and I don't even blame you. You have always deserved better and I wish I could have been the dad you needed, the one who could have guided you, supported you, and showed you both your potential and how much you meant to me. You mean everything to me. But I couldn't be who you needed, and for that, I am deeply sorry. I hope you can forgive me for leaving, for not being stronger. You deserve so much more than I could ever offer or show you. You are the best parts of me and the best thing I ever had a hand in creating.

Alex, my son, please don't let my failures ever define you. You have so much potential, so many dreams that you can still achieve. I want you to know that none of this is your fault. My struggles, my pain, my inability to make anything of myself—these are my burdens, not yours. Don't carry them with you. Don't let my choices, my end, stop you from reaching for the life you deserve. You are capable of so much more than I ever was, and I want you to believe that with all your heart.

Everything I have—whatever little it may be that is left—I leave to you. I want you to use it to build the life that I couldn't give you, to chase your dreams with everything you've got. I hope that one day, you'll look back and know that, despite everything, I loved you more than anything in this world. I never wanted this, never wanted to leave you or cause you more pain, but I see no other option left to me. I've been trapped alone in this darkness that I can't escape, it's always been here and I'm tired of fighting...I'm so tired. But you, you are strong; stronger than me, stronger than I ever was and you can barely drive. You can fight on, you can win, and you can live a life that I could have only dreamt of.

I want you to know that I'm proud of you—proud of all your accomplishments, of the man you're becoming, of your strength, integrity, and your resilience to all of the adversity life has thrown at you. Don't let my weakness be your downfall. You are more than my son—you are my legacy, my hope for something better. Live for yourself, achieve your dreams, and know that in my own broken way, I loved you with all my heart. I want you to find some form of happiness in this life and never let anyone slow you down or stop you from your dreams. Never give up on your dreams for others, in the end all you may have are those dreams.

Please, forgive me, and move forward. That's all I ever wanted for you.

To everyone else, those who watched me crumble while putting on a brave face, I know none of you saw this coming. You couldn't have. But that's the point, isn't it? The brave face, the smile, the forced laughter—it was all a mask, and I wore it so well that none of you thought to look past it. None of you ever thought to ask if I was really okay, if maybe I needed more than a passing conversation or a quick "how are you?" that we both knew I'd never answer truthfully. It's not entirely your fault, I know. I never made it easy to see the cracks, but still, there's a part of me that wonders...if just one of you had stopped, really stopped, and looked beyond the surface, would it have made a difference?

I don't blame you for not seeing it—none of you cared enough to dig deeper, to be a real friend or family member and listen to me. Maybe you were busy with your own lives, your own struggles. Maybe you didn't want to get too close to the darkness you sensed in me. I get it. But in the end, I needed more than casual concern, more than surface-level empathy. I needed someone to truly hear me, to see me, to understand that I was drowning while pretending to swim. But no one did. And now, looking back, I wonder if maybe I was always meant to do this alone.

The truth is, I've been dead inside for a long time—longer than any of you would believe. I mastered the art of looking fine, of keeping up appearances, but inside I've been hollow, a shell of who I used to be. I've tried to reach out in my own way, dropping hints, showing the cracks here and there, but no one ever picked up on them. No one ever saw the person behind the mask, and eventually, I stopped hoping anyone would.

This world was never meant for me, and I've finally accepted that. I fought it for so long—fought to belong, to be enough, to matter. But deep down, I've always known that I was different, that I wasn't cut out for this life. Maybe I wasn't strong enough, or maybe the world was just too harsh, too indifferent. I don't know. What I do know is that I've been holding on to something that was never meant to be mine—a life I was never meant to live.

I truly believe I should have died when I was fifteen, when that aneurysm hit and everything stopped. Or maybe one of those other times when my heart gave out. Those moments felt like fate's way of telling me it was over, that my time had come. But I persisted. I fought to stay alive, for reasons I don't even understand now. And for that, I'm sorry. I'm sorry for holding on when I should have let go, for dragging myself and all of you through years of struggle and pain. I thought I could find something to live for, something to make all of this worth it. But I couldn't. I just couldn't.

So, to those of you who watched and said nothing, who saw my pain and turned away—know that I don't hate you for it. I don't even blame you anymore. But just so that you know, I've been gone for a long time. The person you thought I was, the one you believed had it all together—that person hasn't existed in years. And now, I'm finally ready to let the rest of me go, too.

Maybe now, without me dragging everyone down, you can all find some peace. I never wanted to be a burden to you all and knowing that I was...I apologize.

Goodbye.

Shadows of Atonement

Elizabeth stood on the front porch, the late afternoon sun casting long, slanting shadows across the yard. The warm light painted the tips of the grass in gold, but its touch felt cold against her skin. She hesitated before unlocking the door, her hand trembling slightly as she turned the key. This house—once filled with warmth, laughter, and the cozy chaos of family life—now loomed before her like a hollow, abandoned shell.

The air seemed to hum with a strange emptiness, an echo of the silence that had grown between her and Bryan over the years. She wasn't even sure why she had come today—maybe out of habit, maybe because some sense of duty tugged her back. It had been days since she last spoke to Bryan. Though they were still technically married, they had been living separate lives for months now. Divorce was inevitable as far as Elizabeth was concerned, like a weight hanging over her head, her decision dragging through the court's backlog that had already begun to feel like a distant memory of something they had once shared.

As she pushed the door open, it creaked, a drawn-out groan that sent a shiver up her spine. Their former forever house was unnervingly still—too quiet. The air inside was stale, thick with the smell of dust and disuse, like a place long forgotten. Elizabeth felt the chill creep along her skin, raising goosebumps on her arms. She tried to shrug off the unease, blaming it on the damp, cold air of a house left too long without life. She'd meant to come sooner, but life kept getting in the way—work, friends, and the strange, tentative freedom she had begun to explore on her own. Bryan was supposed to have Alex this week, but their son had decided at the last minute to stay over at a friend's house. She knew Bryan would be alone, and some small part of her felt guilty for not checking in sooner. Maybe that's why she came today, she thought, to assuage the guilt she didn't want to admit she felt.

Elizabeth took a few tentative steps into the living room, her heels clicking against the hardwood floor, each step echoing in the emptiness. The silence here felt different, like a thick, heavy blanket pressing down on her chest, making it hard to breathe. She glanced around, her eyes darting to the familiar corners of the room—the couch where they used to sit together on lazy Sunday afternoons, the bookshelf Bryan had built with his own hands, the family pictures still hanging on the walls, a painful reminder of happier times. But something felt off, something she couldn't quite place. She called out his name, softly at first, "Bryan?" Her voice barely broke the silence. She tried again, louder this time, "Bryan?" But the only response was the low, monotonous hum of the refrigerator in the kitchen, a sound that somehow felt unnaturally loud in the quiet.

Her heart began to quicken as she moved further into the house, her footsteps growing more hesitant. That was when she saw it. A single stack of paper lay on the edge of the kitchen counter, folded neatly in half with her name written across the top in Bryan's familiar, looping handwriting. The sight of it made her stop short, her breath catching in her throat. What the hell is this? she thought. Her fingers reached out slowly, almost unwillingly, as if her body already knew what her mind couldn't yet comprehend. She brushed the edge of the paper, and a cold shiver ran up her spine, the tiny hairs on her arms standing on end. There was something about the way her name was written—so precise, so deliberate—that filled her with an inexplicable dread, a deep, gnawing fear that settled in the pit of her stomach.

She took a deep breath, steadying herself, and picked up the letter. Her fingers trembled as she unfolded it. The paper crackled softly in her hands, the sound unnaturally loud in the oppressive silence. As her eyes skimmed the first line, her heart began to race, her pulse pounding in her ears. The words seemed to blur together for a moment, her mind struggling to process what she was reading. But then the meaning started to sink in, each sentence cutting deeper than the last.

"To those who might care enough to read this..."

Elizabeth felt her breath leave her in a rush, her chest tightening as she read faster, her eyes darting over the words, trying to take them all in. Bryan's words were raw, heavy with a pain she hadn't fully understood before, a pain that seemed to seep from the page like ink bleeding into water. He wrote of his failures, his sense of inadequacy, his desperate attempts to be the man he had always wanted to be, the teacher he had dreamed of becoming, and the husband he thought she needed. He wrote about his love for her—how he had never strayed, never wanted anyone else despite everything that had happened. His words were so full of longing and regret that they seemed to ache off the page, each line a wound reopening.

And then he spoke of their son, Alex. His apology was almost unbearable to read—filled with sorrow and a deep, abiding sense of guilt for not being the father Alex deserved. Each word felt like a stab to her heart, his self-loathing pouring off the page with a weight that was crushing.

But it was the last lines that shattered her completely. Bryan's words turned darker, tinged with a finality that made her blood run cold.

"I've been trapped alone in a darkness that I can't escape, and I'm tired of fighting...I'm so tired. But you, you are strong. You can fight, you can win, and you can live a life that I could have only dreamt of. Please, forgive me, and move forward. That's all I ever wanted for you. Goodbye."

Elizabeth's hands began to shake uncontrollably, the paper fluttering from her grasp as she stumbled back, collapsing against the wall. A strangled sob escaped her lips, her chest heaving with panic and fear as the reality of what she had just read began to sink in, like ice water pouring over her skin. Bryan was gone—he was really gone. She didn't know where he was or what he had done, but there was a finality in his words that left no room for hope. He had meant every word of that letter, and now, somewhere out there, he was alone, facing whatever darkness had driven him to write it.

In an instant, she was up, her body moving on autopilot, tearing through the house with a frantic urgency she didn't know she had. "Bryan!" she screamed, her voice breaking as it echoed through the empty rooms. She ran from room to room, flinging open doors, checking every closet, every dark corner, every place he could possibly be. But the house was empty—there was no sign of him. He was gone.

Her panic grew with every passing second, her breaths coming in short, desperate gasps. She fumbled for her phone, her hands shaking so violently she could barely dial the numbers. When she finally managed to call 911, the dispatcher's calm voice did little to soothe her. She tried to explain, but her words tumbled out in a frantic rush, almost gibberish. They assured her that help was on the way, but it wasn't fast enough. She needed to find Bryan now—or maybe it was already too late.

Elizabeth stared at the phone in her trembling hand, her thumb hovering over Alex's name. She knew this wasn't going to be easy; he hadn't answered her calls in weeks, maybe even months now, and when he did, it was usually with a cold, clipped tone that made it clear he wanted nothing to do with her. But she had no choice. Not now. She dialed the number, pressing the phone to her ear, her heart pounding so hard she thought it might burst.

The line rang once, twice... three times. No answer. Her breath hitched, panic clawing up her throat. She hung up and immediately redialed, her fingers fumbling over the screen. Ring after ring echoed in her ear, each one stretching her nerves thinner, the silence on the other end becoming unbearable.

She hung up and tried again, her hand shaking so violently she almost dropped the phone. Her voice was barely steady as she muttered under her breath, "Pick up, Alex... Please, pick up." But she knew he wouldn't—why would he? She could almost hear his voice in her mind, dripping with contempt, telling her to go to hell, to leave him alone. She remembered the last time he had spoken to her, his words cold and cutting like a knife: "You're nothing but a cheating slut, Mom. You tore this family apart."

She swallowed back the lump in her throat, tried again. And again. Finally, on the fifth attempt, he picked up. She heard a long, irritated sigh on the other end, followed by the sound of him clearing his throat. "What?" His tone was sharp, dismissive. She could almost see him rolling his eyes. "What do you want, Elizabeth?" He used her first name like it was a curse.

"Alex, you need to come home," she blurted out, trying to keep her voice steady, to sound calm, but she knew the fear was slipping through, the tremor in her words betraying her. "It's about your dad... Please, just come home. Right now." She hated the way she sounded—pleading, desperate, the way she had always tried so hard not to be in front of him, the son who had seen her fall from grace and never let her forget it.

There was a long pause on the other end, a silence so heavy it felt like a weight pressing down on her chest. She could feel her pulse racing, hear the blood rushing in her ears. Finally, Alex spoke, his voice quiet but filled with an edge of fear she hadn't heard before. "What's wrong, Elizabeth? What happened?" The way he said her name, not "Mom," but "Elizabeth," sliced through her like a knife.

She swallowed hard, her throat tight, unable to find the right words. How could she explain this to him, to the son who saw her as nothing more than a woman who had destroyed everything good in their lives for some pathetic, broken man? Her voice cracked, the tears starting to flow freely down her cheeks. "Just... just come home, please," she begged, her words barely a whisper. "I'll explain when you get here." She hated the way she sounded, weak and broken, but she had no other choice.

There was another pause, and she could hear him breathing, heavy and uneven, as if weighing his options, deciding whether to hang up and leave her to deal with whatever mess she'd made this time. Her heart twisted in her chest, the tears spilling over, her hands gripping the phone so tightly her knuckles turned white. She waited, praying he would listen, praying he wouldn't just walk away like he had so many times before.

Alex hung up, and Elizabeth was left alone with the deafening silence of the house. She couldn't sit still; her legs moved on their own, pacing the room as her mind raced with a thousand horrible possibilities. She kept replaying her last interactions with Bryan, searching for any clues, any signs she might have missed. How could she not have seen this coming? He had always been quiet, keeping his feelings to himself, but she had thought he was getting better, that he was finally coming to terms with everything. She thought his recent calmness was acceptance, not despair. She had been so wrong.

Elizabeth's mind spiraled, replaying every memory with Bryan, searching for any sign, any warning she had overlooked. The moments she had dismissed as his quiet nature, his way of handling things, suddenly seemed laden with a heavier meaning. She remembered the way he would sit in silence after dinner, staring out the window as if searching for something beyond the horizon, or how his hands would tremble ever so slightly when he thought no one was watching. She thought back to the mornings he left early, before dawn, leaving only a note on the counter: "Went for a hike, needed to clear my head." She had assumed it was just his way of coping, of finding some solitude in a house that was no longer a home, but now those moments took on a sinister clarity.

She couldn't believe how blind she had been. She thought she understood his pain, his struggle, but it was clear now that she had barely scratched the surface. Bryan had been drowning in his own despair, and she had not even seen him slipping under. How many times had she walked past him, a smile on her lips, while he was silently screaming for help? How many times had she chosen to believe that he was fine, that he was just having a bad day, that he would bounce back as he always did? She had told herself he was strong, that he would be okay, even when she sensed something was deeply wrong.

Her breaths became rapid and shallow, panic clawing at her throat. She ran to the front door, flinging it open as if she might see him standing there on the porch, smiling at her with that crooked grin she used to love. But there was nothing — just the quiet rustling of leaves in the gentle evening breeze. She stepped outside, her shoes crunching on the gravel as she scanned the yard, her eyes darting to the empty driveway, to the shadows stretching long and dark under the fading light. "Bryan!" she shouted, her voice raw, breaking into the stillness. The sound seemed to echo off the trees, coming back to her as a hollow, mocking response.

Elizabeth's hands were clammy with sweat as she
clutched her phone, thinking about what to do next.
Her fingers hovered over the screen, itching to call
someone — anyone — but she didn't know who
would understand, who would know what to do.
She called 911 explaining what she knew of the
situation as best as she could and was told police
were on the way. She felt a crushing loneliness settle
over her, a deep, all-encompassing fear that seemed
to tighten around her chest like a vice. She had
never felt so helpless in her life. She had always
been the one to hold things together, to keep
moving forward, but now she was lost, spinning in
a world that no longer made sense.

She looked back at the letter on the floor, crumpled
and stained with her tears, as if it were a living
thing, mocking her for her ignorance, for all the
ways she had failed him. A wave of nausea washed
over her, and she stumbled back into the house,
leaning against the wall for support. Her legs felt
like jelly, barely able to hold her up. The walls
seemed to close in around her, the room shrinking
and stretching in her vision.

She had to do something — anything. She raced to
the kitchen, her eyes scanning the countertops and

the floor for any clue, any sign that might point her in the right direction. She opened drawers, yanked open cabinets, her movements frantic and disjointed. She knocked over a stack of bills that scattered across the floor like dead leaves, her eyes darting over them without registering what they were. The house no longer felt alive with his absence, each corner whispering his name, each shadow stretching out like a hand reaching for her.

She forced herself to breathe, to calm down, to think. She moved to the living room, her hands shaking as she reached for the couch, feeling along the cushions, checking for anything he might have left behind. Her heart pounded in her chest, a steady drumbeat of panic. She flipped through the magazines on the coffee table, tossed aside the throw pillows, her hands moving almost automatically as her mind raced through the possibilities. Where could he have gone? Why hadn't she seen this coming?

Elizabeth's vision blurred with tears, but she blinked them away, trying to focus. She felt her phone buzz in her pocket, and she pulled it out to see Alex's name flashing on the screen. She answered it, her voice tight and choked. "I'm on my way, almost there" Alex said hurriedly, fear evident in his voice. "What's going on? Where is Dad?"

Elizabeth swallowed hard, her mouth dry. "No, Alex I don't know," she whispered, her voice breaking. "But there's... there's a letter he left, Alex. He left a letter. It sounds like... it sounds like he's saying goodbye."

There was a pause on the line, and she could hear Alex's breath catch. "What do you mean, goodbye? Is he... do you think he's...damn it all. I'm almost there."

"I don't know, Alex," she cut him off, her voice trembling. "I just don't know. I need you to get here, okay? Please, just get here fast."

Alex hung up on her, her hands were shaking, and a tremendous wave of dizziness washed over her. She leaned heavily against the wall, closing her eyes, willing herself not to collapse under the weight of it all as she slid slowly down the wall to avoid falling. She needed to stay strong, needed to keep it together for Alex, for Bryan — wherever he was, but how.

3 FRACTURED REALITY

Alex had always been the quiet one in the family, the observer who kept his thoughts close and his emotions closer. But when the divorce came crashing down around him, the walls of his world began to close in. He didn't have the words to explain what he was feeling, not to his mom, not to his dad. The only place that made sense anymore was the dark confines of his room, the glow of his computer screen offering the only semblance of comfort.

He spent hours in his chair, his fingers moving across the keyboard with mechanical precision. It wasn't just about gaming anymore—although that had been his first escape. When his parents' arguments had become too loud, too raw, he'd slip on his headset, disappear into virtual worlds with his friends, where he didn't have to think about the brokenness of the real one. In those games, he could control the chaos. He could be the hero, the one who made the right decisions, saved the day, and got the last laugh. It was everything the real world wasn't: fair, predictable, and, most of all, free of betrayal.

But after the news of the divorce hit, that wasn't

enough anymore. His mom's cheating had torn something inside him that he couldn't ignore. It wasn't just her betrayal of his dad; it felt like a betrayal of him too, of the family he thought they were. Elizabeth had been more than his mother—she'd been the glue that held them all together. Now, she was the one who had ripped them apart.

So he retreated deeper into the digital world. He stopped gaming with friends and started digging—searching for something to make sense of the mess his life had become. The surface web wasn't enough. He found himself diving into the dark web, not to look for anything specific at first, just exploring, trying to see how far he could go. It was exhilarating in a twisted way, being part of something most people didn't even know existed. The thrill of uncovering secrets, of slipping past firewalls and encryptions, was addictive.

Soon enough, his curiosity turned personal. He began searching for information on Elizabeth and her affair with Bishop, the man who had ruined everything. His mom had always been careful, or at least she thought she had been, but Alex had learned things from his dad over the years. He knew how to look beyond the surface, how to track digital footprints. He hacked into her email first, finding the trail she'd left behind—messages exchanged, plans made in secret. Each discovery felt like a punch to the gut, but he couldn't stop. He needed to know the truth, even if it tore him apart.

Bishop, the man who had crept into their lives like a cancer, was next. Alex found his records, his history of violence, his addiction to drugs. He dug deeper, finding connections in Bishop's shady dealings and the people he surrounded himself with. Every piece of information only deepened his hatred, making him feel like a detective in his own personal hell, piecing together the story of how his family had fallen apart.

Meanwhile, Elizabeth had no idea. She kept trying to reach out, kept texting him, calling him, leaving voicemails. He ignored them all. He'd blocked her on social media, blocked her number, cut her out completely. She wasn't his mother anymore—she was just Elizabeth, the woman who had destroyed his father's life and, by extension, his. Her family tried to intervene, too, his aunts and grandparents reaching out, but he kept them at arm's length. They didn't understand. None of them did. He was alone in this.

He felt sorry for his dad, more than anything. Bryan was an amazing man—patient, kind, hardworking. But life had never been fair to him. He watched from the shadows as his father shouldered the weight of the world with quiet resignation. Alex could see it in the way Bryan's shoulders sagged, in the deep lines etched into his face, the way he tried to smile through the pain. His dad was the kind of man who had always put others first, always did what was right, even when it hurt him. And this...this betrayal, this abandonment by Elizabeth, was the final blow.

Alex resented the world for what it had done to his father. It was like Bryan couldn't catch a break. Every job Bryan tried, every effort he made, was met with more resistance, more failure, and now, this. Watching his dad suffer in silence, trying to hold onto some semblance of dignity, was unbearable. But Alex didn't know how to help. So he did what he did best—he buried himself in code, in the digital world where he could at least pretend he was in control.

He became obsessed with finding every detail, every thread that tied Elizabeth and Bishop together, as if by unraveling their lies, he could somehow undo the damage they had caused. But with each new discovery, his anger only grew. He wanted revenge, but more than that, he wanted his family back. He wanted things to go back to the way they were before, when his mom was just his mom and not the woman who had shattered their world.

But he knew that wasn't going to happen. That part of his life was over, and no amount of hacking or digging could change that. The only thing left to do was figure out how to survive the wreckage.

When Alex finally got the call from Elizabeth, it felt like a punch to the gut. His phone had lit up with her name, and his first instinct was to ignore it, like he always did. But something stopped him this time—some nagging sense that this was different, that maybe he needed to answer. His thumb hovered over the screen before he swiped to pick up.

"Alex, you need to come home," her voice was shaky, more fragile than he'd ever heard it. His stomach tightened.

"What's wrong, Elizabeth?" he asked, almost out of habit, the words slipping out before he could stop himself. The fact that he hadn't called her 'Mom' in months hung heavily in the air between them.

"It's about your dad," she said, her voice cracking. "Just come home, okay? Right now."

Alex's heart raced. His dad. The only person who hadn't completely let him down, the one steady presence in his life. He could feel the blood draining from his face as he stood there, frozen for a moment.

"What happened? Is he...?" His voice faltered, fear clutching at his chest.

"I'll explain when you get here, but please, Alex,

just come home. We need to find him."

She hung up before he could ask more. The panic in her voice was unmistakable, and it sent him spiraling. His thoughts raced as he grabbed his keys, barely aware of what he was doing. Bryan was missing? How? When had things gotten so bad that his dad, the one person who had always held it together, was gone?

The drive to their house was a blur. His mind raced faster than his car, each passing second filled with worst-case scenarios. His hands gripped the steering wheel so tightly his knuckles turned white, his heart pounding in his chest. Images of his dad, alone somewhere, lost or worse, flashed in his mind, each one more terrifying than the last. He couldn't let this happen. Not to his dad.

The streets passed in a haze, the sound of his own breathing loud in his ears as he pushed the car faster. He'd been angry at Elizabeth, furious with her for what she'd done to their family, but now all of that seemed to fall away. This was about his dad, about getting him back, and nothing else mattered.

"Please," he whispered to himself, "let him be okay."

He didn't even know if he was praying or begging or just trying to keep from losing it. All he knew was that he had to get there, had to do something, anything, to bring Bryan home.

4 REALITY SETS IN

The sound of police and emergency sirens in the distance snapped her out of her thoughts. She rushed to the front window, watching as the police cars pulled up to the curb. Two officers stepped out, and Elizabeth ran out the door to meet them, her heart pounding in her chest and tears coming down in a torrent.

"Are you Mrs. Black?" one of the officers asked, and she nodded, her voice failing her. "We're here to help," the officer continued. "Have you been able to contact him and Can you show us the letter?"

Elizabeth led them inside, her hands trembling as she handed over the letter. The officers read it quickly, their expressions grave. "We're going to start searching the area starting with going over the house again," one of them said, handing the letter back to her. "Do you know where he might have gone? Any places that were special to him, or where he might go to be alone?"

Elizabeth shook her head no, trying to think. Bryan had always been trying to get her to join him on walks and hikes but she had always been tired or unwilling at the time and found an excuse not to. But there were a few places he had loved—places they had gone together when they were much younger, happier. "There's a park near here," she said finally, her voice barely a whisper. "We used to go there a lot when we were first married. And he loved the hiking trails nearby...he might have gone there."

The officers nodded and relayed the information to their colleagues over the radio. Elizabeth watched as they set up a perimeter around the neighborhood, organizing a search party. More police cars arrived, along with a few of her neighbors who had seen the commotion and come to offer their support. Elizabeth felt numb, her mind reeling from the shock. She could hardly believe this was happening—that Bryan could really be gone, that he had felt so alone, so worthless and hopeless that he saw no other way out.

Alex arrived not long after, bursting through the front door with a look of pure terror on his face.

"Elizabeth!" he cried, rushing to her side. "What's going on? Where's Dad?"

Elizabeth pulled him into a tight hug, tears streaming down her face. "I don't know, sweetheart," she whispered, her voice choked with emotion. "I don't know where he is. But the police are looking for him—they're going to find him."

Alex pulled away slightly, his eyes searching hers for answers. "Why would he do this? What did you do now?" he asked, his voice breaking. "Why didn't he say anything...not even to me?"

Elizabeth shook her head, unable to find the words. How could she explain the depths of Bryan's despair, the darkness that had consumed him? She could barely understand it herself. "I don't know,baby" she said finally, her voice barely audible. "I just...I just want him to be okay."

The hours dragged on, each one more agonizing than the last. Elizabeth and Alex sat together in the living room, surrounded by friends and family, but it all felt surreal, like a nightmare they couldn't wake up from. Every so often, an officer would come in with an update, but there was still no sign of Bryan. The search had expanded to the park and the river, with officers combing the area, but the longer it took, the more Elizabeth's hope began to fade.

Minutes felt like hours as she waited for news. Every time the radio crackled to life, her heart would leap into her throat, only to sink again when it wasn't about Bryan. The house was now filled with people—neighbors, friends, even a few of Bryan's former students who had heard what was happening and came to offer their help. But Elizabeth barely registered their presence. Her thoughts were consumed by Bryan—where he was, what he was doing, and whether they would find him in time.

As night descended on the neighborhood and everyone left, the quiet of the house seemed almost deafening. The tension that had gripped Elizabeth earlier had given way to a dull, gnawing fear. She and Alex sat on opposite ends of the couch, surrounded by a few close friends, alone together for the first time in what seemed like forever, given their strained relationship. The initial flurry of activity from the police had subsided, replaced by a more methodical, yet increasingly desperate search.

Alex sat there, his eyes glued to his phone. He was unusually quiet, but Elizabeth could see the wheels turning in his head. Alex had always been an extraordinarily bright kid—sharp, resourceful, the kind of teenager who could solve a problem faster than most adults and in a dozen different ways. But this wasn't a math equation or a science project. This was real life, and it terrified her to think of what might be running through his mind.

"Alex, honey," Elizabeth said softly, placing a hand on his arm. "Are you okay? Do you want to talk about it?"

Alex looked up at her, his face pale and drawn. His eyes were red, though whether from crying or exhaustion, she couldn't tell. "No, I don't know," he said, his voice hoarse. "I just...I don't understand why he didn't tell me, tell us, or tell someone. Why didn't he say anything?"

Elizabeth's heart ached as she listened to him. She didn't have the answers he was looking for; she barely understood it herself. "I don't know, sweetie," she replied, her voice trembling. "I think he was in a lot of pain, and maybe he didn't want to worry us. But that doesn't mean we don't care. We just need to find him, and then we can help him."

41

Alex nodded, but she could see the frustration building behind his eyes. He wasn't the type to sit idly by when there was a problem to solve. And as much as she wanted to keep him sheltered from the harsh reality of the situation, she knew that holding him back would only make him feel more helpless.

5 GPS not COPS

"Look, Elizabeth. Why do you want to help him now? You caused all of this...nevermind, it's not the time." Alex said suddenly, rapidly sitting up straighter. "Dad always had his phone on him, right? Even when he was feeling down, he should still have it. What if we can track it? Find out where it is?"

Elizabeth blinked, the obvious idea taking her by surprise. She hadn't thought of that and neither had the police, as far as she knew. In the chaos of the last few hours, her mind had been consumed with worst-case scenarios, but Alex was right. If Bryan had his phone on him, they could track it. They might be able to find him before it was too late.

"You think we can do that?" she asked, a glimmer of hope sparking in her chest.

Alex was already moving, his fingers flying across his phone screen. "Yeah, I can do it. Dad's on the family sharing plan, so he and I can see each other's location if our phones are on. Hold on..." He trailed off as he navigated through the settings, his brow furrowed in concentration.

Elizabeth watched him anxiously, her heart pounding excitedly but her brain was feeling the hurt in Alex's words, his blatant contempt for her. She didn't want to get her hopes up, but this was the first lead they'd had all night. If they could find Bryan's phone, they might be able to find him.

Alex's face suddenly lit up, a small gasp escaping his lips. "I've got it!" he exclaimed, holding up his phone for her to see. "It's pinging a location near the river. It's not moving and it's recent, so he must be there."

Elizabeth leaned in, her breath catching as she saw the small dot on the map, indicating Bryan's phone's location. The river was just a few miles away—a secluded spot they used to visit when they first moved to the area. Bryan had always loved the peace and quiet it offered, the way the water seemed to wash away the stresses of the world. She should have thought of it sooner, but she realized she may not have understood Bryan as well as she thought.

"We need to tell the police," Alex said, his voice trembling with urgency. "They need to go there, now. And we are going too".

Alex was already dialing the non-emergency number the officers had given them earlier. He spoke quickly, clearly, relaying the information with a precision that belied his age. Elizabeth could only watch, her emotions swinging wildly between fear, pride, and hope as Alex described the location and their suspicions.

The police response was swift. Within minutes, officers were dispatched to the river, their radios crackling with updates. Elizabeth and Alex were told to stay put, but neither could bear the thought of sitting idly by while Bryan was out there, possibly alone and in pain. They insisted on going and though the police were reluctant, they eventually agreed, realizing there was no way to keep them from going.

The drive to the river was fast and tense, the silence in Elizabeth's car was thick with unspoken fears. Elizabeth's mind raced with what-ifs, each one darker than the last. She couldn't lose him—not like this. The past few months had been hard, yes, but she had never stopped loving Bryan. She just didn't know how to help him and didn't know how to bridge the growing distance between them she had caused. Now, that distance felt insurmountable and impossibly distant.

Alex sat beside her, his eyes fixed on the screen of his phone, watching the small dot that represented Bryan's phone. Every so often, he would glance out the window, as if willing the car to move faster. Elizabeth reached over multiple times and tried to squeeze his hand to offer what little comfort she could, but he jerked his hand away each time.

6 ALWAYS.

Elizabeth and Alex arrived at the river at the same time as the police, the cool night air biting at their skin as they stepped out of the car. The area was eerily quiet, the only sounds coming from the rushing water and the occasional rustle of leaves. Officers moved quickly, spreading out with flashlights as they began their search, the beams of light cutting through the darkness.

Elizabeth's heart pounded in her chest as she was led by Alex and followed the path they used to walk when they visited the river. The memories of those peaceful days felt incredibly distant now, overshadowed by the dread that ensnared her. She had always known this place to be a sanctuary for Bryan, a refuge where he could escape the stresses of the disappointments in everyday life. But now, it feels like it may be the site of something far more sinister.

Alex was beside her, his face pale yet determined, but his eyes were sharp, focused on the task at hand.

He kept glancing at his phone, tracking the location of Bryan's, hoping for any sign of movement, any indication that his father was still nearby. But the dot on the screen remained stationary and had not shown movement in the past few hours, its location just a few yards ahead of them, near the water's edge.

"Over here!" one of the officers called out from just ahead of them, his voice cutting through the silence. Elizabeth's heart leapt into her throat as she and Alex rushed toward the voice, the other officers converging on the location.

As they approached, the beam of a flashlight illuminated a small, familiar object lying on the ground—a phone, Bryan's phone. Elizabeth felt a wave of nausea wash over her as she recognized it, her breath catching in her throat.

Alex rushed past the officers and was the first to reach it, his hands trembling as he picked it up; Bryan's phone. The screen was still on, the battery nearly drained, but the phone was open to the photo gallery. Thousands of pictures filled the screen, each one a snapshot of moments with Alex and Elizabeth—smiling, laughing, even some candid shots they hadn't known he'd taken. The gallery was

48

overflowing with memories, images of a life Bryan had tried so desperately to hold onto, even as he slipped further away from them.

Elizabeth knelt beside Alex, her eyes filling with tears as she looked at the pictures. It was overwhelming—the love, the pain, all of it captured in those photos. She could see how much they meant to Bryan, how much he had tried to keep them close, even when he felt he was losing everything.

But there was something else—something that made Elizabeth's heart ache even more. Beside the phone, resting on a smooth, flat rock, was Bryan's wedding ring. And carved into the surface of the rock was a heart, carefully etched into the stone. Inside the heart were their initials—BEB, CEB, and CAB—and in the center of it all, Bryan had written one word: "ALWAYS!"

Elizabeth felt her breath catch as she reached out to touch the carving, her fingers tracing the lines of the heart, the initials, the word that held so much meaning. "Always." It was a promise, a vow that they had made to each other on their wedding day. A promise she had repeatedly desecrated. But now, it felt like a final farewell, a message from Bryan that he was letting go.

"Hey..." Alex's voice was barely a whisper, his eyes wide with fear as he looked at her. "What does this mean? Where is he...where the hell is he?"

Elizabeth shook her head, tears streaming down her face. "I don't know, Alex. I don't know where he is. But we have to find him. We won't give up."

One of the officers approached them, his expression grim. "Ma'am, we've searched the immediate area, but there's no other signs of him. We're going to expand the search, but it's possible he may have left the area on foot. You did say he was an avid hiker."

Elizabeth nodded emotionally numb, but with her mind racing. Where could Bryan have gone? Where would Bryan have gone? Why would he leave his phone, his wedding ring, and this message behind? It felt like once again he was saying goodbye, but she refused to accept that. He couldn't be gone. Not yet.

Alex stood up, determination in his eyes as he held onto the phone. "We have to keep looking for him, Elizabeth, snap out of it. We have to find him.

Maybe...maybe there's something on the phone that can help us. A clue, or a message."

Elizabeth nodded, trying to hold onto the hope that Alex was right. Bryan had left them something— something that might help them understand what he was thinking, where he might have gone.

They couldn't give up on him.

Not now, not ever.

7 Memories Bring Truth To Life

They returned to the car, one officer having cloned Bryan's phone and took note of the ring and rock as evidence but then returned the items to Elizabeth. The other officers continued their search while Elizabeth and Alex sat in the car, the phone between them both hoping the officers would find some other clues. Alex began scrolling through the gallery, looking for anything that might give them a clue—a location, a recent photo, something that could lead them to Bryan.

As they sifted through the images, Elizabeth found herself lost in the memories they represented. Pictures of Alex's birthdays, holidays, simple moments at home—Bryan had documented it all, capturing the essence of their lives together. It was clear that, despite everything, he had always loved them deeply. But the question that was breaking her brain, and her heart remained—where was he now? What had driven him to leave these mementos behind? Why?

Alex suddenly paused, his finger hovering over a video that had been taken just a few days earlier. "Mom, look at this," he said, his voice trembling.

Elizabeth leaned in, her heart pounding as she watched the video play. It was a short clip of Bryan sitting alone on their back porch, the camera slightly shaky as he adjusted the angle. He was staring off into the distance, his expression weary, his eyes filled with a sadness that made Elizabeth's heart ache.

"I love you both so much," Bryan's voice crackled through the speaker, each word trembling with the weight of unspoken sorrow. His voice was a whisper, quiet and broken, as though it was coming from some deep, hollow place within him, a place that had known too much darkness for too long. There was a rawness in his tone, a rough edge that suggested he had been crying, his breaths coming in short, shaky bursts, as if each word pained him to say.

"I wish I could have been better for you," he continued, his voice faltering slightly, breaking on the word "better," as though the very idea of being anything other than what he had become felt like a cruel impossibility. There was a deep ache in his words, a longing that reached out across the distance between them, pulling at the frayed edges of the bond they still shared. Elizabeth could almost see him in her mind's eye, his shoulders hunched, his head bowed, his hands gripping the phone with a desperation that matched her own.

"I'm sorry," he said, and the words seemed to shatter in the air, fragile and jagged like shards of glass. "I'm sorry for all the ways I've failed you." His voice caught, the apology hanging there, suspended between them, weighted with the unbearable truth of his self-loathing. The regret in his voice was palpable, a heavy, choking thing that seemed to fill the room, wrapping around her chest like a cold, unyielding hand. Each syllable carried a lifetime of pain, of moments lost and dreams deferred, of promises broken and wounds left unhealed.

"But no matter what happens," he continued, his voice barely above a whisper now, as if he was speaking from a place so deep inside himself that it was almost impossible to reach, "please remember—I'll always love you. Always." His voice cracked on the final word, the emotion breaking through despite his best efforts to hold it together. There was a depth to his declaration, a fierce, unyielding truth that seemed to defy the despair that had brought him to this point.

Elizabeth could hear the tears in his voice, could feel them in her own eyes, hot and stinging. She imagined him standing there, alone, his face lined with sorrow, his eyes hollow with the weight of his guilt. She could almost hear the tremor in his breath, the way he would try to steady himself even as his body betrayed him, as if trying to find some strength in his last moments of honesty. She could feel the agony of his words, each one a knife twisting in her heart, carving out all the things she wished she had said to him, all the times she had turned away when he needed her most.

In that moment, the distance between them felt infinite, like a vast, empty chasm that she could never cross. But in his voice, she heard something she had almost forgotten—something tender and fragile, a reminder of the man she had once loved with everything she had. She could feel his love, raw and undiluted, flowing through the phone, reaching out to her and to Alex like a lifeline, a thread that refused to break even in the darkest of times. His words hung in the air, suspended like a prayer or a plea, and she clung to them, knowing they might be the last she would ever hear from him.

The video ended abruptly, leaving Elizabeth and Alex in stunned silence. The words hung in the air, heavy with the weight of what Bryan had been feeling. It was a goodbye, but it was also a plea—for understanding, for forgiveness.

Elizabeth felt tears streaming down her face as she replayed the video in her mind, the pain in Bryan's voice cutting through her. She had known he was struggling, but she hadn't realized just how deep his pain went. And now, he was out there somewhere, alone, carrying the burden of that pain.

"We have to find him, mom." Alex said again, his voice choking with emotion. "We have to bring him home."

Elizabeth reached over and pulled Alex into a tight embrace, her own tears falling freely. "We will, Alex. We will find him. And we'll do everything we can to help him. He's not alone in this—we're in this together."

As they sat there, holding onto each other, the weight of the situation settled over them like a heavy blanket. Bryan was still missing, and this night was far from over. But they had a direction now, a purpose. They would find him, no matter how long it took, no matter how far they had to go or what they had to do. The officers told Elizabeth and Alex they were continuing the search and would keep them informed if they wanted to leave and with the heavy emotional toil of the events they acquiesced and drove home.

As she drove, Elizabeth looked out the window, her mind racing with thoughts of where Bryan could be, what he might be doing. She refused to believe that he was beyond saving. He was still out there, somewhere and as long as there was a chance to bring him home, she would hold onto that hope with everything she had.

The road ahead was uncertain, filled with darkness and doubt. But one thing was clear—Bryan was not alone and never would be again. Elizabeth and Alex would search for him until they found him, help him until they could bring him back to the light, and bring to the life they had built together and the future they had once imagined.

"Always," Elizabeth whispered to herself, the word echoing in her mind as she held onto the memory of that etching on the rock. It was a promise she intended to keep.

8 CONNECTION INTERRUPTED

Elizabeth sat in the dimly lit living room, her eyes fixed on the phone in her hand. The screen flickered with images of a life she once thought she understood—pictures of Alex growing up, of holidays and family trips, moments she had forgotten but Bryan had captured. Every photo felt like a piece of a puzzle she hadn't realized needed solving until now.

Alex was beside her, his gaze similarly glued to the screen as he swiped through the endless gallery of memories. His face was pale, the strain of the last 24 hours evident in the tightness of his jaw, the way his shoulders slumped forward. He had hardly said a word since they left the river, where they'd found Bryan's phone and wedding ring. The image of that heart etched into the rock haunted Elizabeth—BEB, CEB, CAB, and the word "ALWAYS!"—a symbol of a love that now felt lost in the shadows of their collective grief.

"We have to find him, Mom," Alex finally said, his voice barely above a whisper. "We can't let him... we can't lose him like this."

Elizabeth nodded, but the uncertainty gnawed at her. Where could Bryan be? Why had he left them with nothing but a phone full of memories and a carved message on a stone? She knew they couldn't give up, but the path forward seemed so unclear. All they had were these photos and the hope that somewhere in them, Bryan had left a clue.

Alex, ever the problem-solver, had already begun dissecting the details. "Dad didn't just disappear," he said, more to himself than to her. "He's been leaving hints, even if he didn't mean to. He's trying to tell us something. We just have to figure out what."

Elizabeth watched her son, a mixture of pride and sorrow welling up inside her. He had always been so perceptive, so attuned to the world around him. He had inherited Bryan's brilliant analytical mind, his ability to see patterns where others saw nothing but chaos. But it truly broke her heart to see him using that gift now, in this context, trying to piece together the reasons why his father might have felt so lost as to leave them, to leave him.

"What do you think we should do?" she asked softly, wanting to support him but feeling out of her depth.

Alex didn't answer immediately. Instead, he pulled up a recent video, one they hadn't watched yet. Bryan had recorded it just days before his disappearance. In it, he sat alone on the porch, the camera slightly shaky, as though he hadn't bothered to stabilize it. His face was weary, the lines of worry and sadness deeply etched into his features. He looked like a man who had been carrying too much for too long.

"I love you both so much," Bryan said in the video, his voice rough, filled with unspoken pain. "I wish I could have been better for you. I'm sorry for all the ways I've failed you. But no matter what happens, please remember—I'll always love you. Always."

The video was a shorter version of what they watched earlier and ended just as abruptly, leaving both Elizabeth and Alex in silence. He had rehearsed this, even though he was extraordinarily positive this past week to both of them. The weight of Bryan's words hung in the air, heavy and suffocating. Elizabeth felt tears prick at her eyes, and she blinked them away, not wanting to break down in front of Alex. She had to be strong, for him, for both of them.

Alex, however, was more determined than ever. "There's something in these videos," he muttered, his eyes narrowing in concentration. "He's trying to tell us something, maybe where he is or where he is going. I just know it."

"Alex..." Elizabeth started, her voice trembling with the uncertainty she felt. "What if he really doesn't want to be found? What if this... this really is his way of saying goodbye?"

Alex looked at her, his eyes sharp and defiant as he spoke, "We are not giving up on him ever again. He doesn't want to say goodbye, Elizabeth. Not like this. He's scared, he's hurting, and he's in a very bad place mentally but he wouldn't just leave us without a way to find him. He's not that kind of person..right?" His voice trembled and softened, Mom?"

Elizabeth wanted to believe him. She wanted more than anything to believe that Bryan was out there, waiting for them to find him, to bring him back home. But the fear that had been gnawing at her since they found his phone was hard to shake. What if Alex was wrong? What if Bryan truly was beyond their reach, lost in a darkness they couldn't pull him out of?

But then Alex did something that surprised her. He handed her the phone, stating, "You know him better than anyone, Mom. You might be able to see something I missed. I am probably over analyzing things or that is what dad would say."

Elizabeth took the phone, her hands shaking slightly. She began scrolling through the gallery, this time with a different purpose. She wasn't just looking at the pictures as memories; she was looking for patterns, for anything that might give them a clue as to where Bryan could be.

As she did, something began to emerge—an odd but consistent theme. Bryan had taken an unusual number of photos at specific locations around town—places that had been significant to them over the years, decades they had been together. The old mall where they'd gone on their first date, the park where they'd taken Alex so many times when he was a toddler, the coffee shop where they'd spent countless Saturday mornings together. And then there were newer locations—places she hadn't even known Bryan had visited. The photos were all time stamped within the last few weeks, as if Bryan had been on a journey, retracing the steps of their life together and something else. Elizabeth's breath caught in her throat as the realization hit her. Bryan wasn't just documenting memories—he was leading them somewhere, somewhere only she and Alex could understand and figure out.

"Alex, come here and look at this," she said, showing him what might be a pattern she'd noticed. "These places... they're all connected, to us. He's been visiting them, taking photos."

Alex studied the screen, his brow furrowed. "He's leaving a trail," he said, his voice filled with both awe and anxiety. "I bet he wants us to follow it."

Elizabeth nodded. "I want to think maybe he's waiting for us at the last place. The place where it all started."

9 Follow The White Rabbit

The next few hours were a blur of activity. Elizabeth and Alex quickly mapped out the locations Bryan had photographed, using them to trace a path through the town. The realization that Bryan might be waiting for them at one of these places gave them a renewed sense of purpose, a fragile hope that they clung to desperately.

They started with the most recent location—the old mall. It was where Bryan and Elizabeth had gone on their first date, over two decades ago. The building had long since fallen into disrepair, most of its stores shuttered, its halls empty. As they pulled up outside, Elizabeth's heart raced with the possibility that Bryan might be inside, waiting for them. But when they entered, the mall was a ghost town, its once-vibrant atmosphere replaced by a hollow silence that echoed with their footsteps.

The next stop was the park where they used to take Alex to play as a toddler. They searched the area, calling Bryan's name, hoping against hope that he would emerge from the shadows. But once again, they found nothing.

The coffee shop was next. It was one of the few places that still looked the same after all these years. The familiar smell of freshly brewed coffee greeted them as they walked in, and for a moment, Elizabeth felt a pang of nostalgia, remembering the many mornings they had spent there together. But Bryan wasn't there either.

With each stop, their hope dimmed just a little more. But they pressed on, determined to see this journey through to the end.

Finally, they arrived at the last location on their list—a secluded spot near the river, a place that held secrets only they knew. It was hidden away from prying eyes, nestled deep in a grove of towering pines and willows that whispered in the soft breeze, their branches swaying like they were welcoming old friends. The path leading down to the riverbank was overgrown, weeds and wildflowers spilling into the dirt track, their colors vivid against the green. As they made their way down the familiar trail, Elizabeth felt a rush of emotions overwhelm her, a flood of memories sweeping over her like a tidal wave that threatened to pull her under.

Her hands trembled, her fingers gripping the steering wheel tightly even though the car had come to a stop. She could hear the soft murmur of the river in the distance, the water moving slowly over the rocks, a sound she hadn't heard in years. It brought with it a rush of bittersweet nostalgia, the kind that sits heavy in the chest, warm but aching. This had once been their sanctuary, a hidden refuge where they could escape the pressures of life, where they could forget about the world outside, even if only for a little while. She remembered the way Bryan would smile when they reached this place, his eyes lighting up with a quiet joy she rarely saw anywhere else.

She closed her eyes for a moment, taking in the scent of the damp earth, the faint aroma of wild mint that grew along the banks, and the subtle tang of moss that clung to the rocks. Each step she took down the path felt like moving through a veil of time, her feet crunching on the fallen leaves that had gathered like memories waiting to be uncovered. The coolness of the shade brushed against her skin like an old lover's touch, and the air was thick with the hum of cicadas, a sound that always made her feel both comforted and unsettled, as if nature itself were holding its breath.

Elizabeth's heart pounded against her ribs, each beat resonating in her ears. She could feel the uneven ground beneath her feet, the stones and roots shifting underfoot, but she kept moving forward, her legs almost moving on their own. The path twisted and turned, and with each bend, another memory surfaced—Bryan's hand in hers as they walked side by side, the soft murmur of his voice as he told her stories, the way he would pause just to take in the view, his face softening as he watched the river flow. She could almost hear his laughter, carried on the wind, light and carefree, a sound she had missed without even realizing how much.

Her breath hitched as they approached the clearing by the riverbank. She remembered how they used to come here in the early mornings, just after dawn, when the mist would rise from the water like a blanket being pulled back from a sleeping child. The sunlight would filter through the trees, casting dappled shadows on the ground, and they would sit on the rocks, their shoulders touching, listening to the river's secrets. It was a place where everything seemed simpler, where their love felt unburdened, untouched by the complexities that later tore them apart.

Now, the place seemed almost eerie in its stillness, as if it too was waiting, holding onto its breath, watching them approach. The river flowed steadily, its surface glistening in the fading light, but it seemed to move with a slower, more solemn rhythm than she remembered. The air was heavy with the scent of water and earth, mixed with the faintest hint of decay, the smell of leaves that had fallen long ago, decomposing in the dampness. It was a smell she knew well, one that spoke of endings and beginnings, of life constantly moving forward even when everything else seemed to stand still.

As they stepped closer to the river's edge, Elizabeth felt her throat tighten, her heart aching with every step. The shadows seemed to stretch longer here, darker, as if they were trying to swallow the light. The place that once felt like a retreat, a sanctuary, now felt like a ghost of itself, filled with memories that refused to stay buried. She could feel the weight of them pressing down on her shoulders, a heaviness that seemed to seep into her bones, making it hard to breathe, hard to think. The quiet seemed louder here, the kind of silence that speaks louder than words, and she felt a pang of regret that twisted in her chest, sharp and unforgiving.

Bryan had loved this place. It was here he had
taught her to listen, to really listen to the sounds of
the world—the river's whispers, the wind's song
through the leaves, the way the earth seemed to
hum beneath their feet. It was here they had found
solace in each other, in the silence between words,
in the moments that needed no explanation. And
now, it was here that she stood, searching for him,
hoping against hope that this place, this last piece
of their shared world, would somehow hold the
answers she was so desperately seeking.

With each step, her body seemed to tremble more,
her breath quickening, her eyes scanning the
familiar landscape, looking for any sign, any clue
that would tell her he was still here, still with them,
still holding on. But all she saw was the river,
moving slowly, steadily, as if it had all the time in
the world. She reached out, instinctively, grasping at
the cool air, as if she could somehow grab hold of
the past and pull it back, make it alright again. But
there was nothing to hold onto, nothing but the
sound of the water and the memories that clung to
it like mist.

As they approached the clearing, Elizabeth's heart
sank. The spot was empty, just as the others had

been. The late afternoon light filtered through the trees, casting long shadows across the ground. The only sound was the gentle rush of the river, its waters flowing steadily past, oblivious to the turmoil within her.

Alex, however, wasn't ready to give up. He walked around the clearing, his eyes scanning every inch of the ground, searching for any sign that Bryan had been there. But there was nothing—no footprints, no disturbed leaves, nothing that suggested Bryan had come this way.

Elizabeth stood in the middle of the clearing, feeling the weight of despair settle over her. "What if we're too late?" she whispered, more to herself than to Alex. "What if he's already gone?"

Alex looked up at her, his expression a mix of determination and fear. "He's not gone, Elizabeth. He wouldn't do that to us. He's just... he's hiding. He's waiting for us to find him. I can still feel that he is out there...somewhere, whatever his reasons are."

Elizabeth wanted to believe him. She wanted to believe that Bryan was still out there, waiting for them to find him, to bring him back home. But the fear that had been gnawing at her since they found his phone was hard to shake. What if for once Alex was wrong? What if Bryan was beyond their reach, lost in a darkness they couldn't pull him out of?

But then Alex did something that surprised her. He handed her the phone again. "We're missing something," he said, his voice steady. "Dad wouldn't just leave us without a way to find him. He's not that kind of person."

Elizabeth took the phone, her hands shaking slightly as she began scrolling through the photos again. She retraced the path they had followed, revisiting each location in her mind, trying to see it through Bryan's eyes. But nothing new jumped out at her—just the same photos, the same places, the same memories.

Frustrated, she handed the phone back to Alex. "I don't know, Alex. Maybe he didn't want us to find him. Maybe this was his way of saying goodbye."

Alex shook his head, refusing to accept that possibility. "No, just no. He didn't do that to us. He's out there, somewhere. We just have to keep looking and I'm doing that with or without you."

10 A Heart Heavy Moon

By the time they returned home, the sun had set, casting the town in a blanket of darkness. Elizabeth felt utterly defeated, her hope extinguished by the harsh reality of their fruitless search. Alex, though, remained resolute, his mind still racing with possibilities.

As they entered the house, the emptiness seemed to echo their despair. The photos on Bryan's phone haunted them, each image a reminder of what they had lost, what they were still desperately searching for.

But then, as they settled into the quiet of the living room, both ready for a well deserved rest, Alex's phone buzzed with a notification. He glanced at it and froze, his eyes widening in disbelief.

"What is it?" Elizabeth asked, her voice thick with exhaustion.

Alex didn't respond immediately. Instead, he turned his phone toward her, showing her the screen. It was a notification from Bryan's phone, sent from a location-sharing app they hadn't thought to check earlier.

"It says he's at the lake," Alex said, his voice trembling with a mixture of hope and fear. "He's still there, Mom. His watch is still active, mom. We forgot about his damned watch."

Elizabeth's heart leapt at the possibility. Without another word, they were both back in her car, racing toward the lake, their faint hopes rekindled by the GPS signal of a smartwatch of all things.

When they reached the lake, the moon hung high in the sky, a cold, solitary beacon casting its pale silver light over the dark expanse of water. The lake stretched out before them like a vast, endless mirror, its surface smooth and still, as if holding its breath in anticipation. Moonlight shimmered across the water, dancing in fractured patterns, glinting like shards of glass scattered across an obsidian sea. The trees that lined the shore stood as silent sentinels, their dark forms etched against the night sky, their shadows stretching long and thin, merging with the inky blackness of the lake's depths.

The air was heavy with a solemn stillness, the kind that makes every sound seem louder, every movement slower. The only sound was the soft rustling of leaves, a faint whisper carried by the cool night breeze, and the gentle lapping of the water against the rocky shore. The world felt suspended in that moment, as if time itself had stopped to watch the scene unfold. A thin mist clung to the surface of the lake, curling and twisting in delicate tendrils that seemed to reach toward the moonlight, seeking its cold embrace.

The moon's reflection on the water was almost hypnotic, a soft glow that seemed to pulse and breathe with a life of its own. It painted the lake in hues of silver and shadow, casting everything in a ghostly light. The distant call of a lone owl echoed through the night, a mournful cry that seemed to resonate with the ache in their hearts. The lake, so familiar yet so foreign under the moon's glow, felt like a place out of time—a quiet, sacred space where memories whispered in the stillness, and where the weight of what they had lost hung heavy in the cool, damp air.

They rushed toward the shoreline, their eyes scanning the area for any sign of Bryan and then they saw it—the faint glow of a dying camp fire near the water's edge, its embers barely glowing and almost out. But Bryan and his watch were nowhere to be found.

Elizabeth's breath caught in her throat as she reached into her pocket for the phone, her hands shaking. The screen was still on, the photo gallery open to the same endless stream of images—photos of her, of Alex, of their life together. Tears welled up in her eyes as she scrolled through the gallery, each picture a reminder of the man she had loved for half her lifetime, the man she was still trying to save.

Alex stood beside her, his eyes scanning the area, searching for any sign of his father. But the lake was quiet, the night still, as if the world itself was holding its breath, waiting.

"We'll find him, Mom," Alex said softly, his voice filled with determination as he turned and embraced Elizabeth burying his face in her shoulder. "We'll bring him back. We have to."

Elizabeth nodded, her heart heavy with the weight of their task. They hadn't found Bryan, not yet. But they had found a trace of him, a connection to the man they loved, the man they were determined to save. He was still out there. As they stood there, in the quiet of the night, Elizabeth felt a flicker of hope. It wasn't over yet. They still had a chance to bring Bryan back, to heal all the wounds that had driven him away.

They would find him. And when they did, they would bring him home and make him whole again, make their family whole again...no matter what.

Elizabeth's phone buzzed in her pocket, pulling her out of the overwhelming whirlpool of emotions she had been drowning in since finding Bryan's phone and wedding ring by the lake. She hesitated, her fingers trembling as she fished the device out, glancing at the screen. The name on the display sent a fresh wave of guilt and revulsion washing over her—Bishop.

Her hand froze, and for a moment, she considered letting it ring out. She didn't want to hear his voice, not now, not when everything was falling apart around her. But a part of her knew she couldn't avoid it forever. With a shaky breath, she swiped to accept the call and brought the phone to her ear.

"Hello?" Her voice was strained, barely above a whisper, as if the mere act of speaking to him would shatter the fragile state she was in.

"Elizabeth?" Bishop's voice came through, sounding fragile, desperate—the way he always sounded when he needed her to soothe his pain. "Where the hell are you? I've been fucking trying to reach you. I'm tapped out for this week's budget, can I borrow a few bucks 'til Monday?"

"I'm... I'm with Alex," she replied, trying to keep her voice steady. "We're... we're looking for Bryan."

There was a pause on the other end, and she could almost hear the gears turning in Bishop's head as he processed her words. "Looking for Bryan? What the fuck do you mean? Did something happen or are you just playing hide and seek with your boys?"

Elizabeth swallowed hard, her throat tight. How could she explain to Bishop what she barely understood herself? How could she talk about Bryan, about the man she had once loved more than anything, to the person who had become a source of her deepest shame?

"He's missing," she finally said, her voice breaking. "We found his phone, but... but he's gone."

Another silence. Then, Bishop's voice softened, taking on that coaxing tone he used when he wanted to draw her back into his world. "Elizabeth, come here. You shouldn't be out there right now, not like this. When was the last time you ate or slept? Pick up some food and come on over. You need to take care of yourself."

The words were meant to comfort, but they only made her feel more conflicted. Bishop had always known how to play on her vulnerabilities, how to manipulate her and feel like she was the one who needed saving. But right now, she didn't want to be saved by him or have anything to do with him. She wanted to be strong, for Alex, for Bryan—if there even was still a way to bring him back.

"I can't, Bishop," she said, closing her eyes as she leaned against the cold stone near the lake. "I need to be here. For Alex. For Bryan."

"Elizabeth," he sighed, and she could almost picture him on the other end of the line, lying in his bed, his body broken and dependent on the drugs that dulled his pain but never quite erased it. "You can't do this to yourself. You're always trying to fix everyone else, but who's going to take care of you Angel?"

His words struck a nerve, igniting a spark of anger that had been simmering under the surface. "And what about you, Bishop?" she shot back, her voice sharper than she intended. "You always want me to take care of you, to be there for you, but what about Bryan? What about Alex?"

"Elizabeth, that's not fair, I actually care about you" he responded, his voice laced with hurt. "You know what I've been through. I need you—"

"And so does my son!" she interrupted, the words tumbling out before she could stop them. "Alex needs me now more than ever. Bryan... he needs us both. And I can't—I can't just walk away from that. I won't."

Bishop was silent again, and Elizabeth could feel the tension between them stretching thin, like a rubber band about to snap. He had always been the one to pull her in, to make her feel like she was the only one who could help him through his endless cycles of despair and self destruction. But now, in the dark light of Bryan's disappearance, all of that seemed so small, so insignificant compared to what was at stake.

"Elizabeth," Bishop finally said, his voice low and almost pleading. "I don't want to lose you. I can't... I can't do this without you. I won't make it through the night."

His words, once so powerful in their ability to sway her, now felt like a burden she wasn't sure she could carry. She knew that Bishop was broken, just like Bryan had apparently been, but the difference was stark—Bryan had been lost in his pain, hiding it from everyone, while Bishop had always laid his pain at her feet, expecting her to pick up the pieces and mother him through it all.

"I don't know what you want me to say, Bishop," she replied, her voice weary. "But right now, I need to focus on finding Bryan. He's the father of my child. He's... he's my fucking husband."

She heard him draw in a shaky breath on the other end of the line, the reality of her words sinking in. "Elizabeth... I'm sorry," he said, his voice trembling. "I didn't mean to make this about me. I just... I just, I need you too and I don't want to lose you."

There it was—his fear of abandonment, the deep-seated issue that had always driven his neediness, his dependence on her. Elizabeth had once felt a twisted sense of obligation to him, as if she could somehow fill the void left by his absent mother, but now she realized how destructive that dynamic had been.

"Bishop," she said, trying to keep her tone gentle but firm, "you need to take care of yourself. I can't be your everything. Not now, not tonight and possibly not ever. I have to be here for my son, Alex is my number one. For Bryan too. I'm sorry."

There was a long pause, and for a moment, she wondered if he would hang up, if this would be the breaking point that severed whatever connection they had left.

Elizabeth closed her eyes, leaning against the cold stone near the lake. She felt the anger building inside her—anger at herself, at Bishop, and at the entire mess her life had become by her own selfish choices. But before she could respond, Alex's booming voice, sounding so very much like Bryan's, cut through the tension like a knife.

"Mom, hang the fuck up."

She turned to see her son standing just a few feet away, his face set in a hard expression that was far too mature for his age. His eyes were cold, determined—just like Bryan's had been when he was angry. But there was something more in Alex's gaze, something darker, that made Elizabeth's heart sink.

"Alex, I—" she started, but he interrupted her, stepping closer.

"Hang up the damned phone, Mom," he repeated, more forcefully this time. "Now."

Elizabeth hesitated, torn between the pull of Bishop's voice on the other end of the line and the fierce commanding look in her son's eyes. Finally, with a shaky hand, she ended the call, the screen going dark as she lowered the phone.

"Alex, I—" she began, but he cut her off again.

"I know everything, Mom." His voice was low, dangerous, and it sent a shiver down her spine. "About Bishop. About the drugs. About the other women. About everything. Probably more than you even know about that piece of shit."

Elizabeth felt the blood drain from her face. "What... what are you talking about?"

Alex took a deep breath, his expression hardening. "Dad and I shared everything up until recently trying to find a way to reach you and bring you back. We hacked into his phone, social media, and emails. We've known everything for a while. He's a huge piece of shit, Mom. A liar, a drug dealer, a pervert. He's been buying drugs for his own daughter, Mom. When she was hospitalized because of drugs, it was from what he bought her. He's been cheating on you with other women. And the stuff he looks at online... It's fucking disgusting. Sick. Illegal. Immoral stuff."

Elizabeth's breath caught in her throat, the world spinning around her. "Alex... why didn't you...?"

"Why didn't I tell you?" Alex's voice was sharp, cutting. "Because I didn't know how to and dad said you had to make your own choices, that he wouldn't make them for you or manipulate you. For me it was because I didn't want to hurt you more than you already were. But Dad... Dad thought maybe if you knew the truth, you'd see him for what he really is. We didn't know how bad it was until we saw those emails, those messages. And that... that stuff he watches. He's a sick freak, Mom."

Tears welled up in Elizabeth's eyes as the full weight of what her son was saying crashed down on her. She had known Bishop was troubled, that he had issues, but this... this was beyond anything she had imagined.

"I'm so sorry," she whispered, her voice trembling as her tears erupted like a waterfall. "I'm so, so sorry, Alex." She could feel a panic attack coming on and started the breathing exercises Bryan had taught her to calm herself.

Alex's expression softened, but only slightly. "It's not your fault, Mom. Bishop's the one who's messed up. But right now we need to find Dad. We need to bring him back."

Elizabeth nodded, trying to pull herself together. "You're right. You're absolutely right."

For a moment, they stood there in silence, the tension between them easing but not disappearing entirely. Elizabeth's mind was racing, trying to process everything Alex had just revealed, trying to make sense of how her life had spiraled so far out of control.

Finally, Alex broke the silence. "We need to go back to the house," he said, his voice calm but firm. "There has to be something we missed. Maybe Dad left something for us. A clue, or…"

Elizabeth nodded again, swallowing hard. "Okay. Let's go."

As they made their way back to the car, Elizabeth's mind was a blur of thoughts and emotions. She couldn't believe what she had just learned about Bishop, couldn't believe the extent of his deception. But more than that, she couldn't believe how much her son had been forced to endure, how much he had seen and heard without her even realizing it.

When they reached the car, Alex hesitated before getting in. He turned to face her, his eyes still hard but filled with a deep sadness that broke her heart.

"Mom," he said quietly, "I don't blame you. But you need to understand something. Bishop is dangerous. Not just to you, but to everyone. We need to get away from him. You need to get away from him."

Elizabeth nodded, her throat tight with emotion. "I will, Alex. I promise."

12 RUNNING ON EMPTY

As they drove back home, the silence between them was heavy but no longer suffocating. It was a silence filled with understanding, with a newfound resolve to face the truth and to find Bryan before it was too late.

When they arrived back at the house, Elizabeth's hands were shaking as she unlocked the door. Alex was right behind her, his expression focused and determined. They stepped inside, and the air was thick with the weight of everything that had been left unsaid.

Elizabeth walked into the living room, her eyes scanning the room for anything out of place. But everything was exactly as it had been when they left—except for one thing. Sticking out of the drawer of the coffee table, where Bryan's laptop usually sat, was a small, folded piece of paper.

Her heart pounding, Elizabeth walked over and picked it up, unfolding it with trembling hands. But as she read the words scrawled in Bryan's familiar handwriting, her heart sank.

It wasn't a clue, or a message of hope. It was a simple, devastating statement: **"I'm sorry."**

Elizabeth stared at the note, her mind racing. Sorry for what? For leaving? For everything that had gone wrong? For not being enough?

Before she could even process the words, Alex's voice broke through her thoughts. "Mom, look at this."

She turned to see him holding Bryan's laptop, the screen illuminated. He had pulled up a map, one that showed a series of locations Bryan had visited over the past few days. There was a pattern, a trail that led away from the house and towards... the lake.

"He's been here," Alex said, his voice tight with emotion. "He was here, Mom. But where did he go next?"

Elizabeth's heart raced as she looked at the screen. "The lake... the phone... the watch... it's all connected. But where would he go from there?"

Alex's eyes narrowed as he focused on the map. "We'll figure it out. We have to."

As they pored over the map, searching for any sign of where Bryan might have gone, Elizabeth felt a flicker of hope amidst the overwhelming fear and guilt. They weren't giving up. They weren't going to let Bishop, or anyone else, dictate their lives any longer.

And as they worked together, mother and son, to unravel the mystery of Bryan's disappearance, Elizabeth knew one thing for certain: whatever happened next, they would face it together. They would find Bryan, and they would bring him home.

But even as they worked, the shadow of Bishop loomed large, a reminder of the possible dangers that still lurked in the corners of their lives. Elizabeth knew she had to be strong, not just for Alex, but for Bryan—and for herself.

But the darkness that had crept into their lives wouldn't be so easily banished. Elizabeth knew that the road ahead would be long and filled with challenges, but with Alex by her side, she felt stronger, more determined. She wouldn't let Bishop's twisted influence destroy her family any further.

As the minutes ticked by like hours, they continued to search, and continued to hope. But as the sun rose and the house grew brighter, Elizabeth couldn't shake the feeling that they were running out of time. Bryan was out there, somewhere, and they needed to find him before it was too late. With that final thought Elizabeth took the laptop from Alex's lap and covered herself and her amazing son with a blanket so he could rest for a few hours. Because in the end, they were all they had left. And no matter what happened, she wouldn't let them fall apart again.

13 ALEXANDER, THE GREAT

Upon waking, Alex slid out of the blanket and went to use the bathroom and grabbed a protein shake from the fridge. He sat at the kitchen island and his hands trembled slightly as he stared at the map on his father's laptop screen. The blue dots marking Bryan's recent locations pulsed gently, as if urging him to uncover their secrets. His mind was a storm of emotions—anger, confusion, fear—but above all, there was a determination to find his dad and bring him back.

He had always admired his father's mind, his ability to solve problems, to dig into the details until he found the answers he was looking for. Alex had inherited that same analytical mind, and now, as he sat at the kitchen island with the laptop open in front of him, he was determined to use every skill he had learned to figure out where his dad could be.

Elizabeth was still in the living room, just having woken up she was staring blankly at the note Bryan had left. Alex could hear her quiet sobs, but he wouldn't allow himself to be distracted by them. Not right now. Not when so much was at stake.

He zoomed in on the map, his eyes scanning the screen for any details he might have missed. The pattern of locations was clear—his father had been moving in a deliberate path, but it wasn't random. It was like Bryan was following a route, a trail that led from the house, to the lake, and then... somewhere else.

Alex clicked on each individual location, trying to figure out and zero in on what was significant about them. There were a few obvious places—home, the school where Bryan had worked until being forced to resign earlier this year, a park where they had often gone as a family when he was younger. But then there were a few locations that didn't make sense. Places Bryan hadn't mentioned any of them, weird places that weren't part of their usual routine.

"What were you doing, Dad?" Alex muttered to himself as he clicked on a point that was miles away from any familiar spots. The location was a small, out-of-the-way gas station. Nothing special about it, nothing at all but the fact that Bryan had stopped there multiple times recently made it stand out. Alex made a mental note to look into it further.

He continued scanning the map, clicking on each point individually and making detailed notes of anything that seemed out of place or out of the norm. There were several stops along roads leading into the woods, areas where Bryan might have gone to hike and clear his head. But nothing definitive, nothing that screamed, "This is where he went. There couldn't be a "You Are Here!" sign with an arrow pointing to him could it," Alex mused to himself allowing himself to feel humor ever so briefly.

Frustration bubbled up inside him and was ready to erupt. He needed more information, something that would tell him what his dad was thinking, what he was planning. Alex's gaze shifted from the map to the other tabs open on the browser. "Duh," he thought to himself.

One was a search page. He clicked on it and saw a list of recent searches. Most of them were innocent—directions to various places, weather reports, news articles—but a few caught his eye.

One search was for the name of a nearby abandoned military base. Another was for the hiking trails near the lake. There were also searches related to river currents and water depths. Alex's heart sank as he read those. They painted a grim picture, one that he didn't want to believe was true.

"Come on, Dad... don't do this, not like this. Don't leave me." Alex whispered, his voice barely audible.

He clicked on the history tab, scrolling through the list of websites Bryan had visited. He was hoping to find something, anything, that might give him a clue. But most of it was mundane, everyday stuff. Nothing that pointed to a clear plan or location.

Then, an idea struck him. If Bryan had deleted anything, it might still be recoverable. He had learned enough about computers from his dad to know that deleted files didn't disappear immediately. With a bit of effort, they could be retrieved.

Alex opened the laptop's file recovery software. He had used it before, mostly when he or his dad had accidentally deleted photos or documents. But this time, it was different. This time, it had a real life application and could possibly save his father's life.

The software began scanning the hard drive, its digital tendrils creeping through the labyrinth of data, searching for recently deleted files. Alex's eyes were fixed on the screen, watching the thin, green progress bar inch forward with agonizing slowness, as if taunting him with every pixel gained. The room was dark, illuminated only by the pale blue glow of the monitor. His palms were slick with sweat, his fingers tapping anxiously on the edge of the desk, a restless rhythm that betrayed his mounting anxiety.

Each second felt like an eternity, the ticking of the clock on the wall echoing loudly in the quiet room, each tick hammering at his fraying nerves. The soft whirring of the computer fan filled the silence, a low, monotonous drone that seemed to grow louder with every passing moment. Alex's breath was shallow, his chest tight, as if the air around him had thickened, making it hard to draw in a full breath. He leaned forward, his heart pounding in his ears, his eyes darting between the progress bar and the flickering lines of code that flashed across the screen.

His mind raced, thoughts colliding in a frantic jumble. What if he found something important? Something that could change everything, that could lead them to his father, that could explain all the secrets that had been buried for so long? His heart leapt at the possibility, a surge of hope that was almost painful in its intensity. But then, just as quickly, doubt crept in, cold and insidious. What if there was nothing to find? What if all this searching, all this desperate digging, was for nothing? What if he was already too late, and whatever answers were hidden on this hard drive had been lost forever, swallowed up by the digital void?

Alex felt a tremor run through his hands, his fingers tightening around the edge of the desk until his knuckles turned white. His stomach churned with a nauseating mix of fear and anticipation, the kind that gnaws at your insides and makes every second stretch like an hour. He could feel the weight of his own heartbeat, a steady thud against his ribs that seemed to match the slow, torturous pace of the progress bar. He bit his lip, tasting the metallic tang of blood, his jaw clenched so tightly that it ached.

The seconds dragged on, each one heavier than the last. The room seemed to grow colder, the shadows deepening around him, pressing in like a suffocating blanket. The dim light of the screen flickered, casting eerie patterns on the walls, and for a moment, he felt as if the room itself was holding its breath, waiting, just like him. The uncertainty was unbearable, a taut string pulled to its breaking point. He felt a bead of sweat trickle down his temple, his pulse quickening as the progress bar inched forward, painfully slow, mocking his desperation.

What if he found something too late to matter? What if his father had already moved on to another hiding place, or worse, something had happened to him? The thought sent a shiver down his spine, a cold, gnawing dread that made his stomach twist. Alex swallowed hard, his throat dry, his eyes burning with fatigue, but he couldn't look away, couldn't let himself blink. He needed to know. He needed to find something—anything—that could point them in the right direction, that could bring them one step closer to finding Bryan before it was too late.

The bar moved another fraction of an inch, and Alex's breath caught in his throat, his heart pounding so loudly he could barely hear the faint hum of the computer. His hands felt clammy, his pulse racing, his nerves frayed to the breaking point. He leaned in closer, his face inches from the screen, willing it to move faster, to reveal its secrets. Every second felt like a battle against time, a desperate race to find the truth buried in a sea of digital debris, a truth he was terrified to uncover but knew he had to face.

With each moment that passed, Alex's resolve tightened. Whatever he found—or didn't find—he had to keep searching. The progress bar crept forward again, and he whispered a silent plea into the dim, still air, hoping against hope that this time, the computer would finally tell him what he needed to know.

The scan finished, and a list of recoverable files appeared. There were hundreds of them—documents, photos, and videos. Alex's eyes quickly scanned the list, looking for anything that seemed relevant. Most of the files were old, but a few had been deleted within the past few days and that's where he focused.

His curiosity got the better of him and he started with the photos. As the images loaded, Alex's breath caught in his throat. There were pictures of him and his mom—thousands of them, dating back years. Some of them he recognized, but many were moments he hadn't even known were captured. His father had been documenting their lives, quietly, and a bit obsessively. It's like he knew it was all gonna end one day and with him not trusting his own memory, he had to have evidence. And now, it seemed, those images were all that was left of him.

Alex clicked through the photos quickly, his heart pounding. But nothing in the images seemed to indicate where Bryan might have gone. They were just memories, fragments of a life that was slipping away.

Next, he moved on to the documents. Most of them were related to work—lesson plans, grading sheets, notes for classes. But one file, a text document, stood out. It had been deleted just a few hours before Bryan disappeared. Alex opened the file, his heart in his throat. The text was short, barely a paragraph. But what it said sent a chill down his spine.

"I can't do this anymore. I'm tired. I'm sorry, but I need to go. I need to find peace, and this is the only way I know how. I love you both, more than anything, but I can't stay. Please forgive me."

Alex's hands clenched into fists, his nails digging into his palms. He could feel the anger and fear rising inside him, a toxic mix that threatened to overwhelm him. But Alex knew he couldn't afford to lose control, not now.

He forced himself to keep looking using that fear and anger as motivation to continue on, to keep searching for something that could help. He moved on to the emails, hoping there might be a clue there. He had already seen the messages between Bishop and his dad, the vile, disgusting things Bishop had written. But maybe there was something else, something Bryan had kept hidden.

Alex scrolled through the inbox, scanning the subjects and senders. Most of it was junk—spam, newsletters, automated messages. But then he saw one from a name he didn't recognize. It was dated the day before Bryan disappeared.

The subject line read: "I can help."

Alex's curiosity piqued, he opened the email. The message was brief, just a few lines, but it was enough to make his blood run cold.

"Bryan, I know you're struggling. I've been where you are, and I know how hard it is. But there's a way out, a way to find peace. Meet me at the old cabin near the ridge when you are ready. We can talk freely there. I promise you, there's another way. I will leave all the information you need there waiting on you. Anything I leave there is yours."

The email was signed with a name Alex didn't recognize—*D. Mann.*

"Who the hell is D. Mann?" Alex muttered, his mind racing. He had never heard his dad mention anyone by that name. Was this someone Bryan had met recently? Or was it an old friend he had reconnected with?

Alex's fingers flew over the keyboard as he searched for any information about D. Mann. He found a few results, but nothing that seemed relevant. Whoever this person was, they were a mystery.

But the mention of the cabin near the ridge... that was something. Alex knew the area well—he and Bryan had hiked there several times when he was younger. It was remote, quiet, the kind of place someone might go to be alone. Alex's heart pounded as he realized what this meant. His dad might have gone there, to the cabin, to meet this person. It was a lead, the first real lead he had.

He quickly printed out a map of the area, marking the location of the cabin. Then he saved the email and closed the laptop. He needed to tell his mom, and needed to figure out how to get to the cabin as quickly as possible.

As he stood up, the weight of everything he had learned hit him like a ton of bricks. His dad was out there, somewhere, lost and in pain. And Bishop... that son of a bitch was still a threat, a looming storm that could destroy everything if they weren't careful.

But Alex couldn't think about that now. He had to focus on finding his dad, on bringing him home. He couldn't let his emotions cloud his judgment, couldn't let fear take over. He had to stay strong, for his dad, for his mom, for himself.

With a deep breath, he walked into the living room, where his mom was still sitting, staring at the note. She looked up as he approached, he knew her eyes were red and swollen from crying and was glad she had fallen asleep. He knew what he had to do next.

14 Police Business

The sun was just beginning to break over the horizon, casting a soft, pale orange glow over the small town of Springville. The morning light filtered through the dusty windows of the police station, throwing long shadows across the room as officers hurried about, preparing for what was shaping up to be a long day. The station was cramped, cluttered with old desks and filing cabinets that seemed to groan under the weight of years of paperwork. There was a thick tension in the air, a sense of urgency that was almost tangible, like the static that builds before a storm.

Chief Danny Moon, a stocky man in his late fifties with a thick, graying beard and a perpetual scowl, leaned over a table strewn with maps, notes, and hastily printed emails. His eyes, dark and sharp despite his age, scanned the chaos of information spread before him. What had begun as a routine missing person report was quickly evolving into something far more complex and troubling. The pieces didn't fit together neatly, and that made his gut churn with unease. He rubbed a hand across his stubbled chin, the bristles scratching against his palm, as he tried to make sense of the mess.

Detective Sarah Hayes stood beside him, her brow furrowed in concentration as she flipped through a stack of documents they had retrieved from Bryan Black's home earlier that morning. In her early forties, with short, dark hair and a piercing gaze, Hayes was known for her sharp mind and no-nonsense attitude. Today, though, there was a flicker of concern in her eyes, a tightness around her mouth that hinted at the gravity of the situation. The clock on the wall ticked loudly, counting down the minutes Bryan had been missing—over 24 hours now—and each tick seemed to echo the growing apprehension in the room. The discovery of his phone by the river, next to the heart he had carved into the rock, had set the entire town on edge.

"We need to get a better understanding of this guy," Chief Moon muttered, his voice gravelly, thick with both authority and concern. His finger tapped impatiently against the edge of the table, emphasizing his frustration. "What's his state of mind? What's driving him? We can't just search blindly, hoping we stumble upon something."

Hayes nodded, her jaw tightening as she reviewed the contents of the folder in her hands. Her fingers traced the edges of the pages, flipping them over with a soft rustle. "I've been digging into his background, Chief. It's becoming clear this man was deeply troubled—Bryan's been walking a thin line for some time now. We found several warrants he filed against a man named Bishop... Steven Bishop, to be exact. He's a known drug addict, a gun nut, with a long history of violence and fraud. This wasn't just a passing concern for Bryan; it's personal."

She handed a few sheets over to Moon, who took them with a furrowed brow, his eyes scanning the printed words quickly. "These are copies of the warrants," Hayes continued. "Mostly harassment charges, but there's a more serious one in there too—drug trafficking. Bryan swore them out himself. The language in his statements... It's intense, even emotional. It reads like a man who felt trapped, desperate to take action when no one else would."

Moon's frown deepened as he skimmed the documents, his face darkening with the weight of what he was reading. "This doesn't seem like just a legal issue," he muttered, his voice low. "There's something else going on here—something deeper, more personal. What else do we know about Bishop?"

Hayes glanced up, meeting his gaze, her expression grim. "Bishop was having an affair with Bryan's wife, Elizabeth," she said quietly, the words heavy in the room. "Bryan found out, and it looks like it tore him apart. But that's not all. Bryan and his son, Alex, managed to hack into Bishop's phone and emails. What they found was... disturbing, to say the least. Bishop's been involved in some vile stuff—selling drugs, even to his own daughter, indulging in extreme pornography, and worse... making disgusting jokes about bestiality. It's clear Bryan saw Bishop as a direct threat to his family, and maybe even his sanity."

Moon let out a slow, deep breath, the kind you take when trying to process something that doesn't sit right in your gut. His gaze drifted to the old map on the table, the edges curled and yellowed, as if he could somehow find an answer there. "And now Bryan's gone missing," he muttered, almost to himself. "This doesn't bode well. Have we found anything that gives us a clue about where he might have gone?"

Hayes sighed, her eyes scanning the notes scattered across the table. "Not much, but there are a few leads. Alex found something on Bryan's laptop—an email from someone named S. Matthews, suggesting they meet at a cabin near the ridge. It's not much to go on, but it's a start. We've also been combing through Bryan's online presence, and Chief... it's a lot to unpack."

She pulled out more sheets of paper, each filled with excerpts from Bryan's writings—blogs, forum posts, and social media rants. "He's been posting for years. Most of it is about his love for Elizabeth and his admiration for Alex, but after he learned of the affair... it's like something snapped inside him. The posts take a darker turn—anger, betrayal, a festering hurt that bleeds through every word. It's almost like we're dealing with two different people—one still clinging to the idea of his family, the other consumed by rage and despair."

Moon's gaze shifted back to the documents, his lips pressed into a tight line. The writings painted a picture of a man on the edge, someone caught in a tug-of-war between the love he felt for his family and the deepening hatred that seemed to be eating him alive. "We need to handle this delicately," he said, his voice firm. "If we push too hard, we might lose our chance to bring him back safely. But if we don't act fast, this could get a lot worse."

Hayes nodded, feeling the weight of his words. Her mind was racing, already forming a plan. "Agreed. We should start by searching the cabin, but we can't stop there. We need to follow every thread, no matter how small. We can't afford to miss anything. Not with so much at stake."

Moon set the papers down, his expression hardening with determination. "Then let's move. I'll get a team together for the cabin. Hayes, I want you on this from every angle. We need to find out where Bryan's head is at—before it's too late."

15 THE WAR WITHIN

The room buzzed with a renewed energy as officers moved into action, the reality of the situation settling in. Bryan's disappearance wasn't just another missing person case—it was a race against time to find a man who seemed to be at war with himself.

Sample 1: Love for Elizabeth

"Elizabeth, you've always been my guiding light," Bryan's words flowed like a quiet whisper from the page, each one heavy with a mix of devotion and sorrow. "Even when the world seemed to darken around me, and every path I walked felt like it was leading nowhere, you were the single point of light I could always find, the one thing that kept me going. I know I wasn't the perfect husband—I got lost in my own thoughts, my own battles. I faltered, I failed in so many ways, but never once did my love for you waver. Every morning, I'd wake up and thank God for the gift of having you in my life, even if only for a fleeting moment in the grand scheme of things. No matter where this road takes me, no matter how all of this ends, please know that you were always my everything. I loved you with a love that was pure and true, a love that will remain etched in my soul long after everything else has faded. I will carry that love with me to the end of my days."

Sample 2: Admiration for Alex

"Alex, my son, my pride and joy," Bryan's tone shifted here, a mix of awe and pain evident in the words. "I've watched you grow into such an incredible young man, and I'm endlessly proud of who you are becoming. You're strong in ways I never was, smart in ways that constantly amaze me, and your heart... your heart is so much bigger than I could have ever hoped. I'm sorry, son, that I wasn't always the father you deserved. I know I fell short. I wish I could have been better, stronger, more present for you. But please, know this—I have always believed in you, believed in your potential to change the world in ways I never could. You're my legacy, Alex. Even when I'm gone, know that I am with you, in the decisions you make, in the values you uphold, guiding you in some small way. Keep pushing forward, keep striving for those dreams I know are burning inside of you."

Sample 3: The Darker Side

"How could you, Elizabeth?" The words seemed to seethe with a raw, unchecked anger. "How could you betray me like this? I gave you everything I had, every ounce of love and devotion I could muster, and it still wasn't enough. You took all of it—my trust, my loyalty, my very soul—and threw it away for someone like Bishop. Do you have any idea what you've done to me? Can you even comprehend the hell I'm living in now? I hate what I've become because of you. I hate this festering rage that burns in my chest every waking moment, a fire that refuses to die. But more than anything, I hate that despite all of this, I still love you. I'm caught in a tormenting cycle, trapped in this hellish limbo between wanting to pull you close and never wanting to see your face again. I don't know how to escape this pain, and it's eating me alive."

Chief Moon set the papers down, his face darkening as he absorbed the intensity of what he had just read. The room seemed to grow colder as the weight of Bryan's words hung heavy in the air.

"This guy is dangerous," he said finally, his voice steady but filled with concern. "Not just to himself, but maybe to others too. We need to find him before something terrible happens."

Detective Hayes nodded, a determined look in her eyes. She felt the urgency thrumming through her veins, her mind racing as she tried to piece together the fragments of Bryan Black's life that lay scattered before them. "We need to find out who this S. Matthews is," she replied. "Maybe they hold a key to understanding where Bryan might have gone, what he might be planning."

"Agreed," Moon said with a decisive nod. "But we can't rule out the possibility that Bryan is planning something drastic. We need to cover all our bases. Send out a team to search the area around the cabin near the ridge, and keep digging into his online activities. There might be more clues there, something we're missing."

Hayes immediately picked up her phone, her fingers moving swiftly as she made a few urgent calls, instructing officers to begin a comprehensive search of the cabin and its surrounding area. The sound of officers moving, their boots clacking against the floor, filled the station, adding to the tension that seemed to grow with every second. Meanwhile, Hayes returned to Bryan's digital trail, her eyes narrowing as she scrolled through his posts, messages, and search history. The screen's blue light flickered in her tired eyes, but she refused to blink, her determination growing stronger with every passing moment.

She paused as she came across more of Bryan's writings—some filled with an aching love, others steeped in bitterness and rage. The contrast was jarring, like reading the diary of two different men.

Sample 4: Despair and Self-Reflection

"I don't know who I am anymore," the words bled with a deep sense of loss and confusion. "I used to believe I was a good man—a decent husband, a caring father. But now... now all I see is a failure, a shadow of who I once was. Elizabeth's betrayal cut me in ways I never thought possible. It's like a wound that refuses to heal, and I'm bleeding out, drop by drop, day by day. I keep asking myself, what did I do wrong? Why wasn't I enough? Maybe I was always destined for this—destined to end up alone, broken, and forgotten. Maybe this is all I deserve."

Sample 5: A Final Cry for Help

"I'm so tired," the words seemed to waver, filled with a weariness that ran deep. "Tired of pretending that everything's fine when it's not. Tired of clinging to hope when there's none left to find. I've been living in a nightmare, a slow, waking death, and I don't know how to escape it. I keep thinking about the river, about the peace I might find there, the release from all this pain. But then I think about Alex... my boy... and how he'd feel if I was gone. He's the only thing keeping me here, the only thread holding me back from the edge. But I don't know how much longer I can hold on. I just hope he can forgive me when that final thread snaps."

A chill ran down Hayes' spine as she read the last passage. The desperation was palpable, each word heavy with the weight of a man teetering on the brink. The mention of the river, the yearning for peace—it was all too clear. Bryan was on the edge, and if they didn't find him soon, he might slip over it.

She straightened, a steely resolve settling in her chest. She needed to find him, needed to bring him back before the darkness consumed him completely.

As the minutes ticked by, more officers joined the search, combing through the dense woods near the river and scouring the area around the cabin. The tension in the station was electric, every minute that passed without a breakthrough only adding to the sense of impending doom.

Meanwhile, Hayes continued to dig through Bryan's online life, scrolling through post after post that chronicled years of inner turmoil—his silent battles with depression, his fears of losing Elizabeth, his desperate, heartbreaking attempts to keep his family together. Each post was a window into the mind of a man who had been fighting his demons for far longer than anyone had realized.

But it was his most recent writings that sent a fresh wave of fear through her. His posts had grown increasingly erratic, swinging wildly between declarations of undying love and expressions of deep-seated anger and bitterness. Bryan's mental state was deteriorating fast, and Hayes knew they were running out of time.

Sample 6: The Breaking Point

"I can't do this anymore. Every day is a struggle, a fight to keep going when all I want to do is give up. I used to think I was strong enough to handle anything life threw at me, but now... now I'm not so sure."

The words seemed to tremble on the screen, each one pulsing with a raw, aching desperation. Bryan's voice came through in these written lines, not just as text but as a plea, a fragile cry from the depths of a man who had reached his limit. His confession felt like a whisper across a chasm, where darkness had taken root, and hope seemed a distant memory. Each letter was like a heartbeat, faint and fading, teetering on the edge of oblivion.

Detective Sarah Hayes stared at the screen, her fingers hovering over the keyboard, her breath held tight in her chest. She scrolled through Bryan Black's digital footprints, feeling a hollow pit open in her stomach with every new entry. The room felt colder, the faint hum of the fluorescent lights above seemed to grow louder, more oppressive. Every word she read felt like a cry from a man teetering on the edge, one foot already over the precipice, the other struggling to find solid ground. The urgency of the situation gnawed at her, each new discovery adding weight to the fear pressing down on her shoulders—Bryan's online presence painted a picture of a man deeply conflicted, torn between his love for his family and the darkness that seemed to be swallowing him whole. And now, with every passing second, the fear of what Bryan might do next clawed at her, relentless and unforgiving.

"Chief," she called out, her voice tight with concern, the edges frayed with the tension that crackled through the room like static electricity. "We need to escalate this. Bryan's mental state is far worse than we initially thought. His posts, his writings... they're erratic, almost schizophrenic in nature. He swings wildly—from declarations of undying love for his wife and son to angry, hate-filled rants that suggest he's on the brink of something terrible."

Chief Moon looked up sharply from the reports he had been reviewing, his eyes narrowing beneath furrowed brows. His expression was serious, his demeanor that of a man who had seen too much, worn down by the weight of years on the force. "Have we found anything concrete that can lead us to his whereabouts?" His voice was gruff, but there was a hint of urgency, a crack in his normally stoic exterior.

Hayes shook her head, frustration flickering in her eyes. "Nothing yet. The search teams are combing through the area around the cabin, but no sign of him so far." She paused, a knot of anxiety tightening in her stomach. "I'm worried that we might be too late if we don't expand our search quickly."

Moon let out a heavy sigh, his large hands rubbing at his temples as if trying to massage away the tension building there. The weight of the situation pressed down on him like a physical burden, each new piece of information making the case more complex, more urgent. "What about his searches? Is there anything else on that laptop we can use?"

Hayes nodded, her eyes flicking back to the screen as she pulled up a new window. "I've been looking into that as well. Bryan's search history is... troubling." Her voice dropped to a softer, more somber tone. "He's been researching various methods of suicide—ways to make it look accidental, painless. But then there are searches on survival tactics too, like part of him isn't fully committed to the idea. There's a conflict within him, a struggle between giving up and fighting to survive."

She clicked on another folder, opening a list of recently deleted files. The screen filled with fragments—pieces of a life falling apart. "I managed to recover some of the deleted files," she continued, her voice growing more urgent. "They're fragments, but they suggest Bryan was planning something... more coordinated. There are notes about his finances, instructions on what to do in the event of his death, and even a couple of encrypted files that I haven't cracked yet. But the most worrying thing is the maps. He's been mapping out several remote locations around town, places where he could go to be alone, to disappear."

Moon pushed himself up from his desk, his chair scraping loudly against the floor, his expression resolute. "We need to get those locations to the search teams immediately. And we need more manpower. If Bryan's planning to harm himself, every minute counts."

Hayes quickly sent the information to the officers in the field, her fingers flying over the keyboard with a speed born of desperation. Her heart pounded in her chest, a rapid thud that seemed to echo in her ears. The sense of urgency was almost overwhelming; this was no longer just a missing person case—it was a race against time to save a life that seemed to be slipping through their fingers.

As the information was disseminated to the search teams, Hayes turned back to Bryan's laptop, her determination hardening. She had to understand him, to get inside his head if they were going to find him before it was too late. She clicked open another folder, this one containing drafts of unsent emails. The subject lines alone sent chills down her spine.

To Alex: My Final Words
Elizabeth, I'm Sorry
Bishop: You Took Everything from Me

With a deep breath, she clicked on the first email. It was addressed to Alex, and as she began to read, she felt the weight of Bryan's despair pressing against her, his final attempt to reach out to his son.

"Alex, by the time you read this, I'll be gone. I can't do this anymore. I've tried, God knows I've tried, but the pain is too much. I'm sorry for leaving you like this, but I hope one day you'll understand. You're the best thing that ever happened to me, and I'm sorry I couldn't be the father you deserved. I hope you'll forgive me. I hope you'll be able to live the life I never could. I love you, son. More than you'll ever know."

Hayes's throat tightened, her eyes stinging with tears she fought to hold back. The words seemed to blur as she read them, the heartbreak palpable. Her heart ached for the boy who would have to read these words, who might lose his father if they didn't find Bryan in time. She quickly moved on to the next email, addressed to Elizabeth.

"Elizabeth, I loved you more than life itself. Even now, as I write this, I can't stop loving you. But I can't live with the pain of your betrayal. It's eating me alive, tearing me apart from the inside out. I tried to forgive you, to move past it, but I can't. I'm sorry. I'm sorry I wasn't enough for you. I'm sorry I couldn't make you happy. I'm sorry for everything."

Bryan's heartbreak bled through the screen like an open wound. Hayes could almost feel the agony in his words, each one a knife twisting deeper. It was clear that his love for Elizabeth had been his anchor, but her betrayal had shattered him in ways that went far beyond the physical.

Finally, she opened the email to Bishop. The words were short but laced with venom.

"You took everything from me. My wife, my family, my life. You're a monster, and I hope you rot in hell for

what you've done. This is on you, Bishop. You did this."

Hayes sat back in her chair, the gravity of Bryan's words settling over her like a heavy fog. She felt like she was staring into the mind of a man who had nothing left to lose, a man on the brink of making a decision that could not be undone. But there was still hope. As long as they hadn't found a body, there was still a chance to bring him back.

"Chief," she called out, her voice resolute, the determination in her tone clear. "We need to put out an APB on Bishop. He's not directly involved in Bryan's disappearance, but he's clearly a trigger. If Bryan's out there, he might try to confront Bishop before he does anything else."

Moon nodded, his expression hardening as he picked up the phone on his desk. "I'll get it done. Keep digging, Hayes. We need to know everything we can before it's too late."

As Hayes continued her investigation, the search teams spread out across the town, moving with urgency, their flashlights cutting through the early morning fog as they combed through every inch of the remote locations Bryan had mapped out. The air was thick with anticipation, each step weighed down by the fear of what they might find.

The hours ticked by slowly, and with every passing minute, the tension grew. Bryan was still missing, and the fear of finding him too late loomed over them like a dark cloud.

Back at the station, Hayes finally managed to decrypt one of the files on Bryan's laptop. Her heart raced as she opened it—a detailed journal, each entry chronicling the weeks leading up to his disappearance. The words leapt off the screen, filled with love letters to Elizabeth, notes to Alex, and rants that were a whirlwind of anger, despair, and bitterness. But it was the last entry that made her heart stop.

"I don't know how much longer I can keep this up. The pain is too much. I can't sleep, I can't eat, I can't think about anything other than what she did to me. It's like my mind is stuck in a loop, replaying it over and over again, and I can't find the pause button. I thought I could forgive her, but since she chose him I was wrong. Every time I close my eyes, all I see is her with him, and it's like a knife stabbing and slashing into my heart, twisting deeper every day, cutting into and cutting away everything I thought I knew, everything I

thought I was, or could ever be. The betrayal burns to my very soul, and I can't stop it.

I've been thinking about the river. It seems so peaceful from here. Maybe that's where I'll find the silence, the peace I need, where all of this will finally stop. Or maybe where I'll just disappear, and it'll be like none of this ever happened. I don't know. I don't know anything anymore. I just know I can't keep living like this. Something has to change. I can't carry this weight much longer. I'm tired. I'm so tired.

Something has to change."

Hayes felt a cold sweat on her forehead, a chill running down her spine. Bryan's words carried a finality, a resignation that sent a shiver through her. But something else caught her attention, a glimmer of hope buried in his despair.

"The river... Maybe that's where I'll find the silence, the peace."

16 Ashes fall & reveal it all

Hayes wondered if they were looking in the wrong place? Was Bryan trying to mislead them, sending them on a wild goose chase while he headed somewhere else? Hayes quickly sent out an alert, instructing the teams to expand their search to the riverbanks and any nearby locations.

As the officers prepared to move out, Hayes's phone rang. She answered, and the voice on the other end was tense. "Detective Hayes, we've found something. It's not Bryan, but... it may be his, you need to see this."

Her heart skipped a beat. She grabbed her coat and rushed out the door, knowing that whatever they had found, it could be the key to unraveling this case.

One of the officers approached Detective Hayes, holding out a small, blackened notebook. Its cover was scorched, the edges of its pages curled and charred as if they had been licked by flames. A faint, acrid smell of smoke still clung to the air around it. "We found this in the fire pit," the officer said, his voice tinged with a mix of urgency and sorrow. "It's Bryan's. He tried to burn it, but we managed to recover some of it."

Hayes took the notebook with a cautious hand, the charred edges flaking away like ash beneath her touch. The brittle texture of the burned paper crumbled slightly, and the spine crackled, almost as if it were resisting being opened, as though it knew the weight of the secrets it held inside. Her breath caught in her throat as she carefully pried it open, and her eyes quickly narrowed with the weight of what she was seeing. The first few lines were stark and haunting, each word a blade cutting into the silence of the room.

"If you're reading this, it means I didn't make it. I'm sorry. I tried, but I couldn't do it. The pain was too much. I hope you can forgive me. Please, don't blame yourselves. This was my choice. I just couldn't keep going."

The ink on the page was smudged in places, the lines blurred and uneven, as though the words themselves were trembling, struggling to remain on the page. Dark stains marred the paper, marks that looked suspiciously like tears that had soaked through the fibers, making the ink bleed and run, merging letters into a chaotic swirl of desperation and sorrow. The writing seemed to pulse with life, a frantic heartbeat captured in blue and black. As Hayes continued to flip through the notebook, the pages felt heavier in her hands, each one bearing the weight of a man's final, frantic days. The confessions, the apologies, the fragmented thoughts—all scrawled in a hand that grew more jagged, more desperate, with each new entry.

It was not a single letter, but a compilation of torment—a suicide note spread across days, a mosaic of anguish and resignation. Hayes could feel a chill crawl up her spine, an icy tendril wrapping around her bones as she read, her skin prickling with an unsettling awareness. The notebook was like a raw nerve, exposed and throbbing, a window into Bryan's deteriorating psyche. The ink seemed to flow like veins, dark and thick, bleeding out the pain of a man who had lost all hope, a man whose suffering had become too much to bear.

Her fingers trembled as she turned each page, the paper crackling under the pressure of her grip, and she had to force herself to keep going, to see this through to the end. She could almost feel the weight of his despair pressing down on her, as if the darkness of his thoughts were seeping from the pages and filling the air around her, a heavy, cold presence that made it hard to breathe.

The entries began to blur together, the handwriting becoming shakier, the sentences trailing off into broken, frantic scribbles and disjointed thoughts. It was the kind of writing that spoke of a mind grappling with the fraying edges of sanity, a mind that was struggling to hold itself together against an onslaught of pain and loss. The words seemed to stagger across the page like a wounded animal, limping toward an inevitable end.

But amid the chaos, one theme emerged over and over again—a fixation on the river. Each mention seemed to pull her in, almost hypnotically, as if the river itself had a magnetic pull, a dark allure that Bryan could not escape. He wrote of it again and again, how it whispered to him in the quiet moments, how it called to him like a lullaby promising peace. Hayes realized how frequently he returned to this idea, how the river had become a symbol in his mind, a place where he believed he might finally find solace, a place where the noise in his head might finally be quieted.

The river was more than a location; it was a destination, a conclusion, a final resting place for a troubled soul seeking some kind of reprieve from the torment that haunted his every waking moment. The pages seemed to tremble in her hands, and for a moment, Hayes felt as though she could hear the river too, its quiet murmur mingling with Bryan's words, a siren's call that promised to wash everything away.

"The river calls to me. It's peaceful there, quiet. Maybe that's where I'll find the silence I need. Maybe it will wash away the pain. Maybe it's the only place left for me."

The handwriting in these lines was strangely steady, almost calm, as if in the act of writing them, Bryan had found a moment of clarity, a flicker of calm amid the storm raging inside him. Hayes could almost hear the river's distant murmur, its gentle current whispering promises of an end, of relief, of oblivion. She could picture Bryan standing at the water's edge, the cool breeze brushing against his face, the sound of the river a soothing lullaby for his tortured soul.

Hayes closed the notebook slowly, her fingers lingering on the cover as if reluctant to let go. She handed it back to the officer, her face pale and tense. "We need to focus our search on the river," she said, her voice firm but laced with urgency. "He's obsessed with the damned river. If he's still out there, that's where we're gonna find him."

As the team mobilized, the early morning sky began to lighten, the first hints of dawn casting a muted gray hue over the landscape. The search teams, now bolstered by volunteers from the community, moved methodically along the riverbank, their footsteps crunching over the frost-kissed grass. The cold air filled their lungs as their eyes scanned the terrain, looking for any sign of Bryan. The mist rising from the water created a ghostly veil that hovered just above the surface, adding an eerie stillness to the scene. The sound of the river was a constant companion, a low, steady hum that seemed to pulse with the tension in the air.

17 DARK FORUMS

Back at the station, the air was thick with tension. The steady hum of computers and the occasional ring of a phone were the only sounds cutting through the heavy silence. Hayes had enlisted another officer, a tech-savvy younger detective named Miller, to dig deeper into Bryan's digital life. They needed more than surface-level information; they needed to crawl inside his head, to understand the desperation that had driven him to this point. The warrants Bryan had sworn out against Bishop were just a fragment of a much larger, darker picture. The deeper Miller dug, the more layers he uncovered—pages upon pages of online posts, blog entries, and forum discussions that painted a portrait of a man tormented by intense emotions, spiraling downward ever since Elizabeth's betrayal had ripped his life apart.

In one of the forums, buried beneath a maze of pseudonyms and anonymous usernames, Bryan had written about his undying love for his wife. The post read like a confession, each line heavy with the raw, unfiltered pain of a man whose heart was laid bare for all to see. The words bled with yearning, every sentence dripping with longing and loss.

"I loved her more than words can express. She was the sun in my sky, the breath in my lungs. She was my reason for everything, the one who brought meaning to every morning and peace to every night. With her, life was not just something to endure—it was something to cherish, something to revel in. Every laugh, every whispered secret in the dark, every touch of her hand, was a promise of forever, a binding of souls that I thought could never be broken. I saw my future in her eyes, the spark of something pure and beautiful, something I never thought I deserved but had somehow been given anyway. And I would have given anything, everything, to keep that spark alive.

Even now, after everything, I can't stop loving her. I thought love was supposed to bring joy, but this love—this love is a curse. It's an all-consuming fire that refuses to die out, no matter how much it burns. It scorches my insides, every thought of her like a white-hot ember that sears through my veins, reminding me of what I've lost. And yet, I hold onto it, clutching it like a lifeline, like it's the only thing keeping me afloat in a sea of despair. I can't let it go. Not yet. I don't know how.

When I look back, I see the moments that mattered. The small ones, the ones no one else would notice. The way her lips curled up at the corners when she tried not to laugh at one of my terrible jokes, or how her eyes would soften when she looked at me after a long day, as if I were the only one who could understand her heart. I remember the way her hair smelled like lavender in the morning, or how she'd reach for my hand in the middle of the night, even when she was half asleep, needing the comfort of my touch to chase away whatever dreams haunted her. I remember the way we used to dance in the kitchen, barefoot on the cold tiles, with no music except the rhythm of our own beating hearts. These moments were small, inconsequential to anyone but us, but they were everything to me. They were my world, my heaven, my sanctuary.

And now, those same memories cut me like a thousand tiny knives. They tear at my soul, each one a reminder of what was, of what will never be again. I keep asking myself why—why wasn't I enough? Why wasn't the love I gave her enough to hold her, to keep her from drifting away? Was it something I did, or something I failed to do? Was it the way I held her too tight, afraid she might slip through my fingers, or was it the times I let her go, thinking she needed space to breathe? I torture myself with these questions, over and over, but the answers never come. I'm trapped in this endless loop, a cycle of blame and regret that leaves me raw and broken.

But how do you stop loving someone who has become a part of you? How do you rip out a piece of your own heart and pretend it never existed? I loved her with everything I had, with everything I was. She was the center of my universe, and without her, everything feels empty, like I'm floating in a vast, dark void with nothing to hold onto. I keep waiting for the moment when the pain will dull, when the sharp edges of grief will smooth out, but it doesn't come. Instead, the hurt burrows deeper, entwining itself with my very being, until I can't tell where it ends and I begin.

It's killing me, this love. Slowly, painfully, it's tearing me apart from the inside. Every day is a new kind of hell, every breath a reminder that she's not here, that she chose someone else, that she left me standing on the edge of a life we were supposed to build together. I don't know how to exist without her. I don't know how to breathe without feeling like I'm suffocating. It's a torture, a slow, agonizing death that I never saw coming.

But despite the torment, despite the ache that never goes away, I can't let go. Not yet. I don't know if I ever will. Because to let go would mean accepting that she's gone, that everything we were, everything we could have been, is lost forever. And I'm not ready for that. I'm not ready to say goodbye to the only person who ever truly saw me, who ever truly mattered. I'm not ready to admit that the love I thought could conquer anything wasn't strong enough to survive.

So, I hold on. I hold on to the memory of her smile, to the sound of her voice, to the way her laughter felt like sunlight on my skin. I hold on to the hope that somewhere, somehow, she still thinks of me, still feels even a fraction of what I feel for her. Maybe it's foolish, maybe it's pathetic, but it's all I have left. It's the only thing keeping me from falling into the abyss, from letting the darkness swallow me whole.

I loved her more than words can express. I still do. And I don't know how to stop. I don't know if I ever will. Because even now, after everything, she is still the sun in my sky, the breath in my lungs, the beat of my heart. And without her, I am nothing but a shadow, a ghost of the man I used to be. But maybe... maybe that's enough for now. Maybe, for now, just loving her is enough."

Hayes felt the weight of those carefully chosen words settle over her like an impossibly heavy lead blanket, pressing down on her chest. She could almost feel the suffocating intensity of his devotion, a love so powerful it had taken on a life of its own, wrapping itself around his heart like a vice, squeezing tighter with every heartbeat. She could picture him alone in a darkened room, the only light coming from the cold glow of his computer screen, his eyes red and tired but unwavering, staring into the void as he poured his soul out to strangers in the anonymity of the internet. She imagined his fingers trembling on the keyboard, each word typed with the hope of release, yet finding none, only a deepening of the torment that had consumed him.

But just days later, Miller found another post—this one buried deeper, in a different forum, under yet another alias. The tone was drastically different, the words biting and caustic. The love that had seemed so unwavering before now twisted into something darker, a seething, festering anger that felt barely contained.

"She betrayed me. After all we'd been through, after everything I did for her, she threw it all away. I gave her my heart, my soul, every ounce of who I was, and it still wasn't enough. I loved her with a love that went beyond reason, beyond sanity. And for what? For him? For some cheap thrill, for some passing moment that meant nothing compared to the years we built together? I don't know what hurts more—the fact that she did it, or the fact that I still want her, still need her.

It's a pain I can't describe, a kind of torture that reaches into the deepest parts of me. It feels like I've been hollowed out, gutted, like there's this gaping wound that just won't close. The days pass by, and I can't escape the images in my mind—her with him, the way she must have smiled, laughed, the way she touched him with the same hands that once held me so close. I try to push those thoughts away, but they keep creeping back, like shadows that stretch across my heart, darkening everything they touch.

I feel this rage building inside me, this anger that's eating me alive. I hate her for what she's done to me, for what she's made me become. I used to be a good man. I used to believe in love, in trust, in all those things that seem so naive now. But she took that away from me. She took everything. She made me into this... this thing that I don't even recognize when I look in the mirror. I see a man whose eyes are filled with hurt, with fury, with something I can't even name. I see a man who feels lost, abandoned, cast aside like he was nothing.

And yet, despite it all, I can't stop loving her. I wish I could. God, I wish I could. I wish I could tear her out of my heart, rip her from my soul, but she's buried too deep. Even after everything, after all the lies, the deceit, the betrayal, I still crave her. I still need her like I need air to breathe, like I need water to drink. How can I feel this way? How can I still love someone who has broken me in every way possible? How can I still want the very person who has brought me to my knees?

I hate myself for it. I hate myself for wanting her back, for dreaming of a time when we were happy, for remembering the softness of her touch, the warmth of her smile. I hate the way my heart still races when I think of her, the way my chest tightens with longing when I remember the way she looked at me, like I was her world. Was it all a lie? Was it all some cruel joke? How can love turn so quickly into this? Into a war inside myself, between the part that wants to forgive and forget, and the part that wants to scream, to rage, to make her feel even a fraction of the pain she's caused me?

I don't know who I am anymore. I don't recognize this man who feels like he's caught in a storm that will never end, tossed between love and hate, desire and disgust. I look in the mirror, and I see a man who's lost his way, who's been ripped apart by the very person he trusted most. I see a man who wants to make her pay, but also a man who wants to hold her close, to feel her heartbeat against his, to tell her that somehow, some way, it will all be okay.

But it won't be okay. How could it be? She shattered me, broke me into a thousand pieces, and now I'm left here to pick them up, one by one, with hands that are bleeding from the effort. And I don't know if I'll ever be whole again. I don't know if I'll ever be able to look at her without feeling this mixture of longing and loathing, this desperate desire to both pull her back into my arms and push her away forever.

Every day is a battle, a struggle to find some kind of peace in the chaos she left behind. I keep asking myself why. Why did she do it? Why wasn't I enough? Why wasn't our love enough to keep her from straying, from seeking out something else, someone else? Was I too much, or was I not enough? Was I too controlling, or did I give her too much freedom? I don't know the answers, and it's driving me mad, this not knowing, this endless loop of questions that have no answers.

But one thing I do know is that I still love her. I wish I didn't, but I do. I love her in a way that is so deep, so primal, that it feels like a curse, like a poison coursing through my veins. I hate her for what she's done to me, but I hate myself even more for not being able to let go. I hate that I'm still here, waiting, hoping that somehow, she'll come back, that somehow, she'll make it all make sense.

But how do you make sense of betrayal? How do you make sense of loving someone who has taken everything from you, who has torn apart your world and left you to pick up the pieces alone? How do you reconcile the love you still feel with the pain that burns like a wildfire in your chest? I don't have the answers. I don't know if I ever will.

All I know is that I'm stuck in this place between love and hate, between wanting to forget her and needing to remember every single thing. And it's tearing me apart. She's tearing me apart. And I don't know how to stop it. I don't know how to stop loving her, how to stop hating her, how to stop feeling like I'm drowning in a sea of emotions that I can't control, that I can't escape. And I don't know if I ever will."

The contrast between the two posts was stark, a vivid, almost violent portrait of the internal battle, the duality that Bryan's mind and heart were waging, his emotions swinging wildly from one extreme to the other like a pendulum about to snap its chain. His love and hatred intermingled, one feeding off the other, spiraling him further downward at an increasing pace into a dark abyss. The officer assigned to the case flagged these posts and many others, noting the sharp mood swings, the dramatic shifts in tone that seemed to signal a mind fraying at the edges. It was clear that Bryan's mental state had been deteriorating for a long time—far longer than anyone, especially those closest to him, had realized.

18 Visceral Pseudonym

Then came another discovery that sent a fresh wave of concern rippling through the station. Bryan had been writing short stories under a pseudonym, dark, unsettling tales that mirrored his inner turmoil in ways that were disturbingly specific. These stories, posted on obscure corners of the internet, revealed a side of him that no one, not even those closest to him, had likely known existed. Each story was like a confession, a cry from the shadows. The main characters were always men who had been wronged, men betrayed by those they loved, each one seeking revenge with a ferocity that was as relentless as it was terrifying.

The violence in these stories was graphic, visceral—so detailed it felt as if the scenes had been lived rather than imagined. The protagonist's fury was palpable, his rage a living thing brought to life that breathed and snarled on the page. The tone was filled with a bitterness that seemed to seep from every line, a reflection of a man grappling with his own rage and despair, caught in a loop of anger and heartbreak. Hayes read through them, feeling a shiver run down her spine as each story unfolded, each one more disturbing than the last. She could see Bryan's face in every character, hear his voice in every line, his words echoing the thoughts that had been tormenting him, the battles he had been fighting alone in his own mind.

She realized with a cold, unsettling certainty that Bryan's writings weren't just fiction. They were a reflection of his skewed dark reality, a window into a brilliant mind that had been pushed to its breaking point and possibly beyond it. The stories were filled with the kind of details that made it clear these weren't mere fantasies—they were rehearsals, mental manifestations of the darkness that had crept into his heart, scenarios played out in his head so many times they had taken on a life of their own. The imagined actions of a man with nothing left to lose and who is capable of making the decisions most men are incapable.

Hayes closed her eyes for a moment, trying to steady herself. The room felt colder, the fluorescent lights above suddenly too harsh. She could almost feel Bryan's anguish seeping into her, a quiet, relentless damning whisper in her ear, begging for understanding, for someone to see the pain he had been hiding behind a mask of normalcy. She knew they had to find him, and soon, before the stories he had written, the fantasies of vengeance and despair, bled into reality. Before the line between what he had imagined and what he was clearly capable of doing finally snapped.

Meanwhile, Hayes received word that the search teams were continuing their methodical sweep of the riverbanks, their flashlights cutting through the mist as the first rays of the sun began to pierce through the impossible gray. The officers each moved with a quiet determination, their breathing visible in the chilly morning air, their eyes sharp and focused. Somewhere out there, Bryan was waiting, lost in his own darkness, and they were racing against time to find him before it was too late.

Hayes moves on to another one of the stories, the protagonist—a man betrayed by his wife—lured her lover to a secluded spot in the woods, a place where shadows seemed to stretch long and dark, swallowing the light. The air was thick with tension, and the rustle of leaves sounded like whispers of the trees themselves. There, the man exacted a gruesome revenge, his hands steady but his heart racing as he carried out his grim plan. The descriptions were visceral, almost too real, with each word painting a picture of cold calculation mixed with burning rage. The act of violence was detailed in brutal clarity, leaving nothing to the imagination. The protagonist's breaths came in ragged gasps as he stared down at the aftermath, his hands trembling not from fear but from the adrenaline coursing through his veins. And then, in a chilling twist, the man ended his own life, his final moments described in haunting, almost poetic detail. The parallels to Bryan's situation were too close to ignore, and with each sentence, Detective Hayes felt a knot tightening in her stomach, a growing sense of dread creeping up her spine.

"He knew it had to end this way. There was no other choice. It wasn't just a decision; it was a conclusion, an inevitability he had felt coming for a long time, creeping closer with every passing day. She had taken everything from him—his joy, his trust, his belief in the goodness of the world, and most of all, his faith in love. And now it was time to take something back, to reclaim the last scrap of dignity he had left. He had tried to hold on, tried to make sense of it all, but every attempt felt like grasping at smoke, the harder he tried, the more it slipped through his fingers. He had reached his breaking point; something inside him had cracked, splintered under the weight of betrayal, and he knew there was no way to put the pieces back together again.

He remembered the moment he'd found out, the moment the truth had hit him like a physical blow, knocking the air from his lungs and sending him reeling. The world had tilted on its axis, and he'd felt like he was falling, spiraling into a void where nothing made sense anymore. He'd given her everything—every ounce of his love, his loyalty, his life—and she'd thrown it all away for another man. For *him*. The betrayal cut deeper than any wound, a blade twisted in his heart that turned with every breath, every thought, every agonizing moment of awareness.

And now, he had done it. He had taken something back, evened the score in the only way he knew how. But as he stood there, his hands trembling, his heart pounding in his chest, he felt no relief, no satisfaction. Once it was done, once the blood had been spilled, he realized that nothing had changed. The pain was still there, gnawing at his soul like a relentless beast. He had thought it would set him free, that revenge would somehow cleanse him, wash away the darkness that had consumed him.

But instead, it felt like pouring water onto a fire that only grew stronger, feeding on his anguish, his hatred, his despair.

He could still see her face in his mind, her eyes filled with that mixture of fear and disbelief, and for a moment, he almost felt a flicker of guilt, of regret. Almost. But then he remembered—the lies, the deceit, the nights she spent with him instead, the betrayal that had shattered his life, and the guilt melted away like snow in the sun. She had taken everything from him, left him hollow and broken, and he had done what he needed to do to reclaim some semblance of power, some sense of justice. But it hadn't been enough. It could never be enough.

And so he walked to the edge. The river below beckoned him, its dark waters shimmering in the moonlight like liquid silver, promising peace, promising an end. He could hear it whispering to him, calling his name with a soft, seductive murmur that drowned out the noise in his head, the relentless, screaming chaos that had become his constant companion. He felt the pull of the current, felt it tugging at him like an unseen hand, inviting him to let go, to surrender, to find solace in its depths.

He took one last look at the world that had abandoned him—the stars above like cold, indifferent eyes, the trees swaying in the night breeze, the distant lights of the city that had once been his home. He thought of the life he had lost, the dreams that had crumbled into dust, the love that had turned to ashes in his hands. He thought of the future that would never come, the life he would never live, the man he would never be. He saw it all in that final glance, a lifetime's worth of hopes and heartaches compressed into a single, fleeting moment.

And then, he let go. His body felt weightless, suspended in the air for a brief, agonizing second before gravity took hold, pulling him down, down, toward the cold embrace of the river. The wind rushed past his face, a sharp, icy sting against his skin, but he welcomed it, welcomed the sensation of feeling something—anything—other than the gnawing emptiness inside. His mind was strangely calm, clear in those final seconds, as if he had already crossed some unseen threshold, stepped into a space beyond fear, beyond pain.

He closed his eyes, and in that instant, he felt a strange sense of clarity, a quiet acceptance of the end that was rushing to meet him. He thought of her again, thought of the way she used to look at him with love in her eyes, before everything fell apart. He wondered if she would cry when she heard the news, or if she would feel only relief. He wondered if she would ever understand what she had done to him, how she had broken him in ways that could never be repaired.

The water rose up to meet him, and for a moment, he felt nothing—just the cold, the deep, penetrating cold that seeped into his bones, numbing everything it touched. And then, he was submerged, the river closing over his head, muffling the sounds of the world above, the rush of water filling his ears like a lullaby. He let himself sink, the weight of his body pulling him down, down, into the depths where everything was quiet, where everything was still.

He felt the darkness wrap around him like a shroud, soft and comforting, and he surrendered to it, let it carry him away from the pain, away from the memories that had haunted him, away from the love that had turned to hate. He felt his lungs burn, felt the desperate, primal urge to breathe, but he fought against it, fought against the instinct to survive. He didn't want to go back. He didn't want to feel anymore.

And as the last bubbles of air left his lips, as the darkness closed in around him, he felt a strange sense of peace, a fleeting moment of calm that whispered to him that it was over, that he was finally free. But even in that final moment, even as he let himself slip away, he couldn't help but feel the ache of love that refused to die, the stubborn, relentless longing that still clung to his heart, refusing to let go. And he wondered, even as the river took him, if that love would follow him into the dark, if it would be the last thing he felt before everything went black."

Hayes could almost hear the water rushing beneath, the river whispering its dark promises of solace and quiet. She felt the coldness of the night air on her skin, imagined the icy touch of the river as it welcomed him into its depths. The story was not just a piece of fiction—it was a chilling reflection of Bryan's state of mind, a mind that had been planning, perhaps even fantasizing about this ending for a long time. The language was so personal, so painfully intimate, that it felt like she was intruding into the private thoughts of a man who had lost his way. Bryan's inner torment was laid bare, the rawness of his pain spilling across the page like fresh wounds that had never quite healed.

Hayes felt a shiver run through her as she closed the document, her hands slightly unsteady. She had read countless cases, seen more than her share of broken souls, but this... this was different. Bryan's words were like a desperate cry for help, a plea from a man on the edge, teetering between life and death just hoping that someone, anyone would see him where he was mentally and reach out to help. She could sense the rage that had built up inside him, the suffocating grief that had taken root in his heart. It was all there, in stark black and white, and it felt like a ticking time bomb.

"I feel like we're getting closer," she muttered, almost to herself, her voice barely more than a whisper. She could feel the weight of his anguish pressing down on her like a heavy fog.

19 Smoke On The Water

Hayes arrived at the river, stating to her team, "He's here somewhere. He's gotta be. Fan out and let's do this."

With renewed determination, Hayes stepped out onto the riverbank where the morning light had begun to pierce through the thick canopy of trees, casting an eerie, fragmented glow on the water's surface. The river's current moved steadily, not fierce enough to sweep away anything substantial, but certainly capable of hiding something beneath its dark, churning waters. The air was damp, filled with the scent of wet earth and moss, and the sounds of the river were a constant murmur in the background, a steady pulse that seemed to mirror the urgency of their search.

She directed the team to spread out, urging them to expand their search area. The river might not be strong enough to completely hide a body, but it could easily mask a person who was determined to disappear. Hayes could feel the tension in the air, each step heavy with the anticipation of what they might find.

The officers moved quickly down the riverbank, their footsteps crunching against the gravel and dead leaves that covered the ground. They approached the small alcove where Bryan's phone had been found, the place where he had left his wedding ring, and the heart he had carved into the rock—a silent, desperate message etched in stone. The atmosphere was thick with fear and expectation, the kind that makes every breath feel heavy, every heartbeat loud in your ears.

The river flowed steadily beside them, its surface deceptively calm, the gentle ripples hiding whatever secrets it might hold. The trees overhead swayed in the light breeze, their leaves rustling softly like a chorus of hushed voices. The shadows they cast on the water danced in strange patterns, creating an almost hypnotic rhythm that only deepened the sense of unease.

But there was no sign of Bryan himself.

The team began to scour the area for any clue that might lead them closer—footprints in the mud, broken branches, anything that might indicate where he had gone. One of the officers knelt by the water's edge, examining what looked like faint drag marks, barely visible in the soft, damp earth, quickly fading as the ground became softer near the river. They followed the marks, but they seemed to disappear into the forest, swallowed up by the thick underbrush and tall grasses that lined the shore.

"Detective, over here!" an officer called out, his voice cutting through the stillness. Hayes quickly made her way over, her heart pounding in her chest, each step filled with urgency.

The officer pointed to a small patch of ground a few feet from the water's edge. There, scattered carelessly among the leaves and dirt, were several cigarette butts, some of them crushed underfoot, others partially buried in the soft soil. Hayes crouched down, her eyes narrowing as she examined them. It looked like someone had been here recently, maybe even within the last twenty-four hours. The sight of them sent a surge of frustration through her veins—so close, yet still no sign of Bryan himself.

The evidence was clear—he had been here, perhaps contemplating his next move, wrestling with his demons, but where he had gone afterward was still a mystery.

"We need to widen the search area again," Hayes said, her voice firm, trying to suppress the anxiety that threatened to creep in. "He could be anywhere along this river, or he might have moved deeper into the woods. We need to cover all possibilities. Call in anyone that will volunteer."

The team nodded, understanding the gravity of the situation, and the search efforts intensified. More officers arrived along with EMS and firefighters, along with volunteers from the town, their faces set with grim determination to find one of their own. They spread out along the riverbank, moving slowly, methodically, their eyes scanning every detail, every shadow, every ripple in the water.

As the day wore on, the sun climbed higher, and the heat began to rise, turning the search into a grueling effort. Sweat dripped from their brows, their shirts sticking to their backs, but they pushed forward, driven by the urgency of the task at hand. Every potential lead—footprints leading into the forest and what looked like a struggle had taken place, a piece of bloody cloth snagged on a branch—was pursued with relentless focus, but each one turned out to be another dead end. It was as if Bryan had vanished, leaving only the faintest traces of his presence behind.

Hayes knew they couldn't give up. She instructed the officers to search both upstream and downstream, extending their efforts beyond the immediate area. She called in a series of K-9 units, hoping that the dogs might pick up Bryan's scent, that they might find some trail to follow.

Hours passed with no significant breakthroughs. The only new discovery was more cigarette butts further along the riverbank, indicating that Bryan had likely walked along the edge for some distance before perhaps entering the water or continuing on foot into the wilderness. The realization that they might have missed him by mere hours gnawed at Hayes, her frustration mounting with every second that slipped away.

As evening began to fall, casting long, deep shadows across the landscape, the search team was reluctantly forced to pause for the night. The officers regrouped, their faces weary but their resolve unbroken. Hayes gave the order to resume the search at first light, refusing to let the darkness slow their progress she headed back to the station.

Back at the station, Hayes sat down with Chief Moon, reviewing everything they had found so far. It wasn't much—a few cigarette butts, flattened grass, the phone, the ring, the heart etched into the rock—but it was enough to confirm that Bryan had been there, wrestling with his inner turmoil, possibly making a decision that could change everything.

"I don't like this," Hayes admitted, running a hand through her hair, her voice thick with worry. "He's out there somewhere, alone, and we don't know if he's coming back. We don't even know if he's still alive."

Moon nodded, his expression grim, his eyes filled with the weight of his experience. "He's clearly in a dark place, Detective. But in my opinion, we can't give up hope. He left that phone and wedding ring as a message—he's not ready to disappear completely, not yet. There's a part of him that still wants to be found."

Hayes leaned back in her chair, her mind racing with possibilities, her thoughts tangled in the complexity of the situation. "We need to dig deeper into his state of mind. I want more officers on this—checking his digital footprints, talking to

people who knew him, tracing every step he took
before he disappeared. There's more to this story,
and we need to figure it out before it's too late."

As the search team prepared to resume their efforts
at dawn, Hayes felt the weight of the situation
pressing down on her like a heavy stone. Bryan was
out there, somewhere, hiding in the shadows of his
despair, and time was running out. They had found
evidence that he was still alive, but it wasn't
enough. They needed to find him before the
river—or the darkness within him—claimed him for
good. As the good Detective sat down at her desk
she allowed her eyes to close for just a second as she
fell into a deep slumber ending with her head
resting on her arms and snoring. Hours passed and
as the morning sun broke through the station
windows, the morning crew of officers arrived and
startled Hayes awake.

She immediately jumped back onto the discovery of
the cigarette butts at the river and raised an
unsettling question: but Bryan didn't smoke, who
had been there with him? Detective Hayes leaned
over the scattered butts, examining them closely.
They were fresh, not yet fully soaked by the damp
morning dew. This was more than just a piece of

litter; it was evidence that someone else had been at the river around the same time as Bryan.

Hayes picked up one of the cigarette butts carefully with gloved fingers, bringing it closer to her face. The brand was distinctive—Camel, a bold choice often favored by those who had been smoking for years. She placed it into an evidence bag and stood up, her mind spinning with possibilities.

"Bryan doesn't smoke, right?" Hayes asked, glancing over at Officer Daniels, who was reviewing the notes from interviews conducted with Bryan's contacts' list.

Daniels nodded. "That's right. No history of smoking. Health-conscious, for the most part, especially after his aneurysm scare in his teens. And Elizabeth didn't mention any recent changes."

Hayes' brow furrowed. "So who else was there? And why?"

The presence of the cigarette butts suggested that someone else had either met Bryan here or had been watching him. They were scattered around like breadcrumbs left by a ghost, a silent, hidden observer who had kept their distance but had been close enough to witness everything. Hayes crouched down, examining the ashes and the faint impressions in the dirt nearby, her eyes narrowing as she considered the implications. Was this someone who had a more personal interest in Bryan's disappearance, someone who knew him well enough to get close without being seen?

Her mind immediately turned to Bishop—Elizabeth's lover, the man Bryan despised with every fiber of his being for him interjecting himself into their marriage. Bishop was the exact kind of person who would fit into a scene like this, lurking in the shadows, his presence marked by the acrid smell of a stale cigarette. The cigarette butts weren't just a clue, they were a faint trail that could lead them to a potential darker truth. Bishop had always been a wildcard, a man ruled by his worst impulses, driven by jealousy, resentment, and a need for chaos. He was exactly the type of person who might smoke—a man who lived outside the margins of polite society, who toyed with self-destruction like it was a game. And he had every reason to be after Bryan, whether out of spite, jealousy, or something more sinister.

"I want all of the information we have on anyone connected to Bryan—especially Bishop," Hayes said, turning to Daniels, her voice low but urgent. "Let's see if anyone knows if Bishop smokes, and if he has any connection to this brand of cigarette. I want to know what his habits are, who he talks to, where he's been in the last few days." She could feel the tension mounting, a sense of urgency buzzing beneath her skin.

Daniels nodded, already pulling up the information on his laptop. The click of his fingers on the keys was a rapid staccato that matched the quickening pace of Hayes' thoughts. She stepped away, her mind racing through the possibilities, the scenarios, each one more troubling than the last. If Bishop had been here, it opened up an entirely new avenue of concern. He was volatile, a powder keg waiting for a spark, and his past was riddled with poor decisions, drug use, and instability. He had a reputation for lashing out, for using violence when his emotions got the better of him. If he'd been with Bryan, anything could have happened, we could be looking for multiple bodies if Bryan played to his darker self.

"Detective," Daniels called out, his voice slicing through her thoughts, catching her attention. She turned, and his expression told her everything she needed to know before he even spoke. "Bishop does indeed have a history with Camel cigarettes. He's been seen smoking them during a couple of domestic and drug calls we've responded to over the years. He went so far as to put one out on a sheriff's badge a few years ago outside a bar."

Hayes' heart sank. It was a thin lead, but it was something—a thread that might unravel the whole tangled mess. Bishop had the motive, the means, and now, possibly, the opportunity. Her mind flashed through the possibilities again, each one darker than the last. If Bishop had been near Bryan, it could mean he'd confronted him that they could have confronted each other. And knowing Bishop's volatile temper, it wouldn't have been a friendly interaction.

"Get a team over to Bishop's now. He lives in the old trailer park on the edge of town," Hayes ordered, her voice tight with urgency. "We need to know where he was in the last 24 hours, and we need to question him. This might be our first real lead in figuring out what happened to Bryan. I want surveillance, phone records, any recent transactions. Get it all, and get it fast." She turned, her eyes scanning the scene again, searching for something she might have missed, some clue that would point them in the right direction.

As Hayes and her team moved quickly to locate and get eyes on Bishop, a chill ran down her spine, creeping over her skin like a shadow. The air felt thicker, colder, as if it had absorbed the tension of the moment. If Bishop had been at the river, the situation could be far more dangerous than they had initially thought. This wasn't just about a missing person anymore; it was about a confrontation that could have turned deadly in an instant. Bryan might not have just wandered off—he could have been coerced, threatened, or worse. The cigarette butts were a silent witness to something, a moment that had happened here by the water, a moment that could have changed everything.

And Bishop, with his unstable mind and tangled relationship with Elizabeth, could be the key to uncovering what really happened by the river that day. Hayes felt a knot form in her stomach as she considered the possibilities. What if Bishop had followed Bryan here, fueled by jealousy or revenge, determined to confront him about Elizabeth? What if things had escalated, turned violent? Bryan was not a man to back down easily, especially not where his family was concerned, but Bishop had always been unpredictable, always ready to take things too far.

"Stay sharp," Hayes called to her team, the urgency in her voice unmistakable. "If Bishop's involved, this could get ugly. He's got a history, and he's got motive. We're not just looking for Bryan anymore—we're looking for a man who might have every reason to want him gone." She turned back to Daniels, who was still working at his laptop, pulling up every scrap of information he could find on Bishop. She watched his screen fill with details, records of arrests, reports of altercations, a life defined by chaos and conflict.

She couldn't shake the feeling that they were standing on the edge of something, something big, something that could change the course of their search. She knew they were running out of time. Every second counted, and if they didn't find Bishop soon, they might lose their only chance to find out what had really happened to Bryan Black.

20 AND MILES TO GO BEFORE I SLEEP

Alex had sat back at his dad's desk, his eyes scanning the computer screen with relentless determination. He had gone through every folder, every file, meticulously searching for any clue that might lead them to Bryan. It was during a sweep of the browser history that Alex found something peculiar—coordinates, marked as "private." They weren't places Bryan usually visited, but they seemed deliberate, logged at specific times over the past few months.

Alex's heart pounded as he plotted the coordinates on a map. It led to a remote area in the woods, far from where Bryan's phone was found. There was nothing notable on the satellite view—just dense forest and an old, abandoned building that looked more like a hunting cabin. He immediately knew this was where he needed to go.

He didn't tell Elizabeth right away, he was going to but she had cried herself to sleep. She was already on edge, barely holding it together, and he didn't want to get her hopes up without knowing what they would find; especially given the state of her mental health as of late.

Alex's mind was a storm of anxiety and determination as he meticulously prepared his room. He needed to buy himself time—time to find Bryan before Elizabeth got too deep into her own desperation and guilt. He fashioned a makeshift version of himself in his bed using stuffed animals, pillows, and a hoodie, ensuring the silhouette under the blankets would pass for him at a quick glance. The outline was rough, but he knew it would fool Elizabeth long enough.

Grabbing his hiking backpack, he slipped out of the house quietly, the weight of his mission pushing him forward. He had to find the cabin, the secret location Bryan had visited repeatedly—he was sure it held the key to understanding his father's sudden disappearance.

Alex put his car in neutral and pushed it down the street so as to have zero chance of waking Elizabeth. As Alex drove down the dark, winding roads, his mind raced through every possibility. Bryan's laptop had given him more questions than answers, but these coordinates stood out. The location was far from any place Bryan usually went. Why was he there? What did he need to do in such a remote area? Alex had to know and he was going to find out.

The drive was quiet, almost eerily so. If not for the crinkling of the cheeseburger's wrappers and the soda he got at the nearest drive thru it would have probably freaked him out, plus he couldn't remember when he ate last. The forest seemed to close in around him as he ventured deeper into unfamiliar territory. He parked his car on the dirt road near the coordinates, adrenaline pushing him forward as he trekked through the dense woods and found a lightly trodden trail, his flashlight cutting through the shadows.

When Alex finally reached the cabin, it looked even more derelict than he had imagined. Its wooden frame was rotting, windows cracked, and the air around it felt thick with abandonment. But this place was more than just an old building—it was a repository of Bryan's recent life. Inside, Alex found scattered remnants of his father's presence: empty cans, a small fire still smoldering in a crude fireplace, and Bryan's distinct handwriting filling the pages of a notebook left on a dusty table.

Alex's heart pounded as he flipped through the pages. Sketches of him and Elizabeth filled the margins, but it was Bryan's detailed writings that grabbed Alex's attention. The notebook was like an open wound—pages bleeding with Bryan's frustrations, regrets, and unfiltered thoughts about Elizabeth, Alex, and, most shockingly, some of his intentions moving forward.

Bryan's final entries were alarming. The name "D. Mann" appeared repeatedly, accompanied by cryptic notes about a coming confrontation and unfinished business. Alex's blood ran cold when he read the last few lines: "I need to end this. Meeting with D. Mann is the only way. Then, I'll confront the one person who's caused all this pain—Bishop."

Alex snapped the notebook shut, the implications spinning in his mind and quickly sinking in. Bryan had a plan, possibly this whole time, and it was one Alex knew would end badly if he didn't find a way to intervene. He stuffed the notebook into his bag, ready to race back to Elizabeth and warn her of what he had discovered. But as he turned to leave, the faint sound of tires crunching gravel reached his ears.

Alex's eyes widened. Someone else was arriving.

21 Wakeup Call

Elizabeth sat alone in the living room, the walls closing in on her. Every tick of the clock sounded like a hammer to her chest, each moment a painful reminder that Bryan was still out there—missing, alone, possibly even dead. Alex was asleep in his bed, finally.

The river, the phone, the ring—they were symbols of his enduring love, but also of her greatest failures. She replayed every conversation, every argument, every moment when she could have said or done something different. All he had ever asked for was another chance for the constantly improving version of his current self to show her they could be happy...together.

She picked up her phone, her thumb hovering over the contact list. She had received an anonymous message earlier, sent through an encrypted app she had never seen before.

It read: "I know where Bryan is."

The message was followed by a link, but Elizabeth had been too afraid to click on it. What if it was a trap? Or worse, what if it was real?

Elizabeth's mind spiraled. She thought of all the secrets she and Bryan had kept from each other, all the lies she had told, and all the love she had betrayed. Her relationship with Bishop was a constant reminder of her own shortcomings—a toxic escape that had led her further away from her best friend, the man she once swore to love forever.

She stared at the message again, her finger trembling as she finally decided and clicked on the link. The screen changed, displaying a blurred image and an address not too far from where they found Bryan's phone. Her pulse quickened. Was this Bryan reaching out, trying to send her one final message? Or was it someone else entirely, playing on her fears and guilt?

Elizabeth grabbed her keys and rushed out, tears streaming down her face. The guilt was suffocating, but she couldn't ignore the possibility that this might be the clue she had been waiting for. As she drove through the dark, winding roads, she couldn't help but feel that every mile brought her closer to a truth she wasn't prepared to face—a truth about

Bryan, about her, and about the irreversible choices that had led them all to this breaking point.

Elizabeth's hands trembled on the steering wheel, her knuckles white from the grip. The message she received still flashed in her mind—blurred images, an address, and the haunting line: "I know where Bryan is."

The words had burrowed into her, driving her out of the house in a frenzy, not even noticing that Alex's car was missing from the driveway. She didn't think twice; her guilt and fear had swallowed all rational thought.

As she drove, the road became increasingly unfamiliar, winding deeper into a secluded part of town she had never seen or possibly even been to. Her chest tightened with every mile. She didn't know what she would find, but the possibility that Bryan was near pushed her forward like a juggernaut.

The address led her to an old, seemingly abandoned cabin tucked away in the woods. She pulled up next to another car—Alex's car. Elizabeth's breath caught in her throat. Panic flooded her mind as she realized her son had been one step ahead of her.

Bursting out of the car, Elizabeth rushed toward the cabin. The door creaked open under her touch, and she found Alex standing in the dim light, the look on his face a mix of shock and determination.

"Alex!" Elizabeth's voice cracked with a mix of anger and relief. "What are you doing here?"

Alex turned, the notebook still clutched in his hands. "Mom, I... I had to come. I found something on Dad's laptop. There's a lot you need to see. How did you find this place? You were asleep when I left."

Elizabeth's eyes darted to the notebook. She snatched it from Alex's hands, flipping through the pages as tears welled up in her eyes. Sketches of her and Alex, the love and torment tangled in Bryan's mind, stared back at her from the page. But what stopped her cold were Bryan's final entries—the name "D. Mann," cryptic notes, and his seething hatred for Bishop.

Elizabeth read aloud, her voice shaking. "I need to end this. Meeting with D. Mann is the only way. Then, I'll confront the one person who's caused all this pain—Bishop."

Her heart sank. "He's planning something. Something to do with confronting Bishop. Fuck!"

Alex nodded, his own anger bubbling beneath the surface. "Dad fucking hates him, Mom. I hacked into Bishop's phone with Dad, remember? We saw everything—the drugs, the women, all those disgusting things he's into. Dad couldn't stand what Bishop was doing, especially to you. How could you stay with someone that treated you like that? How could you leave us for it...fuck it, its not the time."

Elizabeth felt sick to her stomach, a deep, twisting nausea that started in the pit of her gut and spread throughout her entire body. She could almost feel the bile rising in her throat, a bitter taste that matched the dread coursing through her veins. Bryan's pain, the anguish he had been carrying silently for so long, suddenly felt so close, so real, that it was almost tangible. And now, his plan to confront Bishop, the desperate, reckless edge to his recent actions—it all began to make a terrifying kind of sense. Bishop had poisoned everything—her relationship with Bryan, the bond they once shared with Alex, the fragile peace that had held their family together through the years. Bryan's mind had been shattered, his soul tainted by the corrosive influence of a man who thrived on destruction and chaos.

If they didn't stop him, she realized with a cold, numbing clarity, it wouldn't just be Bryan's heart that was at risk—it would be his soul, his very essence, everything that made him the man she had once loved, everything that made him Alex's father. She could feel her pulse quickening, a frantic, uneven beat that echoed the chaos of her thoughts. And D. Mann, whoever he was, felt like another shadowy figure in this dark and twisted puzzle she could barely comprehend, a piece of the mystery that eluded her grasp, slipping through her fingers like sand.

Her mind raced back to every encounter, every fleeting hint of something darker lurking beneath the surface of Bryan's recent behavior, the small changes she had ignored, the cracks she had been too blind to see. The regret weighed heavy on her chest, pressing down like a physical force. How had she missed it? How had she let it get this far? She felt the sting of tears, hot and burning behind her eyes, but she blinked them away. There was no time for tears, no time for guilt or self-pity. They needed action. They needed to move. They needed to find him.

"We need to find Dad," Alex said, his voice breaking through her spiraling thoughts, cutting through the fog with a clarity that almost startled her. His tone was firm, determined in a way that was so much like Bryan's it sent a pang through her chest. He looked older in that moment, his young face hardened by the weight of the situation, his eyes fierce with a purpose she hadn't seen before. "Before he does something he can't take back. Something that can't be forgiven."

Elizabeth turned to her son, seeing not just a boy but a reflection of Bryan, his spirit, his fire, his capacity to love with a depth that could both save and destroy. Her eyes burned with a mix of fear and guilt, and something else, something new—a fierce, unyielding resolve that had been missing for so long. She knew what she had to do. There was no room for hesitation, no room for doubt. "We will," she whispered, her voice steadier than she felt, gripping the notebook tightly as if it were a lifeline, a map that could lead them back to where they needed to be. "And then we're going to put an end to this once and for all."

She looked at Alex, and in his eyes, she saw that same determination mirrored back at her. It wasn't just a mother and son standing there—it was a team, united by a shared goal, by a love that still held them together even in the darkest of times. They would do whatever it took, cross any line, break any rule, if it meant bringing Bryan back from the edge of the abyss he seemed determined to plunge into. They wouldn't let him face this alone. They couldn't.

They left the cabin together, moving quickly, their footsteps in sync, their hearts pounding with a single, unified purpose. The air was thick with tension, every breath feeling like an effort, every step feeling heavier than the last. Bryan was still out there somewhere, on the brink of doing something that could shatter what little remained of their family. Something that could change everything, irrevocably, forever. And now, Elizabeth and Alex were in a race against time—not just to find Bryan, but to stop the confrontation with Bishop that could destroy them all.

Elizabeth's mind raced as they moved, thoughts colliding in a blur of fear and determination. She felt the weight of her mistakes, of her failure to see the signs, to understand what Bryan had been going through, but she refused to let it paralyze her. She would make it right. She had to. Bryan had been her partner, her best friend, her everything for so many years. And now, she would be his savior if that's what it took. She would be strong enough for both of them, for their son, for the love that still burned bright even in the ashes of their broken marriage.

Alex's face was set in a determined expression, his jaw clenched, his eyes focused ahead as if he could will his father back by sheer force of will. He was scared, she could see that, but he was also resolute. He wasn't a child anymore—he was a young man who had been thrust into a situation far beyond his years, and he was rising to the occasion. For a brief moment, she felt a surge of pride amidst the fear. No matter what happened, Bryan would have been proud of him.

"Mom," Alex said, his voice quieter now, a tremor she almost missed. "We're going to find him, right?"

"Yes," she replied, not allowing any doubt to creep into her voice. "Yes, we are. And when we do, we're going to make this right. We're going to bring him back."

As they made their way through the darkening woods, she prayed silently, to whatever higher power might be listening, that they were not too late as they headed to come face to face with Bishop.

22 QUEEN'S GAMBIT

Alex trailed Elizabeth's car with a laser focus, careful to keep a safe distance as he followed her down the winding backroads of town. He knew exactly where she was heading—the address belonged to Bishop's dilapidated trailer, a place he lived by renting a room from his sketchy roommate, landlord, and drug buddy Matthew. Alex's heart pounded as he replayed the images and writings of Bryan's notebook in his head. The confrontation Bryan was planning was more than just a meeting; it was personal, and Alex couldn't shake the feeling that they were already too late.

Elizabeth's car finally pulled up to the rundown trailer park, and Alex parked a short distance away, his eyes glued to the scene unfolding in front of him. Their trailer stood out among the others—weather-beaten, with broken blinds, rust stains, and an overgrown yard littered with empty beer cans and cigarette butts. It was a fitting home for someone like Bishop, a man whose very

181

existence was a mess of lies, drugs, and manipulation.

Alex watched as Elizabeth sprung out and slammed her car door shut, her movements stiff and determined. She was operating on pure adrenaline, and Alex knew that nothing good could come from this encounter. He slipped out of his car and moved closer, staying in the shadows, close enough to intervene but far enough to stay hidden.

Elizabeth knocked on the trailer door hard, her patience already worn thin with knowledge of what Alex and Bryan had learned of Bishop's true nature.

A few moments later, the door swung open, revealing Bishop. He looked worse than usual—his eyes bloodshot and one nearly swollen shut, a deep purple bruise stretching across his cheekbone. His lip was cracked, caked with dried blood, and his unkempt hair clung to his scalp in greasy clumps. His clothes, wrinkled and stained with a mix of sweat and grime, hung loosely on his gaunt frame. A dark bruise encircled his throat, adding to the general sense of decay. The sour stench of mildew mixed with something more acrid—like rotten eggs, cigarette smoke, and the pungent tang of alcohol—drifted from inside. His pale skin, mottled with fading bruises, looked sallow and sickly under the dim light as he stood hunched, glaring through venomous, bloodshot eyes.

"What the hell do you want, Courtsney?" Bishop slurred, his voice tinged and slurred with annoyance and the telltale signs of another high mixed with whatever injuries he sustained.

"Where's Bryan?" Elizabeth demanded, stepping forward, her tone sharp and unwavering. "I know you've been in contact. What have you done? What the hell is going on?"

Bishop rolled his eyes and let out a dismissive laugh. "Why the hell would I know where Bryan is? Last I checked, your golden boy husband hates my guts and I'm the last person he would ever talk to. Especially after what he did to me up at the river earlier. I'm gonna have him thrown in jail for assault. He walked right up and took my 1911 from me, Elizabeth, and then beat me with it."

Alex inched closer, still hidden from sight but able to hear every word and smiling knowing that Bryan took Bishop's favorite gun and beat his ass with it. He could see the tension between Elizabeth and

Bishop was escalating, like two stormfronts on a collision course.

Elizabeth's eyes burned with anger. "Don't play dumb with me, Bishop. He's planning something—something involving you. So if you know anything, now's the time to speak up."

Bishop sneered, his expression darkening. "You really think Bryan would tell me anything? He said he wanted to talk earlier, but I was done talking and was ready to end things when Bryan blindsided me, stole my "Sweet Lips" and beat me with it. He's too busy trying to play the martyr, dragging everyone down with his faggot bullshit. But you...you've been just as messed up, falling right onto my lap when he couldn't keep his own life together and satisfy you."

"What the hell do you really want?" Bishop sneered, blowing smoke into the cramped space between them. Alex watched from his hiding spot, his breath hitching as he saw his mother's hand move toward her Glock. Bishop, as volatile as he was, could snap at any moment, and Alex knew he had to be ready. Alex's pulse quickened. He knew this was about to explode. He stepped forward, coming out of the shadows and standing directly in front of Elizabeth, his presence catching Bishop off guard.

"What the—" Bishop's gaze shifted to Alex, his face contorted with rage. "Oh, great, the kid's here. Just like his old man, sticking his nose where it doesn't belong."

Alex didn't hesitate for a second, questioning, "Why were you there yesterday, Bishop? At the river? We found your cigarettes and you just admitted to meeting dad...and getting your ass beat *Alex chuckled*."

Bishop's face twitched, a brief flicker of surprise crossing his eyes before he masked it with feigned indifference. "You don't know what you're talking about, kid. Why the hell would I be at the river other than to end your old man?"

Elizabeth, struggling to maintain her composure, stepped forward. "Bishop, don't lie. If you know where Bryan is, you need to tell us. This isn't a game—this is my fucking family."

Bishop's smirk faded, replaced by a darker, more dangerous glint. "Your family? Funny, because I seem to recall your 'family man' wasn't so great to you, Court. And now you're here, accusing me of what, exactly? That I had something to do with him running off? I would have but things happened out there."

Alex stepped closer, his voice low and filled with contempt. "We know what kind of person you are, Bishop. We've seen everything on your phone—your drugs, your sick jokes, everything you're into. So why were you at the river?"

The tension in the room was electric. Bishop's bravado cracked, and for the first time, fear flashed in his eyes. "You have no idea what you're messing with, kid," he hissed, backing away. "I was there, yeah, but Bryan's the one who wanted to talk. Said he needed to set some things straight. He was off his rocker, talking about making things right and wanting Elizabeth to be happy and then about disappearing for good. I told him he could fuck off with all that emotional gayness, and he just... left, walked off into the woods."

Elizabeth's heart sank. Bishop's words were laced with lies and half-truths, but one thing was clear: Bryan had been desperate enough to reach out to the last person anyone would ever expect. And now, whatever had been said between them was buried in the murky depths of Bishop's twisted mind, leaving

Elizabeth and Alex more uncertain—and afraid—than ever.

Elizabeth's hand moved to the waistband of her jeans, her fingers grazing the grip of her pistol—a habit she had picked up after things with Bryan and Bishop spiraled. She had never used it, never even wanted to, but tonight was different. The stakes were higher, and she felt more vulnerable than ever.

Elizabeth's voice dropped lower, each word laced with barely controlled fury. "This is your last chance. Tell me what you know, or I swear to God—"

Bishop cut her off, suddenly stepping closer, his eyes wild with anger and defiance. "You think you're gonna scare me, Elizabeth? You think pulling that little piece makes you tough? I've been through hell today; this is nothing."

Alex kept his composure, his eyes locked onto Bishop's reminding him that he was there too. "You don't know anything about me, Bishop. But I know a lot about you. Dad and I found your messages, your stash, your sick jokes, and proclivities. You're a monster, and you're dragging everyone down with you."

Bishop's face turned a deep red, veins bulging at his temples. He lunged forward, knocking a nearby table and sending a half-empty bottle crashing to the floor. "You little shit! You and your father are ruining everything! You think you're better than me? You're nothing! Just like Bryan—always judging, always fucking things up for people like me! He picked up the broken bottle and started to move towards Alex."

Elizabeth pulled her pistol and pointed it at Bishop, her hands trembling but her eyes steady. "Back off, Bishop. I won't tell you again."

Bishop stopped in his tracks, but his fury didn't subside. He stared down the barrel of the gun, his breath ragged. "You're gonna shoot me? Huh? For what? For telling the truth? I'm the one who has been putting holes in you, not the other way around. You don't have the fucking guts, bitch."

Elizabeth's grip tightened, her mind flashing with memories of every lie, every manipulation, every dark corner she had let Bishop drag her into. She felt sick, but she was determined not to let him hurt

Alex. "You don't know me as well as you think, Bishop. I'm done being scared of you, I'm done with you period."

Alex moved closer to his mother's side, his presence a silent but powerful show of support. "Mom, don't do this. It's what he wants and he's not worth it."

Bishop's demeanor shifted, his bravado faltering as he realized he was done. "You don't get it, do you? Bryan's the one who's out of fucking control. He's got nothing left, and if he comes after me again—"

"Bryan's not the one out of control," Elizabeth snapped. "He's just trying to clean up the mess we made of everything."

Bishop took a step back, his anger replaced by a flash of fear. The power dynamic had shifted entirely, and he knew it. His eyes flicked nervously between Elizabeth's gun and Alex's defiant stance. "Get out. Fucking leave, the both of you. Before I have to make you."

Elizabeth lowered her pistol slightly, keeping it at the ready. "This isn't over, Bishop. Not by a long shot."

She and Alex backed away from the trailer, never turning their backs on Bishop until they were almost to the cars. Bishop had gone inside and the door slammed behind him, and for a moment, the only sound between them was their heavy breathing.

As they reached their cars, Elizabeth finally let the gun fall to her side, her hands shaking with the adrenaline of the confrontation. Alex looked at her, his eyes filled with a mix of pride, relief, and determination. "We need to find Dad. We're close, I can feel it."

Elizabeth nodded, her resolve stronger than ever. "We will. And when we do, we'll make sure Bishop never gets near any of us again." Elizabeth smiled lovingly at Alex.

Together, they climbed into their separate cars, leaving the toxic ruins of Bishop's chaotic world behind and headed home. They were united in their mission, fueled by anger, love, and a desperate need to save Bryan before it was too late. The fight was far from over, but Elizabeth and Alex were ready for whatever came next.

23 Up In Smoke

As Elizabeth and Alex drove away from Bishop's decaying trailer, the tension from the situation hung thick in the air. Elizabeth's grip on the steering wheel was tight, her knuckles white as she replayed the confrontation in her mind. Bishop's venomous words echoed in her ears, but the sight of Alex standing by her side—resilient and determined—gave her a renewed sense of purpose. They had made it out of that hellhole without bloodshed, but the fight for Bryan was just beginning.

Alex's car followed close behind, his eyes flicking between the road and his mother's tail lights. He could still feel the raw adrenaline coursing through his veins, a mixture of fear, anger, and resolve. Every second felt like a countdown, a ticking clock in the search for Bryan. But as they drove out of the trailer park, something caught Alex's attention: speeding Police vehicles with their lights flashing closing the distance rapidly.

Elizabeth noticed them too—four police vehicles speeding passed them towards Bishop's place. SUVs and trucks with sirens blaring, lights flashing in the twilight. She instinctively pulled to the side, watching as they raced past in the opposite direction, dust and gravel flying in their wake as they entered the trailer park. Alex's heart pounded.

"What the hell are they doing here?" Alex muttered to himself, a chill running down his spine. Elizabeth's thoughts mirrored his own, but she kept watching but trying to get away and not get involved, wanting to know but still eager to put as much distance between them and Bishop as possible.

Just as the police vehicles reached Bishop's trailer and a few started to exit their vehicles, Elizabeth glanced in her rearview mirror. The officers began to gather, but before any could even approach the front door, a deafening explosion ripped through the air. The blast was blinding—an intense flash followed by a fireball that roared to life, engulfing the trailer in a violent eruption of flames and shrapnel.

Elizabeth's reflexes kicked in, and she slammed on the brakes, skidding to a halt in the middle of the road. The screech of tires was followed by the loud crunch of metal as Alex's car rear-ended hers. Both vehicles jolted violently, glass shattering, airbags deploying with a sudden, forceful burst. The explosion rocked the entire trailer park, and Elizabeth's breath was knocked out of her as the force sent a shockwave through the ground surrounding their cars.

Through the haze of smoke and debris, Elizabeth saw chaos unfold. The closest police SUV to Bishop's trailer was lifted off its wheels and thrown onto its side, its windows blasted out. Flames erupted from the wreckage, devouring the streams of fuel spilling from the torn metal with a monstrous hunger. The fire raged and crackled, twisting and clawing upward as smoke billowed into the darkened sky. Many officers were thrown to the ground, their bodies battered by the blast wave and shrapnel, some struggling to get up while others lay motionless, dazed and disoriented.

Elizabeth winced as she tried to adjust herself in the driver's seat, a sharp stab of pain shooting through her side. Her ribs felt bruised, the deep ache from where the seatbelt had yanked tight against her chest during the crash—a harsh but necessary grip that had saved her life yet left its painful mark. Every breath was a struggle, a reminder of the impact that had rattled her bones. Her neck throbbed with a relentless, stabbing pain, a flare of agony each time she turned her head, the muscles strained and likely sprained from the violent whiplash. She raised a shaky hand to her forehead and felt the warm, sticky trickle of blood from a small gash where her head had slammed against the steering wheel; the skin split open, the sensation raw and stinging.

Her fingers trembled as she touched her temple, the area tender and swollen, the result of a blunt force she had barely registered in the chaos. Her left shoulder throbbed with a dull, insistent ache, radiating down to her arm, which tingled with a worrying numbness, as if the nerves were still in shock from the collision. Her right knee, pressed awkwardly against the dashboard, sent jolts of pain up her leg whenever she shifted, the joint swollen and bruised from where it had slammed into hard plastic.

Every movement felt like a struggle against her own body, her muscles tight with tension, her skin clammy with sweat. She could feel her pulse racing in her throat, each beat sending a fresh wave of dizziness through her head. Her breathing was shallow, and she fought to steady it, every inhale sending a new jolt of pain through her chest, reminding her just how close they had come to catastrophe. The acrid smell of smoke and burning fuel filled the air, mingling with the metallic tang of blood in her mouth where she had bitten her lip in the crash. For a moment, she closed her eyes, trying to gather her strength, feeling the panic rising in her chest, a cold fear settling into her bones as she wondered how badly she might be hurt and if she had the strength to keep moving forward.

Alex stumbled out of his car, his head spinning, ears ringing from the impact, and his left knee protesting with every step. His chest felt tight and bruised from the impact of the airbag, and his right shoulder throbbed where he'd been thrown against the door. He could feel the sting of glass cuts on his hands and face, minor but painful, each one a stinging reminder of the violent crash. Despite the pain, Alex's focus remained sharp, his determination undeterred by the physical toll. The throbbing aches were nothing compared to the urgent need to find Bryan and piece together the truth of what had just unfolded.. He could taste blood in his mouth, and his vision blurred for a moment before he found his bearings. He rushed to his mom's vehicle, pulling at the passenger door, which was stuck from the collision.

"Mom! Are you okay? Elizabeth, snap out of it and answer me dammit!" Alex shouted, his voice strained and desperate.

Elizabeth nodded, her movements robotic and her mind barely processing the chaos unfolding around her. She shoved the car door open, stumbling out, her legs weak and trembling beneath her. She gripped the doorframe tightly, struggling to find her balance, as her eyes scanned the scene in a haze of shock.

Flames leaped into the night sky, sending up thick, roiling clouds of smoke that turned everything around her into a hellish, red-orange blur. The fire spread with terrifying speed, feeding on the junk scattered around the trailers—old tires ignited in a flash, crackling with intense heat, while stacks of wooden pallets erupted into bright, devouring flames. The discarded appliances hissed and popped as the fire consumed them, each new flare-up sending another wave of heat against her skin. The acrid stench of burning rubber and gasoline filled the air, stinging her eyes and choking her lungs.

Elizabeth's gaze fixed on a nearby car just as the flames reached it, licking at the edges before the vehicle seemed to explode with a violent roar. Glass shattered, and a wall of heat slammed into her, forcing her back. A thick column of black smoke rose from the car, and she could feel the ground tremble under her feet as another wave of flame shot up, the fire growing hotter, hungrier.

Her heart pounded in her chest as she looked around, searching desperately for a way out. The fire was moving too fast, its path unpredictable, devouring everything in its way. The distant wail of sirens pierced the air, but they were still too far away. Elizabeth's breath came in quick, shallow gasps, panic clawing at her throat as the flames grew closer.

She knew she had to move, had to get Alex out of here before the fire trapped them both. The heat was unbearable now, pressing in from all sides, and she could feel the sweat dripping down her back, mingling with the smoke and ash that filled the air.

Elizabeth swallowed hard, her throat dry and raw from the smoke, and pushed herself to get her and Alex away from the danger.

One of the officers, his face bloodied and uniform torn, managed to crawl to his radio. Despite his injuries, he made the urgent call for emergency assistance, his voice crackling with urgency. "Dispatch, we have an explosion at the trailer park—officers down, multiple injuries, fire spreading rapidly. We need fire, EMS, and backup immediately! This place is going up fast! Officers Down!", as he collapsed.

Elizabeth and Alex briefly watched in horror as the fire spread, consuming everything in its path. The officers closest to the blast were moving and trying to assist each other, some dragging their wounded comrades away from the inferno while others staggered toward their damaged vehicles, trying to retrieve equipment or extinguish the flames. The sounds of crackling fire, groaning metal, and pained shouts filled the air, a cacophony of destruction.

Elizabeth's mind raced. "Oh my God, Alex... What the hell just happened? Did Bishop—did he, did he have something to do with this? Did Bryan?"

Alex's face was grim, his eyes fixed on the burning wreckage. "I don't know, but... something doesn't feel right here. We need to leave...now."

They watched as yet another explosion rang out—this time, a propane tank from one of the nearby trailers went off, sending debris flying like shrapnel. More officers took cover, some diving behind vehicles, others desperately trying to control the growing fire. The heat was intense, almost unbearable, and Alex felt it on his skin, a stinging reminder of the peril they were all in.

In the midst of the chaos, Alex's thoughts turned to Bryan. What if this was connected to him somehow? His dad's words from the notebook, the anger, the deep-seated pain, and now this explosion—it all pointed to something bigger, something dangerous.

Elizabeth grabbed Alex's shoulder, pulling him back towards their cars, both heavily damaged but still operable. "We need to get out of here before this whole place goes up. We'll figure out what's going on, but we can't do it here. We can't be here anymore."

Alex nodded, though his eyes remained locked on the burning scene before them. He knew they were just scratching the surface of whatever dark truth lay beneath. Bishop, Bryan, and now the explosion—it was all connected. But for now, all they could do was retreat, regroup, and hope that the answers wouldn't come at the cost of more lives.

They climbed back into their battered vehicles, the doors creaking and groaning as they pulled them shut, each slam echoing through the chaotic night. The smell of burning rubber and scorched metal clung to their clothes, mixing with the thick, acrid smoke that still hung in the air like a shroud. Alex fumbled with his keys, his hands shaking, his heart pounding in his chest. He could feel the adrenaline coursing through his veins, his fingers slick with sweat as he turned the ignition. The engine sputtered once, twice, then caught with a strained, wheezing roar, like an animal wounded and reluctant to move.

Elizabeth glanced over at him, her face drawn and pale, smudged with soot and sweat. Her eyes were wide with a mix of fear and determination, darting between the rearview mirror and the road ahead. The flames in the distance cast an eerie glow across the shattered windshields, flickering shadows dancing across their faces as they moved. She could hear the faint crackle of the fire still raging behind them, the distant shouts of panicked voices, the occasional burst of an exploding tire or gas tank.

Alex gritted his teeth and pressed the gas pedal gently, coaxing the reluctant engine to life, feeling every vibration through the seat, the metal frame rattling like it was about to fall apart. The car lurched forward, hesitating as if unsure of itself, then finally picked up speed. He felt the tension in his muscles begin to ease, but only slightly. His knuckles were white as he gripped the steering wheel, the vibrations making his hands tingle, each bump in the road jarring through his body.

Elizabeth followed close behind, her own car rattling and coughing as if struggling to breathe, the dashboard lights flickering intermittently. Her heart raced as she maneuvered around the debris, her senses hyper-focused on every detail—the glow of the fire still visible in the side mirror, the faint sounds of sirens growing louder in the distance, the acrid taste of smoke lingering on her tongue. She could hear her own heartbeat in her ears, a steady thrum that matched the pounding in her head.

Behind them, the trailer park was a blazing inferno, smoke curling into the night sky, lit from below by the flames that continued to spread. She could see the orange glow reflected in Alex's rear window, shadows flickering as if the darkness itself were on fire. The air was thick with tension, the weight of what they had just escaped pressing heavily on her chest. She took a deep breath, trying to steady her nerves, her hands gripping the wheel so tightly her knuckles ached.

The road stretched out before them, winding and uneven, and Elizabeth could feel every bump and pothole beneath the wheels as if the ground itself were resisting their escape. The smoke followed them, a dark, creeping fog that seemed determined to swallow them whole, curling and twisting in the rearview mirror like the tendrils of some unseen beast. She swallowed hard, her mouth dry, the metallic taste of fear lingering on her tongue as she pressed down harder on the gas.

Alex glanced over at her in his mirror, seeing the same look of grim determination on her face that he felt in his own heart. There was no time to speak, no time to process what had just happened. All that mattered was getting away, putting as much distance between them and the blaze as possible. The world outside the car windows seemed strangely quiet, the usual sounds of crickets and night birds drowned out by the rumble of their engines and the distant wail of approaching sirens.

As they drove away, the smoke and fire trailed behind them like a dark, haunting specter, a reminder of the danger they had narrowly escaped. Every breath felt like a battle against the fear that clawed at their insides, every turn of the wheel a defiant move against the chaos that threatened to consume them. The night was alive with tension, the air thick with unspoken thoughts and a shared resolve that pushed them forward, farther from the flames and closer to the truth.

The sirens of approaching fire trucks and ambulances could be heard in the distance, but the damage was already done. Alex and Elizabeth's mission to find Bryan had taken an unexpected and dangerous turn, one that neither of them could have predicted. The stakes were higher than ever, and as they drove into the night, the only certainty was that nothing would ever be the same again.

24 METAL, FIRE, AND FATE

Elizabeth slumped back in her seat, the leather creaking beneath her, her breath frayed and uneven as she fought to steady herself. Her heart still pounded from the adrenaline coursing through her veins, her fingers gripping the steering wheel as if it were the only thing keeping her tethered to reality. Images of the explosion flickered in her mind like an old film reel—the blast of fire, the police SUVs twisted and overturned, and the sudden eruption of chaos that had unfolded in what felt like seconds. She pressed a hand to her chest, feeling the rapid rise and fall, trying to calm the storm raging inside her.

Her phone buzzed, its sudden vibration startling her, and she glanced down at the screen to see Alex's name glowing back at her. She hesitated for just a moment, wiping a smear of blood from her forehead with the back of her hand, and then pressed the answer button.

"Hey," she said, her voice wavering despite her attempt to sound composed, like she hadn't just escaped a scene from a disaster movie. She grabbed a tissue from the console and dabbed at the cut on her forehead, the sting helping to ground her thoughts, pulling her back to the present.

"Hey, Mom," Alex's voice came through the speaker, tight and strained, but with that familiar note of calm determination she'd always admired, even relied upon, in her son. "You doing okay?"

"Yeah," she replied, glancing up at the rearview mirror, catching a glimpse of the small gash, the blood now smeared into a thin line down her temple. "I'm alright. Just bruised up a bit, nothing serious. How about you? How are you holding up?"

There was a pause on the other end, and she could almost hear him thinking, assessing. Alex's car wasn't in much better shape than hers, the front end crumpled, steam rising in thin wisps from a busted radiator. "I'll live," he finally said, a touch of humor in his voice despite the circumstances. "The car, though... not so much. It's making noises I'm pretty sure it shouldn't be making."

Elizabeth let out a soft chuckle, a release of tension she hadn't realized she was holding in. "Well, that's what happens when you drive like you're in a demolition derby, kiddo."

Alex snorted, a bit of awkward laughter escaping. "Hey, I learned from the best. Remember that time you tried to parallel park on that hill and rolled back into Dad's truck?"

Elizabeth couldn't help but smile, the memory catching her off guard and breaking through the seriousness of the moment. "Touché. Guess we both have a knack for vehicular destruction."

He laughed again, lighter this time, and the tension between them seemed to ease, if only just a little. "I was thinking," he continued, "we should head to Mike's shop. He's not too far from us, and he'll take care of us. Dad wouldn't trust anyone else, right?"

Elizabeth felt a wave of warmth at the mention of Bryan, a comforting thought amid the chaos. "Yeah, Mike's is perfect. I'll give him a call and let him know we're on the way. You think you can make it there without breaking down completely?"

Alex's dry laugh crackled through the phone. "Barely. She's on her last legs, but I think I can manage. We'll just have to cross our fingers and hope she doesn't fall apart on the highway."

"Sounds like a plan," Elizabeth replied, trying to inject a bit of lightness into her voice. "And if she does, well... we can always push it the rest of the way, right?"

Alex chuckled, the sound lifting some of the heaviness from the air. "Right. I could use the workout anyway."

She felt a strange sense of relief in the banter, the small slice of normalcy amidst the madness, but then the weight of the day settled on her shoulders once more, pressing down with renewed intensity. She didn't want to think about logistics, about rentals or mechanics or anything beyond just getting through the next few minutes. But she forced a sense of practicality back into her tone. "I'll see what we can do. Let's just get there first."

There was a pause, a shared moment of quiet understanding between them, a mother and son trying to find their way back to each other in the middle of everything that had gone wrong. Elizabeth could feel the tears pricking at the corners of her eyes, but she blinked them away, knowing she had to stay strong, had to keep moving forward, for Alex, for Bryan, for herself.

"Okay, Mom," Alex said finally, his voice softer, more earnest. "We'll figure it out. Together."

Elizabeth swallowed hard, nodding even though he couldn't see her. "Yeah," she murmured, "together." She put the car in gear, her hand steady on the wheel. They would get through this. They had to.

As they pulled into Mike's garage, the familiar smell of oil and metal hit them, a strangely comforting scent after the chaos they had just escaped. Mike was already outside, wiping his hands on a rag, his expression a mix of worry and familiarity as he watched their battered cars limping into the lot.

"What the hell happened to you two?" Mike called out, rushing over as Elizabeth and Alex stepped out of their vehicles, each movement causing a fresh wave of pain.

"Long story, Mike," Elizabeth said, her voice wavering. "We just… we need your help. Bryan has always trusted you with everything."

Mike looked at the damage, his eyes scanning over the dented frames and shattered glass. He didn't need to hear the details; he could see enough in their exhausted faces to let it go. "Don't you worry about these old gals. I'll get 'em fixed up. But I'm out of rentals right now, and I don't think you two should be stranded right now."

Alex sighed, trying to rub away the pain that throbbed in his shoulder. "Yeah, we were just gonna find something quick to keep moving and get back. We don't want to be a bother."

Mike shook his head and wiped his forehead, smudging grease along his hairline. "You're never a bother. Bryan's practically family to me, and that makes you family too." He gestured toward the corner of the lot, where his personal 4x4 Jeep was parked—mud-splattered, rugged, and dependable. "Take my Jeep. I'm not gonna sit back and let you deal with this on your own."

Elizabeth looked at the Jeep, then back at Mike, her eyes brimming with gratitude and the exhaustion of everything that had happened. "Mike, we can't just—"

"You can, and you will," Mike cut her off, his tone firm but kind. "Bryan would do it for me in a heartbeat. Besides, she's got a full tank and all the bells and whistles Bryan loved and that you two could ever need. She's yours until we get these wrecks sorted out."

Alex ran a hand over the hood of the Jeep, feeling a sense of connection to something familiar, something Bryan would have appreciated. "Thanks, Mike. This means a lot, really."

Mike shrugged it off, handing over the keys without hesitation. "Just bring her back in mostly one piece, alright? And keep your heads on straight. You look like you've got a lot going on right now, and Bryan would want you to stay safe."

Elizabeth nodded, her voice thick with emotion. "We will. Thanks, Mike. For everything."

As they climbed into the Jeep, Elizabeth adjusted the seat, feeling the sturdy frame beneath her. It felt right, more secure than the rental would have, and it was a small comfort in a sea of uncertainty. Alex slid into the passenger seat, his mind still racing from everything that had just unfolded.

They pulled out, the Jeep's tires crunching over gravel, and for a brief moment, it felt like they were just on a regular drive, as if the world hadn't been flipped upside down. The shock was setting in, and the quiet ride gave them both space to process, or at least pretend they could.

Elizabeth glanced at Alex, her voice breaking the silence. "We're gonna get through this, okay? We'll figure it out. Lets get home and get some rest."

Alex nodded, his eyes fixed ahead but his mind somewhere else entirely. "Yeah, Mom. We will figure this out, but after some rest."

But even as they spoke those words, the weight of the day settled heavily around them, and they knew the hardest parts were still ahead.

25 THE UNDEAD AND THE DEMON

Bishop's eyes flickered open, the dim light bulb overhead casting a feeble glow that barely pierced the darkness of the underground cellar. His head throbbed with a relentless, pulsing pain, and he could feel the soreness spreading through his battered body. His vision swam, a haze of darkness and pain, the result of the beating he had received. Every inch of him seemed to pulse with bruises, cuts, and a numbing, sickening ache. The dim light and the steady hum of a small fan and the distant whir of a generator were the only things anchoring him to reality. The raw, metallic scent of blood mingled with the earthy aroma of the dirt walls surrounding him, a stifling reminder of his dire predicament.

The chair he was bound to was cold and unforgiving, its rough wood biting into his back and legs. His wrists were shackled with cuffs so tight they were cutting into his skin, each movement sending a jolt of pain through his arms. His legs were bound with thick ropes, and he could barely shift, let alone stand or run. The cellar's dirt walls seemed to close in on him, the lack of windows or any other light sources only adding to the claustrophobic, oppressive atmosphere.

Bishop's mind raced, a storm of anger, fear, and a gnawing, bitter resentment. The pain was almost secondary to the fury he felt coursing through him. He tried to remember how he had ended up here, but the memories were fragmented, flashes of violence and desperation blending together in a chaotic blur. It was clear that whoever had done this to him wanted him to suffer, and the thought of Bryan and Elizabeth being behind it only fueled his rage.

"How dare they?" he muttered hoarsely, his voice barely more than a rasp. "Those fucking bastards..."

His mind kept circling back to Bryan—Bryan, the man he had despised, the man whose life he had tormented. Bishop's hatred for Bryan was unfathomable, rooted in a twisted combination of envy, spite, and attraction. "It's all your fault," he spat, his voice cracking with the strain of his anger. "You and your stupid, perfect fucking life. You think you're so damn righteous and better than me."

The bitterness in his voice was palpable, a venomous cocktail of anger and fear. He saw Bryan, with his self-righteousness and his insipid sense of justice, having made his life a living hell. Now, as he sat locked down in the dark, damp cellar, the memory of Bryan's face, his smug sense of superiority, only intensified his rage. He seethed, "You think you can just come in and ruin everything? Everything I've worked for, all the power I've had? You and your little family—who the hell do you think you are? You have no idea what I'm capable of, no idea what I'll do to keep what's mine! You think this is over? You think you can just erase me, wipe me away like I never existed? You're fools—all of you! I'll tear you down, I'll make you pay, I'll—I'll make sure you understand—I'll make sure you all understand! You think I'm just some obstacle to be removed, some inconvenience in your little fairy tale? I'm the one who decides how this ends! I'm the one with the control here! Not you, not anyone!"

His voice grew more frantic, rising in pitch as his eyes darted wildly, unable to focus on anything for long. A manic energy radiated from him, his hands gesturing erratically as if trying to grasp something that was slipping away. "You think you can just erase me from this world?" he spat, his face twisted with fury. "You think it's that simple? That you can just take her away and be done with it?" His breathing grew ragged, and he took a step forward, his body shaking with barely contained anger.

"She was *never* yours! Not since I lured her to me." he shrieked, pounding his head against his air. "She's just a pawn in this fucking game, a pathetic little piece I used to get back at Bryan! You really think you have her? You think she loves you? You're nothing but a joke!" His face contorted with disdain as he continued, "She was just a means to an end, and when I'm done with her, you'll be nothing but a forgotten memory! I've fought hard for this, for the chance to destroy you through her. You can't take that away from me! You won't beat me. You were lucky before."

His voice cracked with fury, yet the venom remained. "You don't know the depths I'll sink to. She was my weapon against you, and I'm not about to let you waltz in here and ruin my plans. You think you've won? You haven't seen anything yet!"

Bishop's thoughts then turned to Elizabeth, his means to an end. He had used her, manipulated her, and in return, she had taken his maniacal affections and his faux-power and twisted them into something he could control. "And you, you whore,

215

you're here too aren't you?" he growled, his voice filled with venom. "Fuck you and Bryan. You two fucks were made for each other. You took everything from me. Everything I had left. You think you're both so damned high and mighty? You think you can just walk away? Not from me!"

The bitterness toward Elizabeth was almost as intense as his hatred for Bryan. She had been his means to an end, his way of filling the void in his life—a void he had tried to mask with drugs and deceit. But she had turned on him, her betrayal a final, crushing blow that would have sent him spiraling into a deeper level of pit of despair if he had ever cared at all.

Bishop's breathing became ragged as he struggled against the cuffs, his anger mounting with each futile movement. He wanted to lash out, to scream, to find a way out of this hellish prison. The darkness and confinement only heightened his fear, making his sense of vulnerability all the more acute. He had always been the one in control, the one who dictated terms, but now he was at the mercy of whoever had done this to him.

His mind raced through possible scenarios, each one more desperate and frantic than the last. The pain was almost secondary to the sheer, unrelenting fury that consumed him. "You think this is over?" he shouted into the darkness, his voice echoing off the dirt walls. "You think you've won? I'll get out of here. I'll find you. And when I do, you'll wish you'd never crossed me. You two fucks and your boy. I'll destroy all of you!"

The thought of escape drove him, even though he knew deep down that his chances were slim. The fear of what was to come next—whether it was more violence or a slow, agonizing end—was a constant, gnawing presence. He could feel his resolve weakening, but his anger and hatred were still fierce, giving him a fleeting sense of strength.

Bishop's eyes darted around the cellar, searching for any sign of hope, any hint of an exit. The dim light bulb flickers occasionally, casting eerie shadows that danced on the walls, and the relentless hum of the fan and the generator were the only sounds that filled the oppressive silence.

"Come on," he muttered, his voice trembling with a mix of rage and desperation. "You think you can just leave me here? I'll show you. I'll make you all pay. Bryan, Elizabeth—everyone who's ever wronged me. You think you can just leave me like this? I won't let you. I swear it."

His fury and fear melded together, creating a maelstrom of emotion that left him both enraged and hopeless. The thought of revenge was his only solace, his only way of coping with the torment he was enduring. The pain was undeniable, but his resolve to make everyone who had wronged him suffer in return was even stronger.

Bishop's anger reached a fever pitch, the pain and frustration boiling over as he strained against his restraints. His heart pounded violently in his chest, each beat echoing through his battered body like a drum. The dark, oppressive cellar seemed to close in around him, the dirt walls pressing in, the single flickering light bulb casting long, wavering shadows that danced mockingly in his vision.

"You think you've won?" he shouted, his voice cracking with a mix of rage and desperation. "You think you can just leave me here, forgotten? I'll make you all pay. I'll make you all suff...er!"

The more he struggled and shouted, the more his blood pressure soared, his face flushed with a feverish intensity. His vision blurred at the edges, the dim light bulb appearing as a hazy, dancing orb in his line of sight. He was on the edge of a precipice, the raw, consuming anger driving him to the brink of collapse.

"B-ryan, you spathetic spiece of fshit," he continued, his voice trembling with exertion. "liz-beth, you fthink you're so high and mightsy? I'll shlow you all. You've undergestimated me. You fthink you're safe? You fthink yhou've hwon?'"

His outburst grew more frenzied, his breathing ragged and uneven. The pain in his body seemed to merge with his anger, creating a disorienting, overwhelming sensation. The room around him swayed, the shadows stretching and contracting as if mocking his helplessness. The weight of his rage and the pain from his injuries combined in a perfect storm, pushing him to the brink of consciousness.

With one final, desperate roar, Bishop's vision narrowed, his sight turning dark around the edges. His head lolled to one side, his body slumping as the pressure in his veins became too much to bear. The roar of his fury was abruptly cut off as his consciousness faded, the world around him dissolving into a void of blackness.

As Bishop's body went limp, the cellar door creaked open, and a figure stepped inside. The figure was tall and shrouded in shadow, the dim light bulb casting an elongated silhouette against the dirt walls. The person's movements were deliberate and controlled, a quiet presence that seemed to exude a sense of calm authority despite the chaotic situation.

The figure approached Bishop, their footsteps muffled by the thick layers of dust on the floor. With careful precision, they pulled out a syringe from a leather satchel slung over their shoulder. The needle gleamed menacingly in the low light, a harbinger of the unknown.

The figure knelt beside Bishop, examining his unconscious form with a detached, almost clinical gaze. They took a moment to steady the syringe, their expression unreadable as they prepared to administer the injection.

"Ah, Bishop," the figure began, their voice smooth and contemplative. "You've been quite the problem, haven't you? It's remarkable how one's pride can be so blinding, so utterly self-destructive."

The figure's voice was calm and measured, a stark contrast to the chaos that had preceded their entrance. "You see, there's a certain irony in all of this. You and your grand schemes, your manipulations, your twisted desires. You thought you could control everything around you, that you could bend the world to your will. But here you are, broken and beaten, a mere pawn in a game you never fully understood."

As the needle pierced Bishop's skin, the figure continued their soliloquy, their tone reflecting a deep sense of both satisfaction and detachment. "Your role was never as significant as you thought it was. Your machinations, your attempts to use others—everything you did was part of a larger design. A design you were never meant to see, never meant to comprehend."

The figure injected the syringe's contents into Bishop's vein, watching with an inscrutable expression as the liquid was absorbed. "I've watched you for a long time, Bishop. Your actions, your decisions, they've all been observed and noted. It's fascinating, really, how people like you think they can escape their consequences. But life has a humorous way of catching up with everyone, doesn't it?"

The syringe was withdrawn, and the figure placed it back into the satchel with meticulous care. "And now, as you lie here, unconscious and at the mercy of forces beyond your control, you get a taste of the game you've been so eager to play. The pain you inflicted, the chaos you caused—it all comes full circle."

Standing up, the figure looked down at Bishop's prone form with a hint of pity in their gaze. "You may never understand the full scope of what's happening, but know this: you are just a small piece in a much larger puzzle. And as for Bryan and Elizabeth—well, their roles are far from over. Your actions, your fate, it all intertwines with theirs in ways you could never have anticipated."

With that, the figure turned and walked back toward the cellar door, leaving Bishop bound and unconscious in the dark, his fate uncertain and his role in the larger scheme still shrouded in mystery. The door creaked closed behind them, and the dim light bulb flickered one last time before casting the room back into shadow. The sound of the small fan and the generator hummed on, an unchanging backdrop to the uncertain future awaiting Bishop and those connected to him.

As the figure—D. Mann—turned to leave, he paused, a faint, enigmatic smile playing on his lips. "You know, Bishop," he began, his voice carrying a weight of hidden significance, "the connections between us all are far more intricate than you ever could have imagined. My involvement in your life, Bryan's life, and Elizabeth's—it's not merely a matter of chance or happenstance. There are threads that bind us all together in ways that transcend the ordinary, threads woven through pain, sacrifice, and a shared sense of purpose that runs deeper than you could ever fathom." D. Mann's gaze, though shrouded in shadow, seemed to pierce through the darkness, carrying with it an almost palpable sense of ancient, unspoken truths. "My role in this grand design is one of guardianship, of a duty to protect those who, despite their flaws and failures, represent something profoundly significant. Bryan, with all his struggle and heartache, Alex with his fierce intelligence and potential, and Elizabeth, who embodies a complex mix of love and resilience—each one of them holds a piece of a greater destiny that has been years in the making.

I have endured countless trials, faced my own demons, and made sacrifices that would be unimaginable to most. But it has all been worth it, for their safety and their future. In a world where the forces of darkness and betrayal often seem overwhelming, it is the light they represent—their potential for redemption, for growth, and for the fulfillment of their true purpose—that makes every hardship, every pain, and every cost worth it. I have dedicated my existence to ensuring that they have the chance to fulfill their roles in this vast, intricate tapestry of fate. So, while you languish here in this dark cellar, consumed by your own hatred and misjudgment, remember that their paths are guarded by forces far greater and more determined than you could ever comprehend." With that cryptic declaration, D. Mann stepped out of the cellar and into the night.

26 ASHES AND INQUIRY

The investigation into the explosion at Matt and Bishop's trailer park was intense and exhaustive, marked by a coordinated effort from multiple agencies. The scene was chaotic, with the remnants of the trailer park smoldering and a pervasive cloud of smoke hanging over the area. The damage was extensive, with trailers reduced to twisted metal and heaps of ash. The community was left reeling from the devastation, and the urgency to piece together what had happened was palpable.

As the initial police response continued, specialized teams were brought in to further investigate the explosion. Cadaver dogs were deployed to the scene, their keen noses scanning through the wreckage for any signs of human remains. The dogs worked methodically, their handlers guiding them through the charred debris. Despite their efforts, the search proved challenging. The intense heat of the explosion had incinerated much of the evidence, and the dogs struggled to detect any definitive signals amidst the overwhelming scent of smoke and burnt materials.

The fire marshal's team, equipped with expertise in fire investigation, began their own thorough examination of the site. They meticulously combed through the wreckage, looking for clues that might explain the cause of the explosion. Their initial findings suggested that the blast had been caused by an accidental ignition of propane tanks connected to the trailer.

The investigation revealed a disturbing detail: a series of large propane tanks had been set up near the trailer, linked together in a haphazard and illegal arrangement. These tanks, designed to store gas for heating and cooking, were positioned in close proximity to each other and the trailer's living areas. The fire marshal's team speculated that the explosion was the result of a catastrophic failure of this improvised system. The tanks had been poorly maintained and were not equipped with the necessary safety measures to prevent such a disaster.

The fire marshal's lead investigator, a seasoned professional with years of experience in handling explosive incidents, addressed the gathered reporters. "Our preliminary findings indicate that the explosion was likely caused by an accidental ignition of the propane tanks," he explained. "The tanks were arranged in a manner that was not only illegal but highly dangerous. It appears that a malfunction or leak may have led to a buildup of gas, which was then ignited, resulting in the explosion."

The revelation of the propane tanks added a new layer of complexity to the investigation. It became clear that the explosion was not just a random act of violence but a result of unsafe and illegal practices. The authorities began to investigate the origins of the tanks, trying to determine who had set them up and why they had been connected in such a hazardous manner.

In the meantime, the cadaver dogs and their handlers continued their search for any possible human remains. The search was painstaking, as they sifted through the remains of the trailer and the surrounding area. Despite their best efforts, the intense heat and destruction had left little trace of evidence. The dogs signaled on various spots, but the results were inconclusive, adding to the frustration of the investigators.

As the minutes turned into hours, the focus of the investigation shifted to understanding the broader implications of the explosion. The authorities looked into the history of Matt and Bishop, seeking any connections that might explain the presence of the illegal propane tanks. They interviewed residents and examined the trailer park's past to uncover any patterns or issues that might have contributed to the disaster.

The investigation also prompted a deeper inquiry into the circumstances surrounding Bishop and Matt's activities. The presence of illegal propane tanks suggested a disregard for safety and an involvement in potentially criminal activities. The authorities expanded their search to include any connections between the explosion and the broader network of illegal operations or personal disputes that might have led to such a catastrophic event.

The community, meanwhile, was left to grapple with the fallout of the explosion. The residents, now displaced and without their homes, faced the daunting task of rebuilding their lives. The emotional and psychological impact of the event was significant, with many struggling to come to terms with their loss. Support services and temporary housing were provided, but the sense of upheaval and uncertainty remained.

Matt, who had returned to the scene, experienced a severe mental breakdown, exacerbated by the explosion and his troubled past. His erratic behavior led to his being placed under psychiatric care, where he was evaluated for potential placement in a mental health institution. The mental health professionals worked to address his immediate needs, seeking to provide him with the support and treatment he required.

As the investigation progressed, the authorities remained committed to uncovering the full extent of the explosion and its causes. The discovery of the illegal propane tanks and the subsequent investigation into Matt and Bishop's activities added new layers to the case, hinting at a potentially more complex narrative behind the tragic event.

The once-bustling trailer park, home to a close-knit community, had been reduced to a charred wasteland. The remnants of the trailers were now unrecognizable, their frames twisted and blackened by the intense heat. With nothing left salvageable, the entire trailer park was declared a loss, leaving its residents not only grieving but also homeless.

As the first responders and police conducted their investigation, they interviewed the residents who

229

had witnessed the events leading up to the explosion. Their accounts were filled with a mix of confusion, fear, and anger. Many spoke of the tense interaction they had seen between Elizabeth, Alex, and Bishop just before the blast. It was clear that the confrontation had been heated, but the exact details remained murky.

One elderly resident, Mrs. Hawkins, recounted seeing Alex and Elizabeth's confrontation with Bishop. "I saw them pull up, and it was clear that there was some sort of argument. Bishop looked like he was ready to explode himself before the explosion actually happened," she said, her voice trembling as she relayed her observations. "I didn't know what it was all about, but there was a lot of shouting and anger. It was like the storm was brewing before the storm."

Another resident, Mr. Green, added to the picture. "I saw Bishop pacing around, clearly agitated. Then Alex and Elizabeth showed up. There was a lot of commotion. Next thing I knew, there was this massive explosion. It all happened so fast, I couldn't even process what was going on." His voice was laden with a mix of shock and residual fear. "They had to know something. The way Bishop was reacting, it was like he was about to snap."

The police, piecing together these fragmented accounts, found themselves grappling with the scope of the destruction. The trailers had been utterly incinerated, leaving nothing behind but ashes and twisted metal. The residents, already grappling with the shock of the explosion, were now faced with the harsh reality of their new circumstances. Homeless and without their belongings, they were left to seek shelter and support from local charities and aid organizations.

The emotional toll on the community was palpable. The trailer park had been more than just a collection of homes; it had been a sanctuary for many. Now, with it reduced to rubble, the sense of loss was profound. In addition to the physical damage, the psychological impact on the residents was significant. The trauma of the explosion and the loss of their homes had left many in a state of disarray.

As the community began to rebuild from the ashes, the focus remained on both the physical and emotional recovery. The trailer park residents were offered temporary housing and support as they tried to navigate their new reality. The police continued their investigation, seeking to understand the full scope of the explosion and its implications. The pieces of the puzzle were slowly coming together, but the road ahead was fraught with challenges.

The tragedy at the trailer park had left a lasting impact on everyone involved.

27 Too Early and Too Hungry For This

Alex and Elizabeth had managed to get some very needed sleep, their bodies exhausted and minds heavy from the events of the previous twenty-plus hours. They were both jolted awake by the persistent ringing of their doorbell. Alex, bleary-eyed and disoriented, he rolled out of bed and lurched to the front door. He opened it to find Detective Sarah Hayes standing on the threshold, her smiling demeanor serious yet professional.

"Good morning, Alex" Detective Hayes said, her tone businesslike but sympathetic. "Do you remember me? I'm Detective Sarah Hayes with the local police. I need to ask you and your mom Elizabeth a few questions regarding the explosion at the trailer park. May I come in?"

Alex nodded, stepping aside while waving his arm to invite her in. Elizabeth, still in her pajamas, soon joined them in the living room. Detective Hayes took a seat and began her questioning. She was efficient, her questions precise as she sought to piece together the events leading up to the explosion.

"I understand you and Mr. Bishop had a confrontation just before the explosion," Detective Hayes began. "Can you tell me more about what happened?"

Alex shifted uncomfortably, feeling a gnawing hunger in his stomach. He glanced at Elizabeth, who was clearly grappling with her own emotions. Before she could answer, Alex interrupted.

"Detective Hayes, I think we need a short break. I can't remember the last time either of us ate, and we could really use something to help us think clearly," Alex said, trying to maintain a sense of normalcy amid the chaos. "I'm going to go grab some fast food for us. It shouldn't take very long."

Hayes looked at Alex, understanding the need given the circumstances. "Alright, but please make sure to be back soon. We need to get through this as quickly as possible, but I will just talk with your mom while you are gone"

Alex nodded and left the house, heading to the nearest fast-food with golden arches. The drive was a blur, his mind racing as he tried to process everything that had happened. The streets seemed unusually quiet, the normalcy of everyday life starkly contrasting with the turmoil he felt inside.

At the fast-food drive-thru, Alex ordered a large assortment of items—burgers, fries, and frozen coffee drinks—anything that might provide a brief respite from their distress. He paid and drove back home, the food a small comfort in the midst of the upheaval.

Back at the house, Detective Hayes continued her line of questioning with Elizabeth. "So, Ms. Black, can you tell me about your argument with Bishop? What was it about?"

Elizabeth took a deep breath, her mind replaying the confrontation with Bishop. "It was intense," she admitted. "We had been having issues, and it escalated. I was angry, and so was he. It was a heated exchange, and I'm afraid I can't recall all the details. But it was clear that he was agitated and upset. I had gone there to confront him about some personal issues and to try to understand what was going on with him. I wanted to clear the air and, if possible, find some resolution."

She paused, gathering her thoughts. "During the conversation, Bishop was upset. He was shouting and saying things that didn't make much sense. He kept talking about how everything was falling apart and that it was all someone else's fault. He was particularly angry about how his life had turned out and seemed to be blaming everyone around him for his problems."

Elizabeth looked down, her voice softening. "I tried to stay calm and explain that we needed to address things constructively. I was firm but not confrontational. I really just wanted to get some answers and hopefully work towards something positive."

She continued, "At one point, he mentioned feeling betrayed and cornered, though he didn't go into specifics. It was clear he was struggling with a lot of anger and resentment. I asked him if there was anything he wanted to say or if there was any way we could resolve things peacefully, but he just kept escalating."

Detective Hayes took notes, her expression thoughtful. "And did Bishop mention anything specific about threats or dangers? Did he talk about anyone in particular or any recent events that might be relevant? Involving Bryan maybe?"

Elizabeth shook her head. "Not really. He was too focused on his own grievances to provide clear details. He just kept repeating how everything was ruined and that he was on the edge. He did seem particularly fixated on Bryan and me, though, almost like he was blaming us for his problems."

Detective Hayes paused to let the information sink in. "So, it sounds like the conversation was very charged and emotional. Did you notice anything unusual or out of the ordinary about the situation or Bishop's behavior?"

Elizabeth thought for a moment. "Aside from his anger and frustration, there was nothing particularly unusual that stood out to me. He was just very upset and seemed to be at the end of his rope. I remember feeling a sense of urgency and frustration, but I didn't expect anything like what happened."

Detective Hayes gave her a reassuring nod. "Thank you for sharing that, Ms. Black. It helps us understand the context of the situation better. If you

237

think of anything else or remember more details, please let us know."

Elizabeth nodded, grateful for the detective's understanding. "Of course. I'll keep you updated if anything comes to mind..." Elizabeth just shook her head. "...but I didn't think it would lead to something like this."

As they spoke, Alex returned with the fast food. He set the bags down on the kitchen table and began to distribute the items, trying to keep things as normal as possible.

"I've got food," Alex announced, attempting to lighten the mood. "Let's take a quick break, Detective. We could all use a bite."

Detective Hayes accepted the offer, her professionalism softened by the gesture. She took a moment to eat while continuing to ask questions in between bites. "Thank you, Alex. This is appreciated."

As they ate, Detective Hayes reviewed the information she had gathered. "From what we've pieced together, the explosion seems to be the result of the illegal propane tanks. We're still investigating, but the evidence suggests a significant buildup of gas that was ignited. We're also looking into any connections between Bishop and the tanks."

Alex and Elizabeth listened, their focus divided between the food and the detective's updates. The normalcy of eating in the midst of their crisis provided a brief reprieve from their anxiety. As Detective Hayes wrapped up her questioning, she provided a final set of instructions.

"Please keep your phones on and be available. If you remember anything else or if there are any new developments, let us know immediately. We're trying to piece together everything that led up to the explosion while still looking into any and every lead we unearth about Bryan's whereabouts".

With that, Detective Hayes gathered her things and prepared to leave. Alex and Elizabeth, feeling the weight of the past hours' events pressing down on them, thanked her and said their goodbyes.

Once the detective had left, Alex and Elizabeth finished their meal in solemn silence, their thoughts consumed by the unfolding drama. The fast food provided a momentary yet needed distraction, but the gravity of the situation quickly returned. They were left to navigate their grief, confusion, and fear, all while grappling with the reality of their new and uncertain future.

28 Digging In

As Detective Hayes was leaving, Alex pulled Elizabeth aside, his expression serious and filled with concern. "Mom, we need to talk. I'm worried about whether we've given Detective Hayes the complete picture." He glanced around to ensure their conversation was private. "Did you tell her everything we found? I'm talking about all the disturbing details we uncovered about Bishop—his drug dealings, those vile messages about drugs and his daughter, and the explicit porn and drug stuff he was involved in. And don't forget the threats he made against dad. We've kept this information hidden because it's so fucking creepy."

Alex's voice took on a more urgent tone. "Also, there's the cabin and the notebook we found. It had detailed notes about Bishop's plans and dad's state of mind. Do you think we may need to make sure the detective has that information, too? I am going to email her some photos of lesser journal pages and say they were from the laptop. The cabin might have more clues that could be crucial for the investigation and who knows when or if they will discover it."

He hesitated before continuing, "And there's the laptop. I found some files and recent searches that might shed light on what dad has been thinking and what he was planning. I'm worried about what might happen if the police had all the information we've uncovered. What if they use it in a way that's not in our or dad's best interests, or worse, what if they don't take it seriously?"

Alex's skepticism was clear as he continued, "I also came across a name multiple times, D. Mann, but I haven't mentioned it yet. It seems connected somehow to dad, but I don't know how. I'm concerned that if we give them everything, they might not handle it properly, might miss important connections, or make dad into the bad guy."

He looked at Elizabeth with a mix of anxiety and resolve. "I'm just worried that if the police have all the details, what if they overlook something critical or don't act quickly enough? We've seen how complex and dangerous this situation apparently is. Do you think it's a good idea to share everything, or should we be cautious about what we let them know? I just don't want us to be caught off guard if things don't go as we hope and with them being the police we have no idea what they do or don't already know and that could be the missing pieces we need to find and save dad."

Elizabeth looked at Alex, her eyes heavy with worry and uncertainty. She hadn't considered the possibility that holding back information could be a double-edged sword, especially given how much they'd uncovered on their own. "I don't know, Alex," she said, rubbing her temples. "It's just... all of this. It's so much, and I don't know who we can trust. The police have their protocols, their ways of doing things, and I'm scared that if we give them everything, they might twist it or use it against Bryan somehow."

She paused, her voice wavering. "Your dad's already in a vulnerable position, and I don't want to add to it by giving Detective Hayes something that could be taken out of context. They're looking at everything, and I can't shake the feeling that they're judging all of us—me, you, and especially Bryan. I can almost guarantee they have information they aren't sharing too. If we give them all this stuff... What if they decide Bryan's the problem, not the victim? Between the notebook, the stuff from the laptop, and everything we found at the cabin, I'm worried they'll focus more on Bryan's darker side.

They might see him as unstable, or worse, a threat. You know how these things can get spun in the wrong direction."

She leaned against the wall, feeling the weight of their choices pressing down on her. "It's not just about protecting him. It's about making sure the whole truth doesn't get buried under assumptions and red tape."

Alex nodded, his mind racing through the possibilities. "Exactly mom,that's what I'm afraid of too. They could turn this into something it's not. And D. Mann—whoever that is—I don't even know if the police would take him seriously. If he's connected to Dad, we need to understand how, not just hand it over and hope for the best.

I've been reading Dad's notes, his searches...there's a pattern, but it's not obvious. It's like he's chasing something, maybe even someone, and I don't think we're going to find him by following the police's lead alone. The stuff we've found—none of it paints Bishop in a good light. But you know how it works. If they want to, they can spin it however they like. And D. Mann... the fact that dad was looking into whoever that is right before all of this went down? It's a massive red flag. But what if they don't care?

What if they don't think it's relevant or, worse, they never figure out who he is?"

Alex paused, his voice dropping to a near whisper. "We have to stay one step ahead, Mom. We need to keep digging ourselves. The police are focused on the explosion, on Bishop, on everything but what matters most—finding Dad. And if we tell them everything now, we lose any control we have left. I'm not saying we don't help them, but we have to be smart about this. We need to understand D. Mann's role and what Dad was trying to do, what he was involved in before we decide to turn over anything more."

Elizabeth felt a pang of guilt. She had tried to shield Alex from the worst of this nightmare, but here he was, navigating the dark waters with her. "Do you think this D. Mann could be involved in what's happening to your dad? Do you think he could be dangerous?"

Alex hesitated, torn between his instincts and the lack of concrete answers. "I don't know, I just don't have enough information yet, but it's not just a coincidence. Everything I've found about this guy feels off, and I'm not sure if he's helping dad or if he's the one pulling the strings behind all this chaos. If we hand everything over now, we lose control of what happens next. We lose any advantage we might have in finding dad and getting him out of whatever mess he's in."

Elizabeth sighed, her thoughts a tangled mess. "We have to protect your dad, but we also can't do this alone. We're going to need help, Alex. If we keep all this to ourselves, we're basically flying blind, and I'm terrified of missing something that could save him."

Alex stared at the floor, conflicted. "I know. But I think we need to keep digging on our own, too. Maybe we go back to the cabin, comb through every inch. See if there's anything that the police might miss or won't have the patience to figure out. And I can try to recover more from dad's laptop, see what else he was searching for, who else he was contacting."

Elizabeth nodded, feeling the weight of the decision they were making. "We'll figure this out together. But, Alex, if we do find something—anything—we have to promise to be careful. We can't let our emotions get in the way. This is about finding your dad and keeping us all safe from whatever is going on."

Alex agreed, though the unease lingered. The secrets they held were like a double-edged sword, potentially saving Bryan or pushing him deeper into danger. And for the first time, Alex wondered if they were actually making a little progress.

Elizabeth looked at Alex, realizing that her son was more aware and determined than she had fully appreciated. He was right. The police had their priorities, but so did they. Bryan's notes, the laptop, D. Mann—these were puzzle pieces they needed to keep within their grasp, at least until they could figure out the bigger picture. She reached out and squeezed Alex's shoulder, finding renewed strength in his resolve.

"Okay," she said, her voice steadier. "We'll keep looking. But we have to be very careful, Alex. We're walking a thin line, and if we're not smart about this, we could lose any outside help and with it any chance of finding your dad."

Alex nodded, feeling the weight of the moment but also the flicker of hope that they were still in this together and he wasn't alone. They were fighting to uncover the truth and save him. "We'll find him, Mom. We just have to keep going, one step at a time. One foot in front of the other." Alex thought to himself, that is what dad would say and do and what I will do the same...for him.

29 DARKNESS TO LIGHT

Alex and Elizabeth immediately begin to dive deeper into Bryan's digital world, navigating through his social media accounts, emails, and private messages that had been untouched since his disappearance. With every click and scroll, a hidden side of Bryan's life began to unravel—a side neither of them had fully understood or seen. What they discovered was both heart-wrenching and awe-inspiring: Bryan, while engulfed in his own relentless battles with despair and emotional turmoil, had somehow managed to be a lifeline for dozens of others.

Bryan's inboxes and social media feeds were filled with countless conversations—threads of messages with strangers, friends, former students, and even casual acquaintances. Men and women of all ages reached out to him with their problems, pouring out their fears, doubts, and heartbreaks. And Bryan, always the empathetic listener and wise counselor, responded with patience and sincerity. He guided them through the darkness, offering advice, comfort, and encouragement. Some messages were raw cries for help, riddled with anxiety about failing marriages, troubled children, or the crippling weight of loneliness. Others were subtle thank-yous, expressing deep gratitude for the words Bryan had shared that kept them going through yet another sleepless night.

Alex stared at the screen, reading the conversations with an intensity that tightened his chest. One after another, people thanked Bryan for his kindness, wisdom, and unwavering support. Despite his own crumbling life, Bryan had been a rock for so many others. A middle-aged man from Bryan's old neighborhood wrote about how Bryan had saved his marriage by simply listening and offering thoughtful insights during late-night chats. A young woman, barely out of high school, shared how Bryan had helped her escape an abusive relationship, giving her the courage to stand up to her manipulative boyfriend. And then there were the former students—people Alex vaguely remembered but now saw in a completely different light.

Alex read through one particularly long exchange between Bryan and a former student named Rachel. She had been battling severe depression, exacerbated by a toxic home environment where her stepfather was physically and emotionally abusive. Bryan had been her teacher back in high school, but even after graduation, Rachel had kept in touch, reaching out when her darkest thoughts seemed unbearable. Bryan's responses were gentle yet firm, filled with hope and practical advice. He guided her step-by-step on how to navigate social services, find a counselor, and ultimately move out. The last message she had sent him was a photo of her first apartment, thanking him for saving her life and showing her that she deserved better.

There were even more stories like this—dozens of them. Former students, neighbors, old friends, and complete strangers who Bryan had helped without expecting anything in return. A teenage boy had confessed to having violent thoughts and plans to harm others, feeling trapped in his own anger and confusion. Bryan's approach was careful and compassionate, steering the young man away from his dangerous impulses, helping him find a path to express his emotions safely. Alex couldn't believe how many lives his father had touched. Bryan had been like a silent guardian angel, saving lives one conversation at a time, all while his own was falling apart.

Amid all the stories of Bryan's selflessness, Alex found something that struck a deeper chord. Scrolling further back, Alex noticed subtle flirtations from various men and women. Some were coy, some bold, but all were unmistakable attempts to capture Bryan's attention in ways that went beyond friendship. Alex's breath caught as he read through Bryan's responses. Each time, Bryan gently but firmly redirected the conversations back to platonic terms. He would deflect their advances with humor or kindness, never once taking the bait. Alex saw in every word how Bryan remained unwaveringly loyal to Elizabeth. Even when his own marriage was crumbling, even when Elizabeth had betrayed him in the most painful ways, Bryan never entertained the idea of being with anyone else. He remained committed to his vows, his family, and his own moral compass, refusing to let his integrity waver, even when he was at his lowest.

It was as if Bryan had been grasping at any way to remain a good man, holding onto the last threads of his own identity. And even when the weight of his own heartache seems unbearable, he chose to help others carry theirs. Alex's eyes burned as he continued reading, absorbing the full scope of his father's goodness. He had known Bryan was a kind man, but this—this was something entirely different. Bryan had been drowning in his own sorrow, yet he found the strength to keep others afloat.

Then Alex stumbled upon a hidden folder on Bryan's computer, one that required an extra layer of password protection. His heart pounded as he typed in a few guesses, finally gaining access after using Bryan's old high school football jersey number—a detail only someone as close as Alex would know. Inside, he found scanned letters and typed notes, a private archive of Bryan's deepest thoughts, hopes, and fears. Some were addressed to Alex, others to Elizabeth. They were filled with Bryan's unfiltered emotions, raw and vulnerable. In one letter, Bryan wrote to Alex about the pride he felt watching his son grow up, how he dreamed of seeing Alex achieve his own ambitions. He expressed regret for not being the perfect father but promised that every decision he made was in hopes of giving Alex a better life.

The letters to Elizabeth were even more poignant. They were filled with his love for her, his pain over her betrayal, and his desperate attempts to understand where it all went wrong. Despite everything, Bryan's words reflected a man who still loved deeply, who still held onto the faint hope that they could somehow find their way back to each other.

Alex's eyes lingered on a note Bryan had written shortly after his last brain surgery in 2022. It was a heartbreaking admission of his fears about losing his memory, his grasp on reality, and eventually, himself. Bryan detailed his determination to record his thoughts and dreams because he couldn't trust his own mind anymore. It was both a tragic and beautiful reminder of his relentless fight to hold onto who he was, even when everything else was slipping away.

Alex sat back, overwhelmed by the magnitude of what he had discovered. His father had been a silent hero, a man who gave every last piece of himself to others, asking for nothing in return. As he looked over at Elizabeth, who was also lost in her own thoughts reading the messages, Alex realized they had barely scratched the surface of who Bryan truly was. Bryan's life was far more than the pain and the struggle; it was a testament to his enduring goodness, his loyalty, and his unyielding love.

Alex knew then that they couldn't let the police, or anyone else, control the narrative of Bryan's story.

His father wasn't just another missing person or a man who had lost his way. He was a savior to so many, a protector, and a guiding light even in his own darkest hours. The truth of Bryan's life needed to be told, but it had to be on their terms. And with every message they uncovered, Alex and Elizabeth's determination to find Bryan only grew stronger, fueled by the love and legacy of a man who never stopped giving, even when he had nothing left for himself.

Alex had to find more information to make it all make sense and that is when a social media notification popped up for Bryan on his laptop. Of course, thought Alex...I can't believe I haven't already checked on his personal accounts.

Alex delved deeper into the exchanges on Bryan's social media, feeling a growing sense of connection and understanding with each message. The stories painted a vivid picture of a man who, despite his own crumbling world, was determined to lift others. They revealed the many facets of Bryan Black—a father, husband, teacher, mentor, and friend who consistently put the needs of others above his own, even when he had little left to give. Each story unraveled more of Bryan's complex nature, and

Alex was compelled to explore them further, seeking to understand the true depth of his father's character.

Cherry: The Unexpected Confidante

The thread with Cherry, Elizabeth's mother and Alex's grandmother, was the most painful for Alex to read. Cherry had been a supportive figure in Alex's life, but her sudden shift in allegiance after Elizabeth filed for divorce had left a bitter taste. Yet, Bryan's messages to Cherry were full of patience and empathy. When Cherry's own mother had passed, Bryan was one of the first people she turned to, reaching out in her grief and confusion. The messages showed Bryan's profound ability to be present for others, even when he was drowning in his own despair.

Bryan guided Cherry through her darkest moments, reminding her of the strength she had shown in raising her children and holding her family together. He shared stories about her mother that Cherry herself had long forgotten—details that showed how closely Bryan had observed and cherished their family. His words were a balm to Cherry's aching heart, offering her not just condolences, but genuine companionship in her sorrow. Even as Cherry's demeanor toward Bryan turned cold in the wake of Elizabeth's divorce announcement, Bryan continued to reach out. He asked about her health, her feelings, and her future, maintaining his compassion despite the emotional walls she put up. Alex could see the painful irony: Bryan had been a source of healing for Cherry, even when she later became one of his harshest critics.

Aly: The Student Saved from the Brink

Aly's story was another that resonated deeply with Alex. Bryan had been Alex's history teacher years ago, but their connection had grown beyond the classroom. Her severe anxiety and frequent panic attacks had made everyday life a battle. In the dead of night, feeling completely alone, Aly had reached out to Bryan, confessing that she didn't see the point in continuing. Bryan had responded immediately, his messages a steady stream of reassurance and practical advice. He coached Aly through her breathing, shared grounding techniques, and simply stayed with her virtually, sometimes for hours, until the panic subsided.

But Bryan didn't stop there. He checked in regularly, encouraging Aly to seek professional help while providing an unyielding safety net of support. Bryan's influence helped Aly find the courage to face his anxiety rather than be paralyzed by it. Alex read as Aly's messages evolved from desperation to cautious optimism, each one marked by gratitude for Bryan's unwavering presence. The impact Bryan had on Aly was profound; he had not just been a teacher but a lifeline, someone who cared when Aly felt no one else did.

Kimberly: The Struggling Young Mother

The conversation with Kimberly, a young mother Bryan met at a community event, revealed Bryan's capacity to offer strength to those at their most vulnerable. Kimberly's messages were frantic, filled with fear about her husband's escalating alcoholism and the impact it was having on their children. She had reached out to Bryan almost as a last resort, desperate for guidance and support. Bryan responded with empathy, listening to Kimberly's fears and validating her experiences without judgment. He offered practical advice on setting boundaries, seeking help, and prioritizing her children's safety, but he also gave her something deeper: the belief that she deserved better than the chaos that had come to define her life.

Bryan's words helped Kimberly find the courage to confront her husband, and, with time, she managed to steer her family toward a path of recovery. She credited Bryan with giving her the strength she didn't know she had, and in every message, there was an underlying sense of gratitude for the man who had been there when no one else would listen. Alex could see how Bryan's empathy extended beyond mere words; he had actively helped Kimberly rebuild her life when she was on the verge of losing everything.

Marcus: The Old Friend's Bitter Divorce

The messages with Marcus, an old college friend of Bryan's, were filled with raw emotion and anger. Marcus was in the midst of a nasty divorce, overwhelmed by bitterness and resentment that clouded his every thought. The pain of betrayal had consumed him, and his messages were often laced with rage, directed at his ex-wife, the legal system, and sometimes even at himself. Bryan, however, never shied away from the darkness Marcus was spewing. He listened patiently, offering a balance of tough love and heartfelt empathy.

Bryan's messages reminded Marcus that his anger, while justified, would only continue to harm him if he let it fester. He shared personal reflections on his own struggles with forgiveness and the battles he fought to move past his own pain. Bryan's words didn't just placate Marcus; they challenged him to confront his demons and consider what life could look like if he let go of the past. Over time, Marcus began to shift his focus from vengeance to healing, all thanks to Bryan's steady influence. Alex could feel the respect Marcus had for Bryan—a man who, despite his own broken heart, found the strength to help others pick up their shattered pieces.

Lily: The Young Girl in Crisis

Lastly, Alex came across messages between Bryan and a teenage girl named Lily. She was just sixteen and pregnant, terrified of how her parents would react and paralyzed by fear of the future. Lily's messages were filled with panic and desperation, and Alex could feel the weight of her world crumbling through her words. Bryan's responses were measured and calm. He offered no judgment, only support. He assured Lily that her life wasn't over and that she had options, guiding her step by step through her choices.

Bryan urged her to talk to her parents, offering to be there as moral support if she needed. He shared resources for young mothers and reminded her that every difficult moment could be an opportunity to redefine herself. Bryan's words became a beacon of hope for Lily, who ultimately found the courage to face her situation head-on. Alex was struck by how effortlessly Bryan gave Lily the support she needed, asking for nothing in return, and how his kindness had changed the trajectory of her life.

The Hidden Letters: Bryan's Unspoken Love

Amidst these revelations, Alex discovered a secret stash of scanned letters and notes—personal reflections Bryan had written to both Alex and Elizabeth over the years. These documents revealed Bryan's innermost thoughts, his hopes, dreams, and fears, all preserved because he didn't trust his own memory after his last brain surgery in 2022. The letters were filled with love and longing, not just for a better life but for a renewed connection with his family. Bryan's words were raw and unfiltered, showing a man who, despite all his pain, never stopped believing in the possibility of healing and happiness for those he loved.

Alex was overwhelmed by the sheer depth of Bryan's commitment to others. His father had been a guiding light to so many, saving lives and touching hearts even as his own was breaking. Each message, each act of kindness, was a testament to Bryan's enduring spirit—a man who gave all he had left to those who needed him, while asking nothing for himself.

Alex now understood the true extent of his father's quiet heroism and felt a renewed sense of purpose in uncovering the truth about what had happened to him.

Bryan wasn't just his father; he was a beacon of hope to so many lost souls, and Alex was determined to honor that legacy, no matter what it took.

29 UnPublished Heart

Alex sat in the dimly lit room, the glow from the laptop screen casting long shadows on the walls. The messages from Bryan's social media had already painted a picture of a man who had spent his last reserves of emotional energy on saving others, but the hidden folder he had just uncovered went far deeper. It was a treasure trove of letters—some typed, some scanned handwritten notes, all addressed to him and Elizabeth. They were a mix of private thoughts, reflections, and confessions that Bryan had poured out, often late at night when the weight of his own thoughts was too much to bear. These were not the polished words he had shared with others; they were raw, unfiltered, and deeply personal.

Alex opened the first file, labeled simply "For Alex." As he read, he could feel the weight of his father's struggles, laid bare in the text. Bryan's words were filled with love, advice, and a deep sense of longing for the connection that had been slipping away. Bryan wrote about the early years—coaching Alex's little league games, helping him with his school projects, and the pride he felt watching his son

grow into a young man. But there were darker
entries too, moments where Bryan expressed his
fears of not being enough, of failing as a father, and
of the deep-seated guilt that haunted him for not
being able to shield his family from his own battles.

Letter 1: Reflections of a Father's Love

"Alex, my boy," Bryan's letter began, the words echoing with a gentle, weary tone. "I've watched you grow from a curious little kid into a man with a heart as big as the world. I know I haven't been the perfect dad, and I've let you down more times than I can count. There are days I feel like a shadow of the father you deserve, but you've never once made me feel unloved. I want you to know that every mistake I've made, every bad day I've had, was never about you. You've always been my greatest success, and I'm sorry if my own failures ever made you doubt that."

Alex felt his throat tighten as he read. Bryan spoke about the little moments that had defined their relationship—Alex's first heartbreak, the long drives where they talked about nothing and everything, and the quiet nights where Bryan would watch Alex sleep, wishing he could pause time just to hold onto those fleeting moments of innocence.

The letter shifted, revealing Bryan's inner turmoil as he faced his declining health after the brain surgery in 2022. He expressed his fears of not being around to see Alex graduate, get married, or have kids of his own. Each word was a blend of hope and heartache, capturing Bryan's desperate desire to be present in Alex's life, even as his own was unraveling.

Letter 2: To Elizabeth, With Regret and Love

The next letter was addressed to Elizabeth. Alex hesitated, unsure if he should delve into his parents' private exchanges. But he knew these letters were meant to be read—they were Bryan's last, unspoken attempts to bridge the chasm that had grown between them. This letter was different. It was both a confession and a plea, revealing Bryan's deepest regrets and the undying love he still harbored for his estranged wife.

"Elizabeth," Bryan's writing was messy, as if the words had poured out faster than his pen could keep up. "I don't know where things went wrong, but I feel it every day—the distance, the silence, the coldness that's settled between us. I keep replaying our lives together, trying to pinpoint the moment we stopped being us and became these strangers living under the same roof. You are, and always will be, the love of my life. But I know I haven't been the husband you needed. I let my own darkness pull me away from you, and in doing so, I failed the one person who stood by me through it all."

Bryan wrote about the early days of their marriage—the long nights spent dreaming about their future, the joy of raising Alex together, and the little traditions that had once defined their relationship. But there were also raw admissions: the moments when his own depression had made him distant, the guilt he carried for not being the man Elizabeth deserved, and his unspoken fears that she would one day find solace in someone else. He admitted to sensing her growing unhappiness long before she ever said a word about divorce. Bryan's words were not an attempt to win her back but a heartfelt acknowledgment of the pain they both shared. He ended the letter with a simple, heartbreaking truth: "I'm sorry I couldn't be what you needed, but I will love you, always."

Letter 3: The Notebook of Dreams and Lost Hope

As Alex continued to explore the files, he found what appeared to be a scanned section of a notebook—Bryan's personal journal filled with scattered thoughts, plans, and a list of dreams that never came to fruition. The pages were a heartbreaking mix of mundane musings and profound reflections on life, love, and family. There were entries about the places Bryan had wanted to take his family, the experiences he had dreamed of sharing with Alex and Elizabeth, and the things he still hoped to achieve despite his deteriorating health. Each note was a glimpse into Bryan's mind—a man who, despite his overwhelming sadness, still clung to the hope of a better future.

One page was titled, "Dreams for Alex," where Bryan had listed his hopes for his son's future: graduating college, finding a career he was passionate about, and building a life filled with love and adventure. There were notes of advice Bryan had never given in person, small life lessons he wanted Alex to remember long after he was gone. Another page was a list of things Bryan wished he could say to Elizabeth—apologies, reassurances, and declarations of love that he had never been able to voice aloud.

Letter 4: The Promise to Keep Fighting

A letter labeled "To Myself" caught Alex's attention. It was dated shortly after Bryan's surgery, when his recovery had been slow and painful. The letter was a personal pep talk, a reminder to Bryan that he needed to keep fighting, not just for himself but for his family. It was filled with promises he made to himself: to get better, to be more present, to fix what was broken between him and Elizabeth. But the words also revealed the stark reality Bryan was facing—his fears of losing his mental sharpness, the physical pain that never fully subsided, and the creeping sense that time was running out.

"I can't let this beat me," Bryan wrote, his resolve clear even through the strain of his handwriting. "Alex deserves a father who's here, who's not just a shadow of who he used to be. And Elizabeth... she deserves a partner who can make her feel loved again. I've got to keep trying, even on the days when it feels impossible. I owe them that much."

Letter 5: A Final Goodbye, Never Sent

The last letter was the hardest to read. It was dated just a few days before Bryan's disappearance, and it felt like a final goodbye—a letter Bryan had written but never sent. It was addressed to both Alex and Elizabeth, expressing his undying love for them and his sorrow for the pain his struggles had caused. Bryan spoke about his fears, his regrets, and his overwhelming sense of failure. But even in this, his darkest hour, he reminded them both of how much they meant to him.

"I don't know where this journey ends," Bryan wrote. "But know that wherever I am, I carry you both with me. You are my greatest achievements, my reason for everything. I'm sorry I couldn't be stronger, but please remember me not for my mistakes but for the love I always tried to give. I hope one day you can forgive me and find peace. You two are my world, and I love you more than words can ever say."

Alex finished reading, his eyes blurred with tears. These letters were not just remnants of Bryan's past—they were a testament to his enduring love and his relentless fight against the darkness that had consumed him. They were reminders that even in his lowest moments, Bryan had never stopped caring for his family. As Alex carefully saved each document, he felt a renewed determination to find his father, to bring him back if there was any chance at all, and to finally let Bryan know that his love had never gone unnoticed.

31 BACK IN BLACK

Bryan Black sat in the darkness, the hum of the generator filling the silence around him. The dirt walls of the cellar felt like a tomb, yet it was the only place he had found where he could truly be alone with his thoughts. He rubbed his hands over his face, feeling the roughness of his unshaven beard and the weight of exhaustion settling into his bones. He hadn't intended to disappear—at least not like this—but the events that led him here felt inevitable, like a slow, tragic play that he had been watching unfold without the power to stop.

Bryan's mind drifted back to the beginning, to Elizabeth. She was the light in every dark place he had ever been, a force of nature that swept into his life with a smile that could shatter any sadness. They were young, wild, and consumed by the kind of love that was intoxicating and reckless. He remembered their first apartment, a tiny, dilapidated space that they couldn't really afford but made feel like home with mismatched furniture and walls covered in memories. Elizabeth's laughter had echoed through those walls, and Bryan could still hear it now, clear and bright, even in the silence of the cellar.

They had built a life together, piece by piece. Elizabeth was his anchor, the person who always seemed to know how to pull him back from the edge. When Alex came into their lives, Bryan felt an overwhelming sense of purpose. His son was everything he had ever hoped to be—a bright, inquisitive child who saw the world with a sense of wonder that Bryan had lost somewhere along the way. The three of them had their routines, their quiet moments of connection, and Bryan cherished those times like sacred rites. It wasn't perfect, but it was theirs, and Bryan had given everything to keep it intact.

But things changed slowly, almost imperceptibly. The weight of work, responsibilities, and the endless grind of life began to erode the foundation of their marriage. Bryan knew he wasn't perfect—he was stubborn, quick to anger, and often buried his pain in silence instead of sharing it with Elizabeth. He could see the distance growing between them, a chasm that neither of them seemed capable of bridging. Bryan blamed himself, his failings as a husband, and his inability to be the man Elizabeth needed. But he never doubted his love for her, even when everything else seemed to be slipping away.

Then there was Bishop—a name that felt like a curse every time Bryan thought about it. The moment Bryan found out about the affair was like a thousand cuts with a knife to his heart, a betrayal that shattered everything he believed in. Bryan had always thought he could withstand anything as long as Elizabeth was by his side, but the revelation that she had turned to another man left him feeling hollow and broken. Bishop was the antithesis of everything Bryan stood for: manipulative, self-serving, and morally bankrupt. The worst part was knowing that Elizabeth had chosen him, over everything they had built together and supported each other through.

Bryan could still recall the night Elizabeth told him she wanted a divorce. Her words were calm but final, and Bryan felt like he was watching his world collapse in slow motion. He begged her to reconsider, to think about Alex and the life they had created, but her mind was made up. Bryan was left standing in the wreckage of their marriage, grappling with the reality that the woman he loved was no longer his. He tried to be strong for Alex, to shield his son from the ugliness of it all, but Bryan's own pain was too great to contain. He became a ghost of himself, drifting through each day with a numbness that only deepened as time went on.

The days that followed were a blur of anger, hurt, and desperate attempts to make sense of it all. Bryan's once unshakable belief in the power of love had been tested beyond its limits, and he found himself spiraling into a dark place where hope was a distant memory. He turned to his writing as an outlet, pouring his anguish into letters, journals, and online posts that no one would ever read. It was the only way he knew how to keep himself from drowning. But even those words felt hollow after a while—empty echoes of a man who had lost his way.

Bryan's trajectory from there felt almost predetermined. He couldn't bear to stay in the house that once felt like a home. Every corner reminded him of what he had lost, every photograph a painful reminder of a time when they were all happy. He spent nights driving aimlessly, parking in places that held no significance, just to avoid the suffocating loneliness of his bed. The riverbank became his refuge, a place where he could sit and let his thoughts flow with the current. Bryan found a strange solace there, sketching initials and symbols into rocks like a man trying to leave a mark on a world that no longer made sense to him.

He started planning his disappearance in a way that wasn't entirely conscious—leaving small clues that someone might find if they cared to look, but not enough to truly lead them to him. He didn't want to die; he just wanted to stop existing in the way that hurt.

Bryan knew that if he stayed, he would only continue to unravel, and the thought of Alex watching him deteriorate was unbearable. He couldn't let his son see him as a failure, as a man who had been beaten by life and love. So Bryan did the only thing he thought he could—he walked away from it all. The exhaustion took over as his thoughts drained the last of his energy reserves.

32 A NEW REALITY

Bryan opened his tired eyes, disoriented slightly by the dim glow of the single bulb hanging from the ceiling. The makeshift shelter felt foreign and claustrophobic, but it was his sanctuary for now. He had been on the move for days, drifting between abandoned places, old cabins, and the fringes of towns where no one would recognize him. Bryan had gone from living a life of relative stability to existing on the margins, where every day was a test of endurance.

He had made a makeshift camp in this cellar, a forgotten space beneath an old farmstead that hadn't seen visitors in years. Bryan had found it purely by accident, stumbling upon it during one of his midnight walkabouts. It was damp and cold, but it was safe, and that was all he needed. The solitude gave him time to think, to try and piece together the fragments of his broken life and figure out what came next. Bryan wasn't sure what he was running from anymore—his pain, his past, or the inevitable confrontation with himself.

In this silence, Bryan could reflect on the choices that had led him here. He thought about all the people he had helped over the years—strangers who had reached out in moments of despair, searching for someone who understood their pain or who would simply listen. Bryan had always been that person, that guy, even when he couldn't save himself. He recalled the countless late-night conversations, the messages he'd exchanged with people who were on the brink of giving up or in the worst moments of their lives and needed someone. It had been his way of coping, of reminding himself that he still had something to offer, even if his own life was falling apart.

Bryan's thoughts drifted back to the notebook he had filled with plans and reflections—a final chronicle of his decline and his last attempts to make sense of it all. He had written about Bishop, about the anger that simmered beneath the surface every time he thought of the man who had, along with Elizabeth upended his world and crushed it. Bryan's hate for Bishop was unlike anything he had ever felt, except for his own father; it was raw, unfiltered, and all consuming. He knew it was toxic, but he couldn't let it go and pulled the raw energy from it just to get by day to day.

The notebook was his outlet, filled with half-baked ideas of how to confront Bishop, not in a violent way (not that he hadn't entertained those ideas), but in a way that would make him understand the damage he had caused. In the end there was no way to make a manipulative and narcissistic sociopath understand anything; Bishop would always just be a broken momma's boy in mind, spirit, and body and nothing more.

And then there was D. Mann—a shadowy figure whose name kept appearing in Bryan's research, but always felt just out of reach. Bryan couldn't shake the feeling that D. Mann was connected to everything that had gone wrong, that there was a hidden thread linking him, Elizabeth, and Alex. The thought consumed Bryan's mind, driving him deeper into his obsessive need for answers. He had spent hours on his laptop, tracing digital breadcrumbs that led nowhere, but Bryan knew that D. Mann was out there, somewhere, pulling the strings. The search was maddening, but it was also the only thing keeping him going for now.

Bryan's introspection was broken by the faint sound of footsteps above. He froze, every muscle tense, as he listened for any indication of who—or what—might be coming. The cellar felt smaller, more confined, and Bryan's heart pounded as he realized just how exposed he was. His heart sank when he saw for the first time what looked like drag marks in the dirt and what could be blood or sweat in the dust of the floor. For the first time since his disappearance, Bryan felt the sting of fear, a reminder that even in his self-imposed exile, he wasn't completely alone and he wanted to know what had happened in his sanctuary in the few hours he was away. But for now he has to get away. Bryan checked the doorway from the cellar to the outside and listened for voices, breathing, or anything...nothing. After poking his head out to look around he bolted, at a full sprint, back into the woods while being careful not to make any noise.

33 DISSECTOLOGIST DETECTIVE

Detective Hayes had been putting together the puzzle pieces of Bryan Black's life for days, slowly unraveling the complex web that surrounded his disappearance. Each new clue led her deeper into his troubled world—his bitter love for Elizabeth, his unwavering devotion to Alex, and his spiraling descent into a darkness that no one had fully understood.

The trail had been maddeningly difficult to follow, with gaps and dead ends that only seemed to deepen the mystery. But one lead kept pulling her back: the cabin. Both Alex and Elizabth's phones had both been there separately and together recently and they had not shared anything about it with her. Now, Detective Hayes was determined to see the place for herself.

She arrived at the secluded cabin just past midday, the sun hanging low enough in the sky to cast long shadows through the thick trees that surrounded the area. The place was eerily quiet, save for the occasional rustling of leaves and the distant call of a bird. She parked her car at a safe distance, ensuring she wouldn't be easily spotted if anyone was still around.

As she approached the cabin, she noticed subtle signs that someone had been there recently: fresh tire tracks in the dirt leading up to the cabin, a partially extinguished fire pit with ashes that were still faintly warm, and discarded food wrappers near the front porch that hadn't yet been touched by rain or the wind.

Hayes pushed open the door cautiously, her hand resting on her holstered sidearm. The inside of the cabin was a mess—papers strewn across the table, half-empty coffee cups gathering mold, and a tattered blanket thrown haphazardly on the sofa. She moved methodically through the space, her trained eye scanning for anything out of place.

It was clear that this wasn't just a place Bryan had visited; it was a space he had lived in, if only temporarily. The journal Alex had found was one piece of the puzzle, but Hayes suspected there were more—hidden messages, lost fragments of his state of mind that would help her understand what had driven Bryan to the brink.

In the corner of the cabin, she found a laptop tucked beneath a stack of newspapers. It was old, dusty, and had clearly been used extensively. When she tried to power it on, nothing happened, but she knew that data recovery might reveal more of Bryan's thoughts and communications. On the kitchen counter, she discovered a collection of unopened letters addressed to Bryan from the court, insurance companies, and what appeared to be various legal firms—evidence of the mounting pressures he had faced before his disappearance. Hayes meticulously photographed each item, making sure not to disturb anything that might later be important.

Further searching revealed footprints in the dirt, both inside and outside the cabin. Some were distinctly Bryan's, matching the size and wear pattern of his known shoes, but there were others too—larger prints that suggested someone else had been there, maybe even recently. The thought unsettled her; she couldn't shake the feeling that Bryan wasn't alone in this. It raised more questions about who might be involved—D. Mann? Bishop? Someone she hadn't even considered yet?

As Hayes moved to the small back room of the cabin, she noticed an unsettling detail: a bullet casing on the floor near the window, partially obscured by a curtain. It was out of place, as if it had been discarded in a hurry. The casing suggested the possibility of gunfire, or at the very least, the presence of a weapon.

She checked the window and found faint smudges on the glass, indicating someone had looked out recently, perhaps to check the surroundings or anticipate an approach. The scenario that was beginning to form in her mind was disconcerting; Bryan was not merely hiding—he was preparing for something, something dangerous.

Outside, she meticulously combed the grounds, looking for signs that would confirm her suspicions. She discovered a spot where the grass had been trampled down, suggesting recent foot traffic. Scattered around were cigarette butts, fresh and still pungent with smoke, but there was a glaring issue: Bryan didn't smoke. The presence of these cigarettes meant someone else had been here, someone who was comfortable enough to linger and leave evidence of their presence.

Detective Hayes walked around the back of the cabin, her eyes scanning for any hidden exits. She found a small, partially covered opening at the base of the cabin that led to a crawl space, just big enough for someone to hide in or escape through. She bent down and examined the area closely, finding fresh scuff marks on the wood and dirt, suggesting it had been used recently. Her pulse quickened as she realized Bryan might have been here, hiding just beneath her feet, slipping away as she arrived.

After searching exhaustively for over an hour and finding no sign of anyone currently inside or nearby, Detective Hayes decided it was time to leave and reassess her findings. She closed the door of the cabin behind her, her mind racing with the implications of what she'd seen. Bryan's presence here was undeniable, but so was the presence of others, and that complicated everything. She would send a full forensics team out as soon as one was available.

34 SOLITUDE LOST

Unbeknownst to Hayes, Bryan was there and watching her from the treeline, barely visible amid the thick underbrush. He had bolted from the cabin the moment he heard Hayes' car approach, retreating deep into the woods to ensure he wouldn't be caught. He crouched silently, his breath steady but his heart racing, eyes locked on the scene unfolding at his former refuge. From his vantage point, he could see the detective methodically working her way through the cabin, and though his instincts screamed at him to stay hidden, a part of him felt almost relieved that someone competent was finally piecing together the fragments of his fractured life.

But Bryan knew he couldn't stay here much longer. The cabin was compromised, and now more than ever, he had to remain elusive. As Detective Hayes finally left, Bryan stayed crouched in the shadows, waiting until her car was out of sight. Only then did he emerge, taking one last look at the cabin—a temporary sanctuary that had become a liability. He sprinted silently back into the woods, slipping further into the unknown, where only he understood the path ahead.

The solitude here was both his prison and his protection, a space where he could face, fight, and come to terms with the chaos within himself, away from the judgment and failures that had haunted him for so long. In the quiet of his hiding place, Bryan grappled with the duality of his isolation. It was here, amidst the shadows and the whispering wind, that he could confront the dissonance between who he was and who he had aspired to be.

Memories of Elizabeth's warmth, her laughter and real smile now tinged with the cold sting of betrayal, intermingled with flashes of Alex's youthful determination, naivety, and unspoken hurt. Elizabeth, once the love of his life, now symbolized both the comfort he lost and the reasons for his torment. Her choices for infidelity and the disintegration of their marriage were relentless reminders of his own perceived failures and inadequacies, such that there were things in this world that no matter the effort he could not fix or even repair. Alex, on the other hand, represented the future he had hoped to nurture, but the growing rift between them was a painful reminder of his shortcomings as a father and as a man.

Bryan's solitude was a place where these thoughts churned and clashed, where he faced the raw reality of his mistakes without the veneer of pretense or external judgment. It was both a sanctuary and a house of torment, a place where he could be honest with himself about his broken past and fractured relationships, yet also a place that kept him from reconciling these fragments of his life with the outside world.

35 REALITY CHECK

Alex's hands trembled slightly as he took a deep breath, his gaze locked on the glowing screen of his laptop. The muted hum of the air conditioning in the background was a stark contrast to the whirlwind of emotions and revelations he was about to share with his mother. He glanced at Elizabeth, who stood beside him, her face a mask of concern and curiosity. The light from the laptop cast a faint glow on their faces, emphasizing the gravity of the moment.

"Mom, Elizabeth...Liz" Alex began only finally getting her attention using the name only Bryan ever had, his voice unsteady, "I need you to see something. It's about Dad—about what he was going through and what he did for others." His tone was laden with the weight of his discoveries, and he fought to keep his emotions in check. The half-hidden tears in his eyes betrayed the profound impact the information had on him.

Elizabeth took a seat beside him, her heart aching for her son. The protective instincts that had guided her through so many challenges now flared into action as she reached out and rested a comforting hand on his shoulder. "Show me," she said gently, her voice steady but filled with concern.

Alex nodded, his fingers moving deftly over the keyboard. He brought up Bryan's social media profiles, which were now more than just digital remnants of a man lost to despair—they were a tapestry of his unspoken struggles and unyielding commitment to others.

The first post Alex highlighted was a heartfelt message from Bryan to a woman named Emily. The text was a touching note of encouragement, written after Emily had confided in Bryan about her struggles with depression following a miscarriage. "Look at this, Mom," Alex said, pointing to the screen. "Dad was there for her when she felt like she had no one else. He was always the one reaching out, even when he was on the edge himself."

Elizabeth's eyes softened as she read the words Bryan had written. They were filled with empathy and kindness, a stark contrast to the turmoil Bryan had been enduring. "He never let on just how much he was suffering," she murmured, more to herself than to Alex. "It's like he was trying to save everyone else while drowning in his own pain."

Alex scrolled through more posts—messages to other individuals who had reached out to Bryan during their darkest hours. There was Steven, a former student who had confided in Bryan about his struggle with an abusive home life. Bryan's response was filled with practical advice, support, and a promise to stand by Steven's side. "Dad helped him get out of that situation," Alex said, his voice cracking. "He never mentioned it to us, never wanted any recognition."

Elizabeth's eyes were misty now, reflecting a mixture of admiration and sorrow. "He kept so much to himself. I thought he was just putting on a brave face for us."

Alex nodded, his eyes scanning the screen for more examples. He showed her messages from a teenager named Lisa, who had been on the brink of suicide. Bryan's words were filled with a deep understanding and a genuine effort to pull her back from the edge. "Dad was saving lives," Alex said quietly. "He was reaching out to people who were in desperate need, even though he was battling his own demons."

They continued to sift through the messages, each one a testament to Bryan's selflessness. There were posts about community support, his involvement in local charity events, and countless interactions where he provided a listening ear or a word of encouragement. The more they uncovered, the clearer it became that Bryan's life had been a mosaic of helping others, even as he fell apart internally.

Alex pointed out an email thread between Bryan and an organization that dealt with addiction recovery. "He even offered to speak at events, share his story to help others who were struggling with addiction," Alex said. "He never asked for anything in return. It was like he was determined to make a difference, no matter how much he was suffering."

As they reviewed the materials, Elizabeth's grief was palpable. She saw how Bryan had poured himself into others, trying to make a difference in their lives despite his own deteriorating mental state. The realization of how much he had sacrificed and how deeply he had been affected by Elizabeth's infidelity and the unraveling of their family struck her like a physical blow.

"I had no idea," Elizabeth said, her voice trembling. "I knew he was hurting, but I never saw how deeply it went. I was so focused on my own pain that I didn't see how much he was giving to others, how he was trying to hold onto his own humanity."

Alex took a deep breath, his resolve reaffirming as he closed the laptop. "Mom, we need to find Dad. We need to understand why he disappeared and what's happening with him. All this time, he was fighting for everyone else, and we need to fight for him now."

Elizabeth nodded, her gaze unwavering as she wiped a tear from her cheek. The realization of Bryan's relentless efforts to help others while struggling silently hit her hard. She took a deep breath, steadying herself. "You're right. We owe it to him to understand what drove him to this point and to do everything we can to find him. He was always there for others, and now we need to be there for him."

Alex and Elizabeth began to organize their thoughts and make a plan. Alex started listing the key people Bryan had helped based on the social media interactions they had reviewed. "We should start by reaching out to these people," he said, pointing to a list he had made. "They might have more insights into Dad's state of mind, or they could have noticed something that we missed."

292

Elizabeth agreed. "I'll handle the contacts and try to get in touch with them. You work on the information from the laptop. See if there's anything there that can give us a clue about where he might have gone or what he might have been planning."

Alex nodded, his mind racing with the possibilities. "I'll also try to follow up on any leads we might have missed. We need to cover all our bases." He paused, a worried expression crossing his face. "Mom, you know what's really troubling me? The name D. Mann keeps coming up in the stuff we found. It seems connected somehow to Dad, but I don't understand how. Do you think it's something we should look into more?"

Elizabeth's eyes narrowed as she considered the name. "It definitely seems important. We should look into D. Mann and see if we can find any connections between him and Bryan. Maybe he's someone who has been involved in Bryan's life in ways we don't yet understand."

As they began to coordinate their efforts, the tension in the room was palpable. The weight of their discoveries was heavy, but so was their determination. They knew they were racing against time to find Bryan, and every second counted.

Alex reached for his phone and began to draft messages to the people Bryan had helped, asking if they had any information that could assist in locating Bryan. Meanwhile, Elizabeth sat down at the kitchen table, pulling out her phone and dialing the first contact on her list. The conversation was brief but revealing; the people she spoke to were all grateful for Bryan's help and eager to provide any information they could.

36 STARK UNCERTAINTY

As Alex worked through the files on the laptop, he paused at a particularly telling document—a meticulously compiled list of locations Bryan had visited frequently. Each place was marked with handwritten notes, revealing fragments of his father's thoughts and feelings. One location, however, stood out among the rest: a small, secluded cabin deep in the woods. The notes described it not just as a refuge, but a sanctuary—a place where Bryan went to reflect and escape. It had once belonged to his grandmother, and the words scribbled beside it hinted at its emotional significance. It was clear that the cabin carried the weight of Bryan's past, a place where he could face himself when the world outside became too heavy.

Alex felt a surge of hope, gripping the edge of the table as his heart began to race. This wasn't just another place on the map; this could be the key. "Mom," he said, his voice steady but filled with urgency, "I think we need to check out this cabin. It was important to Dad... maybe he left something there, something that could help us understand where he went or what he's planning."

Elizabeth looked up from her phone, her tired eyes softening with a glimmer of hope. Her face, lined with worry and exhaustion, seemed to relax for the first time in days. "Let's do it," she said, a quiet determination lacing her voice. "We need to follow every lead we can find. If this cabin meant something to your dad, maybe it holds the key to understanding him—and finding him."

The weight of their mission settled heavily between them, propelling them into swift action. Alex packed a backpack with essentials—flashlights, a first aid kit, a few snacks, and some water. He knew they couldn't leave anything to chance. Meanwhile, Elizabeth pulled out an old map and jotted down the directions, her hands moving with a practiced precision as if this small act of control would ground her in the chaos. Despite the dire circumstances, there was something in the air between them, a silent but shared determination that pushed them forward.

As they drove toward the cabin, the landscape around them gradually shifted. The busy streets faded into long, winding roads, the scenery growing more isolated with every passing mile. The trees lining the roads became denser, the world narrowing until it was just them and the vast, quiet wilderness ahead. It felt like they were moving toward the edge of everything they had known—the further they drove, the more distant the rest of their lives seemed. The silence in the car was thick with anticipation, broken only by the soft hum of the engine and the occasional sigh from Elizabeth as she glanced over at Alex.

When they finally arrived, the cabin stood there, weathered and worn, as though time itself had been eroded by the elements. The wood was cracked and splintered in places, the roof sagging slightly under the weight of the years that had passed since Bryan's grandmother had lived there. Yet despite its age, there was something enduring about it, something that seemed to stand resilient against the tide of time.

As they stepped out of the car and approached the cabin, their emotions were a mixture of dread and anticipation. The air was thick with the scent of pine and damp earth, and a light breeze rustled the leaves above them. Alex's heart pounded as they reached the front door. He exchanged a glance with his mother, who nodded resolutely, and together they pushed open the creaky wooden door.

Inside, the cabin was modest, but it carried the unmistakable weight of memory. The air was heavy, almost sacred, as if every inch of the space had absorbed decades of quiet reflection. Dust hung in the air, illuminated by the slanting light coming in through the small windows. Alex immediately began searching, his hands moving with a kind of desperation as he looked through drawers, overturned old books, and opened closets. Elizabeth, meanwhile, moved more slowly, her eyes scanning the room with a quiet reverence. Every item they touched seemed to whisper with the presence of Bryan's past.

They found little things—personal items that Bryan had clearly left behind. An old jacket, frayed at the edges from years of use, hung limply by the door. A book, its pages dog-eared and highlighted, rested on the table, filled with the kind of passages someone reads and rereads when seeking comfort. Near the window was a well-worn chair, slightly pushed back as though Bryan had been sitting there recently, gazing out at the surrounding woods. The fireplace contained the charred remains of a small fire, remnants of a night spent seeking warmth and solace.

Alex's pulse quickened as he searched every corner, opening drawers, lifting cushions, and peering into shadowed alcoves. He had expected more—perhaps a note, a letter, or some sign of where Bryan had gone next. But as the minutes stretched into hours, hope began to slip through his fingers like the dust that coated the surfaces. The cabin, though filled with echoes of Bryan's presence, offered no direct answers.

Elizabeth joined him, her face tight with disappointment. "He was here," she said quietly, her voice barely above a whisper. "But it's like he didn't want to be found."

They stood in silence, both of them absorbing the gravity of the moment. They had hoped for a breakthrough, a clue to bring them closer to Bryan, but all the cabin offered was fragments—pieces of a puzzle that still didn't fit together. As they stepped out into the clearing, the sun beginning to set behind the trees, the overwhelming isolation of the place mirrored the sense of uncertainty they carried with them.

Alex glanced back at the cabin one last time, his shoulders slumping with the weight of it all. "It feels like we're still missing something," he murmured, mostly to himself.

Elizabeth nodded, her eyes scanning the tree line. "We'll find him, Alex. We have to."

With no further clues, they climbed back into the car, the hum of the engine breaking the eerie silence of the woods. As they drove back toward town, the weight of unanswered questions pressed heavily on their chests. They had ventured to the place that once brought Bryan peace, but instead of comfort, they left with more uncertainty, the mystery of his disappearance deepening. Despite the silence between them, one thing remained clear: they couldn't stop searching, not until they found him—wherever he might be.

37 Not Done Yet

Just as they were about to drive away, both Elizabeth and Alex simlutaneously received a mysterious text message on their phones. The message read: "You're not done yet. Meet me where it all began at 2 a.m.."

The sender's number was unfamiliar to Alex, but the message was unmistakable. Elizabeth did recognize the number from the clue that initially led her to the cabin where she and Alex had found Bryan's notebook. It was a cryptic reminder that their quest was far from over. The urgency of the message, combined with the recent revelations, made it clear that they were being led into another phase of their search.

Alex and Elizabeth exchanged worried glances. The message seemed to indicate that they needed to revisit the beginning of their journey—perhaps a place or an event that had significant meaning to Bryan. The weight of the message hung over them as they prepared for the next leg of their search, knowing that their path would likely lead them into even deeper and more challenging territory.

"Mom...what the fuck does this message mean?"
Alex asked Elizabeth; she looked at Alex with all the
love she had and simply said, "We will figure it out
together".

38 LET IT LINGER

As he trudged through the forest towards his next destination, Bryan's mind drifted, his thoughts a storm of regret, love, and aching despair as he walked alone. That cabin had become more than a mere hideout—it was a place where he could strip away the façade he'd worn for so long and face the unvarnished truth of his life. There, surrounded by old journals, tattered notebooks, and letters that held fragments of his past, Bryan could sift through the wreckage of his decisions. As with everything, he was now forced to abandon something else that he loved and gave him the smallest inkling of comfort.

Memories of his early days with Elizabeth flooded back: their shared laughter, the quiet mornings spent together, and the way she'd look at him when he'd catch her off guard with a sweet gesture. Those were the moments that had made him believe they were unbreakable. But the brightness of those memories dimmed when he thought about what came later—the growing distance, the unspoken resentments, and finally, Elizabeth's affair with Bishop, which tore at the very fabric of his heart.

The pain was still visceral, a constant reminder of his failures, not just as a husband, but as the man he had promised himself he would be. Still, every recollection of Elizabeth's smile or Alex's curious gaze was a tether, pulling him back from the edge, reminding him that no matter how far he ran, he could never truly leave them behind.

As Bryan's solitude deepened, he found an odd comfort in the silence, though it was a double-edged sword—both his prison and his sanctuary. In this place, away from the judging eyes of the world, he could confront the chaos within him. He often found himself imagining what Alex was doing, hoping that his son was holding up better than he was. Bryan remembered their late-night conversations about life, school, and everything in between, times when he could be a father in the most honest sense.

The solitude forced him to reckon with his own shortcomings, the guilt of not being there when Alex needed him most, and the crushing reality that he might never see him again. But amidst his pain, there was also a flicker of purpose; he saw his time alone as a way to piece together the broken parts of himself. Every day spent in hiding was an opportunity to regain control, to become the version of himself that he had lost in the spiraling years of his decline. Bryan's thoughts always circled back to Elizabeth and Alex, driving him to hold on a little longer, even when everything inside him screamed to let go.

Bryan's reflections shifted to the many lives he had touched along his path, often without even realizing it. Cherry, Elizabeth's mother, stood out vividly in his mind. She had been a figure of stability in their lives until her world was shattered by her own marriage's breakdown and later, her husband's death. After Elizabeth's announcement of the divorce, Cherry had turned cold toward Bryan, seeing him as the cause of her daughter's pain. But Bryan never forgot the conversations they'd shared when she was at her lowest, contemplating leaving her own husband. He'd listened as Cherry poured out her fears of being alone, of failing her children, and Bryan had offered her comfort without judgment, simply telling her that strength wasn't found in staying or leaving but in making peace with whatever decision she made.

Bryan never realized then how much those words had meant to her; he only knew that for a moment, he had been able to give her something he could never seem to find for himself—a sense of calm amid the storm. But as Cherry's disdain for him grew, Bryan felt the sting of losing yet another person he had once considered family, further isolating him in his emotional exile.

Greg, a former student from Bryan's early teaching years, was another soul Bryan had saved without seeking acknowledgement. Greg's life had been a series of painful events—abandonment by his parents, bullying at school, and a deep sense of not belonging anywhere. One day, Bryan found him on the edge of a bridge, staring into the murky watery abyss below. The boy had been ready to end it all, feeling as though the world had nothing left to offer him.

Bryan didn't approach as a teacher or an authority figure; he simply sat down near him, matching Greg's silence with his own. As the minutes passed into hours, Bryan shared his own struggles, his battles with depression, and the feeling of being constantly overwhelmed by life. He didn't offer solutions or empty platitudes; he just let Greg know that someone else understood what it was like to feel completely lost. That connection, however brief, was enough to pull Greg back from the precipice. Bryan never mentioned the incident to anyone, and Greg never forgot it. Years later, Greg would tell Bryan in a message that the only reason he was alive was because of that conversation, a weighty reminder of the invisible threads Bryan had woven through other people's lives.

Emily's story was another chapter in Bryan's life that spoke to his capacity to give, even when he had nothing left. She had appeared one night at one of Bryan's adult education classes, her face bruised and eyes hollow from fear. Emily was trapped in an abusive relationship, desperate to escape but too terrified to make a move. Bryan had stayed late, offering her his time and attention, meticulously going over her options, from legal advice to contacts at local shelters.

When Emily confessed that she had nowhere to go and feared for her daughter's safety, Bryan didn't hesitate; he drove her to a shelter himself, navigating the dark streets with a quiet determination. That night, as he watched Emily and her daughter walk into the safe house, Bryan felt a

306

rare sense of purpose. For a brief moment, the weight of his own problems lifted because he had been able to protect someone else.

He never expected gratitude or recognition, and Emily's thanks, though heartfelt, were just another echo in the growing chorus of people Bryan had helped. What lingered with him was the knowledge that, even if only temporarily, he had made someone's world a little bit safer.

Jason was another lost soul whom Bryan had guided back from the brink. The young man had been spiraling into drug addiction and anger after his father's death, hanging out with dangerous people and making reckless choices. Bryan recognized the path Jason was on; it was a road paved with anger, self-loathing, and the desperate need to numb the pain.

Bryan spent countless evenings on the phone with Jason, talking him down from doing something he could never take back. He listened to Jason's rants, his plans for revenge against those who had wronged him, and his self-destructive urges. Bryan's advice was never preachy; it was pragmatic, focused on getting through one more day. Slowly, Jason began to see that there were other ways to deal with his grief, other than violence and drugs.

Bryan's constant presence, even from a distance, was a lifeline that kept Jason anchored when he had every reason to drift away. Jason would later tell Bryan that no one had ever cared enough to stay up all night just to make sure he didn't do something stupid, a sentiment that Bryan held onto as proof that his efforts, however small, were never in vain.

Rachel, whose connection with Bryan began through an online support group, became one of his most cherished confidantes. Suffering from severe chronic pain and grappling with her own mental health issues, Rachel found solace in Bryan's late-night messages, which were often filled with humor, empathy, and an unspoken understanding of what it was like to feel trapped in one's own body. Bryan would share details of his own struggles with his health, especially after his last brain surgery in 2022, when his memory began to falter and his confidence in his own mind waned.

Their conversations were a mutual lifeline; Rachel often told Bryan that his words kept her going on days when getting out of bed seemed impossible, while Bryan found comfort in knowing that someone else truly understood his fears. They never met in person, but the bond they formed through shared pain and unfiltered honesty was one of the few things that made Bryan feel less alone.

Among these connections, Bryan also recalled a stranger named Mark, whom he had met at a gas station late one night. Mark was visibly distraught, his car packed with belongings, and his eyes red from crying. Bryan struck up a conversation, learning that Mark had just left his wife after a heated argument and had no idea where he was going or what he was doing. Bryan didn't have all the answers, but he shared a coffee with Mark and listened as he poured out his frustrations, fears, and regrets.

Bryan didn't judge; he simply encouraged Mark to take a step back, consider what he truly wanted, and not make any hasty decisions that he couldn't undo. A few months later, Bryan received a message from Mark, thanking him for that night. Mark had reconciled with his wife, not because of anything Bryan had specifically said, but because Bryan had been there at a moment when Mark felt completely untethered.

Then there was Lily, a young barista Bryan encountered regularly at a local coffee shop. She was bright, witty, but clearly struggling beneath the surface. One day, when Bryan noticed her tears as she wiped down the counter, he struck up a conversation. Lily confessed that she was failing out of college, overwhelmed by family expectations, and battling crippling anxiety. Bryan, recognizing the signs of a young person buckling under pressure, offered to tutor her in history, a subject she found particularly challenging. They met weekly, and their sessions became less about history and more about life.

Bryan helped her see that her worth wasn't tied to academic success, and he encouraged her to seek professional help for her anxiety. Lily often told Bryan that he was the first adult who treated her as more than just a student, seeing her as a whole person rather than a set of grades. Their last session ended with Lily hugging Bryan tightly, thanking him for believing in her when she couldn't believe in herself.

Finally, there was Jake, an older man Bryan had met at a park. They struck up a conversation while watching their dogs play, and Bryan learned that Jake had recently lost his wife of fifty years and was grappling with the immense loneliness that followed. Bryan listened to Jake's stories of love, loss, and the empty house that now felt like a tomb. Bryan would visit the park at the same time each week, just to sit with Jake and let him talk. Jake often said that those moments were the only times he felt alive anymore, a sentiment that Bryan quietly absorbed, knowing all too well the pain of losing someone you love. In his own way, Bryan found solace in these meetings too, as Jake's stories were a reminder of the enduring power of love, even in its absence.

Bryan stared into the void thinking about the letters he had written over the years—some to Alex, others to Elizabeth, and some just ramblings of a man trying to hold on. The words were heavy with emotion, capturing moments of despair, regret, and fleeting hope. In those pages, he had poured out his heart, confessing his fears of being forgotten and his desperate longing to be remembered as more than the sum of his mistakes.

He wasn't sure if he'd ever have the courage to let Alex or Elizabeth read them; part of him feared that they would only see the broken man he had become, rather than the father and husband who had tried, however imperfectly, to do right by them.

Bryan's thoughts lingered on the life he had led, the quiet battles fought in the shadows, and the people he had touched without ever seeking recognition. His solitude was a complex mix of guilt and purpose, and though he remained hidden, he knew that in some small way, he was still making a difference, even if the world never saw it.

39 Discernment at Home

As Bryan wrestled with his past and tried to reconcile the man he was with the man he hoped to be, he pulled out his phone and logged in to the security system at home. There he saw Alex and Elizabeth working together. They were unraveling the threads of his life, slowly piecing together the impact he had made. Each person they spoke to painted a new picture of Bryan, one that neither Alex nor Elizabeth had even known about or fully understood. They began to see the quiet acts of kindness, the sacrifices made, and the burdens carried without complaint.

Bryan's solitude may have been his self-imposed exile, but it was also the place where he continued to be a father, a friend, and a guide to those who needed him most. And as Alex and Elizabeth continued their search, they were no longer just looking for Bryan; they were discovering the man he had always been, hidden beneath the pain and the distance.

Elizabeth and Alex sat side by side at the kitchen island, surrounded by printouts of messages, photos, and Bryan's social media interactions. Alex had meticulously combed through every chat, every private conversation, and every comment Bryan had left behind that he could find, each one revealing a new and deeper layer of his father's hidden life. The air was thick with a mixture of guilt and admiration, and as they began contacting the people Bryan had helped, Elizabeth could feel the weight of her own mistakes pressing down on her. Bryan's relentless kindness, even in his darkest moments, contrasted starkly with her own choices, and she couldn't help but feel that she had failed to see the man he truly was.

The first person they reached out to was Cherry, Elizabeth's own mother. Although their relationship had been strained after Elizabeth's decision to divorce Bryan, Alex knew his grandmother had once leaned on Bryan more than she ever let on. When they called her, Cherry's voice cracked with emotion as she recounted the nights Bryan had stayed up talking to her about her own crumbling marriage, long before Elizabeth's affair with Bishop.

Bryan had been a steadfast listener, offering gentle advice and reassurance when Cherry's world felt like it was falling apart. Even when Cherry had turned against him, Bryan's compassion had never wavered. "He was the only one who didn't judge me," Cherry said softly, her voice tinged with regret. "He made me feel like I wasn't alone, even when I along with everyone else was pushing him away."

Alex and Elizabeth then moved on to Greg, the former student Bryan had saved from the brink of suicide. Greg's voice was filled with gratitude as he spoke about the night on the bridge, when Bryan's quiet presence had made all the difference. "Your dad didn't just pull me back from that edge," Greg said. "He gave me the strength to keep going when I thought I had nothing left. He never asked for anything in return, and I never felt like a burden to him, even when I was at my worst." As Alex listened, he began to realize how many lives his father had touched in ways that he never shared, even when his own life was unraveling.

Emily's call was next, and she tearfully described how Bryan had helped her escape an abusive relationship. Her gratitude was palpable, her voice thick with emotion as she recounted the night Bryan drove her to safety. "I don't think I would have survived if it weren't for him," Emily confessed. "He didn't just save me; he saved my daughter, too. I always thought he was this quiet, unassuming guy, but he was a hero to me. I wish I could have done something for him in return." Elizabeth's eyes welled with tears as she realized how deeply Bryan had been involved in the lives of others, even when he was hurting the most.

Jason's story was equally heartbreaking. He spoke of his descent into addiction and how Bryan had been his lifeline during those darkest nights. "Your dad was the only one who didn't give up on me," Jason said. "He stayed up all night just to make sure I was okay. I was a mess, and he never made me feel like one. He just... cared, you know? In a way no one else did." Elizabeth listened in silence, the ache of her own choices mingling with the understanding of how profoundly Bryan had impacted these strangers while feeling so lost himself.

Next was Rachel, Rachel's voice was soft but steady when she spoke of her conversations with Bryan. The two had bonded over their shared experiences of pain and illness, often spending hours exchanging messages late at night when neither could sleep. "He was a light in the darkness," Rachel said simply. "Bryan never made me feel like my problems were too much. He just... listened. He made me feel seen when I thought I was invisible." Elizabeth thought about the many nights she had spent with Bishop, seeking comfort that Bryan had still been quietly offering to others. The realization was a bitter pill to swallow, knowing that Bryan had been saving lives while she was tearing theirs apart.

As they continued their calls, Alex and Elizabeth found themselves speaking to more people whose lives Bryan had touched since learning of Elizabeth's affair—each story more heartbreaking than the last.

The first was Jennifer, a single mother who had been left by her husband after he drained their savings and abandoned her with two young children. She'd met Bryan at a community event, where he had noticed her crying quietly in a corner. Bryan had sat with her, listening to her story, and later helped connect her with resources for single parents. He had even anonymously sent her groceries when she couldn't make ends meet.

"I was at my breaking point, but your dad... he gave me hope," Jennifer said, her voice quivering. "He told me that it was okay to feel broken but that I wasn't alone. I don't know how he knew, but he always seemed to show up when I needed someone the most."

Next was Duncan, a veteran struggling with PTSD who had crossed paths with Bryan at a gas station late one night. Duncan had been ready to give up, haunted by memories of combat and overwhelmed by his inability to reconnect with his family. Bryan had offered him a cigarette he had taken from a student earlier that day, and struck up a conversation, sharing his own battles with mental health.

"He made me feel normal, like my pain wasn't something to be ashamed of," Duncan explained. "We talked for hours, just sitting on the curb, and I felt seen in a way I hadn't in years. He didn't try to fix me; he just listened. I think that's what I needed most."

Then there was Michelle, a woman who had been contemplating leaving her husband after discovering his infidelity and years of emotional abuse. She met Bryan at a coffee shop, where they had exchanged small talk that quickly turned into a deep conversation about marriage, betrayal, and self-worth. Bryan had shared his own struggles without ever revealing the depth of his personal pain. "He told me that...he didn't push me in any direction; he just helped me see that I had choices. I never knew how much he was dealing with, but he still made time to help me sort through my mess."

Elizabeth and Alex then spoke with Tom, a man Bryan had met in an online support group for men dealing with depression and relationship issues. Tom's wife had left him for his best friend, and he was drowning in bitterness and rage. Bryan had reached out to him privately, offering a listening ear and practical advice on coping with betrayal. "Your dad was the only person who didn't tell me to 'man up' or get over it," Tom said, his voice breaking. "He just let me feel what I was feeling, and he helped me see that my anger was valid but that I didn't have to let it define me. I never knew he was going through something so similar. He was hurting, too, but he never let that stop him from being there for me."

Finally, they spoke with Lisa, a young woman who had grown up in an abusive household and had been on the verge of cutting ties with her entire family. She had met Bryan at a bookstore, where they struck up a conversation about a self-help book she was hesitant to buy. Bryan had encouraged her to prioritize her own mental health and had shared stories of his own complicated family dynamics, subtly referencing his own disappointments and regrets without ever making it about himself. "He told me that family doesn't always mean loyalty and that it's okay to walk away from people who hurt you," Lisa said. "He didn't make me feel guilty for wanting to leave; he just made me feel understood."

Elizabeth and Alex's search led them to another David, whose story was perhaps the most harrowing of all. David had been a successful business owner whose life had spiraled out of control after his wife left him and took their children, leaving him in financial ruin and emotional despair. The day Bryan encountered him, David was sitting by the creek on one of Bryan's favorite hiking trails, a Glock held shakily up to his temple, ready to end it all.

Bryan hadn't hesitated for a moment; he approached David slowly, careful not to startle him, and sat down beside him on the creek's edge without a word. Bryan didn't try to take the gun away or talk David out of his feelings. Instead, he simply began talking about the beauty of the trail, the sound of the water, and how he often found peace there when life became too overwhelming.

David was initially defensive, but Bryan's calm demeanor and genuine presence began to break through his walls. Bryan shared some of his own struggles—his brain surgery, the quiet pain of feeling like a stranger in his own marriage, and the weight of living a life that no longer felt like his. He didn't sugarcoat anything; he didn't offer false hope or cliché advice. He just spoke from the heart, telling David that even though he felt utterly alone, his pain was not something he had to carry by himself.

Bryan told him that he, too, had been to the edge and that sometimes just getting through the next minute was enough. "You don't have to solve it all today," Bryan had said softly, his eyes fixed on the rushing water. "Sometimes it's okay to just sit with the pain and let it be for now."

David listened, the gun slowly lowering from his chin as Bryan's words seeped into the cracks of his despair. Bryan stayed with him for hours, not pressing for details but simply being a quiet, nonjudgmental presence. He offered David his phone number and told him that anytime he needed to talk or just not be alone, he'd be there. The Glock eventually found its way back into David's backpack, and they parted ways with a handshake and a promise that David would at least try to see the sunrise the next morning.

"He didn't save me with grand gestures or by fixing my problems," David later told Elizabeth and Alex, his voice trembling with emotion. "He saved me by just being there, by letting me be broken without feeling worthless. I don't know where he got the strength, but he gave me a reason to hold on, even if just for one more day."

Hearing David's story, Elizabeth felt the sting of tears welling up in her eyes. Bryan's ability to reach people in their darkest moments, to extend his heart even when it was breaking, made her realize just how extraordinary he was. Alex was equally moved, recognizing that his father's quiet acts of heroism had been born from a place of deep personal pain.

His dad had not only saved lives but had done so while drowning in his own struggles, refusing to let his suffering stop him from being a light for others. David's story was a painful reminder of Bryan's relentless compassion and a sobering testament to the unseen battles Bryan had fought every day.

As Elizabeth and Alex listened to David's words, they couldn't help but feel an overwhelming sense of urgency to find Bryan—not just to bring him home, but to finally give him the support and understanding he had so selflessly given to others.

As Elizabeth and Alex hung up agreeing with Alex that this was the last call, they were both left stupefied, in a stunned silence. Each story painted a clearer picture of the man Bryan had been—selfless, compassionate, and endlessly giving, even when his own world was crumbling and he didn't have any more to give. Elizabeth's guilt swelled as she realized how blind she had been to the quiet heroism Bryan had shown to so many. She looked at Alex, her heart heavy with a mixture of love, regret, and a newfound respect for the man they were still searching for.

40 PERFECT IMPERFECTION

Elizabeth sat alone in the quiet of her bedroom, the walls seeming to close in around her as the weight of everything Alex had shared pressed heavily on her chest. She stared at the worn photograph in her hands—a candid shot of her, Bryan, and Alex from years ago, back when their smiles were genuine and untainted by the strain that would later pull them apart. The picture was crinkled at the edges, a testament to how many times it had been handled, folded, and unfolded as if searching for the lost moment it captured.

The past few days had been a whirlwind of revelations, each one cutting deeper than the last. Bryan's sacrifices, his disappearance, and his relentless drive to help others while silently drowning in his own pain, now painted a picture Elizabeth hadn't been ready to see.

Elizabeth's mind was a tangled web of memories and regrets. She thought back to the first time she had met Bryan, the spark in his eyes, the way he made her feel seen in a world that often overlooked her. Back then, he was her rock, her protector, the man who seemed to have it all figured out. They built a life together, and with every argument, every moment of laughter, and every struggle, they had crafted something uniquely their own. But somewhere along the way, things had changed. The pressures of life, the financial stress, and the silent resentments had slowly eaten away at the foundation of their marriage. Her infidelity with Bishop, an act she could barely reconcile with herself, was more than a mistake—it was a breaking point, one she never fully understood until now. Bryan's silence in the face of her betrayal wasn't acceptance; it was his way of fighting a battle she couldn't see.

Sitting there, Elizabeth allowed herself to truly reflect on the moments that led them to this place. She saw the missed connections, the unspoken apologies, and the countless times Bryan had reached out to her in his own way, only for her to pull back. She thought about Bishop, and the hollow comfort she had sought in his arms. It wasn't love; it was a desperate attempt to fill a void that had grown between her and Bryan. But now, she realized that no one could replace what Bryan meant to her. She had been too blind to see that Bryan, even in his darkest hours, never stopped loving her. The messages Alex uncovered showed

Bryan's unwavering commitment—even when the world gave him every reason to walk away, he stayed true. Bryan had been helping others, giving all he had left, while she had been too consumed with her own hurt to see his pain.

Elizabeth's thoughts shifted to Alex. Her son was resilient, smart, and determined, but the cracks in his composure were starting to show. She saw the fear in his eyes when he spoke of Bryan and the worry that his father was slipping further out of reach. Alex had taken on a burden far too heavy for his age, and Elizabeth felt a pang of guilt for being part of the reason why. As she pieced together the puzzle of Bryan's actions through the lens of Alex's discoveries, she couldn't help but feel ashamed. Bryan had never been the villain she had painted him to be in her mind. He was a flawed man, yes, but he was also a man who had loved fiercely, even when that love went unreciprocated.

Elizabeth clenched the photograph tighter, her tears blurring the faces she loved most. She was determined not to let Bryan's story end in the shadows. For the first time in a long while, she felt a flicker of resolve ignite within her. Elizabeth knew she couldn't change the past, but she could fight for the future—for Bryan, for Alex, and for the family they once were.

She thought about every person Bryan had helped, the lives he had touched without ever seeking recognition. He had been a lifeline to so many, yet he had slipped through the cracks himself. Elizabeth realized that Bryan's strength was his willingness to help others, even when he had nothing left to give.

"Bryan, I'm so sorry," she whispered into the quiet room. "I never meant for things to get this far. I never meant to lose you."

Elizabeth's heart ached as she considered how their lives had unraveled. She had always known Bryan as a man of incredible strength and deep compassion. The irony of their situation was that Bryan's strength had become his undoing. While he was out there helping strangers and offering a listening ear, he had been silently suffering, trying to keep the remnants of their life together intact. The realization that Bryan had been using his own pain as a driving force to support others made her reflect on the countless times she had failed to see his needs or offer him the support he had desperately needed. Her betrayal with Bishop seemed like a distant but painful echo now, a mistake that had caused ripples of hurt and regret.

She pulled out her phone and began scrolling through the messages and notes Bryan had left. Each interaction with those he had helped reflected a man who was both deeply flawed and incredibly resilient. His responses were filled with empathy and wisdom, offering advice and solace to people in crises far worse than her own. This stark contrast between Bryan's ability to reach out to others and his silence about his suffering cut Elizabeth deeply. Bryan had poured his heart into helping others navigate their personal storms while his own remained unspoken, unresolved.

Elizabeth reflected on her last conversation with Bryan, just before everything started to unravel. They had argued, her anger a mask for her fear and confusion. Bryan had tried to reach out, but her defensiveness and denial had created a barrier that he could not breach. She remembered the pained look in his eyes, the quiet resignation in his voice. It was at that moment that she realized how distant they had become. The betrayal with Bishop, though a significant breach, had not been the root of their problems but rather a symptom of a deeper disconnect.

She thought about Alex's discovery of Bryan's hidden journal. The entries were a window into Bryan's soul, revealing his internal struggles and the deep love he had for his family. Reading those words made Elizabeth feel as though she had been blind to Bryan's true essence. The journal chronicled his fears, his dreams, and his unrelenting hope that things would get better. The realization that Bryan had written these reflections, knowing how much he had invested in their family despite the pain, filled her with an overwhelming sense of remorse. His words were both a plea for understanding and a testament to his enduring commitment to their family.

Elizabeth's thoughts turned to the people Bryan had helped since learning of her affair. Each story was a testament to his generosity and compassion, a stark reminder of his selflessness. She thought about Sherry, her mother, who had been so cruel to Bryan since the divorce was announced. Bryan had still comforted her, offering a shoulder to cry on even when he was grappling with his own heartbreak, his entire world ending. The complexity of these interactions showed Bryan's ability to compartmentalize his pain while reaching out to others in need. It was a gift and a curse, one that left him isolated even as he was surrounded by people.

As she reviewed the names and stories, Elizabeth's resolve hardened. She had been given so many chances to make things right, to confront the mistakes of her past and to fight for the future. Bryan had been so consistent in his love and desire for her and their future as a family, but she was blinded by her resentments and anger. Elizabeth couldn't help but to think that she was going to need years of therapy no matter what happens and resolved to do that no matter what.

It wouldn't just be for her, but for Alex and anyone else in her life that wanted to really know her...they way Bryan did. He wasn't just her husband, he was her best friend and he knew her better than anyone...even herself. Her mind raced with plans on how to use this newfound understanding to find Bryan and make amends. She knew that Bryan had always acted with integrity and had never sought recognition for his efforts. This realization fueled her determination to honor his legacy and show him that his sacrifices and all the chances he had given her were not in vain.

Elizabeth's reflections also led her to think about how she could be a better support system for Alex. Her son had carried a ridiculously heavy burden, one that was far beyond his years. He was most definitely Bryan's son and took after him in so many ways and she needed to be there for him in ways she hadn't been since this started. She would find a way to help him process the grief and confusion that had consumed him. Their journey to find Bryan was as much about healing their fractured family as it was about locating him. Alex needed her strength and her unwavering support now more than ever.

As Elizabeth finished her thoughts, she felt a renewed sense of purpose. She was ready to face the challenges ahead, to put in the effort required to find Bryan and to make amends for her past mistakes.

Her commitment to solving the mystery of Bryan's disappearance and repairing their relationship was unwavering. She knew it would be a difficult road, but the love she had for Bryan and Alex was a powerful motivator. She picked up her phone again, this time with a sense of clarity and determination, ready to work with Alex to uncover the truth and bring their family back together. The journey ahead would test them in ways they had never imagined, but for the first time in a long while, Elizabeth felt hopeful about the future.

With a deep breath, Elizabeth prepared to face the challenges that lay ahead wondering if she was strong enough. She was determined to make things right, to find Bryan and to rebuild the trust that had been lost. Her newfound resolve was not just about finding her husband but also about rediscovering herself and her capacity to love and support her family. She knew the path would be fraught with difficulties, but she was ready to confront them head-on, with Alex by her side and a renewed sense of purpose guiding her every step.

The guilt was overwhelming, but so was the hope that maybe—just maybe—Bryan could be found and brought back into the light. Elizabeth vowed to set things right, to find him and bring him home, no matter what it took. She would be the anchor this time, the one who didn't give up.

Elizabeth wiped her eyes, her resolve solidifying as she picked up her phone. She knew she couldn't do it alone, and the first step was admitting that she needed help. She dialed Alex's number, her mind already racing with the plans they would make together. As the phone rang, Elizabeth knew that whatever was waiting for them, they would face it together.

She was ready to fight for Bryan, just as he had always fought for her, even when she didn't deserve it. The journey ahead wouldn't be easy, but it was one she was prepared to take. For Bryan. For Alex. For herself. For the life they still had a chance to rebuild.

41 SPECTER, SOLDIER, SAINT

D. Mann sat alone in the dimly lit office of his lakehouse, the glow of his computer screen casting eerie shadows on the walls. His face, chiseled by years of hardship and unrelenting discipline, was set in a contemplative expression. Mann's life had been defined by power, precision, and a relentless pursuit of control—first in the military, then in the unforgiving world of high-stakes business.

He had earned a reputation for his ruthlessness, a man who could make decisions that others would shy away from, whether on the battlefield or in the boardroom. But tonight, as he stared at the digital files before him, he was haunted by a memory that he couldn't quite piece together, a fragment of his past that intertwined with a man who had saved him from his darkest hour.

It had been years ago when Mann's empire—built on grit, blackmail, and blood—had come crashing down. His business was failing, his marriage was crumbling, and he had found himself standing on the precipice of his own destruction. The image of that moment was vague, shrouded in a fog that he could never quite clear. He remembered the cold

334

steel of his service Glock pressed against his temple, his trembling finger on the trigger.

His life had spiraled out of control, a maelstrom of failed ambitions, broken promises, and an overwhelming sense of emptiness and failure. He was ready to end it all when, out of nowhere, Bryan Black had appeared. Bryan's presence that night was like a lighthouse piercing through an impenetrable fog, a stranger who spoke with a sincerity that Mann had never encountered before, ever. Bryan didn't preach or judge; he simply listened, offering him a inhuman perspective that had peeled away the layers of loss and despair he had wrapped himself in.

Mann's gratitude for Bryan's intervention was what initially sparked his obsessive curiosity. He needed to understand who this man was, the one who had unknowingly pulled him back from the brink. Through his extensive military and business networks, Mann began to dig into Bryan's background. What he found was both perplexing and deeply unsettling.

Bryan's life on the surface seemed ordinary, too ordinary—a struggling teacher, a devoted but flawed husband, and a father grappling with his own demons. But as Mann delved deeper, he stumbled upon documents that were never meant to see the light of day: files marked with redacted lines and classified stamps far above TOP SECRET. His military contacts had never seen anything like it, the kind of information that was buried under decades of layers of government black ops and experimental research.

Bryan Black, it turned out, was not just any man; he was the lone survivor of a covert military program designed to create the next step in human evolution. All known participants died of an aneurysm prior to turning sixteen years old and due to a filing error, Bryan's name was included as deceased and the program was summarily terminated.

Mann's hands trembled slightly each time as he scrolled through the documents, each new page revealing a bizarre and unsettling history. The project, codenamed "Re-Genesis," aimed to enhance human capabilities beyond natural limits, blending gene therapy, advanced neurology, and bioengineering in a desperate bid to craft the perfect soldier. Dozens of men and women had been selected, but only one—Bryan—had survived the genetic anomaly that created "a horrendous parietal aneurysm".

The enhancements were designed to remain dormant, a hidden evolution that would pass down genetically to his offspring. This was no ordinary legacy; it was a mutation that would lay dormant until the right conditions were met through frequency manipulation.

Mann's thoughts turned to Alex, Bryan's son, and his mind raced with the implications of what he had uncovered. If Bryan was the prototype, then Alex was the perfected version, the culmination of a secret military ambition to create a flawless human. The classified files detailed Alex's potential, noting that the full range of abilities would only manifest when he turned 21, triggered by a specific sequence of genetic activations built into each and every chromosome in his DNA.

Mann realized with chilling clarity that Alex represented something far beyond what anyone could comprehend: a human who could exceed all known physical and cognitive limits. This wasn't just about strength or intelligence—it was about an entirely new kind of existence, something humanity had never seen before.

Mann leaned back, a cold sweat breaking out on his brow as he processed the enormity of what he had discovered. Bryan's altruism, his tireless dedication to helping others despite his own suffering, took on a new dimension. Bryan had been protecting more than just his family; he was guarding a secret that could change the world and didn't even know it. And what of activating Bryan's own enhancements through this frequency manipulation, was that even possible and what would it do.

Mann's thoughts swirled back to that moment when Bryan had stopped him from ending his life. Bryan had seen something in him, a flicker of humanity that had been all but extinguished. It was that same intuition, Mann realized, that had driven Bryan to safeguard Alex beyond all reasonable parental measures. Bryan unknowingly understood, better than anyone, the importance of protecting what could not yet be understood by the world.

As Mann stared at the digital files, he felt a renewed sense of purpose, a responsibility that extended far beyond personal redemption. Bryan and Alex were more than just two lives intertwined with his; they were the key to something monumental, something that others would kill to control or destroy. Mann's background as a strategist, both in warfare and in business, told him that forces far greater than any of them would be searching for answers—and they would stop at nothing to find Bryan and Alex...if they knew they were still alive.

Mann's mind flashed through every scenario, every potential threat that could be circling around them. His instincts had told him that this was no longer just about paying back a debt of gratitude; it was about ensuring that Bryan and Alex's secrets and very lives remained protected at all costs. He would need to leverage every connection, every ounce of his cunning and experience, and use all of his remaining power to stay one step ahead of those who would seek to exploit this newfound knowledge and safeguard the future.

Mann knew he was no hero, but he understood strategy, loyalty, and the high stakes of what lay before them. He was prepared to do whatever was necessary to keep Bryan and Alex safe, even if it meant embracing the shadows once more.

He pulled out a burner phone, the kind he reserved for operations that required utmost discretion, and began dialing a number. As the line connected, Mann's resolve hardened. Bryan had saved him when he was ready to die, and now it was his turn to return the favor. The world might never know the truth of what Bryan had endured or the potential locked within Alex, but Mann would ensure that they had a fighting chance. Whatever it took, he would protect them. The past had shaped him into a man capable of ruthless decisions, but for the first time in years, he felt as though he was on the right side of the battle. Using the call to instruct his team on ensuring the next steps go off without a hitch, Mann smiles.

As he ended the call, Mann knew that the journey ahead would be fraught with danger and deception. But he welcomed it, fueled by a sense of purpose that transcended his own survival. Bryan and Alex were not just important to the world; they were important to him. And for that, he would go to war with anyone who threatened them, even if it meant facing the demons of his own past.

Protecting Bryan, Alex, and Elizabeth, plus finding those who have been watching and nudging Bryan's entire life and why it is his life's mission; giving it new meaning.

D. Mann had always thrived on control—on knowing every move, every threat, and every possibility long before they unfolded. So when he had fully grasped the importance of Bryan Black, Alex, and even Elizabeth in this unfolding story, he knew his first priority was to ensure their safety, whether they wanted it or not. Mann's background in military intelligence and private security had given him access to resources that most people could only dream of. With a small team of trusted operatives and an arsenal of technology at his disposal, Mann had put Bryan and his family under constant surveillance.

From the moment Bryan disappeared, Mann had eyes on every possible angle, tracking their movements, their communications, and even their most private moments. To the outside world, Bryan, Alex, and Elizabeth were just ordinary people struggling through extraordinary circumstances. To Mann, they were the most critical pieces on a chessboard that could change everything.

Mann's surveillance operation was meticulous and unrelenting. He had cameras discreetly positioned at all of Bryan's favorite places—the cabin, the hiking trails, the cellar, and even key spots around town where Bryan might resurface. Drones patrolled the woods where Bryan had been known to disappear, and listening devices were strategically placed to capture every word spoken within their vicinity.

Mann's team's cyber capabilities were even more formidable; he had hacked into every electronic device that the family used, including phones, computers, and even the police department's secure communications. He knew what the detectives were thinking before they did, and every theory they had about Bryan's disappearance was relayed back to him in real time. Mann's extensive digital network allowed him to stay one step ahead of everyone, ensuring that nothing happened to Bryan or his family without his knowledge.

But Mann's protection wasn't just passive. He had taken active measures to eliminate threats, particularly the one posed by Bishop. Bishop had been a loose cannon for far too long—a ticking time bomb that endangered everyone around him. Mann had seen the potential for disaster and had decided to intervene in a way that only he could. He had infiltrated the trailer park where Bishop was hiding out, meticulously planning a catastrophic event that would seem like a tragic accident. He arranged for a slow gas leak from multiple propane tanks, rigging them to ignite with the slightest spark. The setup was designed to look like a careless mistake, a common occurrence in such a rundown area where maintenance was often neglected. It was a controlled, deliberate act, calculated down to the last second to ensure maximum destruction and cover his tracks.

Mann's real objective, however, was not just to remove Bishop but to make him suffer. He had watched Bishop for weeks, studying his routines, his habits, and his vulnerabilities. On the night of the explosion, Mann had moved swiftly and without mercy. As Bishop stumbled into his trailer after arguing with Alex and Elizabeth, intoxicated, high, and oblivious to the imminent danger, Mann struck with the precision of a predator. Mann moved with silent precision, his steps calculated and his focus razor-sharp.

In one fluid motion, he subdued Bishop with a brutal chokehold, rendering him unconscious in seconds. Mann swiftly dragged Bishop's limp body into a nondescript van parked a safe distance away from the soon-to-be inferno. Just as Mann got

Bishop restrained the blast erupted, a deafening roar that lit up the night sky and sent shockwaves through the trailer park. The fire consumed everything, leaving nothing but rubble and ash. To anyone watching, it was a tragic accident, a fire that had claimed another lost soul. But Mann knew the truth: he had orchestrated every detail with utter perfection.

Mann transported Bishop to the cellar that Bryan had been using as his private sanctuary, a place Bryan thought of as his last refuge. The irony wasn't lost on Mann as he chained Bishop to a chair in the dark, musty basement. It was here that Mann unleashed his full fury. Bishop woke to a world of pain, his vision blurred, his senses overwhelmed by the damp, suffocating air. Mann was relentless, using every tool at his disposal to extract information.

He read through Bryan's journal meticulously, finding Bryan's darkest thoughts and fantasies about what he would do to Bishop if he ever had the chance. One particularly creative entry detailed an imagined punishment involving a homemade device that combined waterboarding with electrified chains—a method designed not just to inflict pain but to break a person's very spirit. Mann, ever resourceful, had brought this vision to life.

The interrogation was brutal and efficient. Mann didn't just seek information; he sought to crush every ounce of defiance in Bishop's broken mind and body. Each question was accompanied by an increasing level of torturous agony, the shocks and suffocation pushing Bishop to the edge of unconsciousness repeatedly. Mann's face remained stoic as Bishop begged, pleaded, and eventually whimpered for mercy. But mercy was not something Mann could afford nor intended to grant. Bishop's very existence was a threat to Bryan and his family.

Mann would see to it that the threat was neutralized once and for all. When Mann had extracted every piece of useful information, he executed the final part of Bryan's imagined punishment. Bishop's body was bound, gagged, and slashed repeatedly but left very much alive, he was then unceremoniously dumped into the area of a local lake known to be inhabited by more than one alligator—a place where no one would ever think to look, not that there would be anything left once the gators had their way.

With Bishop eliminated, Mann intensified his focus on the broader mission: protecting Bryan, Alex, and Elizabeth from all angles. He maintained a rotating team of close knit operatives to keep constant watch over Bryan's known hideouts, ensuring that any movement was immediately reported. The surveillance was sophisticated enough to alert Mann if Bryan so much as took a breath in a new direction. He also monitored Elizabeth's and Alex's phones, intercepting any suspicious calls or messages.

Mann knew that Elizabeth was searching desperately for Bryan, and while he respected her determination, even admired it. He couldn't afford to let her inadvertently lead anyone else to Bryan before the time was right and all of the necessary protections were in place.

Mann's hacking into the police department's communications provided him with an invaluable advantage. He could see their entire playbook—their theories, their dead ends, and every piece of evidence they had collected. It was through this surveillance that Mann learned of Detective Hayes's recent visit to the cabin. He had watched through his own hidden cameras as she meticulously combed through the place, searching for clues.

Mann saw the tension in her eyes, the frustration as she failed to find Bryan but sensed she was close. It was Mann's intention to keep it that way: close but never close enough. He had even taken the precaution of planting misleading evidence, false leads that would send the police chasing shadows while keeping Bryan's true whereabouts hidden.

Mann's surveillance also extended into the digital realm. He had gained access to Bryan's cloud storage, emails, and every file saved on his devices. He had scanned every document, every message, and every piece of data Bryan had ever saved. This exhaustive knowledge allowed Mann to anticipate Bryan's moves before he made them, to understand the depths of his torment and the reasons behind his disappearance.

Mann's team had even pieced together the chronology of Bryan's mental decline, tracking the points where his despair had deepened and his grip on hope had loosened. It was this level of insight that allowed Mann to feel connected to Bryan in a way that was almost personal, as if he were witnessing the unraveling of a man from the inside out.

Mann also had Bryan's journal under constant scrutiny, his operatives regularly checking the cabin and cellar for any new entries. He knew Bryan had been using these pages to process his thoughts, his fears, and his plans. Mann found himself fascinated by Bryan's relentless self-examination and his fierce loyalty to his family, even as he spiraled deeper into his own darkness.

Each entry was a window into Bryan's soul, and Mann couldn't help but feel a profound sense of duty to protect him. Bryan was a man who had given everything of himself to others, even when he had nothing left to give. Mann would not let that kind of man be hunted down and destroyed by a world that would never be able to understand him.

Every day, Mann refined his plans, adjusting his strategy as new information surfaced. He knew that the time would come when Bryan would need to reappear, when he would need to confront the ghosts of his past and make peace with his family. Until then, Mann would remain in the shadows, orchestrating events from a distance, manipulating outcomes to ensure that Bryan and Alex remained safe. He had the skills, the resources, and the unshakeable resolve to see this through. No matter what the world threw at them, Mann was prepared to meet it head-on.

As Mann watched the latest surveillance footage of Elizabeth and Alex reviewing Bryan's social media, he felt a surge of determination. They were piecing together the fragments of Bryan's life, uncovering the hidden battles he had fought for so many others. He understood that this was not just about protecting a family; it was about safeguarding a legacy, a vision of humanity that Bryan had carried alone for too long.

Mann would ensure that Bryan and Alex remained out of reach, hidden from those who would exploit or destroy them. In his eyes, they were more than just people—they were a cause worth fighting for, and Mann was prepared to fight with everything he had.

Mann stared at the monitors in his dimly lit control room, his eyes scanning the screens that displayed the movements of Elizabeth and Alex. Every corner of their lives was under his surveillance, every moment meticulously recorded. He knew they were unraveling, piecing together fragments of Bryan's disappearance while grappling with their own guilt and loss. Mann tapped his fingers rhythmically on the keyboard, a calculated calmness washing over him as he composed the next message.

The time was right to push them further, to guide them toward the truth that lay hidden beneath layers of pain and secrets. He typed out the words with deliberate precision: "You're not done yet. Meet me where it all began at 2 a.m."

He leaned back, satisfied, then prepared the next phase of his plan. Mann carefully placed a burner phone into a small, inconspicuous box, the kind no one would give a second glance. The phone was preloaded with photos and videos that would finally confirm to Elizabeth and Alex that Bryan was still alive.

Images of Bryan captured from a distance: him sitting by a secluded riverbank, wandering through the dense woods, and even entering the cabin where he'd been hiding. Mann had recorded Bryan's every move without ever revealing himself, compiling an undeniable archive of Bryan's ongoing survival.

The phone would be left on the bench in the mall, the exact spot where Bryan had first seen Elizabeth in person on their first date, October 1, 2005—a moment Mann had memorized from his deep dives into Bryan's past. The phone could only be unlocked with an eight-digit code, "10012005," a poignant nod to the date that started it all.

Mann's message was clear: the journey was far from over, in fact it was only just beginning, and only by coming together and confronting their shared history could Elizabeth and Alex find the answers they desperately needed.

42 THE YELLOW BRICK ROAD

Elizabeth paced back and forth in the living room, her mind racing as she read and re-read the cryptic message on her phone. "You're not done yet. Meet me where it all began at 2 a.m." The words taunted her, echoing in her mind as if the sender was sitting in the room with them. Alex sat slumped on the couch, his eyes glued to his own phone, staring at the same message. He ran his hands through his hair, exasperated to the point he wanted to pull it all out.

"Where it all began?" Alex repeated, shaking his head. "What the hell does that even mean? Where do we need to go? It's like this guy wants us to play some kind of twisted scavenger hunt. Why not be more direct? Or is this another type of message within a message? How much do they actually know about us? About dad?"

Elizabeth nodded, still lost in thought. "It could be anywhere. 'Where it all began'... that could mean anything. The night we met, the day we got married, even the hospital when you were born, Alex. There are so many places. And why at 2 a.m.?"

Alex sighed, leaning forward and resting his elbows on his knees. "Why now? What's so special about tonight? There's no anniversary, no specific date that stands out—nothing. Is it just convenient? I hate the unknown."

Elizabeth rubbed her temples, the weight of uncertainty pressing down on her. "What about the hotel where Bryan proposed? Or our old apartment? Or, hell, even one of the hospitals where he got his surgeries?" She trailed off, biting her lip in frustration. "God, there are so many places that hold some kind of beginning for us. I don't even know where to start."

Alex began listing every location they'd ever considered significant. "Could it be Dad's old school? Your first house? Or maybe somewhere we used to go together as a family. Maybe the hiking trail, or even that crappy diner Dad used to love when he was struggling with money. This could mean anything, it could be anywhere dammit."

Minutes passed as they bounced ideas back and forth, dissecting every possibility with growing frustration. The kitchen counter was littered with crumpled notes filled with their scribbled ideas. The clock ticked closer to midnight, heightening their urgency. Alex threw up his hands in frustration. "This could literally be anywhere! And how the hell are we supposed to know which place to choose?"

Elizabeth's eyes flicked to Alex, her voice suddenly calmer, as if the chaos of their thoughts had briefly settled. "Remember what your Dad always used to say? When things get too complicated, you strip it down to the basics. What's the simplest answer?"

Alex stared at her, catching the thread of her thought. "Occam's Razor," he said slowly. "The simplest explanation is usually the right one. So... we go back to the very first thing. The first 'beginning.'"

Elizabeth sat down beside him, her expression softening as she thought back. "It's the mall, isn't it? The mall where we met on our first date. It was October 1st, 2005. Just inside the mall and on the benches outside of Sears he was waiting for me, and we spent hours just talking, eating, and uh *coughing, with a big smile*. That was the first real start for us. That has got to be it."

Alex nodded, relief mixed with disbelief washing over him. "Of course. But how are we supposed to get into a mall in the middle of the night? It's locked down tight, and we can't exactly waltz in there like it's open."

Elizabeth frowned. "We don't. We can't just break in—security cameras, alarms, you name it. Plus, they have night guards. I don't even know how we're supposed to explain ourselves if we get caught."

Alex slumped back, feeling the weight of their predicament. "This feels like a setup, Mom. We don't even know who this guy is or why he's playing games with us. What if it's a trap?"

Elizabeth glanced at the message again, conflicted. "Whoever this is... they've been watching us. They knew about the cabin and what it meant, what we would find there. And they've known other things, too—things we didn't tell anyone. I don't think they're doing this without a plan. I don't feel like they are against us, manipulating us definitely, but in a guiding way."

The tension lingered between them as they mulled over their next steps. Alex finally spoke, his tone determined yet weary. "We'll figure it out. Maybe there's a way that we don't know about, or maybe we just have to trust that whoever sent this has a plan. But either way, we're going to the mall tonight in about an hour, so get ready."

Neither of them realized that the entrance to the mall, normally locked and guarded, would be unlocked and open. D. Mann had ensured it and that every guard scheduled for that night had been reassigned, and every camera facing the entrance conveniently disabled. As Alex and Elizabeth prepared to face whatever lay ahead, Mann watched from his screens, orchestrating every detail with precision, ensuring that the path to their answers remained clear and that they would soon have proof of life and with it...renewed hope.

Elizabeth and Alex left their house in silence, the weight of the message still fresh in their minds. The city lights blurred as they sped through the quiet streets, Elizabeth gripping the wheel with tense determination. Alex's phone buzzed again, the screen illuminating his anxious face with another cryptic message: **"Turn right at the next light. You're being followed."** Alex's stomach tightened as he glanced behind them and spotted the faint silhouette of an unmarked car trailing from a distance.

"Mom, take the next right," Alex said, trying to keep his voice steady.

Elizabeth shot him a sideways glance, catching the edge of panic in his tone. "Why? What's going on?"

"No time to explain. Just do it. We're being followed." Alex's heart pounded as he typed a quick reply: "Who's following us?"

A new message flashed almost instantly. "Hayes. Stay sharp and do exactly as I say."

Elizabeth made the sharp turn, tires squealing as the car's headlights flickered across the deserted street. Alex looked back, seeing the unmarked car briefly hesitate before turning in after them. Detective Hayes was relentless, her car hovering just far enough behind to maintain a discreet distance, but close enough to keep them in sight.

Alex's phone vibrated again: "Left at the gas station. Don't slow down." Alex relayed the directions, his voice clipped with urgency. Elizabeth swerved, narrowly missing a parked car as they darted left past a dimly lit gas station. Hayes hesitated at the turn, momentarily losing sight of them behind a row of rusted delivery trucks.

"Jesus, Alex, what the hell is going on?" Elizabeth asked, her knuckles white against the steering wheel.

"It's Mann. He's giving us directions. He says Detective Hayes is following us. Just keep driving. We have to lose her."

Alex's phone pinged again, the next set of instructions flooding in faster than he could process them. "Straight for two blocks, then cut through the parking garage on your right. Go up two levels, then come down the opposite side."

Elizabeth floored the gas, the engine roaring as they shot down the street. She swung into the entrance of an old, poorly lit parking garage, the concrete walls closing in around them. The sound of their tires echoed in the emptiness, amplifying the adrenaline pulsing through Alex's veins. They spiraled upward, maneuvering between pillars and parked cars, the claustrophobic turns making it hard to tell if they were gaining distance.

Detective Hayes followed, struggling to keep up as she overshot the entrance and had to circle back. She entered the garage just as Elizabeth reached the top level, her headlights casting long, sharp shadows against the grimy walls. Alex read another message: "Take the far ramp down, full speed. Get out before she catches sight again."

Elizabeth whipped the car down the ramp, accelerating as they descended. Alex looked back, catching a glimpse of Hayes's car a level above them, searching the dim expanse for any sign of their escape. Elizabeth took the last turn wide, barely missing a concrete barrier as they shot out of the garage and back onto the street.

Alex's phone buzzed with new instructions: "Left at the next intersection, then cut through the alley behind the bakery."

Elizabeth veered left without hesitation, her focus laser-sharp. The city around them blurred into streaks of light and shadow, the narrow alleyway looming ahead. Trash bins and debris lined the path, forcing Elizabeth to maneuver tightly between obstacles. The unmarked car tried to follow but got temporarily stuck behind a slow-moving delivery van, giving them a precious few seconds to widen the gap.

As they emerged from the alley, Alex's phone buzzed again: "Go straight, then take a sharp right into the industrial yard. It's gated, but the left side is weak. You'll make it through."

Elizabeth hesitated for a split second, glancing at Alex for reassurance. "Do it," Alex urged. Elizabeth swerved into the industrial yard, the car jolting violently as they forced their way through the old, rusted gate. Metal groaned as they tore through the weakened barrier, scattering sparks and debris in their wake. They sped across the gravel lot, the car bouncing on uneven ground, narrowly dodging stacks of wooden pallets and rusted machinery.

Detective Hayes struggled to navigate the same path. The gate, now partially collapsed, slowed her down further, forcing her to choose a more cautious route. Alex looked back, watching as her headlights flickered behind layers of metal and dust.

Another message flashed: "Take the exit on your left. There's a side street that loops back toward the mall. You're almost there. She's too far back now to see you."

Elizabeth followed Mann's instructions, guiding the car out of the industrial yard and back onto a quiet, unmarked street. The unmarked car still trailed, but the distance had widened significantly. Alex's pulse

raced as the mall's silhouette appeared on the
horizon, looming large against the night sky. The
adrenaline rush was nearly unbearable, but they had
made it.

As they pulled into the parking lot, Alex's phone
buzzed one final time: "You've made it. Park under
the entry overhang. Check the bench where it all
began. The evidence is waiting." Elizabeth parked,
both of them breathing heavily, the weight of what
had just transpired sinking in.

Detective Hayes, now far behind, pulled off the
pursuit, momentarily lost in the maze of empty
streets. As Elizabeth and Alex stepped out of the car
and walked toward the familiar bench inside the
mall, a strange calm settled over them. They were
alone, but it didn't feel that way. Every step felt like
a reconnection to a past that was unraveling in the
most surreal way.

Mann watched from a distance, satisfied that the
game was still in play, Elizabeth and Alex were safe,
and that his instructions had led them exactly where
they needed to be—one step closer to uncovering
the truth about Bryan, and one step further away
from the eyes that sought to interfere.

43 What Lies Inside The Box?

Elizabeth and Alex were finally parked in the dimly lit lot, the mall looming like a silent monolith in the chilling night air. The emptiness around them amplified the surreal nature of their mission. The messages, the chase, and now, this—their unexpected arrival at the place where it all began for Bryan and Elizabeth. Alex glanced at the mall entrance, the heavy glass doors locked shut and bathed in the glow of a lone security light.

"I guess we have to break in," Alex said, half-joking but also half-serious. He glanced at Elizabeth, who looked back with a mix of determination and apprehension.

"Looks that way," she said, a nervous smile tugging at her lips. "It's not the first time I've been sneaky in a mall, but it's been a few decades."

They approached the entrance cautiously, sticking close to the wall as if they were in a high-stakes heist movie, not just a late-night rendezvous orchestrated by an unseen benefactor. Alex tried to jimmy the door handle, but it was predictably locked tight. Elizabeth fumbled in her purse, pulling out a bobby pin and a makeup brush as if she were some master lock picker. She bent the pin awkwardly, trying to work it into the door's mechanism while Alex watched, bemused.

"Are you sure you know what you're doing, Mom?" Alex whispered, biting back a laugh as Elizabeth's pin snapped in half, sending her stumbling backward.

"Of course not! But this always works in the movies," she huffed, brushing her hair back with an exasperated grin. "And I thought we'd try the direct approach before we started breaking windows."

Alex tried to stifle his laughter, but the absurdity of the situation got to him. He bent down, searching under the doormat out of sheer habit, then reached up to check the doorframe, feeling like a kid playing hide and seek. To his surprise, his fingers brushed against cold metal, and he pulled down a key that had been duct-taped there.

"You've got to be kidding me," Alex said, showing Elizabeth the key.

"Unbelievable," Elizabeth muttered, shaking her head with a mixture of disbelief and relief. "Our guy thinks of everything."

Alex slipped the key into the lock, and the door clicked open with a faint echo that sent shivers down their spines. They stepped inside, the mall's dark, empty corridors stretching out before them. Their footsteps echoed against the tiled floor, each sound amplified in the stillness of the night.

"Alright, let's find this bench," Elizabeth said, her voice bouncing off the walls. They walked through the mall, passing shuttered stores and forgotten displays that felt like remnants of another life.

Alex's phone buzzed again with a message from Mann: "Bench is near the entrance. Don't rush; you're safe."

Despite Mann's reassurance, they moved cautiously, dodging the occasional security camera and whispering to each other like two bumbling thieves. Elizabeth nearly tripped over an out-of-place mop bucket, catching herself just in time, but not before letting out a surprised yelp that echoed far too loudly. Alex couldn't help but chuckle, and Elizabeth gave him a playful shove.

"Shh! We're supposed to be stealthy," Alex joked, though his own nerves were starting to fray.

"Yeah, tell that to my ankle," Elizabeth replied with a smirk, rubbing her foot as she tried to regain her composure. Despite the tension, there was a lightness between them—an unexpected camaraderie born out of their shared clumsiness.

Finally, they arrived, and there it was: the bench where Bryan had first laid eyes on Elizabeth all those years ago. It looked exactly the same, worn but nostalgic, a simple piece of their past nestled in the heart of this now-mostly empty mall.

On the bench sat a small box, neatly wrapped in plain brown paper, and an old flip phone next to it. Alex picked up the phone, inspecting it with a mixture of curiosity and trepidation. It was a burner phone, no doubt about it, scratched and battered, but functional. Elizabeth opened the box, finding more photos and surveillance footage, some showing glimpses of Bryan in various locations, proving he was still moving, still alive.

Alex stared at the phone, a sense of foreboding creeping in. He tried entering a few random passcodes, but none worked. The phone stubbornly flashed a red "LOCKED" message each time. Elizabeth looked over his shoulder, her brow furrowing in thought.

"What about the date... our first date?" she mused aloud, staring at the phone as if willing it to unlock itself.

"October 1st, 2005," Alex said automatically. He punched in the numbers: **10012005**. The phone screen blinked, then opened up to reveal a cache of files, photos, and videos that laid everything bare.

They scrolled through images of Bryan, weary but alive, taken at various spots around town—places that held meaning to him. There were audio recordings of Bryan's voice, scattered notes he had made, and clips of him pacing in dimly lit rooms, thinking aloud about his next steps.

Alex and Elizabeth exchanged a stunned look as the realization hit them both, a mix of relief and overwhelming emotion flooding their senses.

"He's still alive," Elizabeth whimpered, her voice cracking as tears welled in her eyes. Alex nodded, his heart pounding with a renewed sense of hope, knowing this was just the beginning of the next chapter of their search for Bryan.

44 Porcine Pursuit

Leaving the mall was more harrowing than either Elizabeth or Alex anticipated when just after exiting the mall parking lot Detective Hayes caught sight of the jeep they were in and was back in pursuit. Their thoughts were as clouded as the mist outside, filled with confusion and anticipation.

 They had received D. Mann's cryptic messages, and while they managed to piece together that it referred to the mall where Elizabeth and Bryan had met, they could not fathom why this stranger was guiding them. Nor could they understand why they felt such a desperate urge to follow. As they drove, Alex's phone buzzed again, and he glanced at the screen. Another message from D. Mann. His grip tightened on the phone.

"Take the next left, you are being followed again" the text read. Alex relayed the directions to Elizabeth, who nodded and turned the wheel. "Whoever this person is, they're leading us right to Dad," Alex murmured hopefully, more to himself than to his mother.

"Or they're leading us into a trap," Elizabeth replied, her voice tinged with worry but steadied by determination. "But we have to see it through. We have to find out. They have earned that much trust."

As they continued, the messages from D. Mann came quickly and at regular intervals, guiding them through a maze of backroads, alleys, and unfamiliar neighborhoods. Detective Hayes followed close behind, her unmarked car trying to remain inconspicuous. She could feel the tension in the air, sensing that this chase was more than just a routine surveillance. She wasn't yet aware of an outside presence and their manipulations, and she had been monitoring the situation from a distance, yet as bright as she was always felt a step behind. She knew Alex and Elizabeth were in danger but wasn't certain from whom.

Another buzz. "Turn off your headlights," the next message read.

Alex hesitated but then instructed his mother. "Turn them off, Mom."

Elizabeth, skeptical but trusting, turned off the headlights, plunging them into near darkness. Only the faint glow of the moon provided any visibility.

The road became rougher, unpaved, gravel crunching under the tires. The detective hesitated, her headlights still on, trying to maintain her distance. Suddenly, Alex's phone buzzed again.

"Sharp right, now!"

Without a second thought, Elizabeth jerked the wheel sharply to the right, veering off the gravel path and onto an overgrown side trail. The car bounced and shook, branches scraping against the windows as they barreled through.

Hayes missed the turn, overshooting the exit and skidding to a halt on the gravel as her car balanced on the edge of a small, but steep ravine. She cursed under her breath, reversing, but her car wouldn't get any traction to move; Alex and Elizabeth had vanished safely into the woods.

45 ANTICIPATORY SET

Bryan sits in a borrowed hideout, a small,
dilapidated looking cabin deep in the forest, its
wooden walls lined with maps and photographs. He
stared at the glowing screen in front of him, a
patchwork of surveillance feeds and data streams.
He stumbled upon this innocuous place during a
hike, following a drone that disappeared in the area.
His brow furrowed as he pieced together the clues
about the mysterious D. Mann, the man who
seemed to have an inexplicable interest in his life
and his family's.

Bryan had been following D. Mann's trail for weeks,
using every trick he knew to access surveillance
systems, emails, and encrypted communications.
He had uncovered a complex web of influence
reaching into places he never expected—government
agencies, private corporations, and even military
contacts. Bryan realized that D. Mann had been
manipulating events in his life long before he even
knew of the man's existence.

As he watched the feeds, Bryan noticed a pattern in
Mann's communications. He saw messages that

seemed designed to provoke, guide, and, at times, confuse. There were timestamps that aligned too perfectly with key events in Bryan's recent history, suggesting that D. Mann was always one step ahead, always anticipating his moves. It was maddening, this sense of being manipulated like a piece on a chessboard.

He studied the map again, tracing lines that connected different locations. He had been to most of these places in the past month, following breadcrumbs, but every lead felt like a dead end. The surveillance photos and videos on the burner phone he had found showed glimpses of D. Mann's activities—shadowy meetings, encrypted exchanges, and clandestine rendezvous. But the man himself remained elusive, a ghost lurking in the shadows.

Bryan leaned back in his chair, rubbing his temples. He thought of Elizabeth and Alex, out there somewhere, following their own path to find him. Did they realize they were being manipulated too? Did they understand the danger they were in? Why is all of this happening? The information he had was always just short of explanation and it was frustrating to no end.

He needed to find D. Mann, to end this twisted game once and for all. He needed answers, and he needed them now. The time for the truth was here, no more procrastinating just like earlier...with confronting Bishop.

46 Back To The Beginning

(A few hours after disappearing)

Bryan stood by the river, his breath heavy in the cool night air. His mind swirled with conflicting emotions—anger, betrayal, and the crushing weight of helplessness that had defined so much of his life recently. The letter he'd left for Elizabeth and Alex felt like both an admission of defeat and a twisted act of liberation. But there was one thing he hadn't yet dealt with, one poison in his life that needed to be extracted—Bishop.

The moon hung low, casting a pale glow over the water, shimmering as the currents lapped lazily at the rocks. Bryan's mind was racing, replaying the last few months in painful flashes—Elizabeth's betrayal, the unraveling of their life together, and Bishop's looming presence, a dark specter that had crept in and torn everything apart. He felt the tension in his hands, the fury in his veins, but there was something else too. Something he hadn't felt in years. The deep, gnawing presence of something darker—a part of himself he had buried long ago.

He heard a crunch of footsteps behind him and turned to see Bishop emerging from the trees. His face, twisted in a smug grin, was barely illuminated in the soft light. Bryan could feel his blood boiling, but there was an eerie calm over him as well, like the moments before a storm.

"So, here we are," Bishop drawled, leaning heavily on his cane as he limped forward, his body hunched over from his supposed injuries. "The legendary Bryan Black. The family man, the good guy. But you and I both know better, don't we?"

Bryan said nothing, his jaw tightening as his hands clenched into fists. His eyes burned into Bishop, but something about the way he spoke was off tonight. There was a strange confidence in his voice, an arrogance Bryan hadn't ever heard before.

"You think I wanted her?" Bishop sneered, leaning in closer. "You think this was about love? About Elizabeth?"

Bryan's heart pounded in his chest. He had come here to confront the man who had stolen his wife, the man who had poisoned the life he had worked so hard to build. But now, there was something more—something sinister in Bishop's tone.

"I didn't care about her. Not really. She was just a tool, a good lay, Bryan," Bishop said, his smile widening into something cruel. "This was never about her. It was about you. It's always been about you."

Bryan's breath caught in his throat, a chill running down his spine. "What the hell are you talking about?"

Bishop's laughter was hollow, filled with bitterness. "You don't even remember, do you? You don't remember the night you ruined everything. The night you turned me into this."

Bryan blinked, confusion mixing with the anger that was starting to seethe beneath his skin. "I don't—"

"The bar," Bishop interrupted, his voice sharp and cutting. "That night at the bar. Over two decades ago. You were the bartender, weren't you? Some hero trying to protect that poor little dolled up slut who was asking for all that we could give her. You don't remember me, but I remember you. I remember your fists, your rage. The way you beat the living hell out of me and my three friends. You almost fucking killed us."

375

Bryan's stomach dropped. A flash of memory—the bar, the fight, and Kylie's screams—surged through his mind. He had been in his early twenties, working as a bartender at a dive bar. That night, a group of drunk college kids had been harassing one of the waitresses, cornering her in the back of the bar. When one of the guys hand came down hard slapping her across the face, Bryan had snapped. He'd blacked out, and by the time he came to, the damage was done. In front of him were broken bones, pools of blood, and a few teeth—he had left those men barely clinging to life. He had almost never spoken about it except as his darkest shame and only once to Liz, the memory buried so deep that it had almost disappeared into the ether of his mind.

Bishop's voice cut through the fog of the past. "You destroyed me that night. You didn't just beat me, Bryan. You crippled me. You took away my life, my future. And you don't even remember. You just moved on like nothing happened."

Bryan staggered back, his mind reeling. This couldn't be true. It wasn't possible.

"You think this limp came from a car accident?" Bishop laughed bitterly, leaning into Bryan's shock.

376

"No, that was your doing. Your righteous anger, your fists. You made me into this—this broken shell of a man. And now, after all these years, I've finally made you pay."

Bryan's throat tightened, guilt and horror swirling inside him. He had unleashed something terrible that night, something he had fought to bury ever since. But now, it had all come back to haunt him. He had become the very monster he feared—one that Bishop had been waiting to awaken.

Bishop stepped closer, his face twisted with hatred. "You took everything from me, Bryan. My body, my pride, my future. So, I took the one thing you cared about—your family. I wanted to watch you suffer, to see you brought to your knees, just like you did to me."

Bryan's hands trembled as the memories and emotions crashed over him. He had fought so hard to suppress that side of himself, to bury the rage that lived deep within him. But now, as Bishop stood before him, sneering with triumph, Bryan felt the darkness stir again. He could feel it rising, clawing its way to the surface.

"I came here to destroy you," Bishop whispered, stepping closer. "Just like you destroyed me."

Bryan's vision blurred with anger. His pulse pounded in his ears, the world narrowing to just him and Bishop. He could feel the monster inside him waking up, the same one that had taken over all those years ago. He had sworn never to let it out again, but now, he wasn't sure he could stop it.

Without thinking, Bryan lunged forward, grabbing the handgun that Bishop had tucked into his waistband. The metal felt cold in his hands, the weight of it heavy with the promise of violence. He raised it, aiming it directly at Bishop's face. But instead of pulling the trigger, he smashed the butt of the gun into Bishop's jaw, sending him sprawling to the ground.

Bishop groaned, blood spilling from his mouth as he struggled to get up. But Bryan wasn't done. He slammed the gun down again and again, the force of each blow sending shockwaves through his body. The rage inside him exploded, and for a moment, he lost himself in it. He wasn't thinking about consequences, wasn't thinking about anything except the need to make Bishop feel what he had felt for so long. Hitting him relentlessly with every ounce of anger and strength he had, Bryan was a blur of emotions turned tangible.

When he finally stopped, Bishop was lying on the ground, beaten and bloodied all over. Bryan stood over him, panting, his chest heaving with the exertion of it all. But instead of pulling the trigger, instead of finishing it, Bryan tucked the .38 into his waistband.

"You'll live," Bryan growled, his voice low and cold. "But you'll live with this. Just like you've made me live with it."

Bishop groaned, spitting blood onto the dirt as he glared up at Bryan with a mix of fear and hatred.

Bryan turned and walked away, the rage still burning inside him, but now mingled with something else—relief. He had faced the monster within him, and though he hadn't fully defeated it, he had come close. And in that moment, he knew he wouldn't let Bishop destroy him any further. He had done enough.

But as he left the river behind, Bryan knew this wasn't over. Not yet, not even close.

47 Discovery Nigh?

In his hideout, Bryan continued sifting through data. He was close, so close to uncovering D. Mann's endgame. He had managed to access a secured line that led him to what seemed like D. Mann's operational base, but he needed more confirmation. He began to trace its whereabouts. As he continued scanning through the information, something caught his eye—surveillance footage from a nearby location. He zoomed in, his heart rate spiking.

It was Elizabeth and Alex.

His mind raced. How did they get there? And why, why did they even know about this place? The last time he checked, they were miles away.

D. Mann. Of course, it had to be him. He was leading them to this very spot, to him. Bryan felt a surge of anger and fear, he wasn't ready. He needed to get away before they could find him.

Quickly, he packed up his gear, as he shut down his surveillance feed his trace dinged with a location on a nearby lake, Bryan made a note and slipped out of the cabin, moving swiftly through the forest and leaving the entrance slightly ajar.

He knew these woods well after hiking them for years, every twist and turn was like muscle memory to him. It was time to confront this D. Mann and get some answers. As for Elizabeth and Alex, this was not the time to bring them in, even though the thought of being back with them was the only positive thing left in Bryan's heart. He still needed to be able to protect and provide for them, if they even still wanted him after all this.

48 Near Miss

Alex and Elizabeth's car finally came to a halt at the end of the trail. The silence of the forest enveloped them, broken only by the distant sound of crickets. They exchanged a glance, their breaths coming in short, sharp bursts. They had evaded the detective, but they still had no idea where they were headed.

"Any more messages?" Elizabeth asked, her voice a whisper in the stillness.

Alex checked his phone. Nothing. The screen was blank. He felt a shiver run down his spine. "No... it stopped."

"Why here?" Elizabeth wondered aloud. "What's supposed to be here?"

Before they could speculate further, the phone buzzed again. Alex's hands trembled as he read the message. "Proceed on foot. Follow the path ahead."

Elizabeth took a deep breath. "I guess we have to keep going."

They stepped out of the car, the cool night air hitting their faces. They walked carefully down the path, the overgrown foliage brushing against their legs. The trail led them through dense woods, their footsteps muffled by the soft forest floor. The trees seemed to close in around them, their branches forming a canopy overhead, blocking out the moonlight. The darkness was nearly complete.

The next twenty minutes felt like hours as they walked, and just as they began to doubt the path, they saw a faint glow in the distance—a single light flickering ahead. They quickened their pace, moving toward the light, and soon found themselves standing before a clearing. In the center stood an old, abandoned building, which had at one time been a very nice hunting cabin. The front door was ajar, and the soft glow they had followed emanated from within.

Cautiously, they approached the entrance. Alex pushed the door open with a creak, and they stepped inside. The interior was empty, save for a small table in the center of the room. On the table sat a box, next to it a phone.

Alex's breath caught in his throat. "This is it," he whispered.

They walked closer, examining the box and the phone. The phone was an old model, the screen dark but not dead. Elizabeth reached for it, but Alex stopped her. "Wait... there could be something wrong here. This could be another trick." The box had CAB engraved into it, Alex's initials.

Elizabeth hesitated but nodded. "I think... it's what we're supposed to find. But what's the code?"

Alex stared at the phone, remembering Bryan's love for dates and numbers. His mind flashed back to the stories his father used to tell, the dates that meant so much. He typed in "01312010," the date of his birth.

The phone unlocked. Elizabeth let out a breath she didn't realize she was holding in. They stared at the screen, a series of files and videos began to load.

49 Setting The Table

Miles away, D. Mann sat in a dimly lit room, multiple monitors surrounding him. The glow of the screens cast shadows across his face, giving him an almost ghostly appearance as he stared at the flickering images in front of him. His fingers tapped rhythmically on the desk, a slow, deliberate beat that mirrored the calm chaos unfolding before him. His eyes were fixed on one particular screen, showing Elizabeth and Alex inside the abandoned cabin, their footsteps echoing in the small, quiet space.

They had just missed Bryan.

Mann allowed himself a small, almost imperceptible smile. "Right where I want you," he muttered under his breath. Every movement they made was a step deeper into the web he had spun around them. He had spent years monitoring this family, anticipating their every action, preparing for these moments with surgical precision. He knew Bryan better than Bryan knew himself—his unpredictable predictability, the way his instincts would lead him to this cabin, and how Elizabeth and Alex would follow. It was all part of the plan, every twist and turn engineered to bring them closer to their ultimate revelation.

Leaning back in his chair, Mann opened a secure channel on his laptop, fingers gliding across the keys with practiced ease. The command sequence blinked on the screen as he initiated a signal to his operatives stationed around the perimeter of the cabin. They had been there for hours, silent shadows blending into the forest, waiting for his orders.

The message was simple: "Do not engage unless necessary. We wait for Bryan."

One of Mann's operatives, a man only known by the codename *Jay*, moved swiftly through the dense underbrush, his footsteps silent on the forest floor. His orders had been clear, his timing crucial. As soon as Bryan had left the cabin, moving deeper into the woods, Jay had slipped inside like a wraith, planting the phone on the weathered wooden table just in time for Elizabeth and Alex to arrive. The phone, strategically placed, was loaded with exactly what Mann needed them to see—a breadcrumb leading them deeper into the labyrinth.

Jay worked with the precision of a surgeon, every movement calculated, every second accounted for. He didn't linger, knowing his presence had to remain undetected. Within moments, he had disappeared back into the shadows, blending seamlessly into the environment around him. The cabin now stood silent again, as if no one had ever been there.

Back in his control room, Mann watched it all unfold on the monitors. The placement of the phone was perfect, a small, seemingly innocuous device that would push Elizabeth and Alex further down the path he had laid out for them. He knew it would raise questions, stir suspicions—who had left it? Why? But it was a necessary part of the game, a way to manipulate their emotions, their decisions, and ultimately, their trust.

"They're getting closer," Mann muttered to himself, watching as Alex picked up the phone and began examining it, his brow furrowed in confusion. Mann could almost see the thoughts swirling in Alex's mind—Was this from Dad? Who else would have known about this place?

A flicker of excitement coursed through Mann as he leaned forward, eyes glued to the screen. The game was reaching its next crescendo, and all the movements were finally taking their places. Alex and Elizabeth were pawns, unknowingly advancing toward the inevitable confrontation, but Bryan—Bryan was the key. Mann's eyes narrowed, his anticipation building. Bryan had always been the wildcard, the unpredictable factor that made everything so thrilling.

Mann's fingers danced across the keyboard again,

pulling up a new window. He reviewed Bryan's movements from earlier that day, the trail leading deeper into the woods, the subtle changes in his patterns. There was something in Bryan's gait, the tension in his shoulders, that told Mann the man was close—closer than he had ever been—to figuring out the truth.

But Mann was always one step ahead. He had orchestrated every moment of this, leading Bryan to the precipice of discovery, only to pull him back at the last second. It was a delicate balance—letting Bryan think he had control, that he was making his own choices, when in reality, Mann had been guiding him all along. And now, with Elizabeth and Alex in the picture, the stakes had never been higher.

As the seconds ticked by, Mann opened another secure line of communication, this time sending a private message to one of his other operatives stationed closer to Bryan's last known location. "Maintain visuals. He won't be far. Stay ready."

He leaned back in his chair, a sense of satisfaction washing over him. Everything was moving according to plan. The family had no idea how deep they were in his web, how carefully he had orchestrated every twist and turn of their lives. But soon, very soon, they would understand.

And Bryan, well... Bryan was walking directly into the final act of this carefully crafted play. Mann's eyes flickered with dark amusement. It wouldn't be long now. Everything had led to this moment. The pieces were falling into place, and Mann was ready to watch it all unfold.

50 Convergence

Bryan moved through the dense undergrowth with careful steps, every sense on high alert. He had spent hours tracking the digital clues, the cryptic messages, the hints scattered through the data. Now, they had led him here—to a secluded lake house that felt oddly familiar, though he couldn't place why. The moon cast a shimmering glow across the still waters, the air heavy with the smell of pine and earth. This was the place. He could feel it in his bones.

As he approached, the front door was slightly ajar, a sliver of light seeping out into the night. Bryan pushed it open, quietly stepping into the dimly lit interior. The room was sparsely furnished—a single chair by the window, a table with a few scattered papers, and a man sitting with his back to him. The figure was still, yet there was an unmistakable tension in his posture, as though he had been waiting for this moment.

"Bryan," the man spoke, his voice calm but carrying an edge of anticipation. "I've been expecting you."

Bryan's breath hitched. That voice... he had heard it before, but not in this setting. "Who are you?" he demanded, his voice sharp, a mix of anger and confusion. "Why have you been pulling all these strings, watching me and my family? What do you want from us?"

The man turned slowly, the light catching his features, and Bryan froze. He knew that face. The sharp eyes, the lines etched by both hardship and time. Recognition dawned, and with it, a flood of memories. "David?" Bryan whispered, disbelief creeping into his tone. "David Mann?"

David nodded slowly, a small, knowing smile playing at the corner of his lips. "It's been a long time, Bryan."

Bryan felt a wave of confusion. "You... I saved you that day by the creek. What are you doing here? How are you involved in all this?"

David's expression softened as he stood and turned to face Bryan fully. "You did more than save me, Bryan. You changed the entire course of my life. When you found me that day with a gun under my chin, I had nothing left—no hope, no purpose. But you... you sat with me, you talked to me. You gave me a reason to live when I had none."

Bryan felt his chest tighten as he remembered that day vividly: the despair in David's eyes, the way he had seemed so close to the edge, and the way he had felt compelled to reach out, to offer help to a stranger.

"I just did what anyone would do," Bryan said, his voice quieter now, the anger dissipating into something more uncertain.

David shook his head. "No, Bryan. You did what *you* would do. You saw someone who needed saving and didn't think twice. And that moment... it changed everything for me. It gave me a reason to fight again. And I swore, if I ever had the chance, I'd find a way to repay you."

Bryan stared at him, piecing it together. "So, all of this... the surveillance, the texts, the messages to Elizabeth and Alex... all of it was you? Why? To repay some debt?"

David smiled, but his eyes were serious. "Not just a debt, Bryan. I realized something when I started looking into you—who you were, your background.

I found things that were buried deep, things even you didn't know about yourself."

Bryan's brows knitted together. "What do you mean?"

David took a deep breath, as if preparing himself for a revelation. "You were part of something much bigger than either of us realized. You were the sole survivor of a classified military program—an experiment to create the next evolution of humanity. Gene therapy, genetic enhancements, designed to unlock human potential in ways no one thought possible. But the project was buried, and all records were sealed—except for you."

Bryan felt a cold shiver run down his spine. "I don't... I don't understand. Why me? Why was I the one to survive?"

David stepped closer, his expression earnest. "Because you were the prototype, the first of your kind. Your DNA was unique—anomalies that made you the perfect candidate. But it wasn't just about creating a stronger or faster human. They were trying to build something more, a person who could tap into the full range of human capabilities—physically, mentally, emotionally. But something went wrong, and the project was shut down."

Bryan's mind raced, trying to process the weight of this revelation. "Then why do I feel so... ordinary? If I'm supposed to be some evolved version of humanity, why haven't I felt any different?"

David nodded, understanding the confusion. "Because it wasn't meant to happen all at once. The changes were designed to activate over time, triggered by specific conditions, environments, or even emotional states. You've felt hints of it, haven't you? Moments when you felt something... more?"

Bryan nodded slowly, memories flashing through his mind. Times when he had acted on instinct, with a clarity and strength that felt almost inhuman. He had never questioned it before, chalking it up to adrenaline or luck.

"But why watch me now?" Bryan asked. "Why involve my family?"

David's gaze softened. "Because I needed to know if you were in danger. The people who created you—there are those who want you gone, Bryan, and Alex too. Because what you both represent is a threat to the established order. Alex... he is the culmination of everything they were trying to achieve. The perfect human."

Bryan's heart clenched. "So, what? You're protecting us now?"

David's smile was small but sincere. "Yes. I've kept you safe, kept Alex safe. But there's more at stake here than just you and your family. You're a key, Bryan—a key to something far greater than any of us understand."

Bryan felt a surge of anger mixed with fear. "And you're just playing god with our lives?"

David shook his head. "No, Bryan. I'm trying to give you the choice I never had. To decide your own fate. Because you saved me, and now I'm saving you."

Bryan stood silent for a moment, processing. He realized now why he had always felt different, always felt set apart. There was a reason, a purpose behind it all. He glanced at David, who waited, patient and calm.

"What's your endgame, David?" Bryan asked quietly. "What do you really want?"

David's face grew serious, his voice low. "To make sure that you, and Alex, get the chance to be who you were meant to be. To stop those who would see you as nothing more than an experiment. You saved me, Bryan. Now it's my turn to save you."

Bryan felt a new determination settle over him. "Then we do this my way. I find my family, I protect them, and we figure out the rest together."

David nodded. "Agreed. But be ready, Bryan. The path ahead is full of shadows, and not everyone wants you to see the light."

Bryan took a deep breath, his resolve hardening. He had been searching for answers, for direction, and now he had both. He was ready to face whatever came next, and with his family in mind, he knew exactly what he had to do.

As he turned to leave, David called out, "Remember, Bryan... you're not just a man. You're something more. Never forget that. One day soon I hope to help you unlock that potential. Take this drive with you and review it. There are some good leads on there for you to follow. I will be in contact soon."

Bryan nodded, feeling the weight of those words as he stepped out into the night, his heart steadily beating, and his mind clear. He had a mission now, a purpose. And nothing would stand in his way.

51 Re-emergence

As Bryan stepped out of the lake house, the cold night air hit him like a wave, carrying with it the scent of pine and the faint rustling of leaves. The moon hung high in the sky, casting long shadows across the ground, shadows that stretched and twisted like the doubts still lingering in his mind. But for the first time in a long time, those doubts felt more like challenges to overcome than insurmountable barriers. He had spent too many years feeling lost, drifting from one mistake to another, burdened by the weight of choices that felt out of his control. But now, everything had changed.

He had a purpose. And it wasn't just about finding himself anymore—it was about protecting his family, uncovering the truth, and facing the unknown forces that had manipulated his life from behind the scenes. Bryan felt the adrenaline coursing through his veins, a sharp contrast to the cold air that bit at his skin. He was no longer a pawn in someone else's game; he was taking control of his destiny.

The ground crunched beneath his boots as he walked, every step measured, deliberate. His thoughts raced ahead, forming plans, contingencies. He knew the path ahead would not be straightforward. David had warned him that there were shadows lurking—men and entities that wanted to see him and Alex eliminated, to erase any trace of what they represented. But Bryan wasn't afraid. If anything, the knowledge of danger brought a clarity he hadn't felt in years.

He thought of Alex, the son who had always felt like both his greatest achievement and his deepest mystery. Alex was more than just his child; he was the culmination of something extraordinary, a living testament to the possibilities Bryan had never understood. The boy was still so young, yet he held within him the potential to become something unprecedented. Bryan realized that he had spent too much time focusing on his own failures, his own inadequacies, and not enough on the extraordinary potential that lay within his son. Alex needed him now, more than ever, and Bryan was determined to be the father he had always aspired to be, even if it meant facing the shadows of his past.

He thought of Elizabeth next. The love of his life, the woman who had broken his heart, and yet... she was also the person who had shown him what it meant to love fiercely, to feel alive. He had spent so much time blaming her for the pain, for the betrayal, for the distance that had grown between them. But now, he could see that their story wasn't over. The anger had begun to fade, replaced by a determination to find a way back to each other—not just for their sake, but for Alex's as well. She had made her mistakes, just as he had made his, but they were both bound by something deeper than either had realized. And if David's words were true, if there were forces at play trying to tear them apart, then they had to come together now more than ever.

Bryan felt a surge of determination swell in his chest. The weight of the past few days, the confusion, the revelations—they all sharpened his focus. He had always believed that he was destined for something, but now he understood that his destiny was not something to be found, but something to be shaped. He thought of the people he had helped over the years, the lives he had touched without even realizing it. Every one of those moments had prepared him for this. They had made him strong, compassionate, willing to fight for others even when he couldn't find a reason to fight for himself. And now, it was time to fight for his family.

His mind turned to the enemies David had spoken of—the shadowy figures who wanted him erased. Who were they? What did they know about him that he didn't? He could feel their presence like a distant storm on the horizon, their intentions hidden but unmistakably threatening. He would need to find them before they found him, and he would need to understand exactly what he was up against. His skills, his instincts, his resilience—all of it would be tested in the days to come. But that was fine by him. For once, he felt alive, truly alive, and every fiber of his being was ready for whatever lay ahead.

Bryan reached the edge of the clearing, his gaze drifting back toward the lake house one last time. He could see David watching him from the window, a silhouette framed by the soft glow of the interior light. For all his ruthlessness, all his mysterious machinations, David had helped him find the path forward. Bryan nodded once, a silent acknowledgment of the strange alliance they had formed, before turning away and plunging back into the forest.

The trees closed in around him, their branches reaching out like skeletal fingers. The trail was narrow and uneven, but Bryan moved with a new sense of purpose. He knew he had to move quickly—time was of the essence, and there was so much he needed to do. He needed to find Alex and Elizabeth, to explain everything, to prepare them for what was coming. They needed to understand the stakes, to know that this was bigger than just their family drama or his disappearance. This was about survival, about facing down the very forces that had shaped their lives in ways they had never imagined.

He paused for a moment, catching his breath, his mind racing with the implications of everything David had told him. There were so many questions still unanswered, so many pieces of the puzzle still missing. But Bryan knew that he couldn't afford to wait for all the answers to come to him. He had to act. He had to move forward, to keep pushing, keep searching. The answers would come in time, and when they did, he would be ready.

Bryan continued down the path, his thoughts returning to the task at hand. He needed to make contact with Elizabeth and Alex, but he couldn't risk using any of the usual channels. He knew they were being watched, their every move monitored. David had shown him just how deep the surveillance went, how far the reach of their enemies extended. He needed a secure line, a way to reach them without tipping off anyone who might be listening. He would have to be smart, to think like the enemy, to stay one step ahead.

But that was fine by him. Bryan had spent years honing his instincts, learning how to read people, how to anticipate their moves. He had always been good at seeing the angles, at finding the hidden paths. And now, he would put those skills to the ultimate test. He would find his family, and together, they would face whatever was coming.

As he emerged from the forest, the distant sound of traffic reached his ears. He could see the faint glow of city lights on the horizon, a reminder of the world he was fighting to protect. For the first time in a long time, he felt a sense of hope. He didn't know exactly what the future held, but he knew one thing for certain—he would not let his family go without a fight.

Bryan quickened his pace, his thoughts clear, his heart steady. He had a mission now, a purpose. And he knew that whatever lay ahead, he would face it head-on, with courage and determination. He was ready to fight for his family, to protect them from whatever shadows were lurking in the darkness. He would uncover the truth, no matter the cost, and he would ensure that they had the chance to live the lives they were meant to live.

As he stepped onto the edge of the highway, he looked up at the stars above, feeling a strange sense of calm settle over him. He knew the road ahead would be difficult, filled with danger and uncertainty. But he also knew that he was not alone. He had his family, his purpose, and his newfound knowledge of who he truly was. And with that, he felt an unshakeable confidence that they would make it through this, together.

He began to walk, his steps firm and resolute. The journey was far from over, but Bryan Black was ready for whatever came next. The shadows would not claim him or his family. He would ensure that they found the light, no matter how deep the darkness became. For the first time in years, he felt truly alive. And he knew, deep in his heart, that this was just the beginning.

52 Proof Of Life

Elizabeth and Alex leaned in closer, their faces illuminated by the cold blue glow of the phone screen. The videos load slowly, the small spinning wheel taunting them as they wait. Elizabeth's heart pounded in her chest; she could feel it in her throat, a steady drumming that seemed to echo the anticipation in the room. Alex's hands trembled slightly as he held the phone, his fingers tightening around it like it might slip away, taking all the answers with it.

The first video finally opened. The screen flickered, and they saw Bryan, looking thinner and more worn than Elizabeth had ever seen him. His eyes, normally filled with a quiet resolve, seemed clouded with an exhaustion that was almost palpable. He was sitting in a dimly lit room, the walls behind him bare, a single light casting long shadows on his face. He took a deep breath before speaking, his voice low and rough, as if it had been scraped against something sharp.

"I don't know who will find this... or if anyone ever will," Bryan began, his gaze not quite meeting the camera.

"But if you're watching, it means you've come far enough to know that things aren't what they seem. I'm sorry for all the secrets, for all the things I couldn't say... especially to you, Alex... Elizabeth."

Elizabeth's breath caught in her throat. She could feel Alex's eyes on her, but she couldn't look away from the screen. Bryan's voice was like a knife, cutting through the fog of confusion that had settled over her since he disappeared.

"I know it's been hell," Bryan continued, his expression shifting to something softer, more pained.

"Believe me, I didn't plan for any of this. But there are forces at play here—things I never understood until it was too late. People I trusted... people I thought I knew."

He paused, glancing away as if searching for the right words. "There's a lot you still don't know, but there's one person you should look for. D. Mann. He has the answers, more than I ever did."

Alex's grip on the phone tightened. "He knows D. Mann," he whispered, as if testing the words on his tongue. "He's been in touch with him. Why?"

Elizabeth shook her head, her mind racing. "I don't know. But if Bryan says he has answers, we have to find him. We have to know why D. Mann is involved in all of this."

The next video began to play automatically, and they saw Bryan again, this time sitting by a lake, the wind ruffling his hair. He looked calmer, more at peace. "I've been running for a long time," he said, his voice quieter now, almost a whisper. "Running from the truth, from my past, from... myself. But I can't keep doing it. I need to find out why I've always felt like an outsider in my own life, why I never quite fit in, even with those I loved the most." He swallowed hard, his eyes finally meeting the camera. "I need to know if it's in my blood, if it's something I can or maybe can't control... or if it's just me. Just who I am."

Elizabeth felt a lump form in her throat, a sensation that grew tighter with each second as she watched the video. She had never seen Bryan so vulnerable, so raw, stripped of the usual stoic armor he wore like a second skin. This was a side of him she had almost forgotten existed, buried under years of distance, resentment, and unspoken pain.

She thought back to the beginning, when they first met—Bryan, with his quiet confidence, his intense eyes that seemed to see straight through her, his ability to make her feel understood in a way no one ever had. She remembered the light in his smile, the way he would laugh from his belly when something truly delighted him, how he'd hold her in the night and promise her a lifetime of love. Those were the good years, the years when they felt invincible, like they could take on the world and come out stronger, together.

But then, slowly, that light had started to dim. She could see it now, in hindsight, how he had begun to build walls around himself, one brick at a time. The financial struggles had come first, creeping in like an unseen shadow, slowly squeezing the joy out of their lives. Then the quiet frustrations that grew louder, their conversations turning into arguments, and their silences becoming longer, more suffocating. She could remember the days he would come home, his face clouded with a weariness that no amount of sleep could cure, and she would feel an inexplicable pang of fear, as if some invisible hand was slowly prying them apart. She would watch him retreat further and further into himself, escaping into long hours of work, side projects, and eventually, isolation.

Elizabeth felt a shiver pass through her as she remembered the nights she would lie awake next to him, her heart aching with a loneliness that should have been impossible lying beside the person she loved most. Bryan had become an enigma, a stranger she could no longer reach. She knew he was hurting, but he never let her in—not fully. He had always been the strong one, the protector, the one who held everything together even as the world seemed determined to tear them apart. And yet, here he was in this video, a man she barely recognized—fragile, broken yet together, and yet somehow more human than she had ever seen him.

It was like he had peeled back all the layers he had built around himself, exposing the fragile core he had always tried to hide. For the first time, she saw not just the man who had stood by her side, not just the man who had fought for their family, but the man who had fought battles within himself, alone, in silence. She saw the pain he carried, the fear that perhaps he was not enough, that he would never be enough, that the people he loved most would eventually see through the cracks and walk away.

She realized, with a heavy heart, that she had never truly seen him before—at least, not like this. She had never understood the depth of his struggle, the weight of his loneliness. She had been too busy nursing her own wounds and traumas that she didn't want to deal with, too focused on her own sense of betrayal and anger, to see that Bryan was drowning; how long had his head been barely above water.

And now, seeing him this way, his beautiful soul laid bare and open, she felt a profound sense of guilt wash over her. She had been a major part of his pain and anguish, a beautiful yet burning thread woven into the tapestry of his suffering, and now she was left wondering if she had ever really known him, the real him at all.

Tears filled her eyes as she realized that this version of Bryan, the one in the video, was not just a broken man—he was a man who had fought like hell against forces she still didn't fully understand, against a mysterious destiny he had never asked for. And as the screen went dark, Elizabeth's heart ached with a mix of regret and a fierce, sudden clarity of mind, body, and spirit: she had to find him. She had to help him, somehow. And more than that, she had to know him again, this man who had given so much of himself, only to be left with so little. She wasn't going to lose him—not again, not like this.

"There's a place I have to go," Bryan continued, "a place that might have the answers I'm looking for. If you're watching this, it means I'm either closer than ever to what I'm looking for... or I'm gone. But know this: I never stopped loving you. Either of you. And I never will."

The video cut off abruptly, leaving the screen black. Elizabeth felt a tear slide down her cheek, but she didn't wipe it away. Alex was silent beside her, his face a mix of anger, confusion, and something else—something that looked a lot like hope.

53 Learning To Play

"We need to find him," Alex said finally, his voice barely more than a whisper. "He's out there somewhere, looking for answers. And we're the only ones who can help him find them."

Elizabeth nodded, her resolve hardening with each passing second. "We will," she said, her voice firmer this time. "But we need to start with D. Mann. If Bryan says he has the answers, then that's where we go next."

Just as she spoke, the phone buzzed in Alex's hand, its screen lighting up with a new message. Both of them leaned in closer, tension running through their bodies as they read the cryptic words: *You're not done yet. Meet me where you learned to play and don't forget a golf ball.*

Elizabeth's eyes widened, her heart skipping a beat as she turned to Alex. "What does that mean?" she asked, her voice tinged with urgency, a sense of foreboding creeping into her chest. "Where did you learn to play?"

Alex furrowed his brow, his mind racing back through the years, sifting through memories of his childhood, trying to grasp at the meaning. Then, like a lightbulb switching on, his eyes lit up with sudden understanding. "It's where Dad first taught me to play," he said, his voice soft at first, as if he were speaking more to himself than to his mother. "That having fun could be sweaty, and that he would always be there to pick me up. We used to go there every chance we got when I was little. The playground behind the library."

Elizabeth glanced at her son, seeing not just the boy she had raised but the man he was becoming. There was an intensity in his voice, a quiet strength that reminded her so much of Bryan. Her breath caught for a moment as memories flashed through her mind—images of Bryan standing over Alex on the playground, showing him how to swing a bat for the first time, teaching him how to throw a football, how to ride a bike. Bryan had always been there for Alex, unwavering and steady, even when everything else seemed to fall apart. But now Bryan was the one who needed them, and it was their turn to be his anchor, to find him before he slipped away entirely.

As he spoke, Alex's mind traveled back to those carefree summer afternoons, the ones where time seemed to stretch on endlessly, where nothing mattered except the thrill of running and playing until his muscles ached. He remembered the sound of his dad's laughter ringing out across the grassy field, the way Bryan would call out encouragement from the sidelines. "Good job, buddy! Keep going, you've got this!" He remembered how Bryan would scoop him up when he fell, dusting him off and setting him right back on his feet, no matter how many times he stumbled. It was at that playground where Alex first learned that mistakes didn't matter, that it was the getting back up that counted.

Elizabeth nodded slowly, her own memories intertwining with Alex's. A small smile tugged at the corners of her lips, breaking through the tension that had weighed her down for so long. "Of course," she murmured, her voice full of nostalgia. "I remember... Bryan always said that's where you really learned to play." She closed her eyes for a moment, letting the memories wash over her—the sight of Bryan holding Alex's tiny hand, guiding him through the swings and slides, his face lit up with pride every time Alex mastered something new. "It makes sense," she whispered, more to herself than to Alex.

The urgency of their situation quickly returned, though, and Alex straightened up, his body filled with a renewed sense of purpose. "We need to get there," he said, standing up abruptly. The gravity of their mission pressed down on them once again, but this time there was a spark of hope. "Whatever it is, it's important."

Elizabeth quickly grabbed her keys, and they hurried out the door, a sense of determination pushing them forward. But just as they stepped outside, Alex's phone buzzed again. They exchanged a glance before he unlocked the screen, revealing yet another message—this one far more cryptic: *"Be careful. You're not the only ones watching."*

A shiver ran down Elizabeth's spine. She looked at Alex, her breath hitching slightly. The calm resolve that had carried them this far began to waver, replaced by a growing sense of unease. "What do you think it means?" she asked quietly, though she already had a gnawing suspicion in her gut.

Alex's jaw tightened as he re-read the message, his mind racing. He had known for some time now that they weren't alone in this, that someone else—whether it was D. Mann or someone else entirely—was pulling strings behind the scenes. But the reminder that they were being watched, tracked even, sent a fresh wave of anxiety coursing through him.

"I don't know," he muttered, shoving the phone back into his pocket. He forced himself to breathe, to focus on the task at hand. "But we need to stay sharp. Whoever's watching us... they're not going to stop."

Elizabeth nodded, her mind flashing back to the cabin, to the phone that had been waiting for them.

Someone had been there, someone who knew they were coming, and now this message only solidified that feeling. She swallowed hard, her throat dry as the reality of their situation settled in. They weren't just searching for Bryan anymore; they were being guided, manipulated.

"Let's go," she said, her voice steady, though her insides churned with fear. She unlocked the car, the tension between them palpable as they both climbed in, the weight of the unknown pressing down on them. They had to keep moving, and had to find Bryan before it was too late.

As they drove, the silence in the car was heavy, punctuated only by the hum of the engine and the sound of the wind rushing past the windows. The landscape around them blurred, trees and buildings flashing by as they sped toward the playground, their minds both racing with the possibilities of what they might find.

But even as they pushed forward, a lingering sense of dread hung in the air. They weren't the only ones in this game, and it was becoming clearer with every step they took. The stakes had just been raised, and now, they were playing for more than just answers—they were playing for their lives.

54 A Shadow on the Playground At Night

The Jeep's engine hummed softly as Alex and Elizabeth drove away from the hunting cabin, the tension between them palpable. They were en route to the playground behind the library, guided by the latest cryptic message from D. Mann. The road stretched out before them, illuminated intermittently by the Jeep's headlights that cut through the dense night. The darkness outside was a stark contrast to the light of hope that flickered within them. It was as though they were journeying not only through space but also through time, back to a place imbued with memories and meaning.

As they drove, Alex's mind wandered to the playground—a place that had once been a sanctuary of joy and innocence. It was a location of countless weekend mornings spent with Bryan, a time before the complexities and pain of their current situation had set in. His thoughts were filled with vivid memories of the playground, bringing a rare smile to his face amidst the tension of their quest.

He glanced sideways at Elizabeth, who was driving with a determined look on her face, and felt a pang of nostalgia mixed with an aching sadness. The playground was not just a location but a symbol of the untroubled times they had once shared as a family.

The playground had been more than just a place for Alex; it had been a venue of learning and bonding with Bryan. He remembered the joy of climbing the big slides, the thrill of sliding down with the wind in his face, and the laughter that echoed through the park. Bryan had made these moments special, teaching Alex that having fun could be a full-body experience, one that left them sweaty and exhilarated. It was where Bryan had shown him that fun was not just about play but about connecting with the world in a meaningful way.

Elizabeth, aware of Alex's reflective mood, kept her eyes on the road but noticed the faraway look in his eyes. She knew that the playground held a deep emotional significance for both of them. It was where Bryan had imparted lessons beyond mere play—lessons about the importance of family, the joy of shared experiences, and the value of being present in each other's lives. Those early mornings at the playground had been a foundation for their family's bond, a bond that had since been strained and tested.

As they approached the library, Alex's thoughts continued to roam through the corridors of his memory. He recalled how Bryan had encouraged him to climb higher on the jungle gym, how he had cheered him on as he attempted to swing higher and higher. Those were the days when the world seemed to revolve around simple joys and shared victories, and Bryan's unwavering support had made every success feel monumental.

Elizabeth parked the Jeep near the playground, and the two of them stepped out into the cool night air. The playground was bathed in the soft glow of street lamps, casting long shadows that danced across the swings and slides. The familiar structures seemed almost magical in the moonlight, their outlines shimmering with a quiet, nostalgic allure. The quiet of the night was a stark contrast to the vibrant energy that had once filled this space.

Alex led the way, his footsteps echoing on the pavement as he approached the central play area. The sight of the big slide brought a rush of memories, and he felt a bittersweet pang in his chest. He could almost hear the echoes of their laughter, the cheers of triumph as they raced to the top of the slide, and the comforting presence of Bryan beside him. It was a place that had once been a haven, now transformed into a site of hope and trepidation.

Elizabeth followed closely, her gaze scanning the playground as if trying to reconnect with the past through the present. She had her own memories of this place, of seeing Alex and Bryan enjoying their time together. It had been a rare but precious time when everything seemed simpler and more straightforward. As she looked around, she felt a mix of gratitude and sadness, knowing that these memories were both a comfort and a reminder of what had been lost.

As they reached the bench where the message had directed them, they noticed the stillness of the playground. It felt almost as though time had stood still, holding its breath as they awaited the next phase of their journey. The bench was empty, but there was a palpable sense of anticipation in the air. Alex and Elizabeth exchanged a glance, their expressions reflecting a blend of hope and apprehension.

Alex sat down on the bench, his fingers absentmindedly tracing the grooves in the worn wood, each ridge and scratch a silent witness to years of children coming and going, of memories etched into its surface. He closed his eyes for a moment, letting the sounds of the playground wash over him, though the laughter of children had long since faded. In its place, there was only the soft whisper of the wind rustling through the trees, the creaking of the swings in the distance, and the echo of a time when life was simpler, before everything became so complicated.

He could almost hear Bryan's voice again, that familiar tone of encouragement and warmth, urging him to enjoy the moment, to soak in the pure joy of being a child without a care in the world. *"Don't rush through life, buddy,"* Bryan had said more times than Alex could count. *"Enjoy it. There's magic in the small things—like climbing that wall or making it to the top of the net."*

The climbing net was still there, frayed at the edges but standing strong, just like it had all those years ago. Alex remembered how he used to scramble up the ropes, his small hands gripping tightly as Bryan cheered him on from below. There had been a thrill in reaching the top, that sense of accomplishment when he finally touched the highest point. He'd look down at Bryan, proud of himself, and Bryan's smile would widen, as though Alex had conquered a mountain instead of a playground structure.

The slides had been his second favorite—the long yellow one that twisted around, and the shorter, steep one that felt like a drop straight into the earth. He had a memory of Bryan standing at the bottom, arms outstretched, waiting to catch him if he came down too fast. "Go ahead, kiddo! I've got you!" And Alex, never doubting for a second that his dad would be there, would push himself off the edge and fly down, laughing as the wind rushed past him. Sometimes, when no one was looking, he and the other kids would run up the slides the wrong way, daring each other to make it to the top before someone noticed. Bryan would always catch them in the act and shout playfully, *"You're supposed to go down the slides, not up! Get down here before you break your neck!"*

Then there were the tunnels—the maze of plastic that twisted beneath the playground like secret passageways. Alex would crawl through them, pretending he was on an adventure, sometimes hiding from Bryan for fun. He could picture Bryan now, crouching down, peeking through the openings, pretending to search for him. *"Where's Alex? Is he in here?"* Bryan would call, feigning confusion, only to finally "discover" him and tickle him until they were both laughing so hard it hurt.

Alex's memories drifted to the times they spent with sidewalk chalk, covering the concrete paths in bright, messy drawings of suns, flowers, and random scribbles. Bryan was always right there with him, drawing stick figures of their family or helping Alex sketch out the outlines of imaginary worlds. They'd spend hours drawing together, Alex's imagination running wild, while Bryan made sure to leave room for every idea Alex had, no matter how silly or impossible.

But there was one memory that stood out above the rest—standing in the swings, daring himself to balance like an acrobat while Bryan stood nearby, ready to catch him if he fell. Alex had always loved the thrill of it, of pushing boundaries just a little, knowing that Bryan was always there, steady and dependable, never letting him stray too far or fall too hard.

Now, as Alex sat there, his fingers tracing the familiar bench, he felt the weight of those memories pressing down on him. This playground had been a place of laughter, of pure childhood joy, and it had been *their* place—his and Bryan's. Now, it was something more, something heavier. The message from D. Mann had led them here, but this playground wasn't just a clue in their search for Bryan; it was a thread that tied them to their past, to everything they had once been before their family had started to unravel.

Elizabeth was pacing nearby, her worry clear, but Alex was lost in thought, in the memories of sidewalk chalk and slides, of childhood mischief and the safety that Bryan had always provided. The playground had been more than just a place to play. It had been a place where Alex had learned to trust, to push limits, to believe that his father would always be there for him. And now, they were here again, hoping that this place would lead them back to Bryan, hoping that it still held some of that magic they had both believed in all those years ago.

As Alex stared out at the familiar structures, worn with time but still standing, he felt that surge of determination he hadn't felt in a long time. This playground was a symbol of their bond, and it was here, in the place where he had learned to play, that he would start the search for his father. This was where it had to begin, because this place had always been where Bryan had shown him how to get back up, how to keep going no matter what.

Elizabeth took a seat beside him, her eyes scanning the surroundings as if expecting something to materialize from the shadows. The playground, once a place of carefree play, had become a key to unraveling the complex web of their current situation. She felt a surge of determination, knowing that their quest was far from over, but also sensing that the playground held clues that could lead them closer to the truth.

As they waited in the quiet of the night, the distant sounds of the town seemed to fade away, leaving only the soft whispers of the wind and the occasional creak of the playground equipment. The sense of anticipation grew, and Alex and Elizabeth remained alert, ready for whatever would come next. The playground had been a place of joy and connection in their past, and now it stood as a beacon of hope in their quest for answers.

The minutes ticked by slowly, each one stretching into what felt like an eternity. Alex and Elizabeth's thoughts were a mix of past memories and present concerns, their minds racing with questions about the next steps and the true purpose of their journey. The playground had been a place of learning and growth for Alex, a place where he had learned to embrace life's adventures with a sense of wonder and excitement. Now, it was a place of waiting and hoping, a bridge between their past and the unknown future that lay ahead.

He remembered the giant climbing net, where he had spent hours scaling the ropes with Bryan cheering him on, guiding him through the tangle of challenges until he reached the top, triumphant and breathless. There had been days when the two of them would chalk the sidewalks with colorful designs, covering the ground in a kaleidoscope of dragons, castles, and winding roads, their imaginations running wild. Alex recalled the times when they raced each other up the ladder of the tallest slide, Bryan letting him win more often than not, just so he could feel the rush of victory. The way they'd collapse in the grass, exhausted, their laughter filling the air.

This place had been their sanctuary—a retreat from the world where father and son could bond without the complications of life. It wasn't just a playground. It was where Alex learned to play in the true sense of the word, where Bryan had taught him that play was more than just fun. It was about resilience, about getting back up after a fall, about pushing through the sweat and the scrapes because the reward was the joy they found together. Bryan had been a constant presence, always ready to pick him up if he stumbled, always pushing him to climb higher, slide faster, dream bigger.

Elizabeth watched Alex from the corner of her eye, her own memories flooding back. This was the place where Bryan had brought them together as a family, encouraging her to join in the fun even on days when life felt too overwhelming. She remembered Bryan's arms around her as they watched Alex race from one end of the playground to the other, his energy seemingly endless. Bryan's reassuring words, whispered in her ear, had reminded her that they could still find happiness even in the midst of chaos. Those moments felt like a lifetime ago, before everything had fallen apart.

As Alex stared down at the bench, the weight of their current situation pressed heavily on him. The playground, once a symbol of carefree days, now carried the burden of their search for answers, for Bryan, for closure. He could feel the echoes of his past mingling with the uncertainty of the present. What had once been a haven of childhood joy now felt like the site of something far more ominous. The golf ball that had rolled to their feet moments ago was not just a token of their shared history—it was a signpost, a message from someone who understood the importance of this place, who knew their connection to it and was using that knowledge to lead them.

As the night deepened and the minutes ticked closer to the meet, the playground remained a silent witness to their journey—a place where the echoes of their past mingled with the anticipation of what was to come. Alex and Elizabeth stayed vigilant, their eyes and ears tuned to any sign of movement or change. The playground, with its familiar structures and hauntingly quiet atmosphere, was both a reminder of what they had lost and a symbol of the hope that still guided them forward.

A single gold colored golf ball came rolling across the playground, coming to a stop directly in front of Elizabeth and Alex as they both watched in stunned silence, their gaze following the ball's trajectory back to see a man standing across the playground—D. Mann.

55 LEFT IN THE DUST

Detective Sarah Hayes trudged down the darkened
road, each step echoing her mounting frustration
and fatigue. Her breath came in heavy bursts,
uneven and sharp, her chest heaving as she
struggled to keep her emotions in check. The Jeep
that had sped past her earlier had left a cloud of
gravel dust clinging to her clothes and skin, and she
cursed under her breath as she wiped the grit from
her face, feeling the rough sting of it against her
already raw skin.

Her eyes flicked down to her phone for the
hundredth time. Still no signal. The word
"Searching..." blinked mockingly on the screen, as if
it were taunting her helplessness. The silence from
her cell felt louder than the whisper of the wind, an
unsettling reminder of just how isolated she was. No
backup. No contact. Just an endless stretch of dark
road.

And that Jeep—Alex and Elizabeth's Jeep. She knew
it. The rumble of its engine was unmistakable, the
headlights a familiar blur in the night. They had
been headed somewhere, moving toward answers,
and she was stranded, left behind like an

afterthought. It gnawed at her insides, a bitter resentment building in her chest. They were chasing down leads, possibly getting closer to Bryan, while she was stuck on foot, miles away, useless.

She kicked a rock violently off the road, sending it skittering into the underbrush with a harsh thud. "Damn it," she muttered, the words laced with a mixture of anger and helplessness. The case had unraveled into a twisted mess, with every thread she pulled either snapping or leading to another knot of confusion. Just when she thought she was onto something, it would slip through her fingers like smoke. The whole investigation was turning into a maze, each lead a dead-end or another layer of misdirection.

Hayes clenched her fists, the leather of her gloves creaking with the tension. Her training told her to remain calm, that frustration would only cloud her judgment, but the constant setbacks were pushing her closer to the edge. She had been following this case for weeks now, pouring over every detail, every scrap of evidence, and still, she felt as if she were missing something vital, something that tied all these chaotic pieces together.

D. Mann. His name alone was enough to make her skin crawl. He was a ghost, lurking in the shadows of this investigation, manipulating events from behind the scenes. The more she uncovered about him, the more questions arose. Who was he really? What did he want with Bryan, with the Black family? The deeper she dug, the more it felt like a trap, as though she were being led in circles, always just one step behind. And now, stuck in the middle of nowhere, it felt as if that circle was tightening around her, pulling her deeper into the unknown.

She thought back to the Jeep, to Alex and Elizabeth speeding away. Had they known she was there? Had they left her on purpose? The idea seemed absurd, but still, it nagged at her. There was no mistaking the look of desperation in their eyes the last time she'd seen them. They were following their own lead, running towards something. Bryan? Maybe. Or maybe they were running from something—something bigger than all of them.

She couldn't shake the feeling that she was being watched. The road was quiet, too quiet, the air thick with a sense of unease. The trees loomed like silent sentinels on either side, their branches swaying slightly in the night breeze. Hayes turned, glancing over her shoulder, but saw nothing. Just darkness. Still, the sensation lingered, a prickling at the back of her neck that she couldn't quite shake. Her gut told her that someone was out there, someone who had been keeping tabs on them all along. D. Mann? Possibly. Whoever it was, they were one step ahead. Always one step ahead.

She shifted her focus back to the road, her frustration bubbling just beneath the surface. If only she could get a damn signal, she could call for backup, could catch up with Alex and Elizabeth before they stumbled into something they weren't prepared for. But the phone remained a useless brick in her hand. She cursed again, louder this time, her patience wearing thin. Her whole body ached with exhaustion, her legs heavy, but she pushed forward, determined not to let her own limitations stop her. She was a detective, for God's sake. She had worked her way up through sheer grit, cracking tough cases that had left other officers stumped. But this... this was different. This was personal.

The Black family's tragedy had wormed its way under her skin in a way she hadn't expected. Maybe it was Bryan's desperation, or Elizabeth's quiet strength, or Alex's determination to piece it all together—whatever it was, it had hooked her. This wasn't just another case to solve; it was something more. And she was closing in on something, she could feel it. But what? That was the real question. The answer felt just out of reach, as if she were walking through fog, grasping at shadows.

She kept walking, the road stretching on endlessly before her, each step bringing her closer to the faint glow of the town ahead. Relief swelled in her chest at the sight of the distant lights, but it was fleeting. There was still so much she didn't understand, so much she had yet to uncover. D. Mann was at the center of it all, she was sure of that. But what did he want? What was his endgame? And how did Bryan fit into all of this?

Her mind raced with possibilities as the town lights grew brighter. She had to get back to the investigation, had to get answers before it was too late. The weight of the unanswered questions pressed down on her, tightening around her chest like a vice. But she pushed on, her jaw clenched, her fists still balled at her sides. She wouldn't let this case beat her. Not now. Not when she was so close.

Hayes picked up her pace, determination burning in her veins. She didn't have all the pieces yet, but she had enough to know she was heading in the right direction. Answers were just beyond the horizon, and she was going to find them—one way or another.

56 SHADOWS REVEALED

The playground lay still under the veil of darkness, the quiet only broken by the distant murmur of the city and the occasional rustling of leaves. Alex and Elizabeth sat on a weathered wooden bench, the tension palpable between them. Their earlier revelations from the burner phone had left them anxious and on edge. As they waited, their thoughts swirled with uncertainty and anticipation.

The sudden appearance of the golf ball rolling across the playground caught Alex's attention. It moved with a deliberate purpose, coming to a stop right at their feet. The sight was almost surreal, an odd prelude to what was unfolding before them. Both Alex and Elizabeth watched in silence as the ball rested motionless, a foreboding signal of what was to come.

It wasn't long before a figure emerged from the shadows on the far side of the playground. The man's silhouette was imposing, his movements deliberate and measured. As he drew closer, Alex and Elizabeth could make out more of his features.

The man's presence commanded attention, and there was an air of authority about him.

Alex shifted uncomfortably, his instincts telling him that this meeting was critical. "Elizabeth, mom..." he murmured, his voice barely above a whisper, "we have company."

Elizabeth turned to see the figure approaching. She stood up quickly ready to run or to fight, her expression a mixture of apprehension and resolve. Her hand instinctively moved towards her gun, but she hesitated, sensing that this encounter was different from others and this person had been helping them.

The imposing man finally stepped into the weak light of the streetlamp, revealing his face. He was a tall, rugged individual with a look of intense focus. Alex stared at him, trying to place where he might have seen him before. The man's features were etched with a depth of emotion that spoke of countless burdens carried and secrets held.

"Alex. Elizabeth." the man asked, his voice smooth and authoritative, yet carrying an undertone of familiarity.

Alex's heart raced. "Yes, that's us. Who are you?"

The man's eyes softened, and he smiled faintly. "I'm David, or you might better recognize me as D. Mann, from Bryan's research. I've been waiting to meet you both in person for a very long time. It's good to finally meet you."

Elizabeth's eyebrows furrowed in confusion. "David? The name sounds familiar, why...but I don't—"

David interrupted gently. "I understand, Elizabeth. You don't know me, but I know a lot about you. I've been involved, hidden in the shadows, trying to protect Bryan, Alex, and you."

Alex's mind raced, trying to make sense of David's words. "You've been protecting us? How? Why?"

David nodded, his expression growing more serious. "I was the David that Bryan saved years ago. You see, Bryan's impact on my life was immense and profound. I owe him a great deal, more than I will ever be able to repay and now I'm here in this dark time to return the favor. I've been working behind the scenes, trying to keep you all safe and to protect both Bryan and Alex from those who wish to exploit their potential."

Elizabeth's eyes widened, realization dawning on her. "You were the person Bryan saved from suicide. How did you end up being involved in all this?"

David's gaze grew distant, as if reflecting on past events. "After Bryan helped me, I wanted to make something of my life, to remake it for the better. My background was in both military and business, but Bryan saving me changed my trajectory towards helping others. When I learned the information you two are about to learn and the looming threats against your family I couldn't stand by. I had to act and I have been doing that for years now."

Alex's skepticism was evident. "So, you're saying you've been involved with some sort of secret organization to protect us?"

David sighed, clearly burdened by the weight of his role. "Yes. There's a deeply hidden organization with interests in Bryan and Alex's genetic potentials. They see them as the key to their plans for the future of humanity. My role has been to thwart all of their attempts to find you and to keep you safe, including you Elizabeth."

Elizabeth's frustration was palpable. "And now you're here, but what about Bryan? Where is he? What do we need to do?"

David's expression grew somber. "I wish I could tell you where Bryan is, but revealing his location could put him at greater risk. I just met with him prior to this meeting.What I can tell you is that we all need to be cautious. The organization's reach is extensive, and their plans, while vague, appear far from over."

Alex's mind whirled with the implications of David's revelations. "So, what now? How do we proceed?"

David took a deep breath, the gravity of his role evident in the lines of his face. "There's something crucial you need to understand first, about Bryan's past," he began, his voice tinged with both sadness and urgency. "Before he was born, Bryan was part of a clandestine genetic experiment his mother Darlene had unknowingly signed on for as a nurse needing extra money. The experiment was designed to manipulate the human genome to create what they hoped would be the next evolution of mankind. This experiment was highly secretive and involved altering genetic codes to produce enhanced individuals. Bryan was the only survivor of this process. All twelve of the other test subjects who were subjected to similar modifications perished before they turned sixteen, victims of a genetic flaw that led to aneurysms in the parietal lobe of the brain. Bryan's survival was a freak occurrence and that, along with a paperwork error at the hospital during an emergency medical incident are the only reason he still has any freedoms. After Bryan coded in the ambulance on the way to the emergency room, the hospital lost all records of him. It was this administrative blunder that allowed Bryan to continue living, defying the odds, and being able to create his life with you two."

Alex and Elizabeth exchanged stunned glances as the weight of David's revelation sank in. "So, was Bryan's survival was just a mistake? A fluke?" Alex asked, his voice tinged with disbelief.

David nodded solemnly. "Exactly, but there is more. The experiment was meant to be perfected in the progeny of the participants. Bryan was the beginning, a preliminary test subject, but they intended to refine the process through his offspring, that's you Alex. The genetic alterations in Bryan were incomplete and remain unactivated, and Alex's genetic profile was meant to carry the full potential of the experiment."

Elizabeth's eyes widened with realization, the significance of David's words hitting her like a wave. "So, Bryan was a part of something much bigger, and Alex... Alex is the true culmination of this experiment?"

David's expression was grim. "Yes. Alex's genetic makeup holds the promise of what they were trying to achieve all along. Bryan's survival and Alex's existence represent the unfulfilled potential of a project that was never meant to see the light of day. This is why you both are so crucial now. The organization's interest in Bryan and Alex is driven by their desire to complete what they started back during the Cold War."

The enormity of the situation settled heavily on both Alex and Elizabeth. The realization that both Bryan and Alex's futures and very lives were entwined in a covert genetic experiment added a profound layer to their struggle. The stakes were higher than they had ever imagined, with Bryan's past and Alex's potential now standing at the center of a dangerous and far-reaching conspiracy.

David took a deep breath, clearly weighing his next words. "We need to stay vigilant and continue gathering information. There are four operatives working with me, for me—Mika, Isabella, Jay, and It. They are all part of our effort to keep Bryan and you safe. We'll need to work together to navigate the threats ahead. While Bryan is still not ready, nor does he know I am here with you right now. He is being taken care of and watched over. We won't let anything happen to him. Izzy (Isabella) and It are also researching how to activate Bryan's latent genetic gifts and yes, we think those gifts being inactive are playing a large role in Bryan's mindset and have been for some time. We will find a way to help him and bring you all back together when the time is right. Keep your phones charged and get some rest, you are all being looked after". David walked back into the shadows and disappeared with the same determined steps he had arrived.

As the night deepened, Alex and Elizabeth felt a mix of relief and trepidation. Meeting David was a pivotal moment, but it only led to more questions and uncertainties. The web of intrigue surrounding Bryan's life was more complex than they had imagined, and the path forward was fraught with challenges.

For Alex, the weight of their shared history sat heavily on his shoulders. He had always admired his father's strength, his unwavering commitment to their family. Now, as the pieces of the puzzle slowly came together, Alex couldn't help but wonder how much Bryan had sacrificed, how deeply he had buried his own pain for the sake of those he loved. Alex felt a surge of determination rise within him. He couldn't let his father disappear into the darkness. Not now. Not when they were so close.

David's presence was both a beacon of hope and a reminder of the dangers that lurked in the shadows. With the knowledge that Bryan's safety was intertwined with their own, Alex and Elizabeth faced a daunting task ahead. The answers they sought were within reach, but the road to finding Bryan and uncovering the full extent of the threat against him was just beginning.

As they prepared to leave the playground, the weight of David's revelations settled heavily on their shoulders. The journey to protect Bryan and confront the hidden dangers was far from over, and their next steps would be crucial in unraveling the tangled web of deceit and ensuring their own safety amidst the looming threats.As they rose from the bench, their shared memories lingering like shadows in the night, Alex felt a renewed sense of purpose.

The playground had once been a place of laughter and light. Now, it was the starting point of a new journey—one that would test them in ways they couldn't yet imagine. But no matter what lay ahead, they were ready. They had to be.

57 INTO THE ABYSS

After reviewing the drive David had given him, Bryan begins the arduous trek to a location marked just outside the mostly abandoned military base nearby. Bryan pushed through the thick underbrush of the forest for what seemed like hours if not days, each step carrying him closer to a place he could hardly believe existed. He had caught wind of it through snippets of whispered conversations and fragments of classified documents, always hinting at a hidden sanctuary, a fortress buried deep underground where the world's elite could retreat in times of catastrophe.

As he finally approached the coordinates, his heart beat faster, both from the physical exertion and the realization that this place could be the answer he was looking for — the perfect sanctuary to reunite with Elizabeth and Alex, a place where they could be safe from the threats that loomed over them like storm clouds.

The entrance was almost invisible, concealed behind a tangled curtain of kudzu, ivy and other dense vegetation, blending seamlessly into the surrounding landscape. Only a nondescript concrete structure hinted at what lay beneath. As Bryan approached the thick, reinforced steel door, he noted the biometric scanners and advanced keypad, both strangely out of place in such a secluded area. For a moment, he hesitated, the enormity of the moment weighing on him.

If this bunker was as formidable as he hoped, it would be more than just a place to hide — it would be a fortress, for solitude, a new beginning for Alex, Elizabeth and himself. Steeling himself, he entered the code he had deciphered from a heavily redacted government document. The door groaned, then slid open with a hiss of pressurized air, revealing a dark, sloping corridor that led downward into the earth's depths.

Bryan stepped inside the bunker, a gust of cold, musty air rushing past him. His first impression was one of desolation, the entrance barely more than a dilapidated concrete relic of another era. It looked as if it hadn't seen human presence in years, a forgotten monument to old fears of a world-ending catastrophe. The walls were grimy, cracked in places, and covered with dust. Faded emergency signs hung crooked on the walls, and the steel door clanged shut behind him with a hollow thud that echoed through the corridors. He felt a brief pang of regret—was this truly the place where he'd reunite with his family?

But as Bryan descended further, something began to shift. Soft lights flickered on as if they had sensed his presence, illuminating the path ahead in a warm, golden glow. The farther he ventured, the more the bunker seemed to come alive. What had started as an eerie, abandoned shelter transformed before his eyes into a thriving underground wonderland. The cracked walls smoothed out, the grime vanished, and the once-bleak hallway expanded into a wide atrium. The air itself seemed to change, no longer thick with dust but now cool and crisp, carrying the faintest scent of fresh earth.

He passed the first set of reinforced steel doors, which slid open effortlessly to reveal a massive storage area. His jaw tightened in awe as he looked around. Shelves lined the walls, stretching upward into a space that was far larger than it appeared from the outside. Every possible item of necessity and comfort was there. There were crates of canned goods, but not the usual bland survival fare. There were gourmet meals, preserved to perfection, high-end coffee beans, artisanal chocolates, and wines with labels he recognized as being impossible to come by on the surface. Each row seemed to offer something more luxurious than the last, as if someone had painstakingly prepared for not just survival, but comfort.

Bryan moved forward, and the scent of herbs and vegetables grew stronger, drawing him toward the next level. When he stepped through, the sight took his breath away. The once utilitarian bunker opened up into a lush, thriving hydroponic garden, rows of vibrant green plants bathing in soft, artificial sunlight. The air here was warmer, fragrant with the unmistakable smells of basil, thyme, and tomatoes. Bryan walked slowly, running his hands across the leaves, feeling the life growing in this place. It was surreal—an underground paradise, hidden beneath the earth.

He could already picture Elizabeth here, kneeling down to inspect the plants, her fingers moving carefully through the soil. She had always loved when he cooked with fresh herbs, and the thought of providing that small comfort even in such dire circumstances sent a swell of warmth through him. This garden, this hidden world, was more than a survival mechanism. It was hope. It was a place where they could breathe again, even in the darkest of times. He imagined Alex, wide-eyed and excited, running his hands through the leaves like he had when he was a child, marveling at the sheer impossibility of it all.

The deeper Bryan ventured, the more the bunker seemed to evolve into a masterpiece of modern engineering. The concrete floors gave way to polished marble tiles, the walls smooth and gleaming with state-of-the-art technology.

The medical bay on the next level was equally impressive. It housed every conceivable piece of medical equipment, from surgical suites to an ICU, some equipment he didn't recognize, and a fully stocked pharmacy. Bryan paused for a moment, his mind drifting to the countless days and nights he and Elizabeth had spent fretting over their son's health, and how she would finally find solace in knowing that if anything went wrong, they'd have the best possible care right here.

And Alex — how would he react to all of this? His son had always been brave, but Bryan knew the young man had fears that only deepened with their current journey. Here, he could find reassurance that no matter what he could be okay. Here, Elizabeth wouldn't have to worry about whether they'd make it to a hospital in time, or if they could afford the treatment or anything else. Here, their future was in their hands.

Deeper still, Bryan found the recreation level, and his breath caught in his throat. He could hardly believe what he was seeing: an expansive swimming pool that shimmered under bright, artificial lights designed to mimic natural sunlight, surrounded by a spa complete with hot tubs, saunas, and massage rooms. The gentle sound of water lapping against the pool's edges brought back memories of long-forgotten family vacations, of laughter and splashing under warm summer skies at the beach.

He pictured Alex diving in, his face breaking into a grin as he swam laps, while Elizabeth lounged by the poolside, finally relaxing or at least trying to. He could almost hear their laughter, feel their happiness radiating off them, finding joy in such simple, everyday pleasures. This wasn't just a shelter; it was a place where they could reclaim a semblance of normal life, one they truly deserved after all they had been through.

Moving past the pool and spa, Bryan discovered more — a gym with every type of state-of-the-art equipment, a rock-climbing wall, and even a cinema with plush seats and a library of films. He could almost see the three of them settling in with popcorn, losing themselves in a movie for a few hours, forgetting the world outside. The gym was another marvel; he knew Alex would love the rock climbing wall. The kid had always been athletic, always pushing himself to new heights. And Elizabeth — he could already see her smile at the thought of having a spa day, of unwinding in the hot tub, of letting go of all the stress that had built up over the years. Here, they could be more than survivors; they could find joy again.

As Bryan continued his exploration, he found the residential levels, and he stopped, awe-struck. These were not the cold, cramped quarters he had expected. Each apartment was spacious and filled with modern furnishings, complete with private terraces overlooking a central atrium where green plants climbed upward under soft lighting. The air was filled with the scent of jasmine and lavender, a touch of nature amid the concrete. Smart-home systems controlled the environment with a simple touch, and he could imagine Elizabeth marveling at the comfort, feeling as though they had stepped into another world entirely. The thought of Alex running through these halls, exploring every room, every hidden nook, brought a smile to his face. It wasn't just about safety; it was about giving them a life worth living.

Reaching the seventh level, Bryan entered a room that took his breath away: a command center filled with dozens of screens, each displaying live surveillance feeds from the surface, detailed tactical maps, and weather patterns projected across a giant screen. It was a room built for strategy, to monitor every possible threat, and to coordinate responses with precision. As he took it all in, he felt a surge of determination.

This was more than just a hiding place; it was a stronghold, a vantage point from which he could protect his family and strike back if needed. He thought of how much Alex loved technology, how he would marvel at the gadgets and the power they offered. And Elizabeth, with her innate ability to plan and organize, would quickly recognize the significance of this nerve center. They could be safe here, truly safe, and maybe even begin to take control of their destiny without it being plagued by his failures and manipulation by outside forces.

He moved deeper into the bunker, passing by a fully-equipped data center. Rows of servers hummed softly, indicating a sophisticated network that could connect them securely to the outside world. It was a hacker's paradise, a place Bryan realized he would have to master this network, understand its intricacies if he wanted to keep his enemies at bay. Yet, he also felt a strange sense of relief; if he could figure this out, they could stay hidden as long as they needed. He thought about Alex's curiosity, his eagerness to learn new things — how he would light up at the thought of getting his hands on such advanced tech. And Elizabeth, with her sharp instincts, would quickly grasp the value of such a secure communication hub. Together, they could use this to their advantage.

As he continued to explore, Bryan felt an unexpected sense of calm. Each level of the bunker seemed to offer a new revelation, another piece of the puzzle that could help them rebuild their lives. He found a level dedicated solely to storage — walls lined with shelves holding enough supplies to last decades. Bryan's gaze settled on a vast series of

crates stacked neatly against the stone walls, each
one meticulously labeled and organized. The crates
stretched on as far as the eye could see, arranged in
rows that formed an intricate labyrinth of supplies.
Some were marked with familiar symbols—basic
provisions like canned goods, medical supplies, and
tools—while others were labeled in ways that hinted
at more mysterious contents: "Advanced Tech,"
"Biological Samples," and "Weaponry: Containment
Only." Dust coated the tops of the older crates, but
the sheer quantity of them suggested decades of
careful planning and preparation. This wasn't just a
storage room—it was a treasure trove of survival, a
contingency for every possible scenario, both
known and unforeseen. His attention was drawn to
an imposing stack of human-sized crates, each one
larger and more intimidating than the last. The
crates were uniform in their industrial design, made
of heavy steel, and marked with bold, stenciled
letters: "EXPERIMENTAL" and "TOP SECRET."

Unlike the standard provisions he had seen earlier,
these crates exuded an air of mystery and danger.
The words etched across them were like warnings,
daring anyone to open them. They stretched out in
a seemingly endless series, towering above him,
their contents hidden and heavily secured. Some

had reinforced locks, and others were fitted with what appeared to be biometric scanners, as if only authorized personnel were ever meant to access their secrets.

The cold, sterile air of the storage room felt heavier here, as if the secrets contained within these crates pulsed with a life of their own. Bryan's heart raced with a mix of curiosity and dread. Whatever was inside these crates wasn't meant for ordinary survival—it was something far beyond, buried by time and secrecy. It felt like a time capsule of human resilience, where every crate held a piece of hope, a chance at life beyond whatever catastrophe had driven them underground.

And another, an armory filled with weapons, tactical gear, and enough ammunition to defend against any conceivable threat. He knew it would give Elizabeth peace of mind to know they were so well-equipped, that they wouldn't have to fear for their safety. And for Alex, it would be a chance to learn, to grow stronger, to face whatever lay ahead with courage.

Finally, Bryan reached the lowest levels and found something that felt almost like fate. Before him stretched an underground world, an ecosystem so vast and surreal it defied belief. It was as though he had stepped into another realm, where nature thrived beneath the earth. A crystal-clear river wound its way through the landscape, its gentle current reflecting the soft artificial sunlight that filtered down from an intricate lighting system overhead. Along its banks, fruit trees blossomed—apple, peach, and citrus trees heavy with vibrant, ripe fruit that seemed to glow in the warm light. Beyond the trees, fields of wheat and corn stretched out in neatly cultivated rows, blending seamlessly with patches of untamed wilderness where wildflowers bloomed in a riot of colors.

Farm animals roamed freely in designated areas—cows, goats, and chickens moving about peacefully, their presence adding a sense of normalcy to this hidden paradise. But there were also signs of wildlife—deer grazing on the grass, birds chirping softly from the branches above, and rabbits darting between the trees. The air was filled with the scent of fresh earth, ripened fruit, and the crispness of the river's waters. The temperature was perfect, a controlled environment that felt neither stifling nor cold, balanced in a way that made it seem like a never-ending spring. It was as large as a small city, yet it felt intimate, as though it had been crafted to be a sanctuary for life—a place where humans, animals, and nature coexist in harmony, shielded from the chaos of the world above. It was more than Bryan could have ever imagined, a living world tucked away beneath the earth, waiting for them to find peace.

Off to the side was a vault-like room, reinforced with steel and concrete, filled with everything they could need in a world gone mad. A part of him wanted to collapse with relief. He had found it. He had found the place where they could finally be safe. This place is where they could come back together as a family, away from the chaos and dangers that had plagued them for so long. The air was cool, and the silence was deep, but Bryan felt an unexpected warmth rising in his chest.

As he stared out across the vast underground expanse, he thought of how Elizabeth and Alex would react. He knew there would be questions, doubts, and fears, but he also had faith they would see what he saw: a chance for a new beginning, a place where they could finally start to heal and come back together. He pictured Elizabeth's face, the way her eyes would widen at the sight of the living quarters, the way she would smile at the thought of Alex finally having a safe place to call home. He imagined Alex's excitement, his youthful energy finally given a chance to flourish in this hidden sanctuary. Here, they could find the peace that had eluded them for so long.

58 MAKING THE CALL

With renewed determination, Bryan went to the command center and sent a secure series of texts to David, alerting him to the discovery and asking for his help in bringing Elizabeth and Alex to this place.

Bryan:
David, I found it. The bunker, the crates... everything. This place is beyond anything I could've imagined. You weren't exaggerating. "Top secret" is an understatement.

David:
I told you it was there for a reason. Glad you made it. What's your next move?

Bryan:
I want Elizabeth and Alex here. We need to be together now. Can you bring them—and all their things? It's time we stopped running and started planning.

David:
Already have a plan for that. I'll put it in motion and have everything they need packed up within a

few hours. We've got teams stationed nearby, and once we get clearance, we'll be on our way to you. Every item, every necessity, will be packed and brought to the bunker—no stone left unturned. This place is your new home now.

Bryan:

That's what I need. I want them safe. I've been alone long enough, and we all need to be together here. It feels like we've been scattered for too long. Thank you, David. For everything. Leading me here, for setting this up. It's time to bring them home.

David:

You're welcome, Bryan. This has been a long time coming. They'll be with you soon, safe and sound. Just give us a few hours, and we'll be on the road. By tonight, you'll be reunited—right where you belong.

He knew they couldn't stay hidden forever, but this bunker, this underground haven, was a start. It was a place where they could regroup, where they could plan their next move, and where they could be together again, safe from the world that had tried to tear them apart. As he made his way back to the entrance, Bryan felt a surge of hope and resolve. He had found a sanctuary for his family. Now, he just had to make sure they got here safely and he trusted David enough to do just that.

Bryan took one last look around, knowing he still had work to do. He would have to make sure every corner was secure, every system under his control. But as he prepared to explore the bunker more, he felt a sense of peace he hadn't known in years.

This was a place where they could finally be together, where they could find safety, love, and maybe even a bit of happiness.

He would do whatever it took to protect that which he holds most precious— to provide for and to protect them.

59 PURIFICATION

As Elizabeth and Alex drove home from the playground, the evening air was filled with a mix of tension and hope. The weight of the meeting with David lingered, each word replaying in Elizabeth's mind, but for the first time in months, there was a glimmer of clarity, of the bigger picture. She always knew Bryan was unique but this is so far beyond anything she could have ever imagined. Who or what is he exactly, and Alex too...why did he choose her and always stay by her side, she questioned in her mind.

The headlights illuminated the familiar streets, guiding them back to their house — the house that had once been a home, their forever home they built together. Stepping inside, the comfort of the space felt strangely foreign, yet welcoming. Elizabeth felt a deep yearning to wash away the grime and weariness that had clung to her since Bryan had disappeared and for the months of chaos she had caused. She moved with purpose to the bathroom, feeling the tiled floor beneath her feet for the first time in what seemed like forever.

She turned on the shower, the rush of hot water cascading over her, the initial shock of warmth melting the tension in her muscles. Each drop felt like a release, washing away not only the grime from the day but also the weight of choices she had made—the regrets, the lost moments, the guilt she carried like a second skin. This was her first shower in this place since leaving, since walking away from Bryan and the life they had built together. The water seemed to penetrate deeper than her skin, cleansing the layers of emotional residue that had clung to her since she'd moved into that sterile, miserable condo. It was her first shower in this place since she had left it all behind, since she had moved into that miserable condo by herself. That place had never been hers, just a hollow reminder of the distance she had created between herself and everything that once mattered. Here, in the familiar warmth of this shower, she felt an unexpected pull, as if the home, and Bryan himself, was drawing her back into something she had almost forgotten.

Reaching for one of Bryan's bottles of scented soap—sandalwood and pine, she realized—Elizabeth poured it into her hands, the rich, earthy fragrance filling the air. As she lathered it onto her skin, a warmth spread through her body that went beyond the physical comfort of the heat. It was as though Bryan's presence lingered in the scent, bringing her closer to him, softening the sharp edges of her grief and guilt.

For the first time in what felt like forever, she felt

connected to him again, not just in memory but in spirit. She closed her eyes and let the water rinse over her, imagining his hands gliding all over her, guiding her back to the woman she used to be, the one who laughed freely and loved her two dorks without hesitation. With each breath, the steam curled around her, and a sense of renewal began to blossom within her chest, slowly warming her from the inside out. Maybe, just maybe, this was the first step toward healing—not just her body, but her heart and soul as well.

Afterward, she found Alex already showered and sleeping under the sheets of the master bedroom's king-size bed, Bryan's bed. The overwhelming exhaustion evident in his young face. She joined him a few moments later, pulling the soft blankets over her, feeling the familiar comfort envelop her body. As her head hit the pillow, a deep, consuming fatigue took over, and within moments she drifted into a deep, dreamless sleep, the promise of reunion and safety with both Bryan and Alex easing her into a much-needed rest.

60 Up And At'em

Elizabeth's eyes fluttered open, heavy with exhaustion that seemed to seep down into her bones. She lay there for a moment, her body sinking into the bed as if it were made of lead, every muscle aching from the weight of the past few days. The events that had unraveled so quickly had left her feeling drained, emotionally and physically battered. For a few blissful seconds, she clung to the warmth of her blanket, trying to stay in the protective haze of sleep, but something was pulling her back to reality.

She turned her head, her vision blurry at first, and saw Alex standing at the edge of her bed, his figure still in the soft morning light. He wasn't just awake; he was alert, his body tense with purpose, his face a mask of strange determination she hadn't seen in him before. His fists clenched and unclenched at his sides, and his eyes—sharp, almost unblinking—were fixed on the door. Elizabeth blinked hard, trying to shake the fogginess from her mind, her heart beginning to pick up its pace.

"Alex?" she murmured, her voice rough and barely above a whisper. But he didn't respond immediately, his attention still locked on the door. Her pulse quickened as she turned her head fully toward the doorway, her stomach lurching when she saw it was slightly ajar. Beyond it, she could hear low murmurs, unfamiliar voices drifting through the house. The quiet shuffling of feet. The sound of things being moved. Her heart leaped into her throat, and a surge of panic rose within her. This wasn't normal. These were not the usual sounds of their home.

"What's going on?" she managed, her voice barely steady as she sat up, her body protesting against the sudden movement. Alex finally turned to face her, his expression unreadable but his eyes flashing with something that sent a chill down her spine. He stepped closer, his jaw clenched as if he was holding back a torrent of words or emotions he wasn't ready to release.

"They're here," he said quietly, the weight of his words settling between them like a stone. "David's people. They're packing up everything. They're getting us ready to leave and we're leaving... now. Like right fucking now.."

Elizabeth's mind raced as she tried to process what he was saying. The house wasn't just filled with strangers—these were people sent by David, by the man who had stepped out of the shadows and turned their lives upside down. A rush of anxiety and confusion gripped her. "We're leaving?" she whispered, more to herself than to Alex. The idea of suddenly being swept away from everything they had known, their lives upended and moved like pieces on a chessboard, left her feeling disoriented.

"We don't have much time," Alex added, his voice steady but his eyes flickering with uncertainty. "They said we're going to Dad. That he's found us all a safe place. We need to go. Now."

Elizabeth sat up straight, adrenaline flooding her veins, wiping away any lingering traces of sleep. "What? David's here?" she asked, her voice a mix of confusion and anxiety. She glanced around the room, noticing it was already half-empty. Most of their personal items were gone, only the essentials they had on hand still left untouched. The sudden realization struck her like a blow to the chest — they were leaving, and they were leaving immediately.

Elizabeth's breath caught in her throat as the realization hit her fully. Everything was changing in an instant. Their home, their life, the last remnants of normalcy—they were slipping away. And yet, at the heart of it, there was a spark of hope. Bryan. Bryan had found a place for them, a safe place. The confusion and fear battled with a sense of relief deep inside her. She wanted to ask a hundred questions, but the urgency in Alex's voice and the noises growing louder outside the bedroom made it clear that this wasn't the time for hesitation.

She swung her legs over the edge of the bed, her bare feet hitting the carpeted floor with a soft thud. She looked up at Alex, his determination unwavering, and for a moment, she felt a flicker of pride in her son. He had always been strong, but this—this was something more. He was ready to fight for their family, just like Bryan had always taught him.

"Okay," she whispered, her voice stronger now. "Let's go."

Alex nodded, his face serious, but there was a glimmer of excitement in his eyes. "Yeah, Mom. David and his team, they're packing everything. Dad found a place — a safe place where we can all be together. David said it's secure, and they're getting us there, now. They've already got most of our stuff packed. We have to grab whatever we need for the drive and go."

Elizabeth felt a whirlwind of emotions — relief mixed with apprehension. She swung her legs over the side of the bed, standing up too quickly, causing a momentary wave of dizziness to wash over her. She steadied herself, then nodded. "Okay... okay, let me just—"

Before she could finish, the bedroom door opened wider, and David stepped in, a warm but urgent smile on his face. "Good morning, Elizabeth. Morning, Alex," he greeted, his voice steady, calm. "I'm glad you're awake. I know this is sudden, but we've got to move quickly. Bryan found a secure location, a place where you can all be safe. My team is just finishing up. Maybe 20 minutes and we are on the road. I've got some coffee and breakfast for you both. It's on the kitchen island."

David's calm presence was oddly reassuring amid the chaos. Elizabeth felt a flicker of trust in him, despite the strangeness of the situation. "How did you...?" she began, but David held up a hand, already anticipating the question.

"We've been preparing for this, Elizabeth. Bryan wanted you safe, and he wanted you with him as soon as possible. My team knows how to handle this. We're almost done here, but we need to get moving in the next few minutes. Please, grab anything you need for the road. Everything else, as you may see, is already packed."

Elizabeth moved past David, stepping into the hallway. The house was bustling with quiet activity. Several men in dark clothing, along with David's operatives — Mika, Isabella, Jay, and the silent but efficient It — moved with purpose, their hands carefully packing every item of significance. She noticed how they handled their things with surprising care — photo frames wrapped in thick, protective padding, delicate dishes carefully boxed. It was as if they knew how important these items were to her, to Bryan, and to Alex.

In the kitchen, she spotted two cups waiting on the counter — a steaming cup of coffee with vanilla cream and a dash of cinnamon for her, and an iced vanilla frappe laced with chocolate syrup for Alex. She felt a pang of something she couldn't quite name — gratitude, maybe, or a sense of comfort in the midst of so much upheaval.

She picked up her coffee and took a sip, the warm, spiced flavor instantly calming her nerves, if only for a moment. "Thank you," she whispered, unsure if David had even heard her, but he nodded, a small, knowing smile crossing his face.

Alex grabbed his frappe with an eager grin, taking a sip and sighing in relief. "Mom, it's perfect. They even got it just right... Dad must have told them."

Elizabeth smiled at Alex's small delight. "Yeah, he must have." She glanced around the kitchen, where once there had been clutter and life, now everything was boxed and ready. She felt a strange sadness seeing the house so empty, but also a sense of urgency that pushed her forward. They were finally moving, finally going to be together wherever it was that Bryan had found.

David handed them two backpacks. "You won't need much, but these have essentials for the journey. Anything else, we'll get you when we arrive. It's best to travel light." He gave them both a reassuring nod as if he understood the whirlwind they were in. "We're almost ready. Let's get you to Bryan."

Alex's face lit up at the mention of his father. "Where is he, David? Is he safe?"

David's expression softened, a hint of warmth in his eyes. "Yes, Alex. He's very safe, and he's waiting for you both. It's an amazing and secure location. You'll understand more about whatI mean once we get there. Just trust me a little longer. Bryan told me to tell you the place is "Perfectly Imperfect"" Elizabeth nodded, feeling a swell of emotions for something that definitely came from Bryan's mouth.

She didn't know if she trusted David fully yet, but she trusted Bryan, and Bryan trusted him. That had to be enough for now. She looked around one last time, taking in the now-sterile environment of what was once her forever home — a home they were leaving behind for... who knew how long.

61 ROLL OUT

David's team moved efficiently, almost as if choreographed, placing the last few items into boxes and sealing them. Within moments, the house was stripped bare, the memories they had built over the years now packed away, stored in the back of a series of unmarked trucks. David's operatives moved with precision, and Elizabeth realized they had left nothing behind — no photographs, no dishes, not even a speck of dust. The place was immaculate, almost unnervingly so, as if they had never lived here.

David checked his watch. "Time to go," he said, as he began gently guiding them towards the door. Alex grabbed his mother's hand, squeezing it tightly, sensing her unease and trying to suppress his own.

As they stepped outside, the cold morning air hit them, waking them fully. The team had already loaded everything into the vehicles. David directed them towards the Jeep. "Follow us. We'll take you straight to the bunker, to Bryan. Oh, and we have taken the liberty of blocking all tracking and cell signals to avoid any unwanted company. Just use the handheld radio in the console, Alex. It's the upgraded model from what Bryan trained you to use. Alex smiled at that memory."

Elizabeth felt a surge of adrenaline and something else — hope, maybe. She exchanged a glance with Alex, who nodded, his young face determined, ready for whatever was next. They both climbed into the Jeep, tossing their go bags into the back, and as they turned the key, the engine roared to life and Elizabeth noticed they had even refilled the gas for them.

David's convoy fired up and moved smoothly onto the road, the sound of the engines humming in unison, a low and steady rhythm that seemed to mirror the collective heartbeat of everyone involved. Elizabeth gripped the steering wheel tightly, her knuckles white as she fell in behind one of the trucks, the rest of David's team flanking her car front and back. The security of being surrounded by them was undeniable, but it also filled her with a sense of unease. She wasn't used to being protected like this, being ushered away from her home, her life, toward an uncertain future. And yet, for the first time in a long time, she didn't feel alone.

As they drove away, she glanced in the rearview mirror, her eyes locking on the image of their house fading into the distance, their planned forever home. The place that had once been filled with warmth, laughter, and love was now nothing more than an empty shell, stripped of its memories and belongings. The sight hit her harder than she had expected. There was a weight in that final look, a heaviness that spoke to all the years they had spent there, the moments they had built, both good and bad. Her heart ached with the loss, a bittersweet tug that reminded her of the life they had once dreamed of living.

But there was also a strange sense of closure in watching the house disappear from view, a finality that soothed some of the pain she had been carrying. It was as if, in leaving it behind, she was leaving behind a part of herself that had been stuck, tethered to old wounds and unresolved guilt. There was no going back now, no clinging to what once was. They were moving forward, and that realization washed over her with unexpected relief.

Tears stung her eyes, but she blinked them back, swallowing the lump that had formed in her throat. She couldn't afford to break down now—not when they were so close to finding Bryan, to rebuilding their family, their connection. She glanced over at Alex, sitting in the passenger seat beside her, his face etched with a mixture of determination, excitement, and exhaustion. His silence spoke volumes, and she could see the same emotions swirling in his eyes. He was processing everything, just as she was, trying to come to terms with all they had lost and what they might gain once back with Bryan again.

As the convoy continued down the road, Elizabeth felt a shift within herself. The fear that had gripped her for so long, the uncertainty that had plagued her since Bryan disappeared, began to lift and fade away. In its place, a new sense of purpose bloomed, Bryan had always talked about things being planted in the Fall and Winter time that begin to sprout and bloom as soon as the frost leaves. Whatever awaited them, they would face it together, as a family. And in that unity, there was strength.

She looked back at the road ahead, her gaze steady and resolute. They were no longer running from the past, no longer trapped in a cycle of pain and regret. They were moving toward something better, toward Bryan, and perhaps—just perhaps—toward a future where they could all be safe and whole again. The thought filled her with a hope she hadn't dared to feel in years, a flicker of light that warmed the cold, broken pieces of her heart.

62 Epilogue:
Shadows Before Dawn

The organization that had orchestrated Bryan's existence was more than just a secretive collective; it was a phantom entity with tendrils deeply rooted in every corner of modern society, an entity that operated far beyond the reach of any government or legal system. In its origin, it had been a bold and controversial experiment, an alliance between the world's most clandestine agencies and governments, united by a shared ambition to break through the known boundaries of human potential during the Cold War. Genetic enhancements, psychological conditioning, behavioral modifications — they sought to craft a new breed of humanity, one capable of thriving in circumstances that would break even the strongest of men. Yet, when their results began to tiptoe too close to the ethical precipice, the governments swiftly disavowed any connection. Officially, they had never existed. Unofficially, they thrived in the shadows, cut free from any governing oversight and moral restraint.

Operating now as an independent entity, they had one mission: to shape their one surviving experiment, Bryan, into the man they needed him to become — a man unyielding, shaped by relentless hardship, emotionally impenetrable, and capable of making the kinds of decisions that would break lesser men. Bryan was never meant to be just another participant in their trials. He was the singular outcome of decades of experimentation, the lone survivor of their genetic manipulations. They had selected him because they believed he possessed the rare combination of traits necessary to endure their most rigorous tests. As a child, his mother had been informed of his potential, but after her death to protect him, Bryan had been left alone, a puppet in a game where he did not even know the rules or that it even existed.

Their methods were as subtle as they were insidious. To the outside observer, Bryan's life seemed filled with the normal ebbs and flows of human experience: joys, heartbreaks, successes, and failures. But every event had been carefully orchestrated, every hardship methodically planned to mold him into the weapon they required. From his earliest years, they had observed and manipulated, ensuring every experience pushed him further down the path they had laid out for him. They wove themselves into the tapestry of his life with expert precision, as invisible architects crafting every twist and turn.

Jobs he had excelled at were taken away suddenly, with no reason other than that he was becoming too comfortable, too complacent. Every time he felt like he was getting ahead, something would shift — an unexpected restructuring, a downturn, a change in policy — all orchestrated by their unseen hand. They knew he had to be kept on his toes, perpetually challenged, always striving but never quite reaching his destination. Relationships, too, were not left to chance. His first two fiancées, women who loved him deeply, were nudged by whispers of doubt, insecurity planted like seeds that blossomed into betrayal and cheating. He had watched them slip away into the arms of others, feeling the sting of rejection without ever truly understanding why. Only in his early twenties when he adopted the persona of a douchebag narcissist, did the group leave him to his own devices...he was a monster. His closest friends always drifted away, his family turned distant and dead to him; all guided by the organization's quiet influence. Even Elizabeth, his wife, love of his life, and the mother of his child, was led to believe that leaving him was her path to freedom and peace of mind, convinced that his very presence was suffocating her, when in truth, every thought, every decision had been subtly influenced to make her see him as a worthless burden.

To Bryan, it seemed like the world was dead set against him. But it was more than that — it was a carefully constructed labyrinth, each wall and dead end designed to strengthen his resolve, to make him harder, tougher, more resilient to the point of being unstoppable. The organization believed that only by stripping him of everything he held dear, by forcing him to confront his own demons, could they forge him into the new evolution of man he was meant to be. They were playing a long game, one that stretched out over years and decades, each move calculated to ensure that he was always one step away from the abyss but never quite over it.

Their reach was far and wide, extending into the very algorithms that governed modern life. They were embedded within the social media networks, the financial institutions, the news outlets — all the invisible threads that connected and controlled human behavior in the 21st century. They could manipulate what people saw, what they read, what they believed. A headline here, a social media post there, a targeted ad — all tools in their arsenal. They had the power to shift public opinion, to alter perceptions, to make people question their own realities. It was subtle, almost imperceptible, but it was there, guiding and shaping the thoughts of everyone around Bryan. They could flip a narrative overnight, make a friend an enemy, turn a lover into a stranger. And they did it all without leaving a trace, like shadows moving through the fog.

This wasn't just about Bryan anymore; it was about everyone he might ever come into contact with, every person who could potentially alter the course they had set for him. Each interaction was scrutinized, every conversation monitored, every decision weighed and calculated. The betrayals, the losses, the heartbreaks — they were all deliberate, each one a test, a step in a long, arduous process designed to forge him into something beyond human, something exceptional, something that could not be broken. The perfect weapon, the ultimate decision-maker, the one who could make the hard choices, who could sacrifice what needed to be sacrificed without flinching or blinking an eye.

At the center of this vast web of influence was Ms. GD, the woman who had risen from the ranks of test subjects to become the Director. Her journey had been no less grueling than Bryan's. She was once like him, a pawn in a larger game, a subject in the early stages of experimentation. She had survived the tests, had proven her resilience, and had clawed her way to the top of this secretive hierarchy. She had watched Bryan's life unfold from the moment of his birth, had seen every decision, every failure, every moment of doubt. She knew him better than anyone, perhaps better than he knew himself.

Now, she sat in her dimly lit office, dozens of monitors surrounding her, displaying live feeds of Bryan's movements, his interactions, and even his potential thoughts. She watched with a mixture of fascination and satisfaction, knowing that every step he took brought him closer to the destiny she had planned for him. For Ms. GD, Bryan was not just another experiment — he was the culmination of everything she had worked for in her sixty-five years of life, everything she believed in. She leaned forward, her fingers tapping against her chin, a small, knowing smile playing at her lips as she saw him on the screen, still searching, still fighting, still trying to understand the forces that shaped his life.

But she would never let him see the full picture, not yet. He had more to endure, more to learn. She was not ready to activate his latency and place him into power. The world was changing, becoming darker and more uncertain, and they needed someone like him — someone who could navigate the complexities, who could make the hard choices that others could not. And if that meant bending and breaking him, stripping away every illusion, every comfort, every ounce of weakness, then so be it. Ms. GD was prepared to do whatever it took to make him ready, to make him the man of the future, her vision of the future demanded it.

As she watched, she knew that the real game was only just beginning. And Bryan, for all his struggles, for all his pain, was right where she wanted him — teetering on the edge, ready to be molded into the ultimate monolith of a leader, the final solution for a world that did not yet understand how much it needed him. These thoughts led Ms. GD to reminisce about her beloved projects.

The Birth of the Bunker: The Initial Vision

In the sweltering summer of 1996, Alabama's otherwise tranquil landscape was abruptly transformed by the arrival of a project so clandestine that its implications would ripple through the decades. The land, a vast, undulating expanse nestled on the outskirts of a local military base, was meticulously selected for its strategic isolation and potential for fortification. This location, chosen for its natural security and concealed by a dense forest, was to become the foundation for an apocalyptic bunker that would serve as a sanctuary for the elite leaders of a new world order. At the forefront of this monumental undertaking was Ms. GD, who had recently been appointed as an agent within the organization, marking the beginning of her involvement in a project that would uniquely and significantly impact her life, career and the organization's future.

Ms. GD's appointment was the result of a rigorous selection process, her promotion a testament to her exceptional capabilities and unyielding drive. The project's enormity demanded not only technical expertise but also a leader capable of envisioning and executing a complex and highly secretive operation. Ms. GD, fresh from a series of successful initiatives within the organization, was tasked with overseeing the development of this bunker—a facility that would embody the organization's ideals of safety, resilience, and luxurious living amidst potential global catastrophe.

The Design Phase

The design phase was an intricate and demanding process, marked by her exacting standards and meticulous oversight. Upon being entrusted with the project, Ms. GD assembled a team of elite architects, engineers, and survival experts, each selected for their unparalleled expertise in designing high-security and high-functionality structures. The team was charged with the formidable task of crafting a bunker that would not only withstand any conceivable disaster but also provide a haven for its occupants.

Ms. GD's vision was expansive and detailed, reflecting her high expectations for the facility. The bunker was to encompass twenty levels, each meticulously planned to serve a specific function while ensuring the highest standards of security and comfort. The design included residential quarters, state-of-the-art laboratories, a comprehensive medical facility, recreational areas, and an advanced air filtration system capable of handling multiple types of contaminants. Ms. GD's goal was to create a self-sustaining environment that would ensure the survival and well-being of its inhabitants for an extended period, blending functionality with high quality of life.

Excavation and Construction

With the designs finalized, the project moved into the excavation phase. The selected site, a blend of rolling hills and dense woods, provided natural camouflage and ample space for the ambitious construction. Heavy machinery was mobilized to begin the excavation, a process that required precise coordination and extensive labor. The excavation crews worked around the clock, digging deep into the earth to create the subterranean network necessary for the bunker's infrastructure.

Construction was an equally daunting task, demanding precision and expertise. Reinforced concrete was used to construct the bunker's walls, engineered to withstand extreme external pressures and potential threats. The construction process included the installation of advanced security systems, such as biometric access controls, extensive surveillance cameras, and automated defense mechanisms. Ms. GD played a pivotal role in overseeing every aspect of the construction, ensuring that each detail was executed to meet the highest standards of safety and functionality. Her hands-on approach and relentless scrutiny ensured that the bunker was built to withstand any potential disaster while providing a secure and comfortable environment.

Future-Proofing and Upgrades

Understanding the importance of future-proofing, Ms. GD's team incorporated provisions for regular updates and maintenance into the bunker's design. The facility was engineered to be adaptable, with a comprehensive plan for overhauling its systems every two years. This included integrating emerging technologies and addressing new and evolving threats. Her commitment to maintaining the bunker's cutting-edge status was unwavering, and she personally supervised the implementation of these updates.

The bunker's adaptability was a key feature, ensuring that it could evolve in response to technological advancements and changing security needs. Ms. GD's focus on long-term sustainability was evident in the facility's design, which included modular systems and upgrade pathways. Her leadership in this area further solidified her reputation within the organization, demonstrating her ability to anticipate future needs and ensure the bunker's continued relevance and effectiveness.

Ms. GD's Rise and Legacy

As the bunker neared completion, Ms. GD's status within the organization reached new heights. Her success in managing such a critical and complex project earned her significant accolades and enhanced her influence within the organization. The completion of the bunker was a testament to her vision, leadership, and dedication.

By the time the bunker was officially inaugurated, her role in its creation was well-recognized. The facility stood as a monument to her hard work and strategic acumen, reflecting her ability to transform a concept into a tangible and highly functional reality. The bunker's completion marked a significant milestone in the organization's plans, and Ms. GD's legacy as a key architect of this new world order was firmly established.

The bunker was more than just a physical structure; it was a symbol of the organization's commitment to its vision of the future. As Ms. GD looked over the completed site, she felt a profound sense of accomplishment. The facility she had helped create would play a crucial role in the organization's ambitious plans, and her work had not only met but exceeded expectations. The completion of the bunker marked the beginning of a new chapter for both GD and the organization, setting the stage for the future that had been meticulously planned and prepared for.

Maintenance and Upkeep

The completion of the bunker was merely the beginning of its storied existence. Ms. GD's role evolved from overseer to custodian of a living, breathing testament to the organization's vision. The bunker's ongoing maintenance and enhancement became a critical aspect of her responsibilities, ensuring that it remained not only functional but also a haven of luxury and comfort for its future inhabitants.

From the very start, Ms. GD understood that maintaining such a facility required more than just routine upkeep. The bunker was designed to be self-sustaining, but its complex systems demanded constant attention. Her team was tasked with overseeing the maintenance of the bunker's infrastructure, which included the advanced air filtration systems, power generators, and water recycling plants. Each system was monitored 24/7, with any issues addressed immediately to prevent disruptions.

She also instituted a rigorous schedule for regular inspections and preventive maintenance. Technicians were dispatched regularly to perform checks and repairs, ensuring that every component, from the security systems to the recreational amenities, remained in peak condition. This proactive approach helped to address potential issues before they could become major problems, preserving the bunker's integrity and functionality.

Modifications and Upgrades

As technology advanced, so too did Ms. GD's commitment to keeping the bunker at the cutting edge of innovation. Every two years, a comprehensive overhaul was conducted to integrate new technologies and address evolving threats. This included updating security systems, enhancing communication networks, and incorporating the latest advancements in survival technology.

Ms. GD's involvement in these upgrades was hands-on and meticulous. She worked closely with engineers and technology experts to ensure that each upgrade was seamlessly integrated into the existing systems. Her vision for the bunker extended beyond its initial design, incorporating features that anticipated future needs and challenges.

One of the most significant modifications involved the installation of a state-of-the-art wellness center. Recognizing the importance of mental and physical well-being, Ms. GD ensured that the bunker included amenities such as a fully equipped gym, yoga and meditation rooms, and an extensive spa. The spa featured multiple hot tubs, a sauna, and a massage therapy area, providing a sanctuary for relaxation and stress relief.

One of the most advanced technologies included in the bunker features AI-controlled systems and drones and semi-autonomous androids, designed to ensure both safety and efficiency within the vast underground facility. Once activated, the drones patrolled the various levels, monitoring for any potential structural weaknesses or unauthorized access, while also maintaining an inventory of supplies and performing routine tasks like repairs or adjustments to the environmental controls. Meanwhile, the androids were equipped to assist with everything from daily chores to medical emergencies and even defense of the bunker.

Their advanced AI with adaptive programming, along with synthetic humanoid skin and physical attributes allowed them to interact with residents on a human level, offering personal assistance with tasks, physical therapy, and even companionship. These innovations were not just practical but deeply integrated into the bunker's design, providing the inhabitants with a level of comfort and safety that would make the isolation more bearable. They were built to react to any scenario, ensuring the well-being of those inside while maintaining an atmosphere that felt more like a sanctuary than a shelter.

Luxurious Amenities

Ms. GD's focus on luxury and comfort was evident in every aspect of the bunker. The facility was designed to be a retreat, offering its occupants a range of high-end amenities that would rival any upscale resort. Each level of the bunker was equipped with its own set of amenities, tailored to different aspects of daily life and relaxation.

The recreational areas were particularly noteworthy: One level was dedicated entirely to leisure and entertainment, another featuring a movie theater with plush seating, a game room with the latest arcade and virtual reality games, and a lounge area with a full-service bar. This level was designed to provide a space for relaxation and socialization, offering a respite from the bunker's more functional areas.

Another level was dedicated to gourmet dining. The bunker's kitchen facilities were top-of-the-line, with professional-grade appliances and a dedicated team of chefs. The dining area featured elegant décor, with a range of culinary options to cater to every taste. The emphasis was on providing a dining experience that was both luxurious and comforting, ensuring that occupants could enjoy high-quality meals in a sophisticated setting.

Personal Touches

Ms. GD's attention to detail extended to the personal touches that made the bunker feel like a home. Each residential suite was designed with comfort in mind, featuring high-end furnishings, custom-designed décor, and spacious layouts. The suites were equipped with all the amenities one would expect in a luxury residence, including private bathrooms, state-of-the-art entertainment systems, and panoramic views of the surrounding landscape.

Ms. GD also ensured that the bunker's landscaping and environment was meticulously maintained. Despite being underground, the facility featured simulated natural environments, including artificial skylights and carefully designed greenery. This attention to the aesthetic aspects of the bunker helped to create a sense of normalcy and comfort, providing occupants with an environment that was both functional and pleasing to the eye. The ever expanding facility was one of her two proudest achievements

A Legacy of Preparedness

Ms. GD's role in the bunker's ongoing development was a testament to her dedication and vision. Her commitment to maintaining and enhancing the facility ensured that it remained at the forefront of luxury and functionality, providing a safe and comfortable haven for its occupants.

496

The bunker, with its unparalleled amenities and meticulous upkeep, became a symbol of the organization's ideals. Her work in creating and maintaining this facility reflected her ability to blend practicality with luxury, creating a space that was both a fortress and a retreat. Her legacy was one of foresight and precision, ensuring that the bunker would serve as a model for future projects and a testament to her contributions to the organization.

As Ms. GD looked back on the bunker's evolution, she felt a deep sense of accomplishment. The facility she had helped create was not just a shelter; it was a testament to human ingenuity and the organization's vision for a secure and prosperous future. The bunker stands as a monument to her hard work and dedication, embodying the ideals she had championed throughout her career and knowing that when the time came when he, her son, would use it well.

ABOUT THE AUTHOR

B. Edward Blackmon is an American author known for his emotionally charged and introspective storytelling. Drawing from a diverse background that spans teaching, coaching, and vocational trades to cybersecurity and genetic analytics, Blackmon brings a wealth of life experience to his writing.

His debut novel, Shadows of Atonement, is the first in the "Echoes of Black" series, a deeply personal exploration of family, regret, and redemption. Blackmon's work delves into the complexities of relationships, the lasting consequences of decisions, and the search for meaning amid life's darkest moments.

Born and raised just North of Birmingham, Alabama, Blackmon has long been captivated by the various literary traditions, which all influence his narrative style. When not writing, he enjoys spending time outdoors, engaging in educational initiatives, and fostering meaningful connections within his community.

Made in the USA
Columbia, SC
01 November 2024

9b15ff32-e40d-43dd-8ebe-452f1841723cR01